From Blackpool to Cabrera

Hi Mark
listen to your film review every week
and of course it's my ambition for you to
one day to review "From Blackpool to Cabrera"
who knows

Robert J Roper.

From Blackpool to Cabrera

INTRODUCING MAX WEST

Robert J. Cooper

ISBN-13: 9781518650062
ISBN-10: 1518650066
Library of Congress Control Number: 2015917253
CreateSpace Independent Publishing Platform
North Charleston, South Carolina

for Mrs Anne Cooper
my mum - and biggest fan
X

CHAPTER 1

Seymour Grant III, FBI special agent and Harvard graduate, had had enough—an Olympic-sized swimming pool more than enough. He understood that roughing it on field operations was sometimes necessary, but that didn't stop him from hating it. In Grant's eyes, the only thing worse than roughing it was being left out of the loop. And that was the crux of the problem. Tonight's operation was on a strictly need-to-know basis. And to Grant's dismay, *he* didn't fucking need to know.

How quickly life could change.

Yesterday, he'd been on top of the world—and on top of Special Agent Johnson's country girl, to boot.

Yesterday, life had been beautiful.

But here he was, less than twenty-four hours later, standing in a clump of banana trees, ankle deep in donkey excrement, and with only Special Agent Josh Johnson and the all-American hero Special Agent Dale Richards for company. So, today, life wasn't beautiful anymore. In fact, life was shit. Donkey shit.

Tonight's stakeout was designated as a Dark Watch, meaning who, why, and even where remained highly classified, even to the special agents on the ground. However, nobody had thought fit to tell the Spanish intelligence officer who had dropped them off, as he'd openly plugged their destination into the satellite navigation: No. 11, Avenida Alvarado, Santa Jerez. Not that that helped. Where the fuck was Santa Jerez?

Grant had made calls as soon as they'd landed in Madrid. He'd assumed he wouldn't be in the dark for long, for his ex-Harvard network was legendary. But to his extreme displeasure and surprise, he'd come up blank. Nothing. Fucking *nada*. Even Uncle Owen could only speculate.

"Drug Enforcement Administration boys have this one tighter than a camel's ass in a sandstorm, Seymour. It's a big one. If I had to guess, I'd say major drug bust."

Well, no shit. You didn't need Starsky and Hutch to figure that out. Of course it was a major drug bust. That's all the DEA ever did.

Light-industrial estates and storage depots lined the dual carriageway taking the three special agents away from Adolfo Suárez Madrid-Barajas International Airport. The only thing of interest was a sign in the shape of a large black bull, which was standing majestically on a small hill set back from the road. Advertising brandy, it reminded Grant that he'd not had a decent drink in over twenty-four hours. Eventually, the nondescript, box-like buildings faded away into a nondescript, arid scrubland. A few miles farther on, the driver turned down a nondescript dirt road. They bounced uncomfortably over a small rise where a smooth new paved road cut in. Wherever Santa Jerez was, it was clearly exclusive.

It was dark when they arrived in the small town, but expensive street lighting burned brightly. No problems with money for the electric bill here. Grant peered out sleepily at one luxury villa after another. They were all surrounded by high walls and imposing electric gates. Most were in complete darkness, their wealthy owners electing to spend the working week up in Madrid.

Santa Jerez is affluent but dull, thought Grant. He stretched out, trying unsuccessfully to release the stiffness from his neck.

The car slowed down at a parade of expensive restaurants, beauty salons, and art galleries—all closed—and turned left down a wide avenue of yet more enormous villas. Halfway along, the driver pulled over and killed the engine.

"Señors, that is number twenty over there," said the driver. "It's empty; the owner is away, and the gates are unlocked. Number eleven is right behind it."

Fortunately, both of number eleven's neighboring villas were empty, too, which had made finding a good stakeout position easy, donkey shit aside.

At least the wretched night can't get worse, thought Grant.

Thunder resounded, and fat raindrops began bursting on the top of his head. In five seconds, he was drenched, his hair resembling a sodden tea bag and freshwater running freely down the inside of his shirt.

Life could be so unfair.

Grant slapped an annoying itch on his neck in frustration, grimaced, and then held his hand gingerly out in front of him. The perpetrator, a caterpillar, had exploded. A furry, bulbous section was hanging down from his index finger on a long thread of gut, while the larger, gooier portion had started sliding slowly down his tie.

Grant sighed and kicked Johnson's leg.

"Ouch! What was that for?"

"Sorry, Johnson. Leg spasm," Grant said, unapologetically.

In difficult times, Grant thought about women. He was good with women. Sabrina, Jodie, Stella, and Jasmine were all in play, and all were in the dark. It was a complicated business from a diary point of view, but he enjoyed the secrecy and subterfuge. After all, he was an FBI agent, and he was pleased with himself for including country-boy Johnson's Susie as an extra one-off. However, tonight, it wasn't women but one of Uncle Owen's leadership quotes that came to mind. "Great leaders must tolerate inferiors, Seymour, because they can be sacrificed at no cost." *They would be the DEA, then.* He smiled for the first time in nearly two days.

"I've had enough, Johnson. We're going in."

"We can't, Seymour," said Johnson, who was pressed up against a banana tree in an attempt to avoid the worst of the rain. "You heard what Agent Clark said. 'Until I arrive on site, you do not engage; whatever the *fuck* goes on.' Not much room for misinterpretation there. And like it or not, Seymour, this is a DEA operation."

"Fuck Clark, and fuck the DEA," Grant said, as the butt end of the caterpillar slipped off his tie, leaving a yellow streak. "The FBI is the principal agency here, for God's sake, and we're FBI special agents. And most importantly of all, Johnson, we're the sorry fuckers standing in liquidized donkey shit."

Johnson moved a large, dripping leaf to one side and peered at the villa. Three men were clearly visible in a brightly lit living area. They were sitting, drinking beer, and watching TV, as they had been for the past two and a half hours.

"There are three of them, Seymour. And all we know about them is they are Colombian. And in case you've forgotten, Seymour, we have to pass our probationary period before we become permanent employees. Screw up on our first field operation, and we'll be chucked out. Or at least I will."

Grant tutted. It was a trick that worked well on rednecks like Johnson, who'd studied at some pointless college in Nebraska. "Oh, come on, Johnson. Surely they taught you more than combine-harvester mainte-nance in Hillbillyville. Those three in there have been watching basket-ball, getting hammered, and eating popcorn all night. They're wasted, Johnson. And look around you, man. There are no cameras, no security patrols, and no dogs. It's a two-minute exercise to take them down. It's a 'slam dunk,' in your basketball parlance. Enter through the open bedroom window over on the left, nip smartly across the hallway, and bingo. Old Granny Johnson could do it blindfolded."

"Gran's dead," Johnson said, reviewing the villa floor plan on his iPhone.

Surprisingly, Grant's plan made sense. The unlit room on the far left-hand side of the property was indeed a ground-floor bedroom, and it was straight across from the living room. The living room itself had three entry points, two off the hallway and one off the kitchen, which meant that the three agents could cover them all. Johnson was impressed. Grant's plan was simple to communicate and would be quick to execute, as all good plans should be. So why didn't he want to do it?

"We don't know it's a collar," he said.

Grant tutted again, this time rolling his eyes to double the effect, but knew he'd prevailed. "Oh, come on, Johnson. If Clark hadn't been called away to Madrid, we'd have wrapped this up two hours ago, and you'd be on the plane back home to Stacey."

"*Susie*," said Johnson in exasperation. "I wish you'd remember her name, Seymour. We've been to dinner at your place twice. And we don't know for certain that there are only three of them."

"Apologies, Johnson. Susie. Nice girl. Known her long?"

"Do you listen to *anything* I say, Seymour? We met in high school, as I've told you about ten times."

"I do listen to you; I do," Grant said with oily sarcasm, and then he became serious. "Look, Johnson. These guys are small fries; otherwise, the heavy squad would be here and not us. And think about it: they're off guard and unprofessional. They haven't looked out of the window once since we've been here, so they're expecting no one. We can stroll in, tie them up, wait for Clark inside the villa, and get out of this monsoon." He lifted a shoe, a look of absolute disgust crossing his face. "My new shoes are ruined, Johnson. Did I tell you? Church and Co. of England. Handmade. Cost me over two hundred bucks."

Johnson silently swore. If Grant mentioned his British-handmade shoes ever again, it would be much too soon. If the arrogant buffoon were dumb enough—which he unquestionably was—to come on a field operation in ludicrously inappropriate footwear, then he deserved all he got.

"Richards won't go in without DEA authorization," Johnson said, fervently hoping that that was true. The gripping pains in his stomach were clearly telling him to obey FBI protocol and await orders, but he didn't want to fall out with Seymour Grant, either. Grant was an overconfident fool of the first order, but he was also the nephew of FBI Deputy Director Owen Jefferson and, consequently, was destined for high office someday. The American dream and equality of opportunity it wasn't, but real life it was.

Grant drew his pistol, a Glock 23, standard FBI issue. Then, smiling weirdly at Johnson, he broke cover. There was a loud squelch as syrupy donkey manure sucked hard at smooth leather soles, and Grant stepped onto the lawn. He moved quickly in a half-crouching position over to where Special Agent Richards was hiding behind a pink rhododendron bush.

Johnson followed.

"We've got the go, Dale," Grant whispered, making sure that Johnson couldn't hear him. The Nebraskan country boy had been right about one thing. Dale Richards had graduated from Princeton and wouldn't be intimidated by a measly tut. "I'm taking point, and Johnson will cover our asses."

"Fine. Be good to get out of this rain," Richards whispered. "By the way, Seymour, did you ride Johnson's girl?"

Grant chuckled and felt an element of pride. "Let's just say that little Susie won't be sitting down much this week," he said, patting the other agent on the back. "But for God's sake, keep that to yourself, Dale. I think the dumb schmuck's in love with her."

Grant set off again, treading carefully as his leather shoes kept slipping and sliding on the wet grass. A high hedge bordered the garden on this side, and its shadow concealed the three agents' progress. It was going well.

Grant paused and swept his Glock in a 180-degree arc, smirking as Richards and Johnson followed suit. They were FBI special agents on a mission. They were G-men. They were the untouchables, walking in the footsteps of Eliot Ness, albeit with donkey shit covering their shoes.

A pantomime-villain staccato tiptoe took Grant safely up behind a large, ornamental statue of Venus de Milo. It was a good place to take stock, and he peered cautiously over to the other end of the villa. Light streamed from the living room and across the glistening grass, but nobody was standing in the window. It was all clear. The half-open French doors leading into the empty bedroom were only a few yards away, and Richards and Johnson were still right on his shoulder. He readied himself for a quick dash across the open ground, quelled his fears by remembering Uncle Owen's promise of a rapid promotion, and pushed off.

And slipped.

He went down like a man in a feather suit jumping off a tower block, flailing his arms hopelessly and frantically for an uplift that just wasn't there. Two feet from the ground, the FBI Academy's intensive self-defense training program kicked in, and he started twisting his shoulders in an effort to soften the landing. It wasn't a good strategy. He hit the lawn on the half turn, his elbow spearing into the turf and jarring his forearm.

And trigger finger.

Twice.

The first bullet zipped harmlessly into the rainy night. The second took Venus under the chin and decapitated her with a loud crack. A moment later, Richards shrieked as the statue's four-kilogram head landed on his foot.

The ground vibrated to the open-mouthed Richards's silent hopping as Grant lay on his back, both eyes closed in prayer.

"Seymour," Johnson whispered urgently, "we should go back."

Grant remained motionless.

A minute went by before he opened one eye, as if keeping one closed gave him some form of magical protection. Maybe it did. There was no movement in the villa. Thankfully, Richards had stopped bouncing around like a kangaroo on speed. They'd been incredibly lucky. The Glock's suppressor had silenced the gunshots, and the torrential rain had drowned out Richards's pathetic yelp. Everything was just as it had been before—shitty and raining.

Grant sat up and crawled back behind the statue.

"That never gets fucking mentioned," he said, scowling.

Johnson smirked. "This statue's like the one in Paris now."

"Really?" Grant said sarcastically. "I think you'll find the one in the Louvre has a head but no fucking arms, you dimwit. Was it carrot farming you studied, Johnson?"

Richards was groaning softly. He was sitting up against the headless Venus and vigorously rubbing his foot. "Don't think anything's broken, but it hurts like hell. Which way are the DEA coming in, Seymour?"

"The front," Grant said, lying.

The mission was still on. Despite his unfortunate slip, which clearly had been weather related, and his accidental slotting of a Roman goddess, which was best forgotten, Grant was loving the night's adventure. His mother had said it was better to be lucky than rich, and how right she was, although he'd not felt so after his pop had bankrupted the family business at the Bellagio. Until then, Grant had been looking forward to a life consisting entirely of women and sports cars. However, an ill turn of a roulette wheel—or, more accurately, three hundred ill turns—had put an end to that and left him in the tragic predicament of actually needing a job.

Fortunately, Uncle Owen had stepped up to the plate with a fast-track career in the FBI. Because Grant had nothing else to do, he had reluctantly taken the role. A month later, he was ready to quit. The money was pathetic, and his colleagues were peasants. But then he went to a bar in Orlando and showed his special-agent badge to a bachelorette party from Tallahassee, and he discovered an amazing thing: women *loved* FBI special agents. Money wasn't everything after all.

Grant stepped out again from behind the statue. Five careful strides later, his right shoulder was against the villa's whitewashed wall. Johnson and the hobbling Richards were right behind him.

Showtime.

Grant took a deep breath and raised three fingers into the air. Three, two, one, go. He stepped quickly inside the French doors and breathed out. The large bedroom was dim but not dark. A strip of light was coming in from under the door in the far corner. It was the door that led to the hallway. This was going to be a breeze. It was just brilliant. Three incompetent drug dealers, who were roaring drunk and watching TV, versus the finest the FBI could muster—namely, Seymour Grant III. It was no contest. He almost felt sorry for them. Confidence coursed through him, and he nimbly sidestepped an ornate French dressing table and put his ear flat against the door. He was more excited than he'd ever been in his life.

The hallway was quiet except for the sound of the TV coming from the room beyond.

Grant glanced back at Richards and Johnson with a manic grin. It was another of Uncle Owen's tips. "Seymour," his uncle had said, "a great leader instills confidence in his men, and the best way to do that in the field is to give them a big I-am-here-and-so-you're-going-to-be-OK smile."

Richards looked alarmed but forced a smirk. Johnson seemed to be swallowing a fly.

They must have missed Grant's reassuring smile.

Grant smiled again, just in case, and then raised three fingers.

"Seymour," Johnson whispered urgently.

Grant's glare was caustic. "Shut the fuck up, you imbecile," he silently mouthed.

"Sorry, Seymour," Johnson whispered. "But which doors are we each taking?"

Grant hadn't considered that. And he didn't know how many doors there were.

"I was just coming to that, Johnson."

"Sorry," whispered Johnson.

"Never mind," said Grant, who still had no idea what to do.

Richards came to his rescue. "You take the door opposite, Seymour. I'll take the one by the staircase, and Johnson can come in through the kitchen. We'll need to set a mark, though, so we all enter at the same time."

Grant nodded and put his ear flat against the door again. He could still hear the TV in the living room, and there was no other sound in the hallway. It was all clear to go. "Thanks, Dale," he said. "At least the two of us are on the same page." He patted Richards affectionately on the shoulder and scowled at Johnson before holding up his TAG Heuer watch. "Right, men, on my mark—*one* minute. Three, two, one, and set."

Three tiny beeps sounded in perfect unison, and Grant carefully edged the door open.

The TV noise intensified, but the hallway was deserted. In two strides, Grant was in position outside the living-room door and watched as Johnson moved stealthily past the open staircase and out of view. Then Richards, who was hobbling on after Johnson, also disappeared from view. His entry door was housed underneath the staircase.

Grant gulped. *Shit. That wasn't supposed to happen.* He checked his TAG.

Eight seconds had elapsed since the mark.

Fifty-two seconds to go.

He'd given too long—by about fifty motherfucking seconds.

But there was no going back now. The supreme confidence of eight seconds ago had evaporated like a wisp of cloud in the Sahara sun. Beads of sweat formed on his forehead, and he heard a strange noise. It was his own breathing. It sounded as if he were using a respirator.

Grant could hear the announcer on the TV. "So at the halftime break in this scintillating encounter, it's forty-eight forty-seven, Bulls. Join us again after these messages."

Chairs creaked.

People stood.

It was the commercial break.

Oh my God, they're coming out.

Grant's heart jumped into his throat as a sports-car commercial came on the TV. He heard Uncle Owen speak inside his head. "Buy one of those cars quick, Seymour, and get the hell outta there."

Four seconds later, Grant was stepping back through the bedroom's French doors and out into the rain. Only then did he remember that the three men sitting in the living room were drunk and oblivious to the highly trained FBI agents about to storm in. Even more important, Grant's Glock 23 was cocked and ready for action. It truly was a slam-dunk operation, as he'd told Johnson earlier. It would never get any easier than this. He could do it. He could. He had to. One successful field operation, his uncle had said, and then he'd pull him out and promote him. And this surely was the one. There was absolutely no danger. He could be brave. And if one of the three Colombian motherfuckers so much as blinked in his direction, he'd blow his head off.

Four more seconds. Grant was back in position outside the living room door. Nobody had come out.

Forty-two seconds to go.

He noticed the door handle. It was round and made of brass. It looked heavy. And it was on the right-hand side of the door. *Shit.* He couldn't open the door with his favored right hand and hold the Glock in his right hand at the same time. But he couldn't shoot with his left hand—he'd tried once at the FBI firing range and taken off an instructor's ear. He took two steps to his right. That was better. He could more easily use his left hand to open the door now and keep the Glock in his favored right. That was good, although he was now facing the wall to the right of the door frame and consequently couldn't shoot directly into the room.

Motherfucker.

He heard clinking glasses. Someone was collecting empties.

Thirty-eight seconds to go.

Twenty-two seconds had elapsed since the mark. *How could it possibly be only twenty-two seconds?* It was absurd. Bizarre. Unbelievably unfair, too. God was stretching time to punish him for screwing Johnson's country bitch. It was the only plausible explanation, as the presidential elections could have been held in the time he'd spent outside this fucking door. Hell, there'd been time to clone Elvis, make some new tasseled suits, and have him back at number one with "Return to Heartbreak Hotel."

He studied his TAG Heuer and angrily tapped the glass. Had the second hand stopped? *Come on you bastard, get ticking.*

Another president was elected.

Thirty-three seconds to go.

Fucking Swiss. All they had to do was make watches.

Suddenly, the grainy, pine door six inches from his face transformed into the underside of a coffin lid. It was *his* coffin lid. Seymour Grant III was about to die. A cannonball materialized in the bottom of his stomach, and he broke wind. He needed the toilet urgently. He looked left and right for the restroom, and then he remembered the mission. The restroom wasn't a good idea. *Better to go outside in the garden, in the banana trees.* He could wait there, too, until Richards and Johnson prevailed. It was no good staying here and farting like that again and blowing their cover, as it were. He'd tell Richards there had been voices outside and he'd had to cover their sorry, useless asses. He was gutted to have missed the party, but they would have done the same for him. And if by any chance the two dumb fucks got burned, well, who cared? As Uncle Owen had said, "Inferiors could be sacrificed at no cost."

In any case, FBI procedures were directing him to withdraw. The round door handle clearly prohibited a safe entry, and, consequently, it was too dangerous to proceed. *Health and safety regulations. Important stuff.* He had no option but to leave his position. He was annoyed but saw no other way. He couldn't remember precisely which FBI procedure he was referring to, but the fucking liberal do-gooders were bound to have one about "dangerous, round door handles."

He glanced at his TAG.

Fifteen seconds to go.

Swiss bastards.

Eighteen seconds had gone in the blink of an eye. *Switzerland. A country of parasites. They'd made billions of dollars from being neutral in World War II and now enjoyed higher living standards than the rest of the world by selling overpriced, faulty watches to suckers like me.*

He heard a loud, hacking cough directly behind the door, and he froze solid. He was a stunned rabbit caught in the dazzling halogen lights of a forty-four-ton truck. Schoolboy tears welled up in his eyes and ran silently down his cheeks. His breath caught in his throat. Maybe it was to be his last breath.

The man coughing in the living room was less than two feet away. All that was standing between him and Grant were two inches of pine that a four-year-old kid could undoubtedly bust through in his first karate lesson.

The coughing intensified. It was hideous.

Thirteen seconds.

Strategic retreat.

Grant flexed his knees and jumped backward. Vast supplies of nervous energy were released in a microsecond as he twisted majestically in midair and impressively transferred the Glock into his left hand. He then grabbed and turned the bedroom door handle with his right. Months of high school gym classes had finally proved worthwhile. He'd attended only to get into his best friend's girlfriend's pants, and until now he'd received only a knee into his balls for the effort.

With his supremely elegant maneuver complete and forward momentum maintained, he stiffened the muscles in his right leg, readying for the imminent landing and a speedy getaway.

He needn't have bothered.

The bedroom door was locked.

Twelve seconds.

Grant's bodily momentum drove 250 pounds of body weight into the unyielding wood. It was good-quality wood, too—solid pine, karate black-belt territory. Blood spurted out in a 360-degree arc from the detonation point—his long, slender nose—and he rebounded half unconscious into the hallway.

He never saw the living room door opening behind him.

And he didn't see the two heavily tattooed arms that reached out, grabbed him, and threw him through the open doorway, either. Grant landed heavily on his front, and a heavy boot stamped down on his wrist. Expensive TAG Heuer and fragile bones were crushed and broken, and the Glock 23 slipped from his limp fingers. The heavy boot followed up with a kick into his midriff, and he curled up like an embryo, gasping for breath. The aggressive arms then reached down again and hauled him to his feet. A subsequent punch to his battered face knocked him out. A few seconds later, he returned to consciousness. He was being held upright and had a gun pressed against his ear.

"Welcome, Special Agent Grant," an articulate man with a Spanish accent said. "It's usually stray cats that steal in when it's raining, but it's a foul night to be standing in the flower beds."

Through blurred vision, Grant could see the outline of a man. "My nose is broken."

"Oh, come, come, Agent Grant. The FBI is surely made of sterner stuff than that. At the very least, you should be threatening me with Deputy Director Jefferson's retribution."

Grant's vision cleared a little. The man looked like he'd just walked off a James Bond film set. Although 007 was usually a good guy.

At least the smug bastard knows about Uncle Owen. The man would also be aware that Grant's uncle would hunt him through the fires of hell if they harmed his favorite nephew—his only nephew, to be fair. An awful thought came to mind. *What if they kidnap me and take me back to Colombia?* An FBI deputy director's nephew would be powerful leverage against both the FBI and the DEA. Ten years huddling under a tarpaulin sheet in the South American jungle came to mind. Eating bugs, shitting through straws, and being bent over tree stumps three times a day by sex-starved paramilitaries wasn't his idea of a good time.

"That's my uncle. He'll give you anything you want."

"Yes, yes. I know that, Agent Grant, but I don't need anything from you," Bond said.

Grant's eyes fully cleared. The room was a large rectangle with two fast-whirling ceiling fans and a marble fireplace. He was being held in the middle of the room, between a brown, leather sofa and the fireplace. The window overlooking the garden was directly behind him. Richards's door was to his left, and Johnson's door to the kitchen was facing him.

All three special agents had been caught.

Johnson looked surprisingly calm all things considered. He was being held at gunpoint in the room's far corner, to the right of the kitchen door, by a short, stout man who was continually dipping his free hand into a cardboard bucket. Popcorn was scattered on the floor all around the gunman's bright-blue flip-flops.

However, Richards was clearly terrified, and understandably so. He was standing halfway between Johnson and Grant and was being held by the biggest, scariest, ugliest, and hairiest motherfucker Grant had ever seen. To make matters worse, the huge beast was happily prodding a giant carving knife into the back of the agent's neck.

Grant couldn't take his eyes off the monster. A crop of cauliflower warts covered its left cheek, and its nose was so bulbous that wasps could mistake it for a nest. *Is he an it, or is it a man?* Grant wasn't sure. Certainly, the dirt-festooned facial rug he/it was sporting didn't answer the question because all it suggested was unavailability for dinner dates on full moons—unless, of course, *you* were the main course.

As well as being freaked out by the grisly scene, Grant was also confused. How had they been caught so easily? His face was starting to numb, which he took as good news until he became aware of pains shooting up his broken forearm. His arm was useless, but he knew that he must ignore his injuries. He needed to think.

He steeled himself.

Think.

Bond had just said that the agents had nothing he wanted. Maybe that was good news. Maybe he'd let them go. The DEA would arrive at any second, so surely these criminals would take their chance to leave before they were cornered. The same thinking meant release was a more likely scenario than being taken hostage, too. Grant breathed a sigh of relief, and visions of the South American jungle and tree stumps faded from his imagination. Another jolt of pain from his nose brought fresh tears to his eyes as he suddenly realized that if they were released quickly, then the whole night's fiasco was still redeemable—in other words, Special Agent Grant broke his arm during a heroic pursuit of three armed drug dealers. *Wounded in the line of duty.* He might even get a commendation. And he'd get his promotion. Top result. The alternative scenario, otherwise known as the truth, wasn't as flattering. Three armed FBI agents had been caught cold by low-life drug dealers. He'd be the office laughing stock for months—years, even. Maybe he would fail probation. Uncle Owen could help only so much.

There were four men.

"There were only three of you," Grant whispered.

"Four," Bond said, smiling and gesturing toward the werewolf. "Miguel was in the kitchen all night. He doesn't look much like a chef, but his mama taught him well. He makes wonderful paella. If you had bothered to walk around the villa, Agent Grant, then you'd have seen him at work. Very sloppy and very foolish, but then again, you three agents are all still on probation."

Johnson was shaking his head, clearly reprimanding himself.

"Who are you?" Grant asked.

The irritatingly cool man ignored the question and lit a cigarette. "You must be wondering how we caught you all so easily," he said and blew smoke toward the ceiling.

Grant said nothing.

"When you recently decided to abandon your colleagues, Agent Grant—which, to be honest, I think they took a rather dim view of—I locked the bedroom door from here."

Grant noticed an odd-looking remote-control device on the coffee table next to an open laptop and ten empty cans of Coke. Full recognition dawned when he looked at the computer screen. It was displaying closed-circuit TV footage of the villa, both inside and out. Familiar views of the garden, the hallway stairs, and the still half-open French doors in the bedroom came into view. There had been no need for anybody inside the villa to keep a lookout at the window because all three agents would have been highly visible from the moment they broke cover—even before they broke cover. Grant realized his folly. These men knew their trade, and he obviously didn't. He was a fool.

"As you can see, Agent Grant, the security cameras are excellent and almost impossible to detect unless you know they're there. They're better indoors than out, but the audio pickup works well in the garden." Bond was smiling. "I'm very surprised you acted without the appropriate authority, Agent Grant."

Richards fumed. "You asshole, Seymour. You motherfu—"

He never finished the insult. A long, silver blade emerged from the center of his Adam's apple and glinted in the electric light from above. Richards's face expressed bewilderment at his sudden inability to speak until his darting eyes spotted the strange, metal point protruding below his chin, which might just have had something to do with it. Recognition brought horror and a silent scream as the knife sliced sideways through vocal chords, muscles, and veins as if they were melting butter.

The grinning werewolf dropped the bloody knife, which bounced on the thick carpet with a dull clunk. Using his massive hands, he held Richards's screaming head and ripped it violently to one side. Crunch and snap. The agent's spine broke, and his severed throat tore open to expose a bright-pink stump. The macabre scene was straight out of a Hammer horror movie. Richards's eyes were vertical, and his nose was horizontal. A headless ghost came to Grant's mind, but Richards wasn't holding his own head under his arm; rather, it was lying on his shoulder. Worst of all, he wasn't yet dead. Indeed, the agent's eyes were still blinking as a bright-red geyser spurted from where his head should have been and struck one of the ceiling fan's rotors. Agent Johnson screamed as he and his popcorn-munching captor were showered in blood.

Grant's tensed buttocks gave way as he felt blood spattering down on his suit jacket.

The werewolf laughed and threw the dying body away like a bag of garbage. Mercifully, it landed behind the sofa. Only Richards's twitching feet were visible. After a few seconds, they went still.

Bond hardly seemed to have noticed the horror. "I fear it's too late for you to apologize to Agent Richards for your foolhardiness, Agent Grant. But you do still have time to apologize to Agent Johnson."

Grant was in deep shock but managed a slight hunch of the shoulders, which aggravated the pain in his arm.

Bond continued. "Surely you remember bedding his Susie, Agent Grant. Or is it Stacey?"

Johnson went from screaming to silence in a nanosecond and was about to speak until he remembered Richards's fate of not thirty seconds before. Instead, he looked at Grant and slowly shook his head from side to side, wanting Grant to do the same.

Grant kept his eyes down on his ruined, shit-covered shoes. The gunman covering Agent Johnson laughed hysterically and thrust his crotch toward his captive.

Heavy footsteps echoed in the hallway.

"I'm coming in. So don't fucking shoot," an American with a deep voice said.

A Glock 27, again with a suppressor attached, rounded the door frame, followed very tentatively by a gray-haired head. "Goddamn, it's a goddamned slaughterhouse," the man said, his face screwed up as if he were sucking on a lemon.

To Grant, it felt like the second coming, except the messiah was in the form of DEA Agent Doug Clark. Grant began crying with relief as he recognized his luck. Clark had just saved him from decapitation by a fucking werewolf. Suddenly, a broken arm, an urgent need for new underwear, and months of ridicule were a small price to pay. He was sorry about Richards—nah, who was he kidding? Richards had been the competition, and his death meant one fewer special agent asshole to overcome.

Clark edged slowly into the room, his weapon ready and aimed at the unarmed Bond look-alike.

"About time, Clark," Grant said, closing his eyes and looking up to thank the heavens.

A moment later, his watering eyes snapped open again when he heard two dull slaps. He caught a glimpse of a man being lifted off his feet and thrown backward through the air. The victim fell heavily to the floor, smashing his skull sickeningly against the corner of a marble table en route.

Agent Josh Johnson came literally to rest on his back. Two expanding, red splotches on his shirt pocket were testament to the bullets that had drilled into him and obliterated his heart.

Grant had instinctively ducked to avoid cross fire, but thankfully no more shots came. Bond had shouted for his men to hold fire, and Clark was in no place to kill the gang's leader without being shot himself. It was stalemate.

Thank God.

The FBI was formed in 1908 and today has more than thirty-five thousand employees; in all that time and with such a massive workforce, only thirty-six agents had been killed in the line of duty—service martyrs, the agency calls them—now Richards and Johnson had taken that number to thirty-eight. Clark's entrance had saved Grant from being memorialized as number thirty-nine.

Grant counted slowly to three and gingerly stood.

The shooting had stopped.

He and Clark were outnumbered and needed to exit stage left before it started again.

Bond was calmly smoothing out a crease in his still-pristine white shirt. It was pretty much the only thing in the room that had avoided Richards's metamorphosis into a blood sprinkler system.

Revenge will come later. Fucking liberal, do-gooder regulations didn't apply to agent killers. The FBI would hunt these bastards to Mars, if necessary. And with a bit of luck, he'd get to dispatch the werewolf himself—as long as somebody else nailed down the nightmarish beast first, of course. He shuddered at the thought of a kitchen knife being jabbed into his neck, and he unconsciously lifted his broken arm to touch the spot. Splintered bones cut into swollen tissue, and red-hot pains shot up his arm again, but it didn't matter. He was alive. He was safe. In a few weeks, he'd be as good as new.

A thin wisp of smoke drifted gently up from the end of the gun that had killed Johnson. This wasn't strange. Discharging a weapon indoors would always give rise to gun smoke and the unmistakable smell of burned cordite, which Grant could smell now. But what was strange was that it was DEA Agent Doug Clark's gun that was smoking.

"Clark?" Grant was totally flabbergasted. "Did you just kill Johns—?" He stopped midsentence and turned toward the hallway door.

The hallway was quiet.

Nobody else was there.

Nobody else was coming.

Clark raised the smoking gun again. Grant could see straight down the barrel—as it was pointing at his own head.

"I'm sorry, Seymour," Clark said. "But this is just too big."

Everything went black.

CHAPTER 2

She was calming down now, much to Max's relief, but the woman was still in a state of high excitement. Irritatingly, she kept stroking his forearm as if it were a pet cat.

"I just knew it was you. I just knew it," the woman exclaimed, clapping her hands together in seal like fashion. Lovingly, she then ran her fingertips down his arm again.

The woman stood.

Max thought she was about to leave. *Thank God.*

Oh God.

To his horror, the woman leaned over the table and grabbed both of his ears, using them to haul his face toward hers. Max had no option but to meet her halfway; it was that or lose the ability to hear. The woman's podgy face was looming ever closer, but he was powerless to react.

School blackboards rather than the forthcoming kiss came to mind— or, more accurately, the excruciating sensation when fingernails are drawn slowly down one.

Contact was big and wet, and there was a positive squelch as her lips smacked against the middle of his forehead. A long few seconds elapsed before the airlock was broken, and she pulled away.

Max and the woman were sitting at a table in the swimming-pool cafeteria. It was no place to hold a conversation. Noisy toddlers were screaming with delight as they charged recklessly in between, under, and now on top of the café's bright-blue, plastic tables. A herd of bleary-eyed young mothers looked on, neither seeing nor hearing the chaos surrounding them.

The woman was talking again.

"'Jenny,' I said. 'You are not going to believe this,' I said. 'But it's definitely him,' I said. 'Over there,' I said. 'Standing by the Coke machine,' I said. 'That is the one-and-only *Max West*,' I—"

"Said," Max mumbled under his breath.

The woman had heard. "Said what?" she asked, half glaring.

"Oh, nothing," Max said, wondering if the kiss was about to be followed up with a right hook.

It was a beautiful summer afternoon, and what should have been a welcome breeze from the open skylight created a strangely cool feeling on his brow. It was saliva from the kiss, and it felt gross. Max wasn't sure if wiping it away would be politic, but he had to do something. In his mind's eye, a foamy, white gob the size of a Bassetts Licorice Allsort was about to slide down between his eyebrows.

"Phew, it's so hot," he said and quickly used the back of his hand.

The rouse worked. He relaxed slightly. His forehead had a consistent temperature once again, which confirmed gob removal. Then he noticed the heavy smear of red lipstick.

Christ.

It started on his wrist and widened as it spread across the back of his hand to his knuckles. He must look like Chief Sitting Bull.

"Max, you remember Jenny, right," the woman said. It was a statement rather than a question. She beckoned to a woman on the far side of the pool's viewing area.

"Jenny was top in math and loves baking cakes."

Max's heart sank. *Not another one.* "Well, I, er, th-think so, love," he said while nonchalantly slipping his arms under the table and out of stroking range.

All Max knew about Jenny was what he'd just heard, that she was good at numbers and loved to bake cakes, which presumably the woman sitting opposite him had eaten. Other than that, he was in the dark. *Who the hell are they?* His imagination was searching frantically for answers and was getting nowhere fast. Perhaps the woman had confused him with a contestant from *The X Factor* who was also called Max West, who was his doppelganger, and who could sing. Unfortunately, it was an unlikely scenario, for he could have sorted that out immediately. Three bars of "The Wonder of You" would do it. He couldn't sing a note. The woman would be running for the exit like a dog with earache at a whistle-blowing contest.

However, the most likely scenario here was that they were old school colleagues whom he'd forgotten about over a decade ago. He was racking his brain along those lines, but nothing came. No former schoolmates popped into his head—no former schoolmates' mates, sisters, friends, and no friends of friends' sisters or brothers. The woman opposite wasn't from the council, either; he was sure about that. And he'd never seen her down at the youth club. She definitely didn't go into the Bull's Head, and surely to God she wasn't in his mother's knitting club. *The only rational answer is that I've never met her in the first place.* Therefore, it must be *The X Factor* scenario.

He should sing.

He was depressed to see Jenny waddle over. Four manic kids were in close pursuit.

"Aye up, Maxi. Av just seen your ugly mug shot ont wall over theyre," she bellowed in a thick Yorkshire accent. "Sez you're deputy manager. Very swish, if you don't mind mi saying. Look, mi duck. If there's any jobs going around here, count me in, lad. I'd happily work *under* you for nowt." She finished off this last phrase with an elaborate wink and a Stuka-like squeal.

Max winced as the dozing herd of mothers awoke, all turning as one toward the subject of the loud woman's interest: him. Instantaneous combustion would have been welcome, but he didn't ignite. Instead, the image of a redheaded teenager flashed into his mind. The vision was the beautiful Jennifer Smith. She had been slim, curvaceous, and sweet natured. Jennifer had been the match of a young Nicole Kidman, but only as long as she didn't laugh. Her only flaw was a piercing, witchlike cackle, which had no volume control, and apparently it still didn't. Jennifer Smith—Max suddenly remembered—had a similarly attractive younger sister called Rosie May. Was Rosie May the slobbering kisser?

No way!

It was impossible.

Wasn't it?

Jennifer settled heavily down next to him and started to stroke his forearm under the table. *That probably doesn't look so good.*

His eyes darted back and forth and quickly paused on two young mothers who were staring at him mid–tea sip. His worst fears were realized.

"Oh my God," one of them was mouthing. Her eyes were on stalks. Her worldlier friend wasn't as perturbed. She was smiling warmly at Max while calmly delivering the universally accepted signal for wanking.

Christ.

Max took on the complexion of a human raspberry and quickly slapped both his hands back on the tabletop, grinning as best he could. It was the type of grin a guy pulls after spilling boiling hot coffee into his lap and then tries attempting to avoid further embarrassment by nonchalantly carrying on with whatever task he's undertaking. In these situations, everybody around the hapless chap is fully aware he's just scalded his balls and is in excruciating pain, but that just makes it all the funnier.

"We all fancied the pants off you at school, Maxi," Rosie May said. "On party nights, the girlies voted you the *numero uno* four-minute warning."

Jenny nodded vigorously and held up a chubby finger. "Numero uno, Maxi," she said, staring longingly into his eyes.

"Come on, ladies. That was many lifetimes ago," Max said. "Now, I'm probably going to regret asking this"—he just knew he would—"but just *what* exactly is a four-minute warning?"

Both women looked incredulous.

"Oh, come on, Max. You've got to be kidding," Jenny yelled straight into his ear. "It was your claim to fame."

Both women looked at him expectantly.

Max was taken aback, as well as deafened.

"Er, well, erm…" he said, quickly trying to think of a way to hide his ignorance. But after seeing the women's mounting anticipation, he decided that he'd have to come clean. "Well, to be honest, ladies, I've no idea about the 'four-minute-warning' thing," he said, pulling another boiled-testicle grin. "I must have forgotten. It's an effect of the pool's chlorine fumes combining with the excitement of the over eighties water-aerobics classes."

There went the Stuka squeal again, this time in stereo.

After they'd calmed down, Rosie May explained. "We did it in history, Max. If the Russians had nuked Western Europe, then the early warning radar gave a four-minute warning. Four minutes left to live before hundreds of ballistic missiles brought certain death to the entire nation. Britain would be turned into a nuclear wasteland full of mutant zombies."

"Sounds like Batley," Max said and laughed.

"We live in Batley," Jenny said curtly. She stopped stroking his forearm and glared at him.

"Sorry," Max said. *God, it's actually getting worse.*

"Lighten up, Maxi," Rosie May said. "She's having you on. We live in Birstall, a full two miles from Batley. Birstall has a Marks and Spencer."

Jenny winked at him and started stroking again.

Max didn't know the relevance of living near a Marks and Spencer, unless M&S sold the best radiation suits. It probably did. *This is not just any radiation suit. It's an M&S deluxe radiation suit with built-in earmuffs and chaff-resisting incontinence bottle.*

Rosie May continued. "So, if ninety-nine red balloons went up, the usual rules of engagement don't apply. It would be every woman for herself."

"In other words, only four minutes to get screwed by your *four-minute warning*," Jenny said, suddenly increasing the speed of her stroke. She was starting to sweat profusely.

Max felt sick.

"And *all* the girls in our gang agreed to make a beeline straight for *you*, Maxi," Rosie May added. "I reckon you'd have had about twenty-five of us to sort."

"That's about one every ten seconds," said Jenny, saliva on her lips.

"I'd be all right for the first two or three, then," Max said, squirming in his seat. He now understood what an antelope felt like just before lions tore it apart. He'd seen a wildlife program about it once. The lions crept up real close from different directions and then attacked simultaneously. The antelope became aware of its peril only after half a ton of muscly cats landed on it. The same scenario was playing out here.

Of course, working at the local swimming pool meant bumping into loads of different people all the time. Frequently, those in the thirty something age range knew him, even if he didn't know them. The vast majority were either former school colleagues or people from other council departments. Max had been a reluctant captain of the school's first eleven when Whitcliffe had won the County Schools Football Cup. It was big news in Cleckheaton, and a photo of Max holding the cup aloft was on both the front and back pages of the *Spenborough Guardian* that Friday. That was nearly seventeen years ago; surprisingly, people still remembered.

However, this morning's cringe fest owed more to Max's overdue promotion to deputy manager of the pool. Initially, he'd been as proud as punch to see his photo and nameplate alongside Mr. Thomson's in the lobby. "Max West: Deputy Manager" read the gold lettering. And the photo wasn't a complete horror, either—tie askew and hair suitably ruffled. But from that moment on, the number of people he had no option but to call either "mate" or "love"—he had no idea who they were—had mushroomed. Oddly, in Max's opinion, many were former schoolgirls, and his feelings on the subject weren't helped by an observation from his friend, DG.

"And they're all mingers, mate," DG had said, "every single one of them. It's statistically abnormal, Max. Either ditch your aftershave, or use fly spray in combination because you're attracting bugs."

"Charming," Max had said.

The ex-schoolgirls—or "mums on the pull" or "MoPs," as DG referred to them—had another unfortunate characteristic: they wouldn't take no for an answer. It was just like today, when Rosie May had frog-marched him to the cafeteria. One nasty incident had seen Julie Higginbottom trying to shove her tongue down his throat while her guffawing friend filmed it. She had said it was for the bingo crowd. *So that was happy slapping.* He'd avoided YouTube ever since.

When being honest with himself, which happened every now and then, Max knew that being accosted by ex-schoolgirls wasn't what irked him. And it certainly wasn't being the centerpiece of their teenage sexual fantasies, either. No, what really, really hurt was that all during school and for the fifteen years or so since, he'd absolutely no idea that any of these girls had noticed him at all, never mind the four-minute-warning thing.

He'd recently started thumping the steering wheel as he drove past the old school on his way into work. "Jesus Christ, Maxi," he'd shout in frustration. Just *how* had he missed out on all those girls? It wasn't as if his head had been stuck in a book; that was for sure.

Jennifer and Rosie May Smith, Jane Wheeler, and Carol Jenkins had all been total babes at school, and every one of them—he'd discovered from Rosie May—had had him down as their four-minute warning. Carol Jenkins had been blond dynamite with legs that went on up into the atmosphere. She had been desired by every boy in school—and most of the girls, too.

According to Rosie May, the girls had been attracted by his "air of indifference." A sense of mystery had surrounded him.

"You didn't seem to give a fuck," Jenny said. "The other guys just wanted our knickers off, but you were *different*."

Different!

Christ.

All he'd ever dreamed about for years was removing Carol Jenkins's knickers. Every night of every school day, he'd dreamed it. Every weekend, he'd dreamed it. Even unconscious in the dentist's chair, he'd dreamed it. The thought of pulling down Carol Jenkins's knickers was the only constant thought he'd had as a teenager.

Christ, life is just so unfair.

His tactic of indifference, which he had devised to avoid his anxiety when asking girls out, had actually pulled them in by the busload.

And he'd missed every sodding bus.

Typical.

Max rose from his seat. He'd had enough but didn't want to offend.

"Jenny, Rosie May. Great to see you again, but I'd better get back to work. Hope you and the kids enjoy the pool. If there's anything else I can do whilst you're here, just let me know."

"We'll give you a call over the public address system, then, Maxi," Rosie May said, winking at her sister.

"Yeah," Jenny said. "*Four minutes* before we leave!"

Both women howled as Max hurried back to the pool offices.

Max was thirty-two. He was six feet tall and had dark, wavy hair. According to Mandy on pool reception, his sparkling, blue eyes melted her heart every morning. Occasionally, he was compared to John Cusack, which he liked, for his favorite film was *Grosse Pointe Blank*.

Max had worked at Spenborough Pool since leaving school. His A-level results hadn't been too bad considering the amount of revision he'd done—that is, none—but the early promise he'd shown in primary school hadn't been realized. During sixth form, nobody had advised him on the merits of university, and he'd made no effort to find out about it for himself.

Seeing their only child was going nowhere fast, his parents sent him to see Uncle Norman, who worked at the town council and could be depended on to sort Max out, or so they said. And sure enough, two months later, Max started his working life in Leisure Services as a trainee accountant. From then on, it was a do-your-time, snail-paced climb up the council's long career ladder, with speedier advancement available only if there were unexpected deaths.

Max had laughed at the advice that Mr. Sykes, the human resources manager, had given him on his council induction day.

"Never undervalue the council pension scheme, Mr. West," Mr. Sykes had said. "Get forty years in like me, young man, and you'll never have to worry about the heating bills in your retirement."

Max had bitten his lip to stop himself from sniggering at the man's heartfelt tone. It was a pathetic statement. *Forty years at the council. Give me a break. And shoot me if I do two.* He'd stay long enough to get some cash together, and then he was off. The world was waiting, and he wanted it. New York, Buenos Aires, and Sydney—and by the way, Mr. Sykes, there are no heating bills in Oz.

Fifteen years on from his induction day, Max hadn't been shot. And he didn't need to bite his lip to stop himself from laughing at Mr. Sykes's pension advice, either. As for getting some cash together, his bank account contained exactly the same sum as it did after his first month on the job—sod all—and worldwide travel had consisted of a long weekend in New York and two package Spanish holidays.

Max had always believed that his would be a big life full of excitement, love, and adventure. It would be a life so fulfilling that if he awoke one morning to see Saint Peter standing at the foot of his bed, and Saint Peter asked, "My son, is there anything else you need to do before coming through the gates?" then Max would confidently reply, "No, Saint Peter. There isn't. I've done it *all*, thanks. What's next?"

But Max couldn't say that. He hadn't done it all. In fact, he'd done hardly any of it. If Saint Peter turned up today, the best Max could answer would be, "No, Saint Peter. There isn't anything else I need to do. I've had a weekend in the Big Apple, and I've been to Torremolinos twice. And to be honest, Saint Peter, I'd rather die than go back there a third time."

When Max reflected, he could see that he was falling short, and he knew why. One time, he'd put his name down for the school's French exchange. At first, he'd been anxious, but Henri was brilliant, and they'd gotten on famously well. Max had loved showing Henri around the town. They'd gone to football practice and the youth club most nights. For two whole weeks of warm summer evenings, they'd hung out with the in crowd at the local park. It had been a great time. But when it came time for the return leg twelve months later, Max had made up an excuse and didn't go. He found out later that Tom White, a boy from the year below, his replacement, had had a fantastic time in France and that Henri had invited him back the following January to go skiing in the Alps.

On another occasion, in sixth form, Max and a classmate, Jamie, had discovered that they both had a crush on Jessica Walsh, a long-legged girl in the year below. They'd tossed a coin to see who would ask her out. Max had called right but said he'd *lost*, telling himself he'd pick up the spoils when Jamie was rejected. But Jessica had said yes. Apparently, she'd wanted a boyfriend for ages and had vowed to accept the next boy who asked her.

Jamie had been over the moon.

Max wasn't.

Max feared failure, and it frustrated the hell out of him. His dad was a worrier, too, which was the reason he'd missed much of his only son's growing up.

"Sorry about the football match, Max," his dad would say. "I wanted to come but was scared the boss wouldn't like it if I left early."

Faced with a decision himself, Max was careful to weigh all the possibilities. He'd write down all of the risks and evaluate them—the pros and cons, the upsides and downsides, the advantages and disadvantages, the pluses and minuses, the benefits and costs, the potential opportunities and pitfalls, and so on. Sometimes, he had a full page of benefits and only one negative. But as soon as he neared a decision, that bloody negative seemed to multiply tenfold in strength and throw him back into confusion.

This torturous mind wrestling could carry on for days, weeks, or even months. And, of course, by the time he finally reached a decision, the job vacancy had gone, or the once-available girl was now unavailable, or the better-located flat had been taken.

Max's inner voice of caution didn't so much whisper into the back of his mind; rather, it shouted like a drill sergeant into his ear. Any negatives he would be deliberating at the time would suddenly breed like rabbits—big rabbits, to boot.

Think again, the drill sergeant said. *Don't rush in. It's fools who rush in, and we're not a fool, are we, Max? So let's just wait and see what happens first, and then, and only then, we can reconsider. We must make sure we get the* right *answer. It takes balls to wait. And fortunately for us, we've got balls aplenty.*

And so Max waited, and he didn't rush. He held back and reviewed his choices again and again and again. He evaluated and rescored the endless sets of permutations. Not surprisingly, the drill sergeant's strategy worked perfectly. In summary, over the course of thirty-two years and four months, Max West had survived and avoided serious failure. But his life was as dull as dishwater.

That was yesterday, however.

Today, Max West was reborn. And he felt terrible, unsafe, insecure, and uncertain—vulnerable. He didn't know it yet, but he was getting a second chance at life. He was getting a chance to live the big life he'd always dreamed of living and a chance to succeed and prosper. But he was also getting a chance to utterly fail, wither, and die.

The drill sergeant was gone, thrown unceremoniously into the recycle bin, never to return. In his place stood a much more fearsome foe. It was a part of Max that had been silent for a long time, and it was a part of him that was angry—really angry.

Decades of pent-up frustration poured forth.

"Max West, you're a loser. You've wasted our life. You might as well be dead. *Now wake the fuck up!*"

The words were angry hornets inside his skull, and as they stung, Max began to realize a great truth about himself: his self-promised destiny of a life of great adventure was, in fact, the world's greatest con trick. And it was a trick that he'd played on *himself* and beautifully. He'd constructed the perfect excuse for avoiding every possible failure by convincing himself that all he needed to do to have an amazing life was to wait and see, and then it would all turn out fantastic.

It was pathetic.

He was *pathetic.*

Over the next few months, Max fell into a dark place. He was miserable, bewildered, and confused. He told no one. He didn't know what to say. The stinging in his head continued night and day as his black mood alternated between depressions over wasting the first thirty-two years of his life and a high anxiety that the next thirty-two years would be just the same. For days on end, he'd nervously ask himself the same question: *What if this is all there is? What if this is all there is? Oh God, what if this is all there is?* He'd flinch as the increasingly frustrated voice in his head shrieked in response. *"Yes, you fucking idiot! Yes, that's right. That's the whole point. This is definitely all there fucking is."*

That night, after gazing blankly at the TV set, Max opened a drawer in the sideboard his grandmother had given to him. He took out a pen and paper and made yet another list. But it was a list he'd never made before: a list of his lifetime goals. Two hours of mental ache later, the list stood at only one item, and his numbed and tired mind had had enough.

<u>Life Goals–Max West</u>

1. To swim underwater for two lengths of Spenborough Pool.
2.
3.
4.

He could have put down a multitude of things—climbing Everest, the Volvo Ocean Race, driving US Route 66 on a Harley, going to university and majoring in sports management. But no, his only goal was to swim underwater for one hundred meters. It was embarrassing. So why did he feel such a strong urge to do it? He did swim during his lunch hour, and he did go underwater, even if it was only to retrieve the odd pound coin or piece of cheap jewelry from the pool bottom, but he wasn't exactly Man from Atlantis.

A film he'd seen as a boy came to mind. He thought it starred Doug McClure and had looked for it unsuccessfully one time on the Internet. It was about a traffic cop who gives a Mafia boss a speeding ticket and, as a result, finds himself in an elevator filling up with poisonous gas. The cop survives, wins the girl, and lives happily ever after because of his one and only notable talent: holding his breath for a full three-and-a-half minutes. A gangland rival ends up shooting the godfather dead.

But that was just a forgotten movie. And underwater swimming wasn't about to become an Olympic event. So what was the point? Wasn't this just another distraction from the real world and a childish one at that? Wasn't it just another example of him being pathetic? He started to list the pros and cons but then stopped and listened. There was no sound. Silence. Beautiful silence. The shrieking had stopped. The stinging had stopped. Something, somebody, for some reason, wanted him to under-take this challenge.

He therefore made a decision.

Two lengths underwater of the main pool it was.

It was a small price to pay for internal peace.

And if nothing ever came of it, then so what?

CHAPTER 3

Max stepped out of the taxi a couple of hundred yards before the pub. He often did this in summer to walk past the apple orchard he and his friends had raided as kids.

He strolled along in the evening sunshine. It warmed his face, and he breathed in deeply the sweet scent of the ripening apples. In the breeze, the treetops he'd known all his life gently swayed above him, bringing a host of carefree childhood memories to mind.

Approaching the three-hundred-year-old Bull's Head, he could hear laughter and happy voices. Smiling people in bright summer clothes and sunglasses were sitting on the beer-garden walls, for all of the picnic tables were full. Twenty or so people were leaning against the pub itself.

Max and his friends had first sneaked into the Bull's Head along with the throng on New Year's Eve when they were seventeen. From then on, they called in at least four times a week, never missing either a Wednesday or a Sunday night for reasons long forgotten.

Over the years, the Bull's Head had turned from a second home to what Max had described one day as a place of spiritual significance. He'd been drunk at the time but backed up his claim by calculating that during sixth form, they'd spent more time at the Bull's Head than actually at school, which went some way to explaining his exam results.

The old pub was dark inside and cool.

Max called out hesitantly to the barmaid. "Hi, Marcy."

The girl was very pretty. She was moving efficiently from table to table, picking up empty glasses and admirers as she went. "Oh, Maxi."

She stumbled and dropped a glass, her long, dark curly hair tumbling chaotically across her face as she made a grab for it. She missed, but the glass didn't break. It just bounced and rolled under a chair.

"They're in the taproom, Max, for reasons known only to you lot," she said, reddening. "Go on in, and I'll bring you a Stella." She turned away to collect more empties and thank the man who'd picked up the glass.

"Thanks, Marcy," Max said, pausing in case she turned again.

She didn't.

Marcy and Max had dated for most of the previous year. Then, two months ago, much to Max's shock, Marcy had ended it. Since then, every time they met at the Bull's Head—which, unfortunately, was four or more times a week—they felt more and more uncomfortable.

The Bull's Head taproom was even darker than the main lounge and was in need of serious refurbishment. The white Artexed walls were tinged yellow from preban-era cigarette smoke, and the panes in the window frames rattled with anything above a decent breeze. The burgundy velvet seating upholstery was past its sell-by date. It was bald in places, rubbed away over the years by countless fidgeting legs, and, to add insult to injury, people had picked holes in the exposed weave, which now sprouted tufts of foam. The room's far-end wall housed an old dartboard. It was hung over an unused fireplace and had been so heavily used that the majority of darts fell out unless they were hurled like javelins.

The taproom's centerpiece was the pool table that Max and his pals had played on for almost sixteen years. It had been the scene of many famous victories and even more inglorious defeats. The once-navy-blue felt was faded to at best a light sky blue. Miraculously, however, the balls still ran true, unless they encountered one of three deep cigarette burns.

Stan, Will, and DG were sitting together under the window. They were Max's best friends. Jack, the other member of the "Infamous Five," as others called them, had moved abroad three years before.

"Just in time, Maxi. It's your round," Stan said as Max walked through the open door.

Stan was a short man with a massive chest and a cropped head. He had a grim face, big arms, and small, dark eyes. People who didn't know him often steered clear.

"And nice to see you, Stanley," Max said sarcastically. "You do realize you've said that every single time I've walked into a bar for the last fifteen years."

"Just coincidence." Stan smiled, his eyes nearly disappearing. "Your timing's crap is all."

Max sat down opposite his three friends. "Marcy's bringing me a Stella in. I'll order a round then."

DG winced. "How's the Marcy thing going, mate?"

"Not good, going by the latest episode," Max said, remembering the bouncing beer glass. "Awkward, very awkward."

For the next hour, the chat was about football and the current no-hopers on *Big Brother* as Marcy, always managing to avoid eye contact with Max, trailed back and forth with pints of Stella Artois. Eventually, Will brought the conversation around to the housing market.

"Right, that does it," DG said, banging his empty glass on the table. "Come on, I can't take another session on negative equity and the unfairness of stamp duty. Let's get the meeting over with and go outside." A golden smile suddenly spread across his handsome face. "There're a few young ladies outside in the beer garden that I haven't had the pleasure of yet. In fact, here's an idea: why don't we hold the AGM outside? It's bloody roasting in this shit hole."

Stan was appalled. "Language, please," he said, giving DG a stern look. "There are women on the premises, DG. So watch your *fucking* manners."

DG opened his mouth to protest but then thought better of it. It was always hard to tell if Stan was joking or not.

Stan switched to a formal tone, for which he was ill suited. "The annual general meeting of the Bull's Head Pool Team has only one agenda item—namely, to decide the venue for the annual trip—and has been held in this historic *shit hole* for the last fifteen years straight."

DG started to object. "Hang o—"

Stan waved his objection away. "Yes, yes, DG. I agree. It is a shit hole, but it's also tradition, and there's precious little tradition left. We've chosen such annual trip venues as Blackpool and Newcastle in here, so I'm sorry, but *no* other shit hole will do."

"That's correct up to a point, Stan," Will said. "But it's also a bit of an exaggeration, if you don't mind me saying so. I mean, thirteen out of fifteen years, we've gone to bloody Blackpool. So the taproom's hardly been a creative space for us. Newcastle was a good do, but DG chose that because he'd never laid a Geordie. And don't forget we decided on Weston-super-Whatever in here. I get the tradition, but we all know we're going to bloody *Blackpool*, so let's get it over with and have a beer outside in the sun."

Max pulled an expensive white envelope from his back pocket. "Chaps, it doesn't have to be Blackpool, Newcastle, or even Weston-Whatever this year."

"Bought yourself a ticket for Crufts," DG said, smirking. "At least those hounds are better turned out than your mums on the pull."

Max ignored the comment. "It's from Jack," he said, and he began to read.

Dear Max, Stan, DG, and Will,

I hope that life is treating you kindly. It's been far, far too long since we last met, and I realize that's mainly my fault. Recently, I've been reflecting on the importance of roots and that I'll never know anybody better than the friends I went to school with.

I want to apologize for the last three years. I was shortsighted in not valuing your friendship.

I know it's the AGM coming up, and to make it up to you, I want to organize this year's BHPT annual trip. I know you all love Blackpool, but this year, I'd like you to fly out to Majorca to spend a week aboard my luxury yacht. I'll pay for the flights, organize the internal transfers, and I promise to provide some serious entertainment.

I have asked my executive assistant, Jules, to make all the arrangements. I hope you can all find it in your hearts to accept. It would be fantastic to see all of you again.

Yours hopefully,

Jack

"Do me a favor," DG said sarcastically. "There's absolutely no fuc—sorry—way that he wrote that. For a start, I've seen the Dracula movies, and bloodsucking vampires like Jack don't *reflect* at all. They just vanish into thin air, as our so-called mate did. And as for an apology, he couldn't even spell the word."

Will jumped in. "Any more details, Max?"

"I think this Jules, his executive assistant—bloody posh, ain't it?—must have written the letter," Max said. "She rang yesterday to make sure I'd received it and basically said as much, but she also said that *Mr. North* is desperate to make it up to us for what he calls the 'Blackpool Incident.' He wants to sail us around Majorca, and apparently no expense is to be spared. Although we do have to fly Ryanair, take our own cheese-and-tomato sandwiches, and have no more than fifteen kilos of luggage."

Max paused at the quizzical faces. "I'm only joking, guys. We can take tuna sandwiches, if we want to."

Stan still looked perplexed. "Why just cheese-and-tomato or tuna?"

"Christ, Stan, it's a joke. You can take any kind of sandwiches, even the strawberry-jam-and-cheese ones you like. Anyway…look, Jules said Jack's yacht is being made ready to sail the week after next, which, of course, is 'trip week.' Flights are booked and paid for, and, as the letter says, Jack is arranging some *serious* entertainment."

"*Serious* entertainment?" Will asked.

"Well, I'm hoping for a top comedian," Stan said mockingly, "one who can do brilliant cheese-and-tomato-sandwich jokes like Maxi here. That was a real rib-tickler, mate. I particularly liked the tuna bit."

"Wasted on you lot, that's for sure," Max said and drained another Stella. "Jules doesn't know what he's organizing, Will. She said he wants to surprise us."

"So what do we do?" Will asked.

Max looked at each of his open palms in turn. "That's simple, Will. It's either a week in Blackpool, with trams, amusement arcades, hen parties, and sleet, or a week onboard a luxury yacht in Majorca with no expense spared, serious entertainment—whatever that is—and wall-to-wall sunshine. I'm sure that onlooking bystanders will understand the pain of our dilemma."

"That's all well and good, Max," DG said, who was clearly irritated. "But don't you remember Jack running out on us in the face of a good kicking and leaving us with his hotel bill, including charges for eight porn movies? And since then, he's ignored us for three years."

"Settle down, children," Stan said firmly. "Now, you all know my views on desertion in the field. If a man can't count on his brothers in battle, then the battle is lost. Jack broke that rule; therefore, he's a twat."

DG opened his mouth again to protest, but again thought better of it.

Stan continued. "As chairman of the Bull's Head Pool Team, I need to ensure that we follow the annual general meeting rules. Rule one is that each club member has to state his preferred choice of trip destination and his reasons for that choice, and then we all vote. We've had a proposal, which is Majorca."

"You've just made that rule up, Stan," Will said and laughed.

"No, Will. It's definitely a rule," Stan said, but he was unconvincing. "I devised it after last year's fiasco in Weston-bloody-Nightmare. So, please, chaps, one at a time. What's your preference and why? DG?"

DG had gone from irritated to hurt. "Well, I admit Weston-super-Mare could have gone better."

Stan couldn't contain himself. "Gone better? We never even found the bloody place. You got lost somewhere near Bristol, and then your van broke down. We spent the next three days at a motorway service station, waiting for a new camshaft. Three meals a day for three days at—where was it? Oh yeah, the Happy *fucking* Eater."

"Oh, stop moaning," DG said. "And watch your mouth. Marcy's coming back in."

Marcy placed another four pints of Stella on the table as Max stared down at his shoes.

"Look, guys," DG said. "I'm voting for Blackpool. Don't you remember that amazing Saturday night when we all got smashed and turned over by pickpockets? We kipped on the beach. The stories I've had out of that. So, there you go. We don't need Jack, Majorca, or wall-to-wall sunshine."

"Not wishing to shatter a perfect dream, DG," Max said, "but that night *we* slept on the beach—in the rain, by the way—*you* didn't. You spent the night 'debriefing,' I think you called it, that policewoman who took our crime details. You joined us again at breakfast at the beach hot-dog stand. We all know this very well, DG, because we all sheltered from the pouring rain under that hotdog stand all that *amazing* night."

"WPC Jackson," DG said in a trance. "Sorry, chaps."

"Will, what do you think?" Stan asked.

Will was a mild-mannered, gold-rim-spectacled chartered accountant. He was five foot eight and a little overweight from business lunches, and his light-brown hair was receding by the hour.

He'd met his wife, Jane, also his first girlfriend, at university, where he'd been studying accountancy. After graduation, they'd married, and Will had secured a position in a local accountancy firm. Eight years on, after working ten hours a day for six days a week, he'd made partner, specializing in corporate tax.

Will loved his friends. But Jane, who was from a well-to-do family in Henley-on-Thames, *detested* them with a passion. She would go into a deep sulk before Will was due to meet them.

"You must move on, William," she'd shout. And then for tactical reasons, she'd soothe him. "It's just that they're holding you back, William. You're better than they are, my love. And so am I. *Aren't I*, Will?"

Initially, Will had defended his friends. But over time, he realized that the secret to a bearable life was to nod and go back to work. Over the years, Jane had worn him down, and he'd seen less and less of Max, Stan, and DG. He didn't know how to tell them, but the attrition had finally become too much, and he'd conceded to a delighted Jane that this would be his last-ever Bull's Head Pool Team Trip.

"Well, Jack did let us down badly in Blackpool," Will said. "No doubt about that. And this is the first time he's been in touch. So, while I'm glad he's contacted us, we'll have a great time in Blackpool." *And I really, really don't want to tell Jane we're going to Majorca.*

"OK," Stan said. "Thanks, DG. Thanks, Will. I agree with you both. It's not about where we go. And it's not about fancy bloody restaurants or luxury bleeding yachts, either. They're not important." He took on a Churchillian tone. "No, sir. What's important is that we've all grown up together and that we'll all stand *united* against any bastards that come against us. We trust in our brotherhood, knowing that if one of us is captured, then our three brothers will return."

"Right," Max said, "except when DG has a policewoman to debrief."

Max was disappointed. Blackpool again. He needed something new, something fresh. His friends, however, were clearly comfortable with their decision. "I'm surprised, but I'll go with the majority," he said.

"OK," Stan said. "All that remains to be done before I close the meeting is to formally record the votes in the minutes that Will is taking."

Will hurriedly pulled a gold pen from his jacket pocket and ripped a blank page from his diary.

"Your vote for the minutes, please, Will," Stan said.

"Majorca," Will said, imagining Jane coming toward him with a large carving knife.

"DG."

"Majorca."

Will and DG looked at each other and laughed. Luxury and sunshine had trumped amusement arcades and sleet for sure.

"Yep, Majorca for me, too," Stan said. "It's a no-brainer."

"Christ," Max said. "You had me worried there for a minute, guys. I thought you'd grown principles. Majorca for me, too. Great."

"Excellomundo," Stan said as he slammed down his empty pint glass. "For the record, Will, it's a unanimous agreement for the luxury yacht plus secret entertainment. However, Jack is still a twat, and the Blackpool Incident remains problematic. Meeting closed. Minutes to me by the end of the week."

"Do I have to, Stan? I'm so busy."

"Will, I was joking," Stan said, slapping him on the shoulder. "Calm down. Two weeks will do nicely."

Will, like DG, could never tell when Stan was joking; only Max could. He'd ask him later.

"Right," DG said, rising from his seat. "I was beginning to think we'd be here all night. Time to go and meet the lovely ladies." He rubbed his hands with glee and headed outside.

The others followed.

"Why the change of heart, Stan?" Max asked. "I thought you loved Blackpool."

"I do love Blackpool, Maxi," Stan said. "But you, my friend, need a change. Even *I* can see that. Plus, our ex-pal Jack, the twat, owes us big time. So let's go enjoy some of the ginger-headed bastard's ill-gotten gains."

"Another set, guys?" Marcy asked as they passed by the bar en route to the beer garden.

"That would be great, Marcy," said Max. "Thanks."

He had difficulty pulling away from her eyes because they were locked solidly on his. It wasn't because he felt strong pangs of regret at their breaking up but because he knew that she did. He still didn't fully understand why she'd dumped him. It had taken an age for him to pluck up the courage to ask her out in the first place. Her reply had been a surprise.

"About time, Maxi!" she'd said before wrapping her arms straight around his neck.

They'd had some really good times together, or so he thought. They'd spent a weekend in New York seeing all of the sites and a week on the Costa del Sol with romantic late-night walks on the beach. Marcy had bought a crossword book at Manchester airport, and each day they'd attempted to complete one. They never had.

He laughed even now as eight down—three letters, a policeman?—came to mind.

Quick as a flash Marcy, had replied. "P-I-G."

"Close, darling," he'd said. "But I think you'll find it's C-O-P!"

Marcy had been mortified. "Oh, that's shameful," she'd said before bursting out in laughter.

She had a great laugh.

A few months later, Marcy had broken up with him, saying she knew that he wanted someone else.

"Who?" he'd said, pretty shocked. "There is nobody else. Honestly, Marcy."

Marcy had taken a hold of his hands. Tears were in her eyes. "Max, I know you'd never cheat on me, but I don't think you love me. I think you really care for me, and in time maybe you'd grow to love me, too. But I want more than that. I'm worth more than that."

Max still hadn't understood.

Marcy had tried again. "It's those times in restaurants over coffee or when we're walking together. You get a faraway look in your eyes, and it's obvious that part of you is off searching for something else, for *someone else*. I'm not even sure you know that you do it. But you do, and I need someone with me all the time. It's not meant to be, Maxi. I just know it. It hurts me, but I'd rather be hurt now than devastated later on."

He still hadn't gotten it.

She had tried yet again. "What if I asked if you love me and whether you wanted to spend the rest of your life with me?"

Max had half opened his mouth to speak, but Marcy had gently laid a finger across his lips. "Don't answer," she'd whispered, tears running over her cheeks. "I know you want to say yes, to not to hurt my feelings, but I don't think you can, and you wouldn't lie to me."

Max's brain had searched desperately for an answer that would remedy the situation, but none had come.

Marcy had continued. "The thing is, Maxi, if you asked me that question, then I would say yes in a flash. And that's why I must let you go."

And so he was single again. "How come everybody else seems to know what I think and what I want except for me?" he'd said aloud in the chip shop a few days later. The two elderly ladies in the queue behind him stepped nervously backward in case he became violent.

"If you're not sure, young man, then I'd recommend the fish cakes," one of them had said, trying to be helpful.

Even though it hurt to admit it, Max had finally realized that Marcy was right. He couldn't tell her that he loved her because, as hard as he tried, he just didn't, even though he desperately wanted to. She was also right that he wouldn't lie to her.

He'd learned to be honest with women after an unfortunate episode with DG. They'd been twenty-two at the time. One Friday night, they'd gone to a popular nightclub in Bradford called Cloud Nine. Max had hit it off with a successful businesswoman called Jackie. She'd been ten years

Max's senior, but they'd danced and talked all night and had ended up back at her semi in Morley. They'd arranged to meet again the following Wednesday.

"Wow, great start, Maxi," DG had said the following night. He'd gone off with a cocktail waitress the previous night but had forgotten her name. "Now, what you've got to do, Max, is collect a couple more. Three women on the go should keep you busy. Who's next?"

It didn't feel like *him*, but Max decided to give it a try. After all, DG seemed to be enjoying himself. "Well, I do quite fancy that Sandra who came to watch us play football last week. I thought she gave me the eye."

"Sounds promising," DG had said, "as it's unlikely she was interested in our footballing skills."

"Speak for yourself, DG. I scored the winner."

After Sunday's game, Max had bought Sandra a drink. All had been going according to plan until she asked him what else he'd done that weekend.

"Oh, I went to Cloud Nine on Friday night."

"*That's* a coincidence," Sandra had said. "My friend Jackie went to Cloud Nine on Friday night, too. She's really nice, Max. You'd like her. And she's got this really great job."

A little more questioning had confirmed the inevitable. From that moment on, Max had decided it was one woman at a time for him. That was much less complicated.

DG had cringed when Max told him. "Just beginner's bad luck, mate. Next time will be fine."

"There'll be no next time, DG. I'm not cut out for a harem like you. Too bloody stressful, for a start. Aren't you always worrying that one of your other girlfriends will come into whatever restaurant or bar you're in? I'd be watching the door all night long."

"Nah. For a start, I don't do restaurants. And a lot of my ladies are married, so they're not going to cause any trouble. It works better if they're married."

"Probably not the Church of England's top reason for getting wed, but I see your point."

The BHPT annual trip destination agreed on, all four men were standing in the beer garden. It was a beautiful night, and the sun was still fairly high in the sky, even though it was after eight o'clock. DG was telling jokes to a group of girls from a hairdressing salon, out on a party night, and Stan and Will were busy discussing Majorcan travel arrangements. Max was standing nearby, leaning lazily against the ancient pub's warm stonewall and enjoying the late sunshine.

He felt much better about Marcy. Yes, it had been her decision to end it, and yes, he'd avoided deciding again. But he had given their relationship a go, and even though it felt awkward every time he and Marcy saw each other, he realized that he would never regret the relationship—and that felt good.

Maybe he wasn't quite so pathetic after all.

CHAPTER 4

Jack North left school two weeks before his final exams, finally accepting that he wouldn't pass any of them. He'd worked hard, but academic study just wasn't his bag. His teachers knew this to be a gross understatement.

Jack's last attainable academic objective was to avoid the emotionally excruciating experience that was "results day." The thought of happy, carefree students bounding over to tell him how many *A*s and *B*s they'd gotten—followed by insincere inquiries into Jack's own results—was more than he could bear. He'd want to smash their heads in but wouldn't because they may hit him back.

He resented clever people, and it was all DG's fault. That infuriatingly gifted bastard excelled at almost everything he did, including girls. And DG didn't even try. Top grades and top girls just gravitated toward him. Jack had never had a girlfriend.

After eleven years of torturous schooling, Jack North was entering the job market with just two qualifications—well, sort of two. One was an *E* grade in information communications technology—he'd occasionally copied Max's half-decent course work. The other was a silver star for an apple crumble in year eight—and his mother had baked that.

"All these exams are total bollocks, Maxi," Jack said in his thick Yorkshire accent. "What's the point of all this Romeo and Julie, or whatever his bird is called? And history? Don't get me on to history. Crop rotation and fucking pig iron. Who gives a flying fuck? It's the future that counts, Max, not history, and the future is where I'm going."

They were standing together at the bus stop. Max was going to youth club to help organize a table-football evening, as he regularly did on Tuesday nights. Jack was upset about his school grades, so Max played along.

"I agree, Jack. But most of us aren't as brave as you, or else there'd be more droppi—I mean, moving on to the future."

Jack had a point about the history syllabus, though. Three months of studying the golden age of agriculture was enough to put one off the subject for life.

"What are you going to do, then?" Max asked.

"Had a bit of luck," Jack said, looking really pleased. "I'm off to work with my uncle Cedric. If I shape up, I'll be a manager in no time. Uncle Cedric owns Crossland Weavers."

"Wow," Max said, genuinely surprised. "Crossland's is huge. You haven't mentioned him before."

"Big surprise for me, too. Mum only told me last week. She fell out with Aunty Tracy years ago—that's Uncle Cedric's wife—and they've only just started talking again. Turns out the feud was over Uncle Cedric. Mum swears that she saw him first and that Aunty Tracy is and will always be a gold-digging tart. Anyhow, the bottom line is that good old Cedric is rolling in it, which is just fucktabulous. He also has a machine shop brimming with tasty pussy, which yours truly here intends to work his way through, while you lot write about the bloody Corn Laws. I'm off up to Crossland's now for my induction."

● ● ●

Thirteen years on, Jack was still only a storeroom assistant. The mill's electronic stock system had remained a mystery to him since day one, but worst of all were the machine-shop women.

Mr. Smith, the stores manager, told Cedric Crossland that he'd done the best he could for Jack, but the truth was that his nephew was unreliable and incompetent. Cedric Crossland valued and encouraged honesty from his employees, and he thanked the manager for his candor. If Jack had been any other member of staff, he would have been let go, but Cedric remembered his wife's fragile relationship with her somewhat-scary sister, and he sent his errant nephew on an expensive management-development program instead. He also enrolled him in a number of local information technology courses, including one dedicated to the mill's stock system. Unfortunately, none of the courses added value. Or, as Jack had put it, "Uncle, they're total shit."

The women at the mill became a nightmare after Jack cornered a pretty machinist in the stationery cupboard and demanded a blow job, or else he'd tell his uncle to give her the sack. The girl ran straight to her father, which wouldn't have been so bad if he hadn't been the mill's main union representative, but unfortunately, he was. A two-day strike over sexual harassment ensued, and it only ended after holiday entitlement was increased by two days for all staff groups. Uncle Cedric was less than pleased.

And then Jack's life changed.

And in a very big way.

Very, very big.

During the mill's biannual stocktaking, Uncle Cedric's entire family—except Jack—and three other employees were all tragically burned to death. A firefighter was also killed.

The eight deaths shocked the entire community. Thousands of mourners lined the streets of Cleckheaton as the mass funeral procession wept its way from the town hall to the cemetery.

The fire-service investigation was thorough but inconclusive. The tragedy could have been arson or simply sheer negligence. The investigation report confirmed that the fire had started in the mill's main storeroom and quickly spread. Lives had been lost because of the intense heat; thick, toxic smoke; and a blocked fire exit.

The stockroom itself had been full of wool, yarn, and paraffin—the latter for the heaters. The place had become an inferno in minutes, and the intense heat had melted the flimsy rubber curtaining that separated the stockroom from the stores offices. A few minutes more, and the offices had been consumed. The ground-floor ceiling had caught fire. Old, brittle wooden beams that were saturated in machine oil from over a hundred years of production had proved to be more effective than kindling. Less than half an hour from the first small flame, the old mill's six stories were ablaze. Most employees had reacted as trained when the alarms sounded and were soon safe outside in the car park, but the building itself had been doomed, as was anybody caught in the stores.

Uncle Cedric and his family had been helping administer the stocktaking. They'd been sitting in the store manager's office and checking through computer tabulations, as were the rest of the stores team members. None of them had stood a chance. The manager's office was nearest to the stockroom, and when fire had blasted through the rubber curtaining, it had almost instantly cut them off. In the few seconds it had taken to understand the peril they were in, it was too late. Escape through the ground-floor machine shops had been denied by a fifteen-foot wall of flame.

How the fire had started had been discovered, but *who* had started it had not. The police investigation had been complicated by the number of people going in and out of the stores that day, and the police subsequently failed to identify the single person who had recklessly or purposefully discarded a lighted cigarette.

Jack had always enjoyed a crafty smoke in the stockroom first thing in the morning. It was a perk of being related to the owner. *Christ, it's about the only one*, he thought. He would casually flick the cigarette butt into an old paint tin on the floor and then have forty winks on a wool bale he pulled out in front of the fire door so that he could rest his feet on the crossbar. It was very comfortable.

Two things were different about Jack's normal routine on the morning of the fire, however. First, he'd forgone his forty winks because of the stocktaking. He'd had to. The stores team was milling about, and Uncle Cedric was there, too, as were Aunty bloody Tracy and both of their privately schooled brats. And second, and profoundly perhaps, because of his irritation over the morning's disruption, his aim was off. The still-lighted cigarette butt hit the paint tin's rim and bounced off into some hemp fragments.

As the hemp smoldered away, Jack strolled toward the Merry England Coffee Shop for an early-morning snack. They couldn't expect him to work a Saturday morning without proper sustenance, could they? It wasn't fair. It was unhealthy, too. He'd heard about workplace stress and meant to avoid it. Two bacon sandwiches and three cups of sugary tea later, with a satisfied feeling in his stomach and his iPod wound up to maximum, he turned down Mill Street and stopped dead in his tracks.

Six fire engines were lined up end to end in the street. Firefighters were frantically unreeling hoses while the extendable ladders on the back of the tenders were rising into the air. One was already fully up. A lone firefighter was standing in the gantry seventy feet above the street and was directing a jet of water onto the mill's black slate roof. Two hoses in the street started up. They concentrated on the fourth floor, the powerful water jets blasting through two fourth-floor windows. It was an attempt to contain the flames to the first three floors.

Jack could see that the fire service's valiant efforts were futile. Twenty more fire engines wouldn't make any difference. Compared with the inferno they were trying to quash, the jets of water were pathetic. It was the equivalent of pissing on a large bonfire.

Jack was frozen to the spot. He was mesmerized, staring upward in horror. Flames burst from some fifth-floor windows directly opposite the elevated gantry, and the firefighter up there was consumed by a fireball. A moment later, the ladder he was on began to descend, and the gantry and the firefighter slowly emerged out of a cloud of black smoke. He was helmetless and slumped precariously over the gantry rail. Twenty feet from the ground, he tippled out and crashed onto the fire engine's cab roof, where he remained, unmoving.

Jack screamed at the sight, but the music blaring from his iPod drowned out the sounds of mayhem. Glass crashed into the street, and small fragments began landing on his head. He protected his face with his hands, stumbled backward, and slipped. A firefighter caught hold of him just before he hit the pavement and set him back on his feet. Jack grabbed the firefighter's sleeve—he didn't want him to go; he needed saving too—but the man pulled away and ran toward his stricken colleague.

Jack felt faint. He was still a hundred yards from the burning building, but the heat was rapidly becoming unbearable, and his eyes were watering like taps. All he could see were shadows with yellow pointed hats running in and out of the smoke. His lungs felt hot, and his breath came in small rasps.

He was losing consciousness.

More firefighters ran past him toward the tenders to help raise the remaining ladders. Suddenly, Jack was aware that "Search for the Hero" by M People was blasting into his ears. It filled his world—a truly inspirational song. And it inspired Jack. He now knew what he had to do. Run. And he did without another thought. Up Mill Street like Usain Bolt, and at the top, he kept on going, never looking back.

Jack wasn't a religious guy. Christ, he'd never even been in a church before the fire, but now he attended every memorial service. And he prayed every morning and every night at home, too. He didn't pray for the seven people who'd been burned to cinders, or for the firefighter, or for the grieving families. He didn't pray for the emergency services or even the loss of fifteen hundred jobs either. No, none of those things were important to Jack North. The rest of the town would have been really interested to know that Jack was praying for the opposite of what they wanted—that is, that the name of the individual solely responsible for untold amounts of pain, death, and suffering would always and forever remain *unknown*.

A week after the fire, two police officers called around to check on his whereabouts on the fateful day. Jack claimed that he'd been ill with a painful sore throat. He'd still gone into work at eight, though—after all, he was conscientious—but Mr. Smith, the stores manager, had taken one look at him and sent him straight back home again. The officers were highly suspicious. Jack had been spotted in the Merry England Coffee Shop, but, crucially, no witnesses could place him in the stockroom. This was understandable. The only people who'd been in the stores at the start of the fire—Mr. Smith, the other two storeroom assistants, and Uncle Cedric and his family—were all dead—cremated alive.

A month after the funerals, Jack heard a knock at his door. He and his mother turned to each other in alarm, as they always did now when somebody called. This time, it wasn't the police. It was Mr. Jacobs, Uncle Cedric's lawyer. Initially, Jack feared the worst. New evidence proving his guilt had come to light. His DNA had been discovered on the infamous cigarette stub, or a new eyewitness had come forward who could place him in the stockroom. But it wasn't anything like that at all. It was actually about the most unexpected thing that Jack and his mum could ever imagine.

Jack and his mum were now co-owners of Crossland Weavers. In addition, said Mr. Jacobs, as Cedric Crossland's only surviving relatives, they would also inherit Crossland Hall and a considerable investment portfolio.

Mr. Crossland had been a very successful businessman, Mr. Jacobs said, but he was also prudent. The mill was fully insured, and rebuilding work could begin whenever Mr. North wanted it to.

"Who's that?" Jack asked.

"Why, that's *you*, of course," Mr. Jacobs said, smiling. "You are Mr. Jack North, aren't you?"

"Well, yeah, I am," Jack said in a half daze. "I think so."

His daze didn't last for long.

Mr. Jacobs hadn't even started his car to leave before a huge grin spread across Jack's face. He high-fived his mother, and they hugged for the first time in years. This was an amazing turn of events—a golden opportunity. And he wasn't going to waste it. Deep down, Jack knew that he thoroughly deserved it. True, this good fortune had come about through others' misfortune—or eight deaths, to be precise—but that was life, wasn't it? And it had been an *accident*.

In Uncle Cedric's honor, Jack would transform Crossland Weavers. He'd take it from a small-town operation into a multinational, global force. Aggressive acquisition and diversification would be his strategy.

Jack North, the man with almost no qualifications and a dead-end job, was consigned to history, just like the fucking Corn Laws. And in his place proudly stood a new man, *Mr.* Jack North—the owner, chairman, and chief executive officer of Crossland Weavers, a major manufacturing concern. It boasted fifteen hundred employees and a turnover of more than fifty million pounds. They were impressive numbers, but even more important to Mr. Jack North was what he had inherited in addition to money and power: respect. Jack had craved the respect of others all his life. Now, for the first time, he would command it.

He would begin his new mission immediately.

Four months later, the derelict mill on the other side of town had been refurbished—Crossland Weavers was open for business again.

The very first thing *Mr.* Jack North, the chairman, did on opening day was to find the little bitch who'd refused him a blow job three years before. His elevation to chairman of the board had changed the rules, or so he thought, and he was truly shocked by the woman's venomous reaction. She screamed when he restated his sexual demands, threw a mug of tea on his Savile Row suit, and then shouted at the top of her voice, for the whole machine shop to hear, that she'd rather suck on a dog turd than on his minuscule dick. Oh, and he could stick his crappy job up his fat, lardy arse. Thus, the second thing that the new chairman did on opening day was to sack her.

The incident knocked his confidence somewhat, but other workers, including the woman's father, were beginning to show him some respect, especially after he threatened all their jobs. Mr. Jack North wasn't the proverbial pig rolling in shit just yet, but with time, one day, he would be.

And finally, that day arrived. It was three years after the fire, and Jack was feeling fantastic, the best he'd ever felt. The Aston Martin's roof was down, and he was cruising. The early-morning air was refreshing as it blew through his thick ginger hair, and he smiled in delight at the diamonds twinkling on his Rolex. The Majorcan sun was shining on his life, and everything was rosy. Today was the day he'd get to show his old school chums that he, Mr. Jack North, was the biggest success of them all.

He laughed to himself.

Life couldn't get any better.

He couldn't wait to see the looks of awe on Max, Stan, Will, and Mr. Bloody-Clever-Clogs DG's faces when they clapped eyes on *his* beautiful yacht. He made a mental note to get Jules to film it, and then he laughed again while sliding his buttocks around on the driver's seat; the sumptuous leather felt so good.

He never saw the red Ferrari; he was too busy picturing his triumph.

It cut straight across the Aston's path.

Jack panicked. "Jesu-u-u-u-u-s! Fu-u-u-ck!"

He slammed hard on the brakes and instinctively turned the steering wheel, his fingernails digging into the soft leather. The Aston responded instantly and veered left, missing the Ferrari's back end by inches and swerving across the road.

And directly into the path of an oncoming Texaco petrol tanker.

Time slowed.

All sound died.

And Jack's mind froze.

His unconscious self rose out of his body and floated upward. He found himself unexpectedly watching the unfolding tragedy from above, in a position of surprising calm. His other self was wrestling with the Aston's controls, desperately trying, and utterly failing to steer the supercar back across the road. The oncoming tanker hadn't deviated from its original path.

Sixty tons of steel and petroleum were about to crush his two-ton Aston—at a relative velocity of 180 miles an hour—a giant speeding bomb. DG could have calculated the immense forces and the energy about to be expended, but it wasn't necessary. There was no benefit to Jack to know that the resulting collision would kill him a thousand times over. The impact wasn't going to be a close-run thing. There would be no miracle, no walking out of a broken car with bruised ribs and a black eye. All Jack needed to know was that his forthcoming demise was as certain as night following day. He was about to be obliterated from existence, reduced to the molecular level, and blasted to infinity and beyond. The Texaco tanker driver knew it too. Jack could see. The man's mouth was open wide—presumably, he was screaming—which was severely distorting an otherwise very impressive handlebar mustache.

As Jack watched, the screaming man took his hands off the steering wheel and covered his face.

He's protecting his bloody mustache, thought Jack, just as his mind reentered his body.

Time restarted. There was a cacophony of roaring engines, flashing images, and color. Jack spun the steering wheel. He'd no purpose in mind, but what else was there to do?

Near bursting, the whining, low-profile tires dug deep into the hot tarmac.

The Aston Martin took off, landed heavily, bounced two feet into the air, landed again, slid sideways, and went into a wild spin. It careened across the road and over an area of rough gravel, coming to rest virtually undamaged against an old stonewall, shrouded by a cloud of dust.

"Je-e-e-e-sus Fuckin' H. Christ!"

The supercar was facing directly back the way it had come, an ideal position to see the jackknifing Texaco tanker smash into the jagged roadside cliffs.

One moment, the giant Texaco tanker was there; the next moment, it wasn't. It just vanished, vaporized as eight thousand gallons of highly flammable petrol ignited in an instant. A fireball the size of a small cloud began chasing down the explosion's shockwave, which forced Jack back in his seat and sucked his lungs dry.

Well, that's fucked your mustache good and proper. Jack realized that his head was on fire. Screaming, he furiously patted his skull as the acrid smell of burning human hair—his—caught in his throat.

"Jesus Christ!"

He continued to pat for another five minutes; longer than he thought was necessary and then anxiously peered into the rearview mirror. He was pleasantly surprised. He expected melted ears, at the very least, but they were both still there, and perfectly whole, if a little blackened. His ginger hair and eyebrows were gone, replaced by black scorch marks, but other than that, there was no serious damage. It wasn't a pretty sight, yet as his mother would have told him, it hadn't been a pretty sight before, either.

He laughed.

Jack's one real strength was resilience and a maniacal sense of humor in the face of adversity. Yes, he cried, screamed, and ran away, but he could also laugh about it, at himself, and his predicament.

His instinctual crisis strategy kicked in. "Right, we're off," he said to himself. Nothing could be done for the tanker driver, anyway. He was floating somewhere up by the hole in the ozone layer, and Jack was buggered if he was going to stick around to fill out bloody police forms.

The Aston Martin's engine was still running.

"What a fucking car!" he shouted and punched the air. "Come on, you beauty. Take Daddy home."

He pulled up to the main road just as three black Audis emerged out of the destroyed tanker's smoke pall. He paused to let them pass by, but then he found himself screaming again as the Audi column suddenly veered off the road and straight toward him. Another collision seemed inevitable, and this time it was Jack covering his face, as three expertly delivered hand-brake turns boxed him in—front, side, and rear.

"Jesus, fuck. Will it ever end?"

He watched in horror as the Audis doors flew open and huge men in black overalls jumped out, their black boots thudding on the hard, dusty ground.

In the time it took for him to lock the Aston's doors—which wasn't going to be much use in a soft top, particularly with the roof down—the twelve SWAT members had him encircled and were aiming a heady mixture of machine guns and automatic handguns at the only bit of Jack they could see—his head.

Jack was terrified. He could only focus his eyes on the little black holes at the ends of the many gun barrels coming toward him, and those holes were rapidly increasing in size. He froze as one cold barrel jabbed into his blackened left ear. Another poked at his cheek.

"Jesu—"

His breathing failed, and he passed out.

CHAPTER 5

I t was five o'clock Saturday morning.

The white minivan taxi had just picked up Max.

"Morning, mate," Max said sleepily. He hated getting up so early. It always felt like a shock to his system, as if he were a computer forced to start even though problems persisted. "We've three more to pick up," he said wearily. "I'll direct you."

The first stop was Stan's. There was no need to knock at his door. He was already outside waiting on the drive and looking eager, his khaki shorts and T-shirt bouncing as he limbered up on the spot. Stan loved the mornings; the earlier the start, the better.

Tina was standing by his side in full battle dress.

Max powered down the window and did his best to sound awake. "Hi, Tina. You look marvelous."

"Thanks, Maxi," Tina said, beaming. "I thought I'd make the effort. You know, to make sure that Stanley knows what he's missing."

There's certainly nothing left to doubt. Max rubbed the last bit of sleep from his eyes.

Tina was fully made up. She was wearing a pink Barbie-doll crop top and a yellow miniskirt with leg warmers. Stardust sparkled on her face and fingernails, and diamond ankle bracelets sparkled on top of her fluffy slippers. The whole outfit was topped off by the Princess Aurora tiara that Stan had bought for her at Disneyland Paris.

"You're late," Stan said to Max in a bark. "We said five!"

"Jesus, Stanley. It's all of three minutes past. I thought I was grumpy early doors."

"Timeliness is critical," Stan said in a serious tone. "Whether it's the army or plumbing, it doesn't matter. I didn't get a reputation for being the most reliable plumber in town by being three minutes late for a job, you know." He winked at Tina and picked up his bag.

"Timeliness can be of importance," Max said, yawning. "Like the bomb is set to go off in seven minutes, or the air ambulance will be here in three minutes, but we're flying civilian, Stanley—well, Ryanair. We'll be waiting around for hours in queues at the airport, and we'll still have time for a fry-up."

"Timeliness is discipline, and indiscipline is what gets you killed. My old sergeant major used to drill that into me, God rest his soul." Stan opened the taxi's rear door and threw in his luggage.

"What happened to him? KIA?" Max asked.

"Nah. It's a bit embarrassing, actually. Old Ramsden slept in during parachute training and didn't pack his chute properly. He hit the ground at one hundred twenty-five miles an hour."

"At least he was on time, though, aye," Max said, smiling. "Helluva role model, Stanley."

• • •

Stanley Winston Longbottom had a passion for the military and conflict. At his insistence, they'd played cowboys and Indians at junior school after he'd watched a John Wayne movie. The school bike shed served as a rudimentary fort, and the sports field was the open prairie, as Stan's Union army slaughtered the lower-school pupils, who were unfortunately designated the Sioux Nation.

Years later, cowboys and Indians gave way to pitch battles between the comprehensive school and the local grammar school. For decades, the interschool fighting, which consisted of baseball bats and chains, had blighted the town in the last week or two before the summer holidays. Surprisingly, however, other than cuts and bruises and the odd broken limb, it sounded worse than it was.

At fourteen, Stan organized the comprehensive school's campaign, and they'd given the grammar-school boys a real hiding. The following year, the grammar school refused to fight. Their leader, a lanky boy called Ralph Emerson-Smyth Tomkins, summed up their reasoning.

"That Longbottom chap thinks he's Rambo. He's really going to damage one of us. If he's in, then we're out."

Stan's response was confusion mixed with pride. "I thought damaging 'em was the whole bloody idea. Rambo damaged plenty."

First Blood was Stan's favorite film, and he religiously watched a Rambo movie once a month. For him to be compared with his action hero was indeed the ultimate compliment.

A few weeks before Stan's sixteenth birthday, the day he would enlist in the British Army, two incidents occurred that would reshape the rest of his life. The first was reading *Bravo Two Zero*, which Max had bought him for Christmas.

"Max, it's all about the SAS, the Special Air Service," Stan said, barely able to contain his excitement. "They're British Army Special Forces, the finest in the world, and I'm going to join 'em."

The second incident occurred two weeks later. Stan and his mum were at the bingo in Bradford. He'd never been before, but Aunty Hilda, his mum's usual partner, had the gout, so he drove his mum there and decided to have a go. Unbelievably, and to the unanimous resentment of regulars, he won. "House," he shouted and leaped on stage to claim one hundred pounds in Marks and Spencer vouchers. While doing so, he met Tina, who was the blond bingo caller, and instantly fell hopelessly in love.

"Tina's the love of my life, Max, and I'm hers. I know it," Stan said the day after. He was besotted.

The next couple of weeks saw Stan struggling with a heart-breaking dilemma: the British Army and his lifelong military calling versus Tina, the newly found love of his life. It was a complete stalemate. It was mountain versus mountain, Goliath versus Goliath. Stan couldn't bear the thought of not being in the army, but he equally couldn't contemplate a life without Tina. The predicament overwhelmed him. It was a classic no-win situation. In a drunken depression, he explained it all, yet again, to Max.

"Look, Stan," Max said after patiently listening to his friend's distress again. "I know you're the military expert here, but I've done a little research of my own. You do know that you could join the Territorial Army and stay at home with Tina, don't you? I know it's the reserve and not the full-time regulars, and you'll have to wait until you're nearly eighteen, but they must use all the same weaponry, and you'd be called up in a war situation. The best bit, of course, is that they have two SAS regiments, 21 SAS and 23 SAS. So you could have both, couldn't you—the Special Air Service and Tina. And you could train as a plumber in the time before joining up. What do you think?"

Stan was speechless. He'd been so caught up in his seemingly impossible situation that he'd never thought of any other options. But Max was right. The Territorial Army was serious military, and they did have SAS regiments. Why hadn't he seen it himself? It was so bloody obvious, it was so bloody brilliant, and it was so absolutely totally bloody sodding salvation. He'd grunted with a primitive, guttural relief and hugged Max so tightly that he bruised his ribs.

A decade and a half later, Sergeant Longbottom, SAS veteran, and Tina the bingo caller were still unmarried but still very much together. Whereas the grammar school boys and a number of other armies around the world were no match for Stan, little Tina was in full control of her man. She had her little pinkie, as she liked to call it, wrapped tightly around his carrot, another of Tina's words.

As far as Max knew, only one thing on the planet scared Sergeant Longbottom: his woman's temper. It wasn't violent or raging in the conventional red-mist sense, but the excruciating pains inflicted by Tina's window-exploding shrieks pierced one's soul and made a person beg for death—or that's how it felt to Max, anyway.

● ● ●

"Is that all the luggage you're taking, Stan?" Max asked.

"Toothbrush, sun cream, change of underwear, T-shirts, shorts, and some military stuff. It's all I need." Stan walked back over to Tina to say his good-byes.

"*Bravo Two Zero* in there?"

"Never go anywhere without it, Maxi, and a couple of Andy McNab's newer ones, too. Want to borrow one?"

"May do," Max said, meaning "no thanks."

Stan tenderly kissed Tina and then slid into the back of the taxi.

"Be careful, boys," Tina said through the open window in a voice and manner that were at odds with her look as a fairy princess. Her arms were tightly crossed over her chest, and she was tapping one fluffy pink slipper on the tarmac. "You really don't want me coming over there to bring you back!"

Stan went pale, but he did his best to engineer a smile. "Don't worry, Tinker Bell," he said. "It's strictly a boys-only trip. Fishing and football talk." He prodded the taxi driver's shoulder. "Come on, lad. Get us moving," he whispered out of the corner of his mouth.

Max watched the departure scene of Stan and Tina's extravagantly blown kisses with a slight sense of envy. On one level, their relationship was rather frightening, but on another, the two were clearly in love and would likely do anything for each other—including mass murder.

Five minutes later, the taxi swept up a drive, crunching the gravel, and pulled noisily to a stop outside an old coach house. Next to the beautiful, ivy-covered home was an open double garage. A black Range Rover Vogue and a two-seater Audi sports car, both with personalized number plates, were parked inside.

"He's done well this time," Stan said. "Married?"

"Of course," Max said. "She's a good looker, too, apparently."

"They always are."

"True. This one's husband is an IT consultant, spends a lot of time in Europe. DG texted me the address last night."

The coach-house door swung open, and a man emerged. He was six foot two and lean and had wavy, unkempt dark-brown hair. He was pretty good-looking, but his smile set him apart from other men. To those who knew him well, DG's movie-star smile gave him an almost limitless ability to act outrageously with women and get away with it.

As Marcy had once said, "DG is gorgeous in a rough-around-the-edges, cheeky-boy sort of way. Gorgeous and untamed—that's DG. And most women can't resist a combination like that."

That had all proved very true, time and time again.

• • •

DG's nickname was courtesy of a lower-sixth former called Alison Smith. Graham Turner, DG's real name, had dated Alison for a week before she'd found out that Graham, her lovely boyfriend, had four other girlfriends. Not unexpectedly, she dumped him. However, what was unexpected—for Alison, anyway—was returning home after netball practice and finding Graham tucked up in bed with her mother. Alison went ballistic and chased a half-dressed Graham down the street while attempting to whack him with a frying pan.

"You're bloody *disgusting Graham*," she shrieked over and over again to the amusement of onlookers—hence, "DG."

DG sold used cars at Patel's Quality Motors in Cleckheaton, and he was brilliant at it. In fact, he was so brilliant that Mr. Patel, the owner, wanted him to be general manager.

DG turned him down. "I'm sorry, Mr. Patel. But I'm happy just selling the cars."

DG wasn't interested in money. Only women motivated him. He adored everything about them, and women adored him right back. Even when his womanizing habit messed up his plans, as it often did, he refused to change. Being bright, DG had flown through school, a straight-A student, and he was offered a place at Durham University to study economics. At the last moment, he rejected the offer and took a job with his father's firm as an insurance claim adjuster.

"University life isn't for me," he'd said at the Bull's Head. "I really want to work with Dad."

The truth was different. He was besotted with a girl named Sadie from the grammar school. Sadie had flunked her exams and was consequently going to work at the local Tesco. She wasn't going to university; therefore, neither was DG. Four months later, the red rose of young love had withered and died. And when DG checked, so had his offer to study at Durham.

It was the claims-adjusting world for him, whether he liked it or not. And he didn't like it. He loathed it. So-called adjusting seemed to mean reducing legitimate claims by any means possible, fair or foul. DG became an unwilling expert in identifying unapproved window locks and spotting errors on long, complicated forms. He hated it more and more and eventually refused to comply, which cost his dad a fortune. One drizzly Monday morning, his in-tray overflowing with the mundane or unfair, DG stood at his desk and announced that he was leaving to do something else. "Anything else!"

"Well, thank the fuck for that, Graham," his dad said calmly. "Son, you've finally realized what we've all known for months. You are absolutely *crap* at claims adjusting."

DG was amazed. "Why didn't you say so before, Dad?"

A golden smile spread across his dad's handsome face. "Some lessons you have to learn for yourself, lad. That way, they stay learned. Now, fuck off and enjoy yourself."

DG took the sales job at Patel's Quality Motors after a string of temporary jobs. Initially, Mr. Patel was infuriated by his new recruit's timekeeping—half an hour late was on time for DG—and he considered letting him go, but that was before monthly sales doubled.

DG's ability to sell used cars was unmatched. He sold three times as many cars as the other two salesmen put together. In addition, most customers paid the price on the car windscreen and took the service, warranty, and finance packages, too. However, what really shocked Mr. Patel was that positive customer feedback had gone through the roof at the same time.

DG was a sales phenomenon.

How did he do it?

Mr. Patel made it his job to find out. But after a month of observation, he was still none the wiser. *Must be a sophisticated selling patter*, he thought. The next day, he lingered by the coffee machine to listen in on DG and a Mr. Thompson, who'd been eyeing a blue Ford Focus.

"Henry, your car will be ready on Friday," DG said. "And don't forget to bring in the CD."

Mr. Thompson laughed. "You betcha, lad. Not had a first-timer in a while."

As yet another satisfied customer left the showroom Mr. Patel wandered over to his mysterious protégé.

DG was relaxing in his swivel chair.

"What's the CD thing about, Graham?" Mr. Patel asked.

"Oh, hi, Mr. Patel," DG said, putting his boots on the desk. "Well, it's a silly thing, but the customers seem to like it. You see, in my view, the very *first time* you do something is also the most memorable, if you know what I mean."

Mr. Patel looked embarrassed.

"Well, anyway," DG said, feeling a bit awkward himself. "I ask the customer to bring in one of their favorite songs, a song that reminds them of a great moment in their lives. Everybody has at least one. Then we play it nice and loud as they turn the ignition key in their new car for the first time. As I explain to the customers, if they play that song every morning, then they'll feel great every morning, too—guaranteed. But here's the best bit, Mr. Patel. Every morning they'll also remember Patel's Quality Motors, and also in a great way. How cool is that?"

● ● ●

Max realized that DG was hooked on that "first-time feeling" full stop, which explained his prolific record with the opposite sex. DG had lost count of his "ladies" years ago, but one thing was for sure: he had an addiction and gave no sign of wanting to go cold turkey, and neither did the ladies.

DG's technique for picking up girls, as well as selling cars, had been honed to perfection over the years. Now it was instinctual behavior. At its core was his ability to connect with people. Most folks took a while to get to know somebody new, but DG managed it in minutes, and half the time he didn't even have to speak. Young women; older women; beautiful, single women; beautiful, married women—it didn't matter, for they all fell under his charm. If Max had to guess how many times he'd heard the phrase, "I feel I've known your friend DG for years," he'd have been out by hundreds.

DG's uncanny ability, combined with good looks and a natural sense of harmony, was an irresistible cocktail to women. They flocked to him in droves. A few relationships had lasted a month or two, but sooner or later, generally sooner, DG would feel the urge for that first-time feeling, and he'd stray again.

Surprisingly, however, in addition to being absolutely gorgeous, most of DG's conquests were also extremely forgiving. Some were married, of course, and could hardly complain themselves, but many of the ladies were single, and even these women didn't seem to mind being part of a bunch. Two or three had cut up rough over the years. But Max believed that if most of them were given the chance, they'd take DG back.

DG's latest girlfriend, Linda, another stunner, worked at the Estée Lauder counter at Debenhams in Leeds. She'd been seeing him for nearly three months—a near record—until DG unfortunately, if not unpredictably, succumbed to a Zumba-class instructor at the DW gym. He was as philosophical as ever the night a tearful Linda dumped him.

"Max, life is beautiful, and women are a gift from the gods."

Max didn't know what religion DG was practicing, but it wasn't Catholicism.

• • •

DG stood in the coach-house doorway and stretched his arms high above his head. "Ain't life just fab-fuckin'-tastic?" he said, taking in a breath of fresh morning air. He smiled broadly and stepped onto the driveway, casually flicking his old and worn leather jacket over a shoulder. He was immediately followed out by a blond woman, who appeared to be wearing one of her husband's work shirts. Giggling, she jumped up into DG's arms, wrapping her arms around his neck and her legs around his waist.

"Take me with you, DG," she said. "Please take me with you."

DG spun her around playfully. "I'd love to, Sheila. But you've worn me out, girl. I'll be back in a week all rested and ready for you again."

Max watched the scene, feeling unsure of whether it was admiration, jealousy, or disgust he felt. He settled on jealousy.

The taxi driver laughed. "I've picked DG up in the early hours from dozens of houses around here," he said.

"You know DG?" Max asked, surprised.

The taxi driver laughed again. "Mate, everybody on the cabbie circuit knows DG; he's a living legend. I saved his skin last year, too. Husband came home early at a lovely place over in the next village. Your mate, DG, there, was sprinting down the road trying to do his trousers up, and the raging hubby was in hot pursuit. Was like an episode of *Footballers' Wives* but funnier. I picked him up, him being a regular fare an' all. One of the other cabbies told me that the cheeky bastard was back at the same address the week after. Apparently, DG said he couldn't leave a job half done. Talk about balls. I'm telling you guys, these women just can't get enough of him. You two know him well. What's his secret? How does he do it?"

"He's only got a two-inch cock," Stan said, looking irritated. "They all feel sorry for him."

Max was laughing. "If we knew DG's secret, we'd have bottled it and sold it on eBay years ago," he said. "We'd be millionaires by now. As to how he does it, the only thing we can all agree on is that it's not his ability to commit." Max lowered the window. "Come on, DG. Put her down," he called over. "And morning, love. Nice shirt you're nearly wearing."

Sheila giggled again. "I'm not letting him go." She tightened her legs.

After another flurry of spinning and canoodling, DG eventually made it into the taxi. "Morning, chaps," he said, and then recognized the driver. "Hi, Shazad. I've not forgotten that you saved my bacon, mate. Thought I was in for a right mauling." He held his hand out, and the taxi driver shook it enthusiastically.

"Where's your luggage?" asked Max.

DG pulled a toothbrush from his inside pocket.

"Traveling light," he said with a wide grin. "But I must have fresh breath for the ladies."

"Seriously, is that it?" Max asked.

"Afraid so. Most of my stuff is at Linda's, and it's best I give her some space. I'll borrow some stuff from you guys. It's no sweat."

The last pickup was Will.

"Nice pad," DG said, as they pulled up outside a five-bedroom, red-brick detached house complete with a conservatory, manicured lawn, and carved-stone bird table.

"I'm surprised you've not already been here," Stan said sarcastically. "Looks like an easy stretch from the drainpipe across to the bedroom window."

"Not much point," DG said. "Jane's up her own, already."

At the front door, Max gave the shiny brass lion's head a good rap. A moment later, Jane answered and scowled. She turned away with a *tut* and walked back into the house, leaving Max standing on the doorstep.

"Hi, Jane. Nice to see you," Max called after her.

Will appeared. He was wearing new Levi's that were too tight and a lumberjack shirt that was too big. Over his shoulder was an enormous holdall. "Can you get my other bag, Maxi? It's in the study. Come in, come in."

"Jane looks well," Max said as he hauled an even larger holdall up the drive. "You do know it's only the week, Will?"

Both men staggered to the rear of the taxi and crammed the luggage in. The rear door clicked shut on the fifth attempt after Will forced his backside against it.

"Right, men, we're all present and correct," Stan said excitedly. "So start your engine, Shazad, and let's move 'em out." He whirled his hand theatrically around his head and pointed forward. "To the transit area."

"Shazad," said DG, "in case you're wondering, that means Leeds and Bradford Airport."

The taxi pulled away.

They were off.

CHAPTER 6

The dusty, potholed Majorcan street was baking like an oven.

The sky was cloudless. There wasn't even the whisper of a breeze. The only sound came from a solitary cricket squatting on a drainpipe outside the bank. Anything else living and with a choice was resting in the shade, waiting for cooler temperatures later in the afternoon. The rest of the day's tasks could wait till then.

Only the old café bar was open for business.

And so the man using the pay phone outside the pharmacy stood out, not only because he was the only person standing on the street but also because his Armani suit and diamond-studded belt cost more than most people in the village earned in a year.

But something was amiss in the man's world. Otherwise, why had he stopped in Guadalest to use the pay phone?

His demeanor was odd.

He was watchful.

His senses were alert.

Every few seconds, he removed the telephone receiver from his ear and listened hard while carefully resurveying the street. He was doing it now, his mirrored sunglasses briefly pausing as they passed over the elderly men sipping espressos under the café bar's awning.

Apparently satisfied, he continued with his call.

The man was thirty-three years old. He was born in Medellín, Colombia, and so he was a very long way from home. But that didn't worry him, as he was back in control now. He oozed confidence and self-belief—traits developed after making countless decisions every day, life-and-death decisions: who would live, and who would die?

Carlo Ortega was dangerous. He'd spent much of the past week evading a posse of law-enforcement agencies all across southern Spain. He'd escaped, but it had been a close-run thing—too close. He was lucky to be alive, and he knew it. Two of his men hadn't been so fortunate, but the Russian syndicate had fared worse, losing six men, including Rostov's deputy. Alex Rostov himself had been late for the meeting and so avoided the attack. If he'd been on time, the DEA would have killed him, too, and the cocaine deal of the century would have died with him.

Eight men and counting were dead, but it would take much more than that for either Carlo or Rostov to walk away from $3 billion a year. The Russians had taken the brunt, which was fortunate. All men were expendable, but he'd rather they were Rostov's men than his; it cost money to train men.

The Ivans had been unprofessional. They'd been roaring drunk and closest to the Radisson suite's double doors. They'd been merrily toasting everyone from Anna Kournikova to Yuri Gagarin and back again, while waiting for their boss to arrive. The Colombians had shunned the vodka and been ridiculed for it right up until the doors blew off and stun grenades were thrown in. They'd all been taken by surprise, but the Russians were the easiest targets, slumped on sofas and slow to react as the masked assailants opened fire.

Carlo and his four men had been standing together at the suite's far end, away from the vodka and next to the open windows. As Russian bodies shuddered from multiple bullet wounds, the Colombians jumped blindly from the balcony. Fortunately, it was a first-floor suite, and the dense smoke from the stun grenades gave good cover for their escape.

The old road to Toledo, running southwest out of Madrid, ran straight outside the hotel, and the five Colombians had landed heavily on it. They fell and went sprawling across the hot tarmac. No gunshots followed. The authorities wouldn't fire into the street for fear of hitting innocent citizens—one major advantage of being a crook.

Carlo recognized a new danger and rolled quickly into the gutter, as did the two men nearest him. The two younger Colombians—brothers—hadn't been as quick or as clever.

They'd tried to stand.

A BMW X5 hit them. It was traveling at over eighty miles an hour and accelerating as it overtook a lorry. The eldest brother, nearest the center of the carriageway, was struck squarely in the chest. The massive collision forced the man's rib cage straight out through the back of his leather jacket and launched his body half a block down the road, where it crashed straight through the window of a tapas bar.

The younger brother had been lower to the ground and so avoided any serious chest injuries; unfortunately, the BMW's bull bars decapitated him. His severed head pounded into the side of the hotel with the force of a cannonball. However, a human head isn't made of twelve pounds of solid iron but, rather, brittle bone and soft tissue, so it exploded like a ripe, oversized tomato. What remained intact—half a skull containing two eye sockets, with one open eye, and an empty brain cavity—landed with a thud next to Carlo's face as he lay at the roadside.

The shaken BMW driver reversed back to the gory scene just as Carlo got to his feet. The motorist was as white as a ghost but was clearly a model citizen, duty bound not to leave the scene of an accident and determined to help in any way he could. He shouldn't have been. All he received for his trouble was a shot from a nine-millimeter Parabellum. The bullet went through his right eye and obliterated his neocortex, taking out a piece of skull the size of a fried egg on exit, before ending its short-but-deadly journey in the rear seat, buried in an empty baby chair.

The dying motorist was still twitching on the sidewalk as Carlo and his two remaining men drove away.

● ● ●

An ordinary man with an ordinary job couldn't dream of staying calm in this situation, but Carlo Ortega wasn't an ordinary man, and his job was extraordinary. Death was an everyday occurrence in Carlo's world, an occupational hazard; everybody died someday.

As a young man, his father, Andre Ortega, had started a coffee business called the Bogota Coffee Company. Competition was fierce in those days, and profits were hard to come by. Initially, the company had done well, but problems with suppliers and cheap coffee from Brazil meant financial problems. Receivership was only days away when a rich family friend helped out with a loan.

Twenty years later, the Bogota Coffee Company was still trading, which was surprising because it had never made much in the way of profit. In contrast, the family friend's business, cocaine production, was now turning over tens of millions of dollars each year. Unfortunately, the family friend, along with his wife, had been shot dead twenty years before, and his lucrative business interests had passed smoothly into the ownership of the assassin, Andre Ortega.

However, tens of millions of dollars weren't nearly enough for Andre. He wanted billions, tens of billions. And the newly formed supercartel, combined with the Rostov deal, would deliver exactly that. Five years from now, the Ortega family would be richer than half the countries in South America, and with that kind of wealth would come great power. Armies could be bought, technology and people could be bought, land and property could be bought, and governments, parliaments, and presidents could be bought, too. The Colombian state police could be directed away from his organization, and laws could be changed. The threat of extradition to the United States for drug trafficking would be revoked. In five years, the Ortega family wouldn't be above the law; they would actually *be* the law.

And now that dream was threatened. The damned Americans had discovered the Rostov deal. Worse still, the DEA had trailed Carlo to Europe. And the Yanks weren't playing by their usual soft government rules, either; six dead Ivans were testament to that.

In times of adversity, Carlo drew on the advice of his father, rules that had been drilled into him in childhood. "Be ruthless. Be cruel," his father had said over and over again. "Sympathy is for fools, and it will kill you. It will kill us both."

Occasionally, his father would test him. "Carlo, what are the two most important attributes our people must have?"

"Intelligence and loyalty, Father," Carlo would say, having heard the answer a hundred times before.

"Yes, Carlo. That is good."

His father would then elaborate. "Intelligence. The ability to outthink our enemies requires information. We must have the latest surveillance technology, and of course, we must hire the best people, particularly law-yers." His father always laughed at that. "And loyalty. Loyalty most of all. The most important attribute. I have told you how to ensure the loyalty of our people; it is the foundation of our strength."

Carlo learned his lessons well. On his return from Massachusetts Institute of Technology, he rapidly advanced through the company ranks. First, his father put him in charge of a small poppy farm and prod-uct manufacturing. Next came some time in logistics and distribution, then security, and, finally, marketing. Andre Ortega was delighted with his son's performance and made him a full partner, with sole responsibil-ity for developing overseas markets and, most significantly, the Rostov deal.

● ● ●

The moped rounded the corner of the pharmacy building in Guadalest. Its high-pitched, two-stroke engine cut sharply into the hot stillness of the afternoon. Carlo was still standing at the pay phone. He held the receiver in one hand; the other was behind his back holding a Beretta PX4 semiautomatic.

Carlo's red Ferrari was parked a few yards farther on, its driver door open wide into the street, should the need for a hasty exit arise.

The moped rider, a long-haired teenager, glanced carelessly in Carlo's direction, and knew instantly that for some reason, he wasn't supposed to look. Just in time, he remembered the dusty road in front of him.

Youthful reflexes kicked in. The old Vespa's back wheel skidded and slid sideways as the boy leaned to his left, desperately trying to balance the weight of his veering machine. Somehow, he missed the Ferrari, the only car on the entire street, and was now wobbling erratically back to his original course.

Carlo smiled as the teenager accelerated away.

To the three village elders sitting in the café bar opposite, the blister-ing sun didn't seem to touch the man across the street. Everything outside was hot and getting hotter by the minute, but the stranger seemed imper-vious to the overpowering heat. He seemed cool, as if he were cocooned in a small cloud of air-conditioned air. Maybe he was.

The elders were pretty much right, but Carlo Ortega wasn't merely cool—he was cold—an efficient, cold-blooded killer.

His father had tutored him in murder. Initially, Andre Ortega had worried that his boy was squeamish and hesitant. He was wrong on both counts. Carlo wasn't squeamish. He was highly capable and aware of the need to cover his tracks. He wasn't hesitant, either, but he did plan thoroughly. Carlo's first contract had been to dispatch a thieving farmhand. He'd been told just to pull the trigger, but shots in both knees had persuaded the thief to name his associates. Carlo shot them all to the head the following day.

The moped had disappeared from view, its shrill whining engine still just audible.

Carlo was speaking quickly now.

He'd been in the open too long.

"Miguel, listen carefully. Cell phones are too easy to track and intercept, so ditch them all. We have to change our departure plans. I'll lie low today and meet you at my fiancée's at nine tomorrow morning. Bring Diego and Fernando. Do you understand me, Miguel?"

"*Si*, Carlo. I understand. Is everything OK?" Miguel sounded concerned.

"Si, Miguel. But we have to be careful. I overtook that idiot, North, this morning. He lost control of his car and caused a major accident. I was lucky. Clark's men thought it was me that had crashed and gave away their cover. It's as we were informed, Miguel. But don't worry. I've lost them for now. The Americans have missed their chance, and they won't be getting another. We'll be sipping tequilas in Medellin soon enough, *mi amigo*. Nine o'clock, Miguel."

"Si, Carlo."

"*Hasta mañana.*"

CHAPTER 7

Leeds and Bradford Airport is a small, regional airport with flights to European holiday destinations and a few scheduled domestic routes aimed at local businesspeople. The taxi ride to the airport was trouble free, and Max, Stan, DG, and Will arrived early, at six. They were first in the queue at the Ryanair check-in desk.

The desk clerk, an oily-haired and spotty teenager called Rufus, held out his hand without looking up, and Max placed four passports into it. The clerk's lifeless eyes barely registered the travel documentation or Max's and Stan's baggage. He asked all the usual security questions in high-speed monotone, not waiting for, or clearly wanting, any answers before checking all the bags through.

DG was next in line. He placed his solitary toothbrush on the scales, luggage label attached, and waited with a wry grin.

Rufus's dull expression remained unchanged—it was just another bloody comedian with a toothbrush, after all—and he passed it through—but then Will stepped forward with his massive holdall, and Rufus's spotty, pockmarked face lit up like a Christmas tree.

"Oooo, you bloody beauty," he said and jumped up from his seat to help Will pull the holdall up onto the weighing scale. The electronic readout settled on an improbably large number as a warm, friendly smile spread out across Rufus's face.

"Sir, this is going to cost you a bloody fortune," he said, his once-dull eyes sparkling like sapphires.

Will bent down and pulled forward his other bag.

"Oh, don't tease me, baby," Rufus said, looking gratefully to the heavens. He was absolutely ecstatic. "It looks even bigger than the other one."

Will heaved the second bulging bag onto the scales, going red in the face with the effort.

"That's it, fella," said Rufus, who was holding his breath and peering eagerly at the scale.

"Yes," he screamed, and he punched the air with delight as if he'd scored the winner at Wembley. "Oh, you bloody diamond, sir." He stood on his chair. "Hey, Stevie! Stevie!'" he shouted to another spotty youth five desks along at Jet 2. "Stevie! Stevie!"

Stevie, looking just as bored as Rufus had been earlier, paused from checking in a young couple and raised his weary head toward his animated colleague.

"The ten quid's mine this week, Stevie, my boy." Rufus pointed to a disconsolate-looking Will. "This superstar here is twelve kilos over on bag one and—wait for it—seventeen kilos over on bag two! That's the record. You may as well just cough up now, buddy. Nobody's going to beat that, ever."

Rufus sat down again and returned to Will, straightening his jacket and tie as he did so. He took on a professional manner.

"I'm sorry, sir," he said, slightly smirking. "But there appears to be an excess-baggage charge to pay." He then pulled a calculator out of his jacket pocket.

Max and Stan were buying newspapers in WH Smith's across the hall but turned instinctively toward the Ryanair desk, as did everyone else in the terminal.

Will had screamed.

"How much? That's ridiculous! It's almost ten times the cost of the bloody flight."

"Want me to twat him, Will?" Stan, who'd walked back over, asked.

"No, no. Don't, Stan," Will said, trying to calm himself while handing over a large wad of twenty-pound notes, "unless he keeps on smiling like that."

Rufus was grinning from ear to ear, but a glance at Stan's frightening expression turned his face pale. "Sorry," he said sheepishly. "Only doing my job. I hate it, guys. Really, I do. The company's rules on excess baggage are a disgrace."

Checking that he couldn't be overheard by any other Ryanair staff, Rufus beckoned Will closer. "Bit of advice for you, mate," he whispered. "Next time, just give one of your bags to the comic who checked the toothbrush. Would have saved you over a hundred pounds!"

"That's great," Will said. "I'll do that now."

Rufus almost swallowed his tongue. "Oh, no-o-o, no, no, no. Sorry, matey. No can do. More than my job's worth, I'm afraid. But, you know, *I would if I could.*" Rufus was beaming again.

They passed quickly through into the departure lounge, a sullen Will bringing up the rear, and sat for a breakfast of coffee, bacon sandwiches, and a read of the morning papers. An hour and a half later, an announcement called them to gate two, where another spotty Ryanair teenager, a girl this time, herded them into what looked like cattle pens.

"Move right to the back of the holding area," the girl, who clearly enjoyed authority over adults, said. "Come on, ladies and gents. Now, squeeze up, squeeze up, we need to pack you in—I mean, accommodate a few more passengers."

The few more, a group of twenty prospective Weight Watchers clients, were either eating burgers or drinking milk shakes or both—and clearly had been doing so for some years. They were unceremoniously packed inside, and a metal crossbar snapped shut. Fifteen minutes later, everyone was still standing there, and all were totally pissed off. One hundred twenty-two sweaty people crammed into a tiny corner of the departure gate—a tin of sardines neatly positioned on the corner of a dining table.

The sound of footsteps echoed around the building.

Max craned his neck and saw two columns of people marching through the gate, flanked by another spotty Ryanair teenager. *Do they only employ people with acne?*

The columns passed without so much as a sideways glance and carried on up to the gate, arriving with a collective smirk.

"Who are that lot?" asked Stan.

"Priority-boarding passengers," Max said, twisting away from the metal barrier uncomfortably pressing against his hip.

"Nice," Stan said. "How much is priority boarding?"

"About five pounds," said Max.

"Jack's a twat," Stan said. "No expense spared. Who's he kidding?"

It was raining hard outside on the runway. And for reasons not shared by the Ryanair staff, the no-frills passengers were made to wait in the downpour at the bottom of the plane's steps. The priority boarders were already onboard. *Another ruse to increase future priority-boarding bookings*, Max thought as raindrops ran down his back. If it were a ruse, it worked; he'd definitely be paying the extra five pounds the next time around.

A few minutes later, the Boeing 737 had risen above the clouds and into the sunshine. Max forgot all about the endless queuing and the rain. His mood lifted. It was amazing that condensed water vapor could have such an impact on how he felt. On the ground, the wet day had matched his demeanor: gray. But up here, it was bright and sunny and warm, and he felt optimistic for the first time in months. The week ahead was going to be great. This trip was going to be the beginning of something new; something special was going to happen. He laid his head back against the padded headrest and enjoyed the warmth radiating through the window.

"Sir, can I get you a drink?" the flight attendant asked.

Max ordered vodka and tonic, which he always did on flights, although he never drank it elsewhere. Why was that?

Bizarrely, the vodka arrived in a little sachet.

"It's like ketchup. It's less bother for us," the flight attendant said. "Doesn't spill like bottles, and they don't roll under the seats." She laughed. "And when passengers get drunk, like that lot up there"—she directed her eyes toward the front of the plane—"then the sachets are too difficult for them to open."

Max half stood. There were a number of Inter Milan shirts bobbing up and down three rows from the toilets. So that was where the horrendous "singing" was coming from. The vodka sachets obviously weren't posing too much of a problem so far.

"They're off to see Real Majorca," said the flight attendant.

"So why the Inter Milan shirts?" asked Max.

"I asked them that. My boyfriend is Italian, so I need to know a bit about football. Apparently, they first booked for Milan, and then they couldn't get tickets for the San Siro. The shop wouldn't take the shirts back."

Not the sharpest tools in the box, Max thought. *Always best to get the game tickets sorted first. They're harder to come by than flights.* The names printed on the backs of the Inter shirts didn't make much sense, either. ION, BLO, BUC, NHS, THE, and UL were the ones he could make out. *Jesus, whatever happened to traditional nicknames like Spud, Maca, or Jonesy? It isn't that hard to come up with a decent nickname, is it? These days, perhaps just having your initials on the back of your shirt is the in thing. But why on earth would anybody want "THE" on his or her shirt? THE what?*

An hour into the flight, Max heard the unmistakable sound of retching and shouts of alarm from in and around the Inter Milan zone. Flight attendants rushed to the grisly scene, resignation and disgust on their faces in equal measure. Half the plane was standing to see what was going on.

It was *THE.*

THE one who gets smashed on two sachets of vodka and vomits uncontrollably over the seats, then.

There was another commotion behind him. Max turned to see that two hen parties were seated at the back of the plane. The two groups—*What's the collective term for "hen parties"? A gaggle? A troop? A busload? Perhaps "a nightmare of hen parties" is best*—were wearing pink cowboy hats and sparkling cropped tops. They were chatting ferociously and seemed to be checking out who'd gotten the most condoms attached to her top.

Max sat back in his seat and tried again to open his sachet of vodka. *Bloody thing.*

An hour later, the plane touched down at Palma Airport to the cheery sound of a trumpet fanfare, followed by an announcement that yet another Ryanair flight had landed on time. This seemed pretty inevitable to Max, as long as they didn't smash into a mountain, as the flight duration on his ticket was a good twenty minutes longer than the actual flying time.

Passport control was surprisingly smooth, and the luggage carousel was already moving when they walked in.

"Un-fucking-believable," Stan said, shaking his head in disbelief as DG's toothbrush slowly crawled by. "He actually put it through, and it's the first bloody thing out." He reached down and picked it up.

"Check that it's mine, Stan," DG called out from the other side of the conveyor belt.

Palma Airport was a model of efficiency. The remainder of the luggage emerged quickly. Even though the airport's arrivals-and-pickup area seemed miles away, travelators conveyed the masses effortlessly. To his amusement, Max found that if he walked on the moving walkway, he positively zoomed by, passing hundreds of tourists who had elected to walk alongside.

"Look at those numpties," DG said.

It was the Inter Milan boys. They were walking—staggering—in three semi-choreographed rows. Side by side, the lettering on the shirt backs now made sense, cringingly. The five drunks bringing up the rear spelled out "E JAC UL AT ION." Five yards in front of them was "ICU MIN BUC KETS." And leading the way was a call for "BLO WJ OBS ON THE NHS." Fellow travelers at first looked confused before realization dawned. Then they either laughed or turned away in disgust.

The pride of West Yorkshire, thought Max. *Jesus.*

His attention was distracted by a nippy four-year-old boy sprinting beside the travelator, trying to beat him to the end. *No chance, sunshine.* A short, well-timed sprint saw him off, but Max miscalculated the jumping-off point and ruined his intended victory celebration by stumbling into the path of a businesswoman. With a rather panicky sidestep followed by two hops and a skip, he narrowly avoided a head-on collision, and the woman helped enormously by jumping smartly to one side. Max didn't look back—he was too embarrassed—and dashed on, as if he was racing to catch the last plane to New York.

"Max? Are you Max?"

Shit. He was going to be told off for running. *Humiliation or what?* He slowed to a halt and turned to see that it was the businesswoman who had called after him. She was busily rearranging her dark-brown hair, no doubt a result of the evasive action she'd taken to avoid the madman.

Max remembered that she'd called his name. "Yeah, I'm Max," he said, puzzled, as Stan, DG, and Will caught up.

"Great," she said, offering her hand.

Max shook it tentatively.

"I'm Jules, Mr. North's executive assistant."

"Oh, hi," Max said. "I'm sorry, Jules. We were expecting to meet you out front. Great to finally meet you, and apologies for nearly knocking you over."

"No harm done. Children love the walkways," she said, making Max feel even sillier. "Well, gentlemen, a warm welcome to beautiful Majorca. I was going to meet you outside, but something unexpected has come up, and Mr. North needs to liaise with me urgently."

"Bet he does," DG said.

Stan butted in. "That's no problem, darlin'," he said. "We don't envy the poor bugger that has to liaise with Jack. Lay out plan B, love, and we're good to go."

Jules clearly hadn't understood most of what Stan had said, but urgency was spurring her on. "Yes, gentlemen. Thank you. These are your return-flight details." She handed Max a set of documents. "The taxi is outside in bay six, and the driver, Antonio, will take you all straight to Porto Colom. That's where Mr. North's yacht is moored. It's at the end of the marina; you can't miss it. He says it's easily the largest yacht there. I'm looking forward to having a tour later today myself. There are a few bars overlooking the marina, so you can all enjoy a cold beer before Mr. North arrives. We shouldn't be too long." The phone in her hand rang. "I have to go, I'm afraid." She moved off but then paused. "Oh, I nearly forgot. Please don't board until Mr. North gets there. He's really looking forward to showing you around personally." And then she was gone.

"See you later, Jules," Max called after her.

"Very, very nice," DG said. "Very nice, indeed. I'll be amazed if Jack is liaising in the way he'd like to with her. She's way out of his league, or used to be at any rate." A golden smile spread across his face, and his eyes twinkled mischievously. "However, she's *not* out of mine."

● ● ●

Antonio drove them away from the airport and Palma and into a country-side that was in sharp contrast to the modern city behind them. Donkeys stood unmoving under ancient yew trees, out of the midday heat, as the scorched fields of grass around them shimmered. Rustic farmhouses, old barns with sun-bleached roofs, olive groves, and vineyards all portrayed a simple life away from the rat race.

After an hour's drive, the taxi cleared the brow of a small hill. The deep-blue sea stretched out across the entire horizon—the Mediterranean. It filled the whole windscreen as a refreshingly cool breeze blew in through Max's open window. He closed his eyes and breathed in deeply, tasting the salt. Tension drained from his chest and shoulders as he slowly exhaled. His eyelids suddenly felt heavy, and he dozed off with a smile.

He awoke as the taxi pulled to a stop outside a line of small bars. They looked out over Porto Colom's natural harbor and the town's small yacht club, which was all contained in a small bay, surrounded by tree-covered hills dotted with whitewashed houses and large villas. The town center was also pleasantly undeveloped, with no buildings over three stories high.

After tipping Antonio and piling the luggage, most of which was Will's, on the dock, the men eagerly headed for the nearest bar and sat down under a faded green-and-white-striped awning.

The bar owner sensed urgency and immediately brought over a cold pitcher of San Miguel and four frosted glasses.

"Ah, that is so good," DG said, taking a large mouthful. His feelings were shared around the circular wooden table.

"It's enormous," Stan said.

"Eh?" DG said. "It's not that big. We need to order another jug already."

Max followed Stan's gaze. He wasn't looking at the nearly empty pitcher of beer but above it and out along the marina walkway, toward a row of yachts slightly obscured from view by the harbormaster's hut.

Max stood up.

The sailing yachts were all somewhere between twenty and fifty feet in length, with motor yachts of similar sizes interspersed. There were about thirty vessels in total. Max blinked as the bright sunshine reflected off the pristine white hulls and into his eyes. He could hear a soft humming sound. It was made by the sailing yachts' rigging as the wires gently vibrated in the breeze.

And then he caught sight of it—*the* yacht.

If you could call it a yacht, he thought.

All the boats in the marina were unquestionably beautiful things, and they were a testament to a set of incredible lifestyles that Max and his friends could only dream about. But in comparison to the magnificent *superyacht* at the end of the walkway, all of those yachts were but toys.

"It's bigger than the one mum cruised the fjords on," DG said.

"It's a ship," Will said.

"Looks like Jack's finally got it together, big time," said Max. "It must be worth millions. He'll need a crew to sail it."

"Jack's a twat," Stan said. He looked really annoyed.

"Let's get a closer look," Max said, setting off down the concrete walkway.

"Jules said to wait here, Max," Will said.

"You stay here, then. We're only having a look," Max said.

The closer they got, the more super the superyacht became, and they ended up jogging the last stretch with mounting excitement.

"She's a beauty," Will said, panting. "A Sunseeker. I read about Sunseeker in a yachting magazine at the dentist's. They're built in Dorset, and this one is top of the range. It's well over a hundred feet. Wow, what a boat! She's fantastic."

"*Conchita*," said Stan, reading the name painted on the stern. "Concheat-er. Apt for Jack North, that, him being a conning, cheating bastard an' all. Cheek of the twat, he's even bloody advertising it."

A gangplank with little, white ropes and tassels extended from the marina walkway and over to the main deck. There, four padded sun beds and a quadrangle of luxurious, white, leather sofas sat invitingly in the shade provided by the overhanging flybridge. The main saloon's glass doors were just beyond, but the dark tinting made it impossible to see inside.

"I'm feeling the urge to bag a sun bed before the Germans parachute in," DG said, and he stepped onto the gangplank and quickly crossed over. The other three men looked at each other once, nodded, and then followed suit.

"The *Conchita* will have cost Jack the best part of twenty million pounds," said Will.

Stan didn't look convinced.

"I'm not kidding, guys," Will said. "This is one serious piece of kit. It'll cost him twenty thousand pounds to fill it with diesel, although Jack has saved some money on mooring charges. Porto Colom will be a third of the cost of Palma."

"Typical fucking Jack, that," Stan said with undisguised scorn. "Spends twenty million pounds on a boat and then scrimps on storage. It's like buying a new Rolls Royce and keeping it in the garden shed. The man's got no bloody class," he said, scratching his balls.

Max looked skyward.

"What?" Stan asked.

"Nothing," Max said, smiling.

DG tried the saloon doors.

Will protested, but they were locked, anyway.

They sat on the sun beds for a few minutes. Max was sunbathing with his eyes closed. When he opened them, Stan had gone.

"Where is he?" he asked, just as the saloon's glass doors slid smoothly open behind him. Stan was inside sporting a huge grin.

"Window left unlocked up at the front. Couldn't resist having a look inside. It's a palace, and I've already bagged my cabin."

"Christ, Stan," Max said, but he got up and ventured inside.

The saloon was dim and cool and quiet, and it took a moment for Max's eyes to adjust. It was hard to see colors in this light, and the soft carpet absorbed the sound of their footsteps.

Max walked slowly forward. He felt like he was an unwanted guest in somebody's house at night, and the owner was asleep upstairs. But he kept moving forward, quietly, placing each step.

The saloon's centerpiece was another quadrangle of white leather sofas but much larger than the set outside on the main deck. A square wooden coffee table sat in the middle with an enormous, empty silver fruit bowl sitting on it. The only other items of furniture in the saloon were two wooden cabinets, one on each side of the main doors. They displayed an assortment of wine glasses, books, and dried flowers.

Max's eyes were drawn to a spiral cast-iron staircase, which appeared out of the gloom in the saloon's far left-hand corner. Getting closer, he could see that it corkscrewed through a hole in the ceiling, presumably up to the flybridge. In the other corner of the saloon, a conventional staircase disappeared below decks. It was too dim to see much more, so Max unlatched the large window next to him. The glass panel slid effortlessly and silently to one side, revealing a small balcony that protruded over the yacht's side and a stunning view of Porto Colom bay.

Light flashed painfully into Max's eyes. He raised a hand to shield them and moved away from the window. Strangely, the dazzling light still blazed.

It was coming from inside the saloon.

Max moved farther inside.

A cocktail bar filled the area between the two staircases at the saloon's far end. It had been hard to see in the dimness, but direct sunlight had illuminated it as effectively as a thousand neon bulbs would have.

It wasn't hard to see why.

Mirrored tiles covered the back wall. The long bar itself was a mirror, and so was all the bottle shelving. In fact, with the exception of a dark rectangular space, located in the center above the top bottle shelf and just below the ceiling, every other square inch of the bar was mirrored.

Max was intrigued, and he moved out of the reflections to get a better look, just as Will switched on the saloon lights.

Max's breath caught in his throat.

The rectangle above the bar wasn't just space. It was an oil painting. An oil painting of the most beautiful woman Max had ever seen. He stood stock-still, unable to move, thoroughly transfixed by the woman's sparkling emerald eyes.

She was young, maybe early twenties, with long, glossy black hair. For some reason, Max felt that she didn't want to be there. She was sitting on a bed of pale-blue silk and looking out into the real world. She wore no makeup. She didn't need any. Her face was spellbindingly beautiful—kind, clever, incredibly warm, sexy, and embarrassed all at the same time. Angelic. Her mouth was slightly open as if she were about to smile or speak. She was holding a ruffled sheet over her breasts.

Max breathed in as his brain reminded him of the need for oxygen. His heart was beating like a drum, and his stomach felt weak.

Christ, it's only a bloody painting.

He heard a long, low whistle behind him; turned; and saw that DG had walked over.

"It doesn't get any better than that, Maxi," he said. "No expensive clothes, no jewelry, no makeup. Just her. If that's our Jack's girl, then even I'll take my hat off to him."

"I know this sounds a bit stupid, DG. But I thought she was going to speak to me." And as soon as he'd said it, he felt really, really, stupid.

Both men burst out laughing.

"Get behind the bar and pour me a bourbon, and then maybe, just maybe, I won't tell Stan and Will you said that," DG said, punching him on the shoulder.

"Fair enough." Max tore his gaze away from the woman's eyes. *It's a bloody painting*, he reminded himself. "Bourbon on the rocks, coming up."

He made two large measures of Maker's Mark, his favorite bourbon, with ice. The cut-glass crystal tumblers added to the effect. The American whiskey smelled and looked as good as it tasted, as it always did.

"Don't see her working behind the bar at the Bull's Head," Max said, and he instantly felt guilty about Marcy.

"True," DG said. "For a start, our cultured landlord, Ronny, wouldn't employ her. Her tits are too small. That's Ronny's number-one criterion, his only criterion, actually. Says he walks applicants up to the wall with their elbows stuck out. Elbows hit the wall first, and they're out."

"Ronny is a Neanderthal," said Max.

Shouts came from above.

It was Will.

"Up here, guys!"

Max and DG climbed up the spiral staircase and emerged onto the open-sided flybridge, next to the drive station. It was like an airplane cockpit. A multitude of buttons, switches, and screens were facing them, as was a ridiculously small steering wheel. Two large leather seats, one of which was raised up slightly higher, looked out over the foredeck.

"Captain Jack's," DG said. "He wouldn't be able to see properly, otherwise."

Will shouted again. He was standing with Stan on the foredeck.

"Come down here and check this beauty out," he said, looking up at Max and DG. "You'll need to go back down the staircase to the main deck, though, and then walk along the side of the yacht."

Two minutes later, they were all sitting in the empty hot tub.

"Top man, our Jack," DG said. "I've done lengths in pools smaller than this."

"And look at this," Will said, sliding back a small panel that was integrated into the deck. "State-of-the-art music system with surround sound. At full volume, they'll hear us in Palma."

"Nice," DG said. "Love my music."

"And finally, chaps," Will said, "the pièce de résistance."

He depressed a square black button. A whirring sound was accompanied by a huge TV screen rising straight out of the deck.

"And I was worried about missing *Newsnight*," Max said.

"Does it play DVDs?" Stan asked.

"We are not watching *Rambo*," Max said.

"Oh, come on, Maxi. It's Saturday night, and I brought 'em special. Saturday night is Rambo night. Won't be the same without a Sly killing spree."

"Jesus H. Christ," DG said. "Don't you ever get tired of seeing the same bloody films? Let's go and check out the sleeping quarters."

"I'm sure Jack will have something to say about that, DG," Will said. "We should go back up to the bar and wait. We did agree to wait for Jack to arrive."

A compromise was hastily agreed. A quick "shifty" below decks—as Stan described it—to review the guest quarters, and then they'd park themselves on the sun loungers near the stern and have a few beers, remembering to relock the saloon doors.

"Jack won't mind us sitting there, will he? He'll have meant for us not to go inside, that's all," said Stan. "We'll just have to go, 'Oo-o-o-o,' and 'Wow, that's fuckin' amazing, Jacko,' when he gives us the royal tour."

The *Conchita* had five berths—four doubles and a master stateroom. The double rooms were luxurious, boasting marble-tiled en suites with high-tech entertainment systems and cocktail cabinets bursting with crystal champagne, but it was the master stateroom that took the eye. It had an altogether more splendid grandeur. It was sheer opulence. Its centerpiece was an enormous, circular bed with white silken sheets and puffed-up golden pillows. It reminded Max of the bed in the girl's portrait.

The four friends were sitting on the edge of the bed, facing a colossal TV screen that was sunken into the wall and surrounded by a diamond-studded frame. DG was trying unsuccessfully to switch it on using a remote control he'd picked up from an ornate side table.

"Nothing's happening," he said, pressing most of the buttons in a fit of irritation.

The whole bed suddenly began to revolve.

The men leaned with the motion, except for Will, who slipped off and landed on the crimson carpet. It didn't hurt; the pile was about an inch thick. The bed turned fully through 180 degrees as luxurious red velvet curtains simultaneously swept back to reveal a panoramic view of the large yacht moored next door.

"Now, *that* is class," Max said.

The rest of the stateroom didn't disappoint, either. A Roman-style marble bathroom with a Jacuzzi and two multijet showers was just as incredible as the bedroom, and the walk-in dressing room with automated wardrobes full of designer clothes wasn't far behind.

• • •

"Pass me another beer, Will," said DG, who was lying on a sun bed.

After they'd brought the luggage onboard Stan had volunteered to make a return trip to the bar next to the marina to pick up some booze, but Max had discovered a ready-and-refrigerated supply under the bench seating that ran around the whole stern area.

They drank all afternoon and into the early evening as they waited for Jack, who didn't arrive. The sun dropped in the sky, and a light breeze took up as the sky began to darken. They were hungry and ordered pizzas and ice cream.

A couple of hours later brought nightfall, and there was still no sign of Jack. The moon shone alone in the sky directly above them, silver and perfectly round.

Max's phone rang, interrupting Stan's animated explanation of SAS tactics in Iraq.

"Oh, hi, Jules. Great. We were getting a bit worried about you," he said, quickly trying to sober up. "We'd have rung, but we don't have your number."

Stan sat up. He could see that Max was listening hard. Finally, Max spoke again. He sounded calm but totally deflated. His shoulders had visibly slumped.

"OK, Jules. I understand...Of course it's not your fault...We know there's nothing you can do about it...Yes, it's not Jack's fault, either...Yes, we've got the return-flight tickets, and don't worry. We can sort ourselves out back to the airport."

DG and Will were listening now, too, looking at each other in confusion.

"No, Jules," Max said, avoiding the eyes staring at him. "Don't worry about that, either. We've not been near the yacht...Yeah, me, too. Bye."

He clicked off the phone and dropped it on the sun bed. It bounced off the edge and skittered across the deck. He couldn't be bothered picking it up.

"Fuck."

"What?" DG asked.

"I'm sorry, guys," Max said. "You heard most of it. Jack was involved in a car accident on his way over here. He was injured, but he's OK."

"That's a fucking shame," said Stan.

"Stan," Will said, looking shocked.

"Well, anyway," Max said. "The upshot is that Jack's in no fit state to sail, and so the trip's off. We're to book into a local hotel tonight, send the bill to Jules, and then fly home tomorrow—we can change the ticket dates at the airport."

As Max was speaking, he could feel all of the excitement and energy the trip had generated in him draining away. For reasons he couldn't totally fathom, he'd actually begun to believe that maybe, just maybe, this trip was going to be the start of something new—something good and fresh and real. Maybe the pause button holding his life in limbo for so long was finally being released. But what had looked so full of promise and adventure had turned out to be just another false dawn, a cruel trick devised to raise his hopes before unceremoniously dashing them again. Wednesdays at the Bull's Head beckoned, and most other days, too.

"We're staying onboard tonight," said Stan. "I can't be arsed moving to a crappy hotel. We'll get sozzled here and fuck off after breakfast."

Nobody argued. The mood was grim.

"Let's crack open some more beers, then," said DG, doing his best to feign enthusiasm. He wasn't very convincing, but at least he was trying. "There's about another six hundred bottles in that cooler to get through before breakfast."

Six or seven bottles each later, the mood had lightened. Even Max had decided to not feel as sorry for himself.

"It's a pity Jules couldn't join us for the evening," said DG. "I do like the professional look." He was lying back and staring up at the clear night sky. "Long, dark-brown hair tied up in a bun; bright, immaculate makeup, not overdone, mind you, as that gets tarty; and perhaps a little suit. A black jacket is good, and a tight white blouse tucked into a thigh-hugging black skirt. And stockings, of course. Oh, and high heels."

"Sounds like Stephanie, the management consultant you brought into the Bull's Head last New Year's Eve," Will said, opening another four bottles. "Jane said she was too ambitious for you, DG. Said she'd eat you alive."

DG laughed. "Jane was right, then," he said. "Stephanie ate me alive about four times that night, if I remember correctly. And it was Stephanie I was thinking of, right down to the stockings and suspender belt. She wears gorgeous underwear, not that it stayed on for long," he said, winking. He sported a huge smile. "Pass me one of those, mate."

Will had positioned his sun bed up against the beer store. He was able to reach in and grab bottles and then pass them out as required, without the inconvenience of having to stand up.

"Do you think you'll ever settle down with just one woman, DG?" Will asked. "I mean, all of your ladies are beauties and everything, but…well, don't you ever want to have a meaningful relationship?"

"Define 'meaningful,'" said DG.

Stan and Max rolled their eyes.

Will thought hard. How could he get across the meaning of true love to a man who had bedded more women than the Beatles?

"Well, a meaningful relationship is based on the love that two people have for each other. A relationship that has trust at its core. One where you can rely on the other person to give you an honest opinion, even if it's not what you want to hear, in the certain knowledge that they will have your best interests at heart. Someone who will *always* put you first and never let you down, no matter what happens. Yes, that's it, that's what a meaningful relationship is." Will was satisfied with his answer.

"Sounds like the relationship I have with my mum, Will," DG said, sitting upright and placing his bottle of beer down on the deck. He was searching for the right words himself now.

"Will, you know when you and Jane are making love, and you both reach that incredible moment when the bed, the town, and the country—no—when even the whole universe just disappears? Yeah, you know that feeling, Will. Yeah?"

Will was embarrassed and confused. "When the whole universe disappears?"

"Yeah, you know, Will. That moment, when you and Jane become the same person. It happened with Sheila last night, and we'd only been at it for three or four hours. One minute, we were enjoying each other, and the next, we were one being. One body, one heart, one mind, and one soul. Our spirits had melded. It was like…like…like being born again. Yes, that's it. Reborn. Cleansed and new."

Will was wondering which planet DG had beamed in from. Stan and Max, who had heard it all before, just kept on drinking.

"Why are you looking at me like that, Will?" DG asked. "What did I say?"

"Beats me, DG. Something about yours and Sheila's spirits melding, presumably, her vodka and your bourbon." He turned to Max for a more sensible conversation, he hoped—understandable, at least. "Have you a woman on the go yet, Max?"

"Met Jennifer and Rosie Smith the other week," Max said, tossing another empty bottle into the wheelie bin they'd carried over from the walkway. "Remember them?"

"Sure do. They were both corkers."

"They were, too," Max said. "But a few too many Krispy Kremes, I'm afraid. Didn't recognize them until they came over. No girl for me since Marcy last summer." He felt awkward again. "Anyway, how's it going with you? How are Juliet and Harriet?"

Love shone in Will's eyes. "Juliet and Harriet are brilliant, mate," Will said. "They're both at prep school now, which costs a bloody fortune, but they love it. You should see them in their red-and-blue-striped blazers, Max. They look adorable."

"Still horse riding?"

"They are. Ponies. They spend most evenings and weekends up at the riding center. Jane is sorting some show-jumping lessons. She wants the girls to compete in the Olympics." Will smiled. "The girls are absolutely desperate for a pony of their own, and I think I've found them a little beauty through a client."

"That's fantastic," Max said. "You must be really proud of them, mate. And you should be." Max paused for a second. "Will, I know this is a bit awkward for you, but if you don't mind me saying, I do know that Jane can't stand me. It's not a problem, honestly, as I very rarely see her. It's just that I don't know what I've done to offend her."

Will shifted uneasily. "No, Max," he said, looking at DG, too. "Honestly, Jane thinks you're all great. She keeps going on about inviting you all over for dinner, but it's just I'm so busy at work. There's never any time, you know, with all the changes in tax legislation."

Stan emerged through the saloon doors. He'd broken in again to go to the toilet. "No bog roll in the bar toilet, so I nipped into the master stateroom."

"Oh, that's just brilliant, Stan," Will said, looking alarmed. "You did flush it properly, didn't you?"

Stan was noncommittal.

"Oh, for Christ's sake," Will said, sitting up. "One of yours festering for two weeks, and the whole yacht will need fumigating. Couldn't you have had a dump onshore?"

Stan looked mightily aggrieved. "For your information, Will, I didn't have a dump, but you can't dab your end without toilet paper, can you?"

"*Dab* your end!" Max said.

DG had jumped up from his sun bed as if there'd been an explosion below decks, and he was now staring at Stan in utter amazement. Eventually, he managed to mouth, "Dabs his end." The incredulity on his face soon gave way to side-splitting laughter, which quickly spread to Max and Will.

Max was in absolute stitches. He was taking in controlled breaths; otherwise, he couldn't speak. "Stanley, I...I...remember you telling me that behind enemy lines, it was...was...was...standard SAS procedure to collect all turds in little, plastic bags, but I'm sure even the world's finest special forces don't warrant it necessary to dab the end of your cock with tissue paper. Andy McNab doesn't seem the dabbing type to me. I reckon he just shakes the drips off like everybody else."

DG had crumpled to the deck and was unable to speak.

"Oh, very fucking funny, Maxi," Stan said angrily. "Anyway, Tina says it's unhygienic not to dab your end; otherwise, pee gets in your pants. And as you know full well, merely shaking leaves a drop on your end, which, over the course of the day, can accumulate. Tina told me that women sit down and dab every time, and I think it's a good idea." He suddenly remembered the point he thought would clinch the argument. "In fact, I always sit down to piss now, too, as it's much more comfortable, and Tina says the toilet's cleaner."

DG paused from laughing just long enough to mouth "sits down" and then began rolling around the deck, howling with hysterical laughter.

Max looked closely at the hardest man he'd ever known. "Anything else you want to share with us, Stan?" he asked. "You may as well get it all out into the open now, buddy. There can't be much left to declare, unless you've started shaving your legs, sporting a Brazilian, and having your nails done after Pilates class. My bet's the Brazilian, yes?"

"Fuck off, you wankers. Tina just gives me a quick trim every now and then."

It was well over an hour before Max, DG, and Will could even look in Stan's direction without ending up in stitches.

"Get a bottle of bourbon, DG," Max said. "I need to numb my stomach."

CHAPTER 8

Jack awoke in a sweat.

"Nightmare," he mumbled. "Fucking nightmare. No-o-o-o. Don't shoot; don't fucking shoot."

He was unable to get comfortable. He rolled over and became aware of the stench of stale urine as the bad dream faded away. He checked his pants. Dry. *Still smells like old piss*, he thought. He stretched out his right leg as it began to cramp, and his foot bumped into cold stone.

Don't have a wall there, he thought, and he rolled over again.

He fell right off the bed.

Fortunately, something soft cushioned his fall.

He heard a scream.

"A-a-a-argh."

For a moment, Jack thought he'd been caught in an earthquake until he realized that somebody was trying to wriggle out from under him. He lay still for a moment until the squirming had stopped, and then he strained his eyes. A dirty old tramp was staring at him. The man was rubbing his head and chest; presumably the areas Jack had landed on. He was filthy, and he stank. He had long, gray hair; a straggly beard; and disgustingly long, mucky yellow fingernails. His clothing was no better, consisting of a Nike tracksuit filled with holes, mismatching trainers, and what looked like a navy blue Ralph Lauren blazer, although this one had no collar and was covered in black motor-oil stains.

Jack's head began to spin. Images of exploding tankers, handlebar mustaches, and SWAT police swirled around in his brain.

"It's a *living nightmare!*" he said and held his head.

"Señor, what is wrong?" the old man asked. He sounded concerned and placed a comforting hand on Jack's shoulder. Jack pulled it roughly away.

"Get off me."

Jack shrank against the side of the bed and leaned back, resting his head on the dirty sheets and looking up at the damp, stone ceiling. He was past being scared. He just wanted to know what was going on. The situation was ridiculous. It was a mad game show where some unsuspecting, poor bastard—him—was being elaborately set up and forced to endure one hellish event after another as a thrilled nation of reality-show freaks watched and laughed their socks off. He sighed and scanned the walls. No little red lights. There were no cameras—at least, none that he could see.

His arm itched. He'd been scratching since the moment he awoke, thinking that the dust and gravel inside his clothing was irritating his mild burns.

Something bit his arm.

Something bit his scorched head.

Fleas.

The bed was practically alive with them. He lurched forward and found himself looking into the old tramp's eyes.

"Just who the fuck are you, Pedro?" Jack asked angrily while still scratching vigorously.

The tramp looked confused. "Señor, how did you know my name was Pedro?"

"Christ."

Jack couldn't be bothered to answer the old fool. He stood instead and looked around.

He was in a cell. A Wild West sheriff's cell with one whole wall of bars. Or was he inside a caged sewer? The smell of old piss seemed to have intensified.

He hobbled weakly over to the steel bars and grabbed them. They were cold, rusty, and locked, and about six inches apart. His sore face wouldn't go all the way through, but he managed to push in up to his ears, and turned his head forty-five degrees.

There wasn't much to see.

He saw a dim, empty corridor; another three cells like the one he was in; and, at the end of the passageway, a thick, wooden door with a caged light above it.

"Hello?" he called out. The word reverberated in the empty silence. He called again, this time louder. "Hello-o-o-o-? I think there's been a terrible mistake here. Hello-o-o? Hello-o-o-o?"

Ten minutes of "hello" brought about no response. Jack's anger was on the rise. "You can't just keep me here. I'm English, you know. Hello-o-o-o? Whoever you are, let me out. *Now*."

Another twenty minutes went by, and Jack lost it. He bellowed down the corridor. "Right, you dago bastards. Telephone and a lawyer right now, or it'll be the fucking Armada all over again."

There was still no response, not even the sound of another door opening or closing in the building. Nothing. Pure silence. It was like standing in a vacuum.

"Fucking dago bastards!"

Jack shook the bars. Specks of rust were showering down on his head and shoulders as he worked hard to sustain a continuous barrage of insults. Everything Spanish got the treatment—everything he could think of, anyway.

"King Juan Carlos is an imbecile. Placido Domingo, Real Madrid, and Barcelona are shite. Churros are shit, too, as are paella, seat cars, and flamenco dancing. And Ibiza and Lisbon"—*Is Lisbon in Spain? I don't care!*—"they're shite, too!"

On and on he went, round and round the same material for the next two hours solid. Occasionally, he'd remember something new.

"And Gibraltar's British, you bastards."

Finally, exhausted and nearly hoarse, he sat down on the flea-ridden bed and once again noticed his companion.

"How long have you been in here, Pedro?" he whispered.

"Two days, señor," the tramp said, smiling through stained teeth. "But sometimes it's a week before I have to go."

"*Have* to go? You mean you actually stay here voluntarily?" Jack was astounded. "Even Butlins is better than this, man." His spirits rose. "Does that mean I can go when I want to?"

The filthy old man looked sad. He'd sat quietly on the cell floor while the mad Englishman had been delivering his marathon tirade.

"It's too hot for me outside, señor. And they feed me well in here. I have no house. My father was a policeman, you see, and so they look after me. I'm sorry, but I don't think you can go, señor. But you should ask Sergeant Hernandez. He'll know. He called by just before you woke and told me to tell you he'd be back in about three hours."

Jack's eyes nearly popped out of his head. "Well, why the fuck didn't you say so?" He was totally exasperated. "Didn't you hear me shouting my guts out down that fucking corridor for over two bloody hours?"

"Sorry, señor," the tramp said, shrinking into the dim corner of the cell. "It's just that you seemed to know better."

"Jesuuuus!" Jack screamed at him before slumping heavily down onto the bed, causing the weak, tubular frame to bend within an inch of the concrete floor.

Jack remembered the fleas but was past caring.

Half an hour later, the wooden door at the end of the passageway creaked open, and in waddled Sergeant Hernandez. He was a potbellied police officer with a big, happy face, most of which was covered up by the handkerchief he was holding over his nose.

He unlocked the cell door with a large, old, rusty key and began pulling it open. Both hinges were deeply corroded, and they screeched with shock at once again being forced to perform the task they were designed for.

"Señor, follow me," the sergeant said, and he immediately walked off, leaving the cell door wide open.

Jack hauled himself off the broken bed and edged into the passageway. For a horrible moment, he worried that the sergeant may have been talking to the tramp and not to him, for Pedro, too, had quickly stood. But Pedro had just wanted to reclaim the now-empty bed for himself—if he discounted the million or so fleas, that is.

Jack winced. *How could anybody be so desperate as to want that old, dirty thing?*

"Come on, Mr. North," Sergeant Hernandez called.

Jack smiled at the tramp.

"*Hasta la vista*, Pedro," Jack said, waving. "It appears that your lot have regained their senses at last, thank God." And with that and a sense of optimistic glee, he hurried to catch up to the sergeant, who was waiting for him in the open doorway.

"Take me home, please, Sergeant Hernandez, and all is forgiven. I'm in need of a shower, as I'm sure you can tell. Pongs down here."

The sergeant ushered Jack past him and up an old stone staircase. "Up, please, señor."

The steps were worn and smooth, betraying a century or more of use, and Jack took them two at a time. He was feeling positive. A bright, electric light was flooding in from the open doorway at the top of the staircase, and that signaled civilization, food, and warmth. All of a sudden, he was there, in the light, breathing hard and squinting.

His eyes took a few moments to adjust. When they did, he could see that a little, bald man wearing small, round spectacles and a dark-gray suit with a matching gray tie was standing in front of him. Charles Montgomery Burns from *The Simpsons* came to mind. The guy looked ridiculous, like some sort of Dickensian clerk. In different times, Jack would have laughed at him, ridiculed him, but the two enormous men flanking the man put a stop to that. The soldiers were both wearing black fatigues. They had grim faces, and they'd planted their shiny black boots solidly on the tiled floor to better balance the submachine guns they were carrying.

Jack felt faint again.

There was to be no shower.

The little man wheeled on his heel, a 180-degree spin that most ice dancers would have been proud of, and strode off down the corridor.

Jack took a step backward—*It might be better, safer, to go back down below*—but Sergeant Hernandez cut off his retreat and pushed him forward, and one of the soldiers grabbed his arm.

They fell in two steps behind the little man. Men and women, some in police uniforms, stared at them from open-plan offices.

Jack was doing his best to remain calm, but it was a losing battle. His legs were wobbling as if his bones had melted, and his head was swimming. Only the soldiers' grip kept him upright. The many onlookers weren't helping his state of mind, either. A policewoman in the water-cooler crowd was pointing at him, while covering her mouth as if in shock, and the other people around her were now walking over to gawk.

His mind went into overdrive. *Oh God, the dead tanker driver. I'm going to be charged with murder.*

No way, screamed his rational brain. *That's bollocks. In the UK, the worst you're facing is reckless driving.*

But we're not in the UK, his alter ego shouted back. *And maybe the Spanish take killing innocent road users seriously. English courts are soft as shit on motoring offenses. Maybe these bastards aren't.*

Rubbish. No speed cameras and no witnesses. The dagos can't prove a thing, his rational self said but not as confidently.

No evidence? Wake up, man. You mean no evidence other than an exploding petrol tanker and a burnt corpse. Jack's sneering negativity threatened to overwhelm him.

Even the most optimistic parts of Jack knew that his situation wasn't good. Damning evidence was certainly there. There was the twat in the Ferrari, too. He was a witness. Maybe he was the bastard who had grassed him up.

"Shit."

Nah. That's definitely not right. That maniac was going twice as fast as I was. He caused the whole fucking accident. He should be sitting here.

Jack took a deep breath. In for seven and out for eleven, as the child psychologist had taught him.

Back home, it'd be "driving without due care and attention." Three points and a fifty-quid fine. That's all. And it can't be much different in Spain. This must just be standard Spanish procedure. A man had died, and obviously the dagos take that seriously. Fair enough. If I had died, and I nearly had, then I'd want some fucker to pay as well. Tough Spanish procedures. All fatal road accidents are treated in exactly the same way; I'm no exception. Not treated any better or any worse than anybody else would be. However, Spain is in the EU, and European courts believe in that human-rights bollocks, and so eventually I'll walk free.

He relaxed.

All he had to do was wait it out.

Worst-case scenario was another day without a shower and three points on his license. A fine wasn't going to bother him; that was for sure. He smiled. He was a fucking multimillionaire.

Then he remembered the mill fire.

And crumbled.

Lord, have mercy.

He was finished.

New forensic technology could now prove it had been his cigarette butt. Or video footage had come to light showing him standing in Mill Street while his uncle's family and work colleagues were burning to death in the stores. Perhaps new evidence could prove he'd lied to the police. He was going to jail for a very, very long time.

Mr. Jack North was finished.

"Oh God, no-o-o," he said under his breath.

Sweat began dripping into his eyebrow-less eyes. The salt stung, and his eyes filled with tears. The bright police station and the moving, staring, and pointing figures all around him became a blur. His legs began to wobble.

It was the mill. He'd never see the light of day or Coronation Street ever again.

A violent, bubbling sensation formed in the bottom of his stomach.

Followed by an eruption.

Before he'd realized what was happening, Jack had vomited—volcano style—right over the little man's back.

"*Que es—*" The startled little man spun around, but he never finished his question.

Jack's second heave was much more powerful than his first. It was deep and guttural and powered by terror. It caught the still-unsuspecting official squarely in the face. Runny, custard-like vomit ran over the man's smooth pate; it squirted into his ears; it went up his nose; it ran inside his shirt and jacket; and, worst of all, it forced its way through his partly open mouth and slipped down his throat.

The two soldiers looked on in horror.

What was the protocol?

Should they execute the spewing man?

Instead, they grabbed the offender's shoulders and turned him to face the wall. It was a sensible action, if a little late, although it did have the benefit of protecting them just in case of a third eruption.

A heavy silence fell.

Jack knew he was about to die. He turned his head slightly to see who was going to kill him.

The little man was staring straight at him.

If Jack's mouth hadn't been still full of spew, he'd have gulped; instead, he clamped his lips tightly together. The little man had spat the unwelcome contents of his own mouth on his jacket sleeve and was now clearly thinking about how he would exact a terrible revenge. And who could blame him?

Jack felt another retch building but managed to keep it down.

After being vomited on, most men would launch into some sort of furious assault, but this strange chap did nothing. He simply stood stock still; somehow, that seemed even worse. He was unmoving but thinking. The cogs in his head were undoubtedly whirring at breakneck speed, no doubt considering the darkest of evil plans. *Why couldn't I have thrown up on a normal guy?* Jack thought. *By now, at least I'd be halfway through my beating or else already dead.*

Jack was frozen stiff, not breathing; awaiting the guillotine's heavy blade or whatever else was about to terminate his miserable existence.

And they all waited.

And waited.

And waited.

And then with a third of the speed a bomb-disposal expert takes to remove a delicate, magnetic time switch from a nuclear warhead, the little man removed the stained spectacles from his face and carefully inspected them as if they were a priceless, ancient relic. He then painstakingly wiped the lenses clean with a handkerchief from his trouser pocket.

It took him an age.

Finally satisfied that all of the alien material had been removed, he replaced the shining temple arms back behind his sticky ears and nodded to his men.

The corridor's fearful silence was instantly shattered by the harsh clacking of machine guns being cocked.

Jack fell to his knees.

"Holy fuck," he sobbed. "Please don't shoot me. Please don't. You've got to believe me, I didn't mean to block the fire exit, and I didn't mean to kill anybody. It was an accident. I'll give the mill to charity. I'll give it to you. But please don't kill me."

"Mr. North," said the little man in an ear-splitting voice that would have suited a cartoon rat. "It would indeed give me great pleasure to shoot you many, many times. But, unfortunately for me, His Spanish Majesty's government would be displeased. *Probably.*"

He addressed the slightly larger of the two soldiers. "Captain, get a bucket, and take this man to interrogation room 1. I'll meet you there. I need to change." He turned on his heel and walked off briskly down the corridor, vomit splattering onto the floor in his wake.

"Sir," the captain said. The huge captain, wearing a grin that he'd masterfully contained until his superior had left, placed his cold gun barrel under Jack's wet chin and raised him to his feet. "Señor, if you please. This way."

• • •

Interrogation room 1 was sparse: one door, four walls of battleship gray, and a white tiled floor. A large rectangular mirror hung on one wall. Jack sat on a gray plastic chair at a square Formica table, which had a pink bucket on top of it.

The two soldiers were standing behind their captive—which made sense—out of the line of fire, so to speak—but they needn't have worried. Jack's stomach had settled, not that there was anything left in it to cause further trouble. His mind had calmed a little, too, even though he couldn't deny the size of the hole he was in. *If you could call it a hole. More like a canyon, and the Grand fucking Canyon, no less.* Every couple of minutes, his hands would shake and betray his mind-set. He'd resorted to putting them into his pockets so he didn't have to see them, and he felt all the better for it. He needed to think straight, and he was desperately trying to.

The mill fire had finally caught up with him, and apparently in a country where they didn't piss about. *No soft liberal shites here.* He attempted to look for the bright side, as Max had taught him to do, but the best he came up with was that the vile smell of stale urine that had followed him from the cell had finally left—due to the crusty vomit lining the inside of his nose, which somewhat reduced the perceived benefit. Maddeningly, his scorched eyebrows were itching, and scratching them had made them bleed.

The little man returned half an hour later wearing an oversized white work shirt and no jacket. He'd retained his original dark-gray trousers, which now sported an even darker-gray wet crotch. *Not a good look*, Jack thought, noticing that the man's shoes had been newly polished.

The little man tentatively checked the contents of the pink bucket, which was empty, and placed it on the floor. "Mr. North, my name is Alberto Masa, and I work for the Colombian government. Colombia is in South America."

"I—"

"Quiet!" said Masa in a high-pitched shriek.

Jack jumped in shock and went quiet.

"Listen. Please, Mr. North."

Jack was listening.

"I apologize for the conditions in the detention area, but the new high-security cells are still under construction. Funding issues, the Spanish authorities tell me. Until they're completed, we have to use the old cellars. I'm told they're fit for purpose but can be a bit damp and smelly."

"A *bit*. I can tel—"

Masa slapped him across the face. The force of the blow made Jack bite into his tongue. His mouth filled with blood.

"I'm still speaking, Mr. North."

Jack was silent. Harsh words didn't scare him, and neither did a slap. They never had. His dad hadn't used harsh words or slapped him; he'd used his fists. And he'd hit a lot harder than this bastard did. Right now, Jack would happily accept forty years in jail and many more slappings just so long as the torturous itching above his eyes would stop. His eyebrows were aflame, alive with an all-consuming itch that mosquitos could only dream of creating.

Masa walked slowly around the room, stalking his quarry. *Domination*, Masa was thinking. Stage one of his own tried-and-tested interrogation technique.

Alberto Masa was the unrivaled master interrogator—so thought Alberto Masa—and this fool, this idiot Englishman, this prisoner, was his ignorant pupil.

He spoke again. "Mr. North, we all know why you are here, and so it would be very much appreciated if you would fully cooperate. I hope for your sake that you agree. You may now speak."

Jack stopped scratching. He'd used the time waiting for Masa to clean up to think of a plan. Only one idea had come to mind: he would play dumb. He was good at that. He'd resigned himself to his fate, too. If they had enough evidence to charge him with starting the fire, then so be it, and he'd be royally stuffed. But if they didn't, then he wouldn't be giving it to them by confessing. He wasn't going to convict himself. He'd usefully remembered an old *Scooby Doo* episode where the janitor "fesses up" to running the entire counterfeiting operation; yet Shaggy and Thelma later admitted they had no idea who the culprit actually was. That had surprised Jack; it was always the janitor. Shaggy should have known.

"Señor Masa, if you know why I'm here, then please fill me in. As for your cells being *fit for purpose*, they would have been condemned by Henry VIII—"

"Mr. North!" Masa squealed.

Jack jumped in his chair again, expecting another blow.

None came.

"You are lying, lying, lying," Masa screamed.

Crumbs, he's going to have a thrombi, thought Jack, and tried his best to sound reasonable. He needed to get on with this guy. He'd seen that in a Hollywood hostage movie. Get on the bad guy's side.

"Well, it's not exactly the Holiday Inn, Señor Masa. There's no running water for a start, and—"

"Not the cells, you imbecile. You're lying about not knowing why you're here."

Masa was still screaming, but Jack could tell that the nasty little fucker was feigning. He wasn't angry. Jack had seen plenty of angry people in his time, and this guy wasn't even slightly miffed. Jack's dad's face and neck would go bright red, for a start, and this guy's skin hadn't changed color at all.

Still, Jack thought it in his best interests to explain. "Señor Masa, there's been a major identity cock-up. Somehow, you're confusing me with Al Qaeda. It's just a case of mistaken identity, so please let me go."

Masa was listening, so Jack continued. He was getting somewhere at last. He was making a connection.

"I know I've been involved in a major crash, and the poor dago—sorry, the poor *fella*—driving the petrol tanker is dead, but it really wasn't my fault, Señor Masa. Honestly. If anybody was at fault, it was the lunatic in the Ferrari."

Masa's interest perked up.

Jack pounced. "Surely, one of your guys saw him. He drove me off the road, and then your lot surrounded me in seconds. They must have seen him."

Jack paused. He was convinced that he'd done enough to persuade the man, but just to make sure of the home run, he added, "And I'm really sorry about spewing up all over your head, Señor Masa."

The Colombian bent forward and placed both of his tiny hands on the table. He stared kindly into Jack's burned and bleeding face.

"You are Mr. Jack North. Yes?"

"Yes, I am. Yes. But don't you see? There must be another Jack North. Yes? One you're mixing me up with. You see that now. Yes?" Jack nodded animatedly.

Stage two of Masa's interrogation process was to humiliate and confuse the prisoner to ensure that he understands how weak and vulnerable he really is.

Masa pulled a damp notebook from his shirt pocket. "Well, let me see," he said, opening it and taking a high and mighty tone. "Ah, yes. Here we are. The Jack North we want is thirty-two years old. You are much older, of course. How old are you exactly?"

"Well, I'm thirty-two, but—"

"Really? Oh dear, that's not helpful. Tough life, perhaps. They do say an extra stone of fat adds a year. I'd have put you at midforties. Well, let me see what other details I have here." Masa flicked through a few more pages before stopping. "Right, here we are. The Jack North we want is from England and lives in a small village, Gomersal, in West Yorkshire. His mother still lives there, apparently. He was educated at Birkenshaw Primary School."

Masa put the pages down by his side. "Where were you educated, Mr. North?"

"Well, Birkenshaw Primary but—"

Masa cut in again. "But that's incredible." Masa feigned amazement. "Another Jack North, same age and same school. What a coincidence. We do need to be sure, though, don't we? Make absolutely certain. It would be truly awful if we sentenced the wrong Mr. North to fifty years in jail. Just awful. How would I ever live with myself?"

Masa smiled with a deepening pleasure. Humiliate and confuse. "So let me just check a few more details, Mr. North," he said, working on humiliation. "Details are important, and details are what I'm all about." He scanned the next blank page in his notebook with his finger and paused halfway down. "Ah, yes. Here we are. The Jack North we want owns a large villa in Puerto Portals, just up the coast from here. He's also the owner of a company called Crossland Weavers in a place called Hal-i-fax. Is that how you pronounce it?"

Jack nodded glumly.

Masa steamed on. "The Jack North we want inherited this company, in Hal-i-fax, following a suspected arson attack in which eight people were killed."

Oh God, thought Jack. *Here it comes. It* is *the mill.*

"The murderer"—Masa paused for effect—"or, more accurately, *the mass murderer*, has never been apprehended. However…"

Jack was crying inside.

Masa could smell panic. The prisoner was on the run.

Jack knew he was finished. Life imprisonment—or rather, eight life imprisonments, to be precise. For each of the eight poor souls he'd cremated in that blazing mill, he would now spend his remaining lifetime in a hellhole like the one downstairs. He would be forever hungry, in the dark, and with nobody but a mangy old tramp and the smell of stale piss for company.

The Colombian had stopped talking. "Are you listening, Mr. North? You seem distracted. No wonder your school record is so abysmal, if this is the extent of your ability to concentrate."

Masa was glowing.

The prisoner was falling apart.

He truly was the master interrogator.

"What could possibly be more important to you than what I have to say, Mr. North?"

Jack realized that he was about to be unveiled as Cleckheaton's most infamous son. He could picture the headlines in the *Spenborough Guardian*: "Jack North Is the Crossland Weavers Mass Murderer."

Tears welled in his eyes, and his hands were shaking again. He tensed his jaw. He was a boxer who knew that the vicious knockout blow was coming but was powerless to block it. Strangely, however, the fear he'd felt at the thought of being unmasked was starting to subside, replaced by a building anger. In short, Jack was transitioning from shit scared to absolutely furious. He had an intense hatred of authority, specifically those people with direct authority over him. *Like teachers.* And Masa was acting like a fucking teacher, the worst kind, too—a bully. The little, bald-headed bastard had just mentioned the most embarrassing thing that Jack could ever think of—his school record—and fear had gone out of the window. He was buggered if he was going to show any fear to a teacher, and that's who this guy thought he was. Jack had done enough of that at school. He hated teachers—hated, hated, *hated* them.

Masa continued.

Humiliate and confuse. Stage two of his interrogation process was in the bag.

"We thought you were a legitimate businessman, Mr. North. Incompetent but legitimate. There's no law against being incompetent, of course. Otherwise, the jails would be fit to bursting with people like you." Masa giggled like an eleven-year-old. "But you made a mistake, Mr. North. People like you don't learn. You purchased Lovebirds, a night-club in Palma, and then proceeded to install a brothel on the top floor. I understand that you visit Lovebirds religiously, if that's an appropriate term. Tuesday and Friday nights—my agents aren't sure why those two nights in particular."

Jack was sure. Consuela, his housekeeper, visited her mama on Tuesdays and Fridays. He had his reasons for keeping secret his twice-weekly habit from Consuela—and so he offered no explanation.

Suddenly, Jack realized that Masa hadn't condemned him as the Crossland Weavers mass murderer. He hadn't even mentioned the fire again. Jack's fury began turning to hope and then joy.

He doesn't know! The little, nasty bastard doesn't know that I started the fire. Nobody knows.

A huge smile spread across Jack's filthy, scab-encrusted, and scorched face. The itching started up again, but he didn't care anymore. He was safe.

Masa doesn't know.

Masa was smug. He knew he'd won. "And the Jack North we want owns a motor yacht that's moored in Porto Colom."

Masa paused. "Just *what* is there for *you* to smile about?"

Jack was chuckling. He couldn't help it; he felt gloriously happy. The only thought going round and round in his head was that nobody knew about the mill fire. The relief it inspired was immense. Dark thoughts of countless lifetimes spent in fleapits had vanished, and whatever this ludicrous situation was, it couldn't possibly be as bad as being unveiled as a mass-fucking-murderer. He knew he shouldn't show his glee, but he couldn't hide it. He attempted to force his aching face muscles to hold the corners of his mouth down, and it worked for a moment. He looked glum for about two seconds. Then the corners of his mouth turned upward again and created a clown-like grin.

"And fin-n-nally," Masa said, stuttering and losing confidence. What was happening? It had been going so well, but now the prisoner, instead of capitulating, had seemed to relax. The English pig was smiling like a buffoon, and he, Masa, the master interrogator, was confused and humiliated.

Masa bumbled on, trying to recover. "The…er…Jack North we want has a housekeeper, a Miss Consuela Fonseca, who is also his—"

"All right," Jack said. "That's enough, Señor Masa. If I may be permitted to speak?"

Masa nodded.

"Yes, it does appear that I'm *that* Jack North. I was brought up in Gomersal, and I did inherit Crossland Weavers, but what's illegal about that?"

He paused, waiting for a reply, but Masa remained silent.

Jack relaxed further. He was home and dry. He'd asked directly about the legality of his inheritance, and Masa had said nothing. Hallelujah. "Señor Masa," said Jack. "The mill fire robbed me of my dear uncle and all his beautiful family and some of my closest friends, too. So, I'll ask you to respect my grievous losses. As for the rest of your information, with the exception of my yacht, it's total tosh."

"Tosh?" Masa asked.

"Tosheo. In-accurateo. Bollockseo," Jack said, in a shockingly bad Spanish accent.

"Inaccurate, Mr. North?" Masa asked calmly, trying to wrestle back control of the interview. "Are you sure about that, Mr. North? Or are you saying you attend your dirty little brothel on Saturdays, too?"

The truthful answer to that question was *sometimes*, but Jack wasn't worried about being made fun of. He'd endured plenty of that before.

"Very funny, Señor Masa. Good joke." Jack was pleased that he'd vomited all over the nasty, little sod. "It does seem that I'm bang to rights on Lovebirds, if you've any evidence to back those charges up, that is. So get me a lawyer, and then I can get the hell out of here. I need a shower."

"Admitting you need a shower are the first words of truth you've spoken," Masa said, spitting like an attacking snake.

Jack was startled by the venom and involuntarily sat back in his chair. Masa was almost hissing.

"I'm not interested in your sordid sexual habits, you imbecile."

That worried Jack again. Not the imbecile bit. He was scouring his brain for any other reasons the Majorcan police might want him if it wasn't the fire; didn't appear to be the car crash, even though the tanker driver had bought it; and wasn't Lovebirds or his "sordid sexual habits." And just what did Masa mean by that? Sordid? Schoolgirl outfits weren't sordid, were they? He remembered asking the girls' permission first. They were all in their twenties and had seemed happy enough to comply. The main problem had been getting their bras off afterward, as they'd been really tight and had cut deep into his back.

"You won't be having a shower until you cooperate, Mr. North. Until then you will stay either in this room or in the detention cell—"

"Dungeon, you mean," shouted Jack.

Masa ignored him. "Until you cooperate by fully explaining your connection to the Medellín drug cartel."

Jack's mouth dropped open. He'd been about to demand his right to a telephone call.

What had Masa said? It certainly wasn't anything about schoolgirl outfits, arson, or prostitution. He tried to remember and repeated it aloud.

"The meddling cartel?"

Masa bent over the table again, his rodent-shaped, reddening face within an inch of the insolent Englishman's.

"Not the 'meddling cartel,'" he said in a whisper that threatened imminent violence. "The Medellín Cartel. Until Pablo Escobar was shot dead by the Colombian police in 1993, the Medellín drug cartel was the biggest cocaine producer and distribution network that the world has ever seen and its most violent."

Jack was beginning to make sense of what Masa was saying. The guy seemed to be accusing him of being a *drug lord!* And not just any old drug lord, either, but rather, the world's biggest-fucking drug lord ever, with the world's biggest fucking drug empire to boot. Analysis complete, all worry left him, and he burst into riotous laughter.

"You think I'm a drug lord! Ha-ha-ha-ha! What a joke. Ha-ha-ha-ha-ha!"

Tears of laughter ran down his face. "The only drug I do, Señor Masa, is Viagra, but you don't need any of that. You're stiff enough already."

The look of shock on his interrogator's face caused Jack to laugh even louder.

"Just call me Godfather North from now on, Masa. Let's dispense with the 'Mr. North' shite."

"Mr. North—"

"Godfather North. Call me that. Go on, Masa, go on. You're a good-fella. Ha-ha-ha! Get it, Masa? *Goodfellas.* The film. Ha-ha-ha-ha!"

Alberto Masa was totally humiliated and confused. Prisoners had deployed all kinds of strategies to beat interrogation. Faking illness, mental breakdowns, and blaming others were very popular, as was feigning ignorance. Occasionally, interrogees had shown incredible levels of stamina. Either that, or they'd been telling the truth all along, which sometimes happened, although this was only usually discovered well after the event. A handful of prisoners had been subjected to stronger techniques. Masa wasn't proud of this, though on some occasions, the ends had mostly justified the means. But all of that was a long time ago and on his home turf in Colombia. However, in a career spanning more than thirty years, and consisting of thousands of interrogations of some of the nastiest, cleverest, and most ruthless people ever imaginable, he'd never been laughed at.

Masa thought of himself as an expert in his trade, the master of interrogation, and so after a few moments of thought, he rallied and recognized the sheer brilliance of Jack North's strategy. The man was using raucous laughter to simultaneously create the appearance of innocence and humiliate the poor interrogator. It was genius. It was brilliant.

Masa smiled. His confidence was back. This Englishman was no fool after all; he was an expert masquerading as a fool, and he was playing his part with Oscar-winning talent. He was a real specialist for sure. Masa almost felt admiration. He'd heard that the cartels were training their people in psychological techniques. Well, here was the proof. This foul-mouthed, fat, sweaty, and stinking Englishman would be a tough nut to crack, but he'd met his match. Alberto Gonzalez Philippe Romeo Masa was a *nutcracker*.

Two can play the Englishman's game, thought Masa. He'd been momentarily shaken—badly knocked, in fact—but his training and years of experience had quickly kicked in. Most importantly, he'd controlled his emotions well, although a nerve just above his left eye was twitching—making him wink involuntarily.

He noticed that the prisoner was winking back at him.

Jack began to laugh raucously again, and Masa's twitching nerve got worse.

He slammed a hand over the eye.

Jack laughed even more; his interrogator looked like a pirate.

"Captain, wipe that smile off your face," Masa squealed to one of the soldiers standing behind Jack. He was in a fury. "Can't you recognize a defensive interrogation technique when you see one?"

The captain bit down hard on his lip and stared at the floor.

"Take the prisoner back to the cells," Masa barked. "And strip him to his underwear. Take his shoes, too. And he's allowed no food. Let's see if Mr. North finds that funny."

"Señor Masa," Jack said as he was being frog-marched to the door.

"What?"

A grin stretched right across Jack's grubby, burned, and bleeding face. He looked grotesque. He was soot stained, beaten, and tattered but gloriously happy. "Masa," he said with a chuckle. "You're a right fucking *winker*. Get it Masa, not wanker, *winker*. Ha-ha-ha-ha-ha! Ha-ha-ha-ha-ha-ha-ha!"

CHAPTER 9

Max awoke from a recurring dream. He'd been journeying alone through deep space, cryogenically frozen so as not to age or die on the five-hundred-year voyage. As usual, he'd woken before being defrosted.

Wonder if I ever arrive, he pondered as he became aware of painful throbbing and hammering sensations inside his head. He closed his eyes and tried to go back to sleep but couldn't, so he just lay there feeling lousy. Half an hour passed before he realized the throbbing and hammering were coming from different sources. The sensation of a metal hammer hitting a granite block and showering sparks was definitely in his head, but the throbbing pulses were from the *Conchita's* engines.

"Stan!"

He swung his legs off the bed, stood, and then sat again, feeling faint. After a few moments, the blood climbed its way back up into his head, and he quickly pulled on an old T-shirt and shorts and headed up top.

Stan was on the flybridge. He had a big smirk on his face and was sitting comfortably in Jack's helm seat. He was smoking a Marlboro Light. The rocky south Majorcan coast was smoothly passing by a few hundred yards to starboard. Puerto Colom wasn't even in sight. It was long gone.

"Morning, Maxi," Stan said. "Lovely day for a sail, ain't it?"

"Bloody hell, Stan." Max shielded his eyes from the painful, bright sunlight. "We'll get ten years apiece for this. You've nicked a twenty-million-quid superyacht. And just what the hell are you wearing?"

Stan looked down at his garb. He was wearing a light-blue polo shirt with "Conchita" embroidered on the pocket in gold italics. The shirt went rather well with his dark-blue shorts and white deck shoes.

"Thought you'd not clocked the outfit," Stan said, looking very pleased with his new attire.

"Difficult to miss, Stanley."

"And what do you think about this for the cherry on top?" Stan held up an ornate captain's hat. It was pristine white with a dark-blue rim. More gold braiding flanked each side of the hat's centerpiece, which was a bright-blue star. Stan plonked it on his bald head. "What do you think?"

"Well..."

"Don't be jealous, Maxi. There's a full crew uniform for everybody down below. Some formal gear, too. You know, blazers, trousers, and patent-leather shoes, in case we hold a ball like. Play your cards right, mate, and I'll get you an invite to the captain's table."

"I can assure you I'm not in the least bit jealous, Stan," Max said, getting angry. "But, gee, that's great to know, as we'll all look really smart in court when we get sentenced. In case you'd forgotten, this is Jack's yacht."

"Oh, chill out," said Stan. "And fuck Jack. He's the one who invited us out here for a sailing trip to make up for the so-called Blackpool Incident, remember? In my book, we deserve a day or two on the Med before we head home. Hey, we could it sail back to Blighty."

"Don't be a dick," Max said, but he sat in the other helm chair. His head felt no better, and he was feeling nauseated now, too. "None of us have a clue how to sail a dinghy, Stan, never mind this bloody thing. How the hell did you start the engines?"

"Type the PIN into the console, and Bob's your uncle. No key required," Stan said. The breeze was picking up, so he pulled the captain's hat down tighter on his head. "Very secure, unless you write the code on a Post-it and stick it underneath the captain's chair, as our dipstick Jack did. God, he's thick. And the *Conchita*'s easy to drive. Is that the term? Easier to drive than a heavy-goods vehicle anyway, although I've not worked out how to stop it yet. Can't find the brakes. Will can sort that out when he wakes up. He knows all about yachts and stuff."

Max groaned. "The only experience Will has of sailing is from flicking through the yachting magazines at his dentist's," he said, feeling totally exasperated. "I grant you that's more than the rest of us have, but in my view, it's still lacking."

"Fair comment," Stan said and chuckled. "He'll crap himself when I tell him he's our new skipper. Jane's apparently been talking about a cruise, though, so this'll be good experience for him. Nothing like learning on the job."

A pair of Ray-Ban sunglasses was lying on the console, and Max put them on. That was better. He could open his eyes properly, and the deeper colors were pleasant. Now all he needed was a neurosurgeon to sort out the thumping in his head.

"Come on, Maxi," said Stan, taking on a conciliatory tone. He'd been on a negotiation course the previous year. "A couple of days won't hurt us, will they? And they won't hurt Jack, either. It does sound like he'll be out of action for a while. So where's the harm? Two days trundling up and down the coast, and then we'll take her back. I promise. The sea's a millpond. What could possibly go wrong?"

"And when Jack finds out?" asked Max.

"*If* Jack finds out, we'll claim it was all a big misunderstanding, just like he'll be saying the Blackpool Incident was. It's done now, so you may as well enjoy the ride. We can come over all remorseful and apologetic if we need to. It's not hard to fake. I do it with Tina all the time."

Max's head was finally clearing, and he took in the scene. It was beautiful out at sea and peaceful, too—relaxing. The *Conchita* was easing along parallel to a coastline of shallow hills and deserted sandy beaches. Sea gulls flew high overhead across a clear, blue sky. Max saw no houses, factories, roads, smog, drizzle, or other people. To port, the horizon was a straight, blue line; the ocean and sky merged in seemingly endless space. No other boats disturbed the scene. Surfers and oil rigs were absent. Nothing was around but deep-blue water, space, and peace.

A couple of days, thought Max. *Not much to ask.* He didn't quite share Stan's optimism that nothing could go wrong, but Stan was right about Jack: he wouldn't be doing any sailing for a while. So, maybe a spot of cruising and sunbathing, a few beers, and a laugh or two were reasonable as long as they didn't sink the bloody thing.

"And I need some leave from Tina, mate," said Stan, seeing that his friend was coming around. "I love her to bits, but she's a powder keg. The tension in the house gets unbearable."

DG and Will's faces appeared as they came up the stairs. Both had confused expressions.

"Don't ask," Max said. "Your uniforms are downstairs."

"Uniforms?" Will asked.

He spotted Stan's regalia. "Great," he said. "And what's for breakfast? I'm starving."

"San Miguels for breakfast," Stan said. "The captain's favorite beer."

"That's my favorite beer, too," Will said, stretching his arms above his head and yawning before reality dawned. "Oh, come on, guys. You're joking?"

They weren't.

"But I'm not qualified," Will said.

"You're not formally qualified," said Max. "However, we've reviewed everybody's sailing qualifications, and it does appear that you are the most *informally* qualified. It was that quick scan through the *Yachting Monthly* at your dental checkup that sealed it. Plus, I remember you telling me that your mum watched reruns of *Howards' Way.*"

Will was in shock.

"Snap out of it, Will," DG said. "You know you want to be *el capitano.*"

Stan held out the impressive captain's hat. Will went to snatch it but Stan pulled it away at the last moment and hid it behind his back.

"Only el capitano can have the hat," DG said.

Stan held the hat out again. The blue star above the center of the brim caught the sunlight and shone.

Will was quicker this time and grabbed it to cheers. He took two quick steps backward to ensure he kept hold of it.

"Jane will skin me alive," he said, looking adoringly at his prize. He placed it lovingly on his head, as if it were the crown of England.

Coronation complete and a look of deep satisfaction on his face, Will eased Stan authoritatively aside and sat down at the main helm to a round of applause.

"Long live El Capitano," DG cheered.

"Shipmates," Will said, becoming serious, "I need to check direction, depth, and speed. Max, turn on the navigation system. It's the green-screen, the round thing. Stan, check the oil pressure. And, DG, you can get me a San Miguel from the main deck. I'm needed on the bridge."

"Aye, aye, El Capitano," came back the reply in triplicate with salutes.

Max could see that Will was scanning the superyacht's controls with genuine enthusiasm. He seemed totally in his element. *He looks bigger, like he's grown two inches in the last minute.*

El Capitano slowly pulled back two levers and bubbling white seawater mushroomed up behind the *Conchita*. The great yacht was responding to her powerful engines and surged forward, sea spray splashing up and over the bow rail.

Max's lungs filled with revitalizing fresh sea air. This was what he'd imagined the trip would be like after first receiving Jack's invitation, only this was a thousand times better. It was real. The power of the engines, the wind blowing through his hair, the sea spray, the smell of salt, and the bumping along were fantastic. He could see DG, Will, and Stan all grinning inanely from ear to ear, and then realized that he was doing the same.

He threw back his head and laughed. "This is just fucking great."

• • •

The *Conchita* raced west throughout the morning and into the early afternoon. It was still a beautiful day, not a cloud was in the sky. The southern Majorcan shoreline was in sight but over three miles away to starboard. They'd moved out to sea to avoid a host of smaller craft and intrepid tourists on pedalos, one of whom they awoke with a blast of the *Conchita*'s foghorn. The guy nearly had a heart attack, particularly when seeing how far he had to pedal back.

Max and DG had donned *Conchita* crew T-shirts and shorts like Stan wore, but Will had gone for the formal outfit and was sporting a white blazer with gold epaulets and gold buttons and pressed white trousers. Will thought that the outfit emphasized his newfound authority.

The men's excitement at finding themselves to be modern-day luxury pirates lasted well into the afternoon, and they joked about escaping across the Atlantic, spending their lives circumnavigating the globe, or exiling themselves in Brazil as Ronnie Biggs, the Great Train Robber, had done.

"I thought old Ronnie got nicked in the end, though," DG said, who was lying on the deck and drinking in the sunshine. "I'm sure he was extradited to a jail in the UK."

"Biggs came home for NHS treatment," Will said, straightening his shirt collar. "Makes you bloody laugh. He spent thirty years on the run, most of it with a young Brazilian girl that he'd got pregnant to avoid extradition in the first place. And then after the girl wears him out, UK taxpayers have to cough up for his medical bills. It could only happen in Britain."

"That's actually quite a comforting thought," Max said. "We've just stolen a yacht worth probably ten times as much as the Great Train Robbers nicked in the first place."

"And there are worse things in life than spending thirty years with a Brazilian girl," DG said.

Captain Will decided to keep the coastline in sight until they'd mastered the satellite navigational system, or at least worked out how to turn it on. Fortunately, Max had discovered a pair of binoculars and a large map of Majorca in a small cupboard under the main instrument console. He'd begun navigating by landmark after spotting Palma Cathedral. The huge building's twelfth-century walls were easily visible to the naked eye from three miles out and dominated the view of Majorca's capital city, but other small villages required the use of the binoculars.

Late afternoon saw them fast approaching Andratx, a small town and bay in the southwest of the island. Max was sitting alone on the foredeck, resting his back against the flybridge superstructure. Between dozes, he'd been watching DG and Stan as they waved at passing yachts. They were sitting at the bow rail, dangling their bare legs over the side and into the refreshing spray. Every now and then, they'd cheer wildly as fellow sailors waved back.

It reminded Max of their junior-school trips. He and his friends would all squeeze on the coach's backseat and give a thumbs-up signal to whatever vehicles were traveling behind. If a driver acknowledged, then the students in the backseat would cheer maniacally. But if the driver ignored them, as quite a few of the miserable sods did, then they got the treatment: full-scale jeering and a coordinated middle finger. On one occasion, a particularly sour-looking woman had scowled at them for miles. Stan had mooned her. The woman's eyes had nearly popped out of her head as she finally realized that a hairy backside had just appeared in the window. She'd duly slammed on her brakes and turned off at the next exit, as the students in the backseat sang a rousing chorus of "Moon River, wider than a mile."

Max closed his eyes. The sound of the metronomic splashing of the bow waves was relaxing, as was the sun's warmth.

Then he remembered Jack. *Is he really OK?*

His inner voice answered. *Shouldn't you be finding out? Just what kind of friend are you, anyway? He was in a car accident, and all you've done is fuck off on his yacht. Hope you're enjoying yourself, Maxi.*

It's true, he thought. *It's bad.*

What with all the booze, the dabbing revelations, a stinking hangover, the surprise of finding himself all at sea—literally—and then the even bigger surprise of wanting to stay there, he'd forgotten all about Jack. No. That wasn't true, was it? He was lying to himself again. He hadn't forgotten about Jack; he'd just been having too great a time to care, and now guilt was kicking in big time.

He dug the mobile out of his pocket, saw that there was a signal, and dialed Jules's number. He didn't have Jack's, which made him feel guiltier still.

Jules had told them at the airport that Jack was OK, which was reassuring, to a point. But they didn't know that for certain. And clearly, Jack wasn't really OK; otherwise, he'd be with them on the yacht.

The call went to voice mail.

"Jules, it's Max. We're worried about Jack. Give me call when you get this message, please."

He felt really unhappy with himself, so he stood and went to see Will on the flybridge. Will was busily avoiding a small sailing dinghy that was about to cross their path.

"I'm worried about Jack," said Max. "I've just left Jules a message."

"Just look at those two wallies," said Will, smiling, and turning the *Conchita* slightly to port.

DG and Stan were both waving frantically at the two teenage boys on the dinghy to get out of the way. There was no danger of a collision, and both teenagers seemed bemused, but they waved back a "thanks," anyway—better to keep the scary men happy.

"I'm worried about Jack, too," Will said. "But Jules did say that he was all right."

The dinghy was behind them now, so Will straightened up back along the coast.

"And Jules did get a call from Jack," he said. "Remember, at the airport? So he must be pretty much OK, although I'd like to check in with him, too." Will's brow furrowed. "Although it would be lousy to get back into port and find out he was hurt real bad or worse."

"You're not reassuring me, Will," Max said.

● ● ●

Max had seated himself on the foredeck. He was still feeling like crap but had more or less convinced himself that Jack was just shaken up. As Will had reminded him, Jules had taken a call from her boss after the accident, so it couldn't be too bad. *You don't make calls from intensive care.* That thought eased his mind, and he hoped that Jules would return his voice mail soon, too.

A speedboat coming directly out from the coast caught his eye. It was still the best part of a mile away, but it was traveling at high speed. Its bright-red bow was raised prominently out of the water and pointing straight at the *Conchita*. If it stayed on its present course, it would intercept them very soon.

"Seen the speedboat, Will?" Max called out.

"Yeah," Will shouted. "Looks like it's making straight for us. I'll change course to see if she follows. Here goes. Hang on."

Will spun the ridiculously small steering wheel hard to port, and the *Conchita* responded immediately, her stern port side digging deep down into the sea. The superyacht almost stopped in her tracks as she turned on a sixpence through thirty degrees. Max held on to the starboard rail. Turn complete, the *Conchita* surged forward again on a course that took her inshore.

Both men watched for the speedboat's reaction.

There was none.

Good.

Max breathed a sigh of relief just as a wave of white water shot up from one side of the approaching vessel. It signaled a high-speed turn, and, once again, its red bow pointed straight at the *Conchita.*

"Shit. Could be the bloody cops," Max said.

Will began to panic. "Oh God. Oh God. What are we going to do?" He took off his captain's hat and held it behind his back.

"We're going to meet whoever it is, is what we're going to do," Max said. "We've not enough fuel for Brazil."

Max raised the binoculars. The speedboat was well within range, but it was difficult to focus on any detail because it was bobbing about so much. "It's red. That's about it at the moment. Can't see any police markings, and there's nobody visible in uniform. Nobody visible full stop. They're definitely coming here, though."

"Fuck me," DG said, clambering up to the flybridge. "What was the hairpin turn all about, Will? You nearly tipped me and Rambo into the drink. Stan's balls got crushed against the metal railing post. Funny in many ways, but not pleasant to see or hear, especially for him. He's less than amused, might even take the captain's hat back. If you had it on, that is. Where is it?"

Will still had the hat behind his back. He was sure that the longest jail sentence would be reserved for the captain. "Sorry, DG. We were just checking whether we're being followed," he said, pointing to the fast-approaching speedboat.

Stan appeared. He was groaning, both hands tucked down his shorts. "Fucking hell, Will. Did we miss the iceberg? If so, let's go back and get some ice to soothe my bollocks."

"Sorry, Stan, but look," Will said.

The speedboat was slowing up a hundred yards away. Five figures were now clearly visible in the small cockpit. Four of them were jumping up and down, as if they'd each won the lottery.

"If I'm dreaming, then do not wake me up," DG said.

"Andy McNab's testicles," Stan said, the pain in his groin instantly forgotten.

"This must be Jack's *secret entertainment*," DG said, a look of awe on his face. "I'm forgiving him for Blackpool, and he's got my vote for mayor." With that, he turned and ran for the stairway leading down to the main deck.

"The fat bastard's played a blinder, that's for sure, but he's not forgiven," said Stan, following DG. "I'll go meet and greet and save 'em from Casanova."

Will cut the *Conchita*'s engines. A few moments later, the speedboat did the same and freewheeled up alongside the *Conchita*'s stern. Its driver was standing at the wheel. He was a young Spaniard wearing dark sunglasses and a pair of tattered old shorts.

He called over. "Hola, *Conchita*."

DG threw a rope to him.

Max and Will watched the bizarre scene from the flybridge.

Four bikini-clad girls were also in the boat. They were still jumping up and down and screaming with excitement. The speedboat was rocking wildly from one side to the other.

"They're all bloody gorgeous," Will said. "It's like a beauty pageant."

"More like Monday through Thursday in the *Sun*," Max said. "But they're definitely not here to arrest us."

"Eh?" Will said.

"Page Three girls, Will. Keep up, mate."

"Hola, señors," the young Spaniard shouted. He was struggling to make himself heard over the high-pitched frivolity going on around him. "Sorry we're late, but I was told to meet you off Porto Colom this morning. I saw you leaving and followed down the coast. It's lucky for me that you slowed, as I'm low on fuel. Have the arrangements changed, señors? Do you still want the girls?" He held one cupped hand to his ear in an attempt to hear the reply.

"Is the pope a Catholic, son?" DG shouted. He was grinning like the proverbial Cheshire cat.

The boy was confused. "Si, señor, he is."

"Well, there you go, mi amigo," DG said. "No change of plan, then." He began pulling on the mooring rope, easing the speedboat in.

"Lower your platform," the Spaniard shouted.

Now it was DG who was confused.

"The black button in the housing next to the rail, to your left," Will shouted from above.

DG pressed it. An electric motor started up, and a two-meter square section of decking over the stern rail began sinking into the water. It was a bathing platform, and it allowed ease of entry to the yacht from the sea, usually for swimmers, but it worked well for mooring up small craft, too.

DG jumped down on it, his feet disappearing into the shallow water, and offered his hand Sir Walter Raleigh style.

"Pass them on over to me, DG, and I'll pull them up on deck," Stan said, sounding very eager.

"God, look at them both," Max said to Will. "It's embarrassing. They're drooling."

The gorgeous blonde stepping out of the speedboat didn't seem to mind. She took DG's hand and fell into his arms. He held her for a moment, the two seemingly reluctant to part, before Stan reached over and grabbed one of her arms.

"Come on, DG," Stan said. "There's three more waiting, so get on with it. All this rocking about is making me feel sick."

A minute later, all four women were safely aboard.

"Catch, señor."

Stan just managed to pull his eyes off a short, busty brunette before the holdall landed on his head. Three other bags quickly followed.

Embarkation complete, DG untied the speedboat's mooring rope and threw it back across to the smiling speedboat driver.

"Enjoy yourselves, señors," he said before powering up and heading back for the coast.

● ● ●

The four giggling women stood in a line on the main deck. The four men stood opposite, gawking. Max broke the ice.

"Hi, girls," he said. "Very nice of you to join us." He felt uncomfortable. This was ridiculous but exciting in a trashy, *FHM* lads' magazine sort of way. It was the sort of article/bathing-suit photo shoot that men like him completely ignored when anybody else was in the room but picked up again immediately when they were alone, having accidently hidden the offending magazine under the sofa. "Let me introduce you to my friends," he said. "Left to right. DG and Stan, whom you've already met, and this is Will, our captain."

Will remembered that the captain's hat was still behind his back. He quickly stuck it back on his head.

"Hola, ladies," DG said, beaming a golden smile.

"Aye up," Stan said. His eyes had fixed again on the small brunette—or, more accurately, on her enormous boobs.

"Er...Hello, ladies," Will said, finding it difficult to speak. But as captain, he knew that he had to. He then clammed up totally when he noticed the tall redhead at the end of the line staring at him.

"And I'm Max." He felt anxious, as he usually did when meeting women for the first time, although the surreal circumstances had made it less of a problem than usual. *Jack used to freak out around girls. He'd changed his ways. He was usually hopeless.* "Welcome aboard the *Conchita.*"

"So now you all know us," DG said. "But who are we going to have the pleasure of?"

"For Christ's sake, DG, give it a rest," Stan said. "We don't even know their names."

The short brunette whom Stan had already bagged in his mind ignored DG's comment. She'd heard it all before.

"Hello, Max, guys. I'm Tracy from Sheffield," she said in a thick Yorkshire accent. "Is there a hot tub? I love hot tubs."

Tracy was the shortest of the four women but had easily the biggest boobs, which were being improbably held in place by a rather flimsy-looking bikini. Surely, it was at least two sizes too small. Stan's eyes focused like laser beams on the small green triangles of material covering her protruding nipples in anticipation that the thin straps must soon give way. And he wasn't going to miss it.

"Nice, aren't they, darling?" Tracy said.

Stan was in a trance. "Absolutely magnificent," he said with a sense of awe. He hadn't even realized that it was Tracy who had spoken. His gaze was lower down than her face, eyes still locked on the incredible, bursting bikini top. He suddenly became aware that all eyes were now on him. He also realized what he'd just said. It broke the moment.

"I mean, er, yes, very nice, love," he muttered. He tried again to rees-tablish an ounce of credibility. "Er, hello, Tracy. Love. Nice to meet them… I mean…er…you. I mean, all you girls."

He stopped talking and put on a cheesy grin. He looked ridiculous, but it was the best he could do. He'd been in this position with Tina a few times—that is, making a right pillock of himself—and had found that silence was the best option.

"Charmer," DG whispered.

"Hi there," the tall redhead said. "I'm Lisa." She spoke directly to Will. Her voice was slightly husky.

Lisa was the tallest of the four, a full head above Tracy. Her red hair was aflame in the hot sunshine, even though it was tied up in a bun. She was slim and had long, slender arms and legs and pale-white skin. She reminded Max of Wilma Flintstone.

All Will could manage in response was to open and close his mouth, twice—like a goldfish—and with as much sound.

The two remaining women were stunning. They were standing together, shoulder to shoulder, and they were exactly the same height and looked the same weight. They both had long, wavy blond hair and dark-hazelnut eyes, wore the same makeup, had on the same style of bikini, and had matching jewelry. If no two people could be carbon copies, then these two women disproved the rule.

"Max, there are two of them, right?" whispered DG.

The twin on the left spoke. "Hello," she said with a warm smile of pure-white teeth. "It's great to be on your beautiful yacht. My name is Kylie." She turned toward the other blonde. "And this is my sist—"

"Don't tell me," Max said, stepping forward to shake her sister's hand. "Then you must be Dannii."

"That's right," the woman said in surprise. "Have we met you before, Max? How did you know my name?"

"Just a lucky guess," Max said. "Well, ladies, before you arrived, we were just about to have an afternoon drink. Care to join us?"

"Max," Will whispered anxiously into his ear as the women were filing through the saloon doors. "Please, we've got to get rid of them. There aren't enough cabins, and Jane will kill me if she finds out. I told her we were going fishing, for Pete's sake."

Max took him to one side. "Will, we're out in the middle of the bloody Mediterranean. I can't even get a mobile phone signal, and there's no way either Jane or your mother-in-law can call around. Jane will be playing bridge or having lunch at Harvey Nichols, so she's well occupied. And don't worry about Lisa, as I'm sure DG will take her off your hands."

Will looked shocked. "Tell DG to keep his fucking hands off her," he said and strode quickly to catch up with the women.

Jesus, Will's managed to fall head over heels in love, and he's actually not even spoken to her yet.

It was DG's turn to pull Max to one side.

"Maxi," he whispered, knocking him playfully on the shoulder. "It's my all-time dream fantasy: blond twins. That was funny, by the way, the Kylie and Dannii Minogue thing. Gorgeous sisters. What was the name of that Kylie song?"

"Not that I'm her biggest fan, DG, but she's done a few. Although I think the one that sums up your current situation is 'I Should Be So Lucky.'"

"Totally," DG said, grinning. "I should be so very fucking lucky."

Kylie and Dannii were visible from outside the saloon, for they were standing at the cocktail bar and waiting for Stan to make drinks.

"Awesome, aren't they?" DG said. "I used to daydream about spending a weekend with Kylie and Dannii. Never thought I'd get the chance, though. Although if I do, there's a mathematical problem, as it leaves one of us with only a book for bedtime."

"Don't worry yourself, DG," Max said. "If fate has brought Kylie and Dannii to you, then who am I to get in the way, even if they are two different pairs of sisters? I can always borrow *Bravo Two Zero* from Stanley."

"Very unselfish of you," DG said, and then he laughed at Will, who was hovering about next to Lisa but still not speaking. "It's just what he did at the school discos."

"Most of us were like that," Max said, remembering strutting his stuff around many girls without actually having the nerve to talk to them. Not that you could hear a word anybody said because the music was so loud. But that hadn't stopped DG. He just waltzed onto the floor, and girls came over to him, as if he had his own personal gravity pulling them in—which, of course, he did.

"I'll go on watch," Max said. "Women are too complicated."

"Don't be soft," DG said. "You need to research the market just as much as me. And you can; I've seen you in action. Granted, I've a different approach—more hands on, so to speak—but I find it very enjoyable. It's therapeutic, even. And it's certainly less stressful than the tortuous process you go through, with all due respect, Maxi."

Max wasn't offended. "Hmm, but it's only less stressful as long as her husband doesn't come home early."

"True, but that keeps me alert and fit," DG said, patting his flat stomach and jogging on the spot comically. "Anyway, my point is that I have *my* way of market testing—for *the one*, as you'd put it—and you obviously have *another*."

"Which is what?" Max asked.

"Oh, nothing. You know."

"Come on, spit it out. You may as well."

DG clearly wanted to get something off his chest. "Well, your way sucks. You've been getting all serious about *the one* again lately, and all it does is piss you off. I know I'm not exactly the good practice guide of *How to Find Your Soul Mate*, but—"

"You can say that again," Max said. "What is it that Jane calls you?"

DG smiled. "That would be 'a shallow excuse for a man and a waste of human tissue.'" He looked proud.

"There you go," Max said. "Not a ringing endorsement of your approach, and it's from a member of the opposite sex."

"Jane is a right piece of work, though, Max. You can't go by her opinions. And poor Will. All I'm saying is enjoy yourself, and leave it to the gods."

"Eh?"

"The gods. Fate. Leave it to fate. Who knows what fate has lined up for you? And you can't predict it, which is good; otherwise, life would be boring. Just think—you could be in Eastern Spice with Jennifer Smith, and her *bhuna* is off. She feels unwell and needs to go home. The owner's daughter—'the one'—feels responsible and drives you both home. After Jenny and her stomach cramps exit, the violins start to play, and love blossoms. Happy ever after with boundless love and free curries for life. Bliss."

"You've been smoking that funny weed again."

"Touch obscure, perhaps. For a start, the Eastern's bhuna is never off. You're my best friend, Max, and I know you could be me if you wanted to, but you don't, and that's cool. But please consider that just maybe this is the week to be a shallow excuse for a man and a waste of human tissue and live it up. I mean, come on, buddy, we're just about to party on a luxury yacht with the Pussycat Dolls. And just how much more cool can life get? So I intend to remember this time forever, and I do not want part of that memory to be that all you did was to go on watch. There, I said it."

"Blimey," Max said. He was more surprised than hurt. "Where did that lot come from?"

DG was staring through the saloon and at the portrait above the bar.

"If *she* was real, Maxi, then I'd say you'd found her."

Max looked, too. And the beautiful woman's emerald eyes stared back as sunlight fell over the canvas. He felt the tingling sensation in his stomach again, and his heart missed a beat.

He knew that she was *real*. The portrait could have been painted years before, he supposed. *She could be eighty.* But he knew she wasn't. More likely, she was married or working in New York as a journalist. Perhaps she was an investigative journalist at the *Daily Planet*, with Superman already on her arm.

He felt a playful slap.

"Back to reality Maxi," DG said, and he ushered Max toward the saloon. "Let's go and talk to the ladies. Sit yourself down, dreamer boy, and I'll fix us some drinks."

After a couple of hours and more than a few get-to-know-you drinks, an unsteady Captain Will managed to steer the *Conchita* into a small bay and shut down the engines. It was beautifully calm. A few minutes later, as they were drifting aimlessly toward the shore, Captain Will clambered drunkenly back to the helm and dropped anchor.

● ● ●

Fourteen empty bottles of champagne ringed the hot tub, in which four men and four women were sitting. It had been raucous for an hour—giggling, laughter, and jokes—but now there was a moment of quiet. The solar system's star, a perfect disk of orange, was majestically slipping into the darkening waters of the Mediterranean. It was an awe-inspiring sight.

"Right, it's gone. Stick some more music on, somebody," DG said.

Tracy stood. "My turn to be disc jockey. I love music."

It transpired that Tracy was also an expert in hot tubs and Jacuzzis. Her father sold bathroom fittings, and she'd instantly recognized the make and model. An Evolution 10 could seat eight and was self-sanitizing. It had a high-power pump system, eighty-seven hydrotherapy jets, illuminated jet fountains, and air diverters. "It's the dog's bollocks," said Tracy.

Stan had monopolized the music selection, and his musical taste was a touch limited—pretty much only AC/DC. He'd loved the Australian band ever since finding out that the US infantry went into battle with "Highway to Hell" pumping out of huge speakers mounted on the backs of Humvees. Apparently, it helped overcome a man's fear of dying and brought on the battle rage. In Stan's opinion, the rock song was fantastic but superfluous. Americans didn't need extra motivation. Whether it was a well-defended fortress surrounded by thick, high concrete walls or a derelict, rickety wooden hut in the middle of an open field, the US military's strategy was always the same. Blast it to kingdom come. Not a bullet, missile, bomb, grenade, or firecracker was to be spared. Nothing was to be left in the tank, literally, other than its crew. The Yanks took absolutely no chances.

"Highway to Hell" three times in a row was more than enough for Tracy. She declared it "old man's music," turned it off, and played Calvin Stewart, Maroon 5, and a special song for Stan by Seasick Steve.

He was pleased until "You Can't Teach an Old Dog New Tricks" croaked out into the balmy night. Tracy thought it was hilarious until Stan retaliated with Queen's "Fat Bottomed Girls."

"Definitely touched a raw nerve there," DG said.

The escalation jumped up another notch when Tracy grabbed *First Blood* and feigned to throw it overboard.

Stan panicked. "Give that back now," he barked.

The first Rambo flick was Stan's favorite film, and it was the DVD that Tina had bought him when he passed SAS selection. Stan ejected himself from the hot tub like a submarine-launched Trident missile in hot pursuit of what turned out to be a very agile young woman.

Tracy flitted this way and that, moving lightly from one foot to the other. She was the veritable moving target. Stan was mesmerized, not knowing whether to focus on his favorite DVD or Tracy's enormous breasts, which were swaying in the opposite direction to where she moved.

"You couldn't catch a cold, Stan," DG shouted from the hot tub as Tracy evaded him again.

"Naff off."

Stan lunged at his quarry. It was a desperate and unsuccessful move. Not only did he miss, but he also crashed through the ring of empty champagne bottles. Moët & Chandon labels rolled over and over as they dispersed to all four corners of the deck.

Stan needed a new tactic. He stretched his arms out wide in a large arc and crept slowly forward, as if trying to gather up long grass. He was resisting the urge to pounce. *Wait*, he was thinking. *Have patience; wait for the right moment to strike. You are the tiger, and she is the helpless wildebeest. Wait some more. Wait.* He was six feet away and began to move his arms up and down like a defensive basketball player, or possibly a man standing in the fast lane of the M1 and desperately trying to stop traffic.

Two feet away, Stan filled with elation. "Got you now," he shouted in triumph.

Tracy was cornered against the wheelhouse station.

Now.

Strike.

Stan pounced.

Somehow, he missed. He grabbed in vain at the warm, balmy air with his strong hands, which now filled the space where Tracy had been standing only a third of a second before.

Clang.

Stan's shiny onrushing head collided with one of the six pillars holding up the flybridge's fiberglass roof—an unintentional ferocious head butt.

The tubular stainless-steel pillar caved in at one side.

Stan fell back, dazed, as a small cut on his forehead began to bleed, and a raised bump began to show. However, the injury was nothing compared with the grievous mauling his pride had just suffered. Not that he would ever show it, but he was mightily embarrassed. He stood upright and steadied himself, playfully slapping the offending pillar.

Max, DG, and Will weren't buying it.

"I've seen faster slugs," DG shouted through tears of laughter.

"Don't use your head anymore," Will said.

"How many of us do you see, Stan? Six, twelve, or eighteen?"

"Fuck off," Stan said, holding the damaged pillar for support.

Tracy had clambered up onto the flybridge roof using the captain's chair as a makeshift staircase. She'd avoided the human tank and its bizarre, flailing arms by ducking down and then neatly sidestepping from a standing start. It hadn't been an easy maneuver, but she'd pulled it off with the aplomb of an international rugby player.

Stan was not happy. Early on in the ill-fated chase, he'd applied little effort. Tracy was a girl, after all, even though she was great fun. But she had nicked *First Blood*, and now she was making him look like a right pillock in front of his mates. And he was SAS. It couldn't be allowed to continue.

The hot-tub crowd had thought that seeing Sergeant Longbottom being given the runaround was great sport, and they cheered every time Tracy evaded capture, which only served to increase Stan's frustration.

"Lovely move, Tracy," DG had said as Tracy escaped onto the roof. "It's just like an episode of *Tom and Jerry*. Actually, more like Jerry and that big, fat, gray dog, the one with the spiky collar. What was he called?"

"That would be Spike," Max said.

"Oh yeah," DG said. "Stan's definitely more of a Spike than a Tom."

Stan had gone from frustrated to exasperated. Normally, as in a battle, he'd have just shot her. War was simple: raise, aim, and fire. And that would be the end of the problem. No more looking like a worn-out pit pony. He was doing his best to cover his stressing emotions, but he was never going to make it in the movies.

"This is pretty good fun," he said, gasping for air and still holding on to the bent pillar.

Tracy was peering over the roof's edge at him.

"Times up now, missy," Stan said.

He gulped down a chest full of air and ran at the captain's chair. One step, two steps, a push from his immensely strong arms, and he was sliding across the shiny white roofing to where Tracy had been.

Impressive.

But Tracy had climbed onto the radar housing at the back of the roof and was now well out of reach again. She waited there a moment as Stan resigned himself to a humiliating defeat, and then jumped over to other side of the roof and climbed down the way she'd first come up. She dropped the last couple of feet to the decking and slipped, twisting her ankle. *It's a fake injury, for sure,* thought Max. *She'd get a game for Liverpool any day. Definite yellow card, at the very least.*

Stan came chugging around the other side of the flybridge like Thomas the Tank Engine and pinned her down. "Stamina is the most important weapon in a soldier's armory," he said, gasping for air and sweating profusely.

"You remind me of Sylvester Stallone," Max said. "Not Rambo, though. More like Rocky Balboa in the first movie, where his trainer has him trying to catch that chicken. You're unfit, Stanley. I thought you ran up and down the Brecon Beacons all week."

"Fuck off." Stan was wheezing. He was still pinning Tracy to the deck but hadn't managed to retrieve his DVD.

Tracy, for her part, just lay still, waiting patiently for Stan to get to his feet. He finally did so while keeping a tight hold on her hand.

"She's like Sonic the bleeding Hedgehog," he said, not without an element of pride.

Another hour and another eight bottles of champagne later, things moved on in the hot tub.

Stan was now wearing Tracy's bikini top, and she was sitting happily on his knee without the need for handcuffs. Her boobs, much to Stan's fascination, were covered in foam and floating freely on the water's bubbling surface.

Sitting primly next to Stan and Tracy were Lisa and Will. They were obviously holding hands under the water but had refrained from any other overt touching—or, in Will's case, even any direct acknowledgment that Lisa was actually there. He was staring straight ahead, clearly in two minds. One refused to accept that a beautiful redhead was caressing his fingers, and the other was straining his peripheral vision to assure himself that Lisa wasn't looking at DG.

In actual fact, Lisa's big brown eyes had never left Will's face ever since they'd sat down together in the tub. Even during the madcap Stan-and-Tracy show, her gaze hadn't faltered.

DG was sitting between Kylie and Dannii, his arms hanging languidly over their shoulders. He'd impressed the twins earlier by simultaneously unclipping their bikini tops. The fingertips of his right hand were gently stroking the top of Kylie's right breast, while those of his left hand were stroking the nipple on Dannii's left. He was also smoking a large Montecristo cigar. Once in a while, Kylie removed it from his mouth, and DG would emit a perfectly formed smoke ring.

"There goes another message of thanks to the gods," he said. "That one said, 'Don't wake me up.'"

Max was smoking a Montecristo, too, and blowing his own smoke rings.

"What's the message?" DG asked.

"It's a request for a bigger bikini top for Stanley," Max said.

Will came to life. "Give us one of your jokes, DG, a really good one, one that the girls will like, too."

DG closed his eyes. He was in rapture. The beautiful sisters were kissing his throat and caressing his chest, their hands leaving little swirling patterns across his torso.

Kylie took his cigar.

"All my jokes are *really* good, Will," DG said. "But for this one, I'll need some help. I can never remember any decent French names. Max?"

"Sure," Max said. "You sure about this one? It may spoil your fun later."

"Can't resist it, mate," said DG, sitting up straight. "Plus, I find the international element spurs 'em on a treat."

DG winked at Kylie, who Max felt required absolutely no additional encouragement whatsoever. "Right, then, shipmates," he said.

Tracy, Kylie, and Dannii were listening intently. Lisa still had her eyes locked on Will.

"Picture this: a beautiful summer's day on the outskirts of a small village in Provence. And—"

"Where's that?" Dannii asked.

"France, babe," DG said, thrown off track. "Right, I'll start again. It's a beautiful summer's day on the outskirts of a small village in France, and a young—"

"What's an outskirt?" asked Kylie.

"You joking?"

"No. Sorry."

"Well, it's not an overgarment, babe," DG said, looking mildly irritated. "Third time lucky, then. It's a beautiful summer's day near a small village in France, and a young man called—"

"Jacques," said Max.

"*Oui*," DG said in his best French accent, which wasn't half bad. He waited a moment in case further clarification or simplification was required. None was needed. He continued.

"A young man called Jacques is strolling down the lane. He's enjoying the sun's warmth and the clean country air when *suddenly*, he hears some unusual noises from behind a hedgerow.

"He investigates. And peeping through a *petit* gap in the bushes, he spies a couple making love.

"'Ah,' says Jacques. 'Love eez a beautiful thing. Eet iz magical. Zee birds, zee beees, zee flowerz-z-z-z. It eeez l'amour-r-r-r.'"

DG was loving it. Max and Stan were rolling their eyes, and Will was staring straight forward. The girls were lapping it up.

DG continued. "But then, Jacques gasps. 'Oh *non, non*,' he says. 'Surely, it cannot be.' He jumps back into the lane in shock and bumps into—"

"That would be Jean-Claude," said Max.

"*Oui*. Jean-Claude. 'Jean-Claude,' says Jacques, in fright. 'Up there in the field, behind the hedgerow, a couple is making love!'

"Jean-Claude has concern on his face for a moment but then smiles.

"'Ah-h,' he says. 'That eez a beautiful thing. Zee scent of *l'amour* is all around us, my friend. Eet is a magical thing, yes?'

"'*Non*, Jean-Claude, eet isn't. *Vous ne compris pas. Ecoutez*,' says Jacques. 'The woman in the field. She is *dead!*'"

"No!" Kylie, Dannii, Tracy, and Lisa gasped in unison.

DG moved into top gear. "'*Zut alors!*' cries Jean-Claude, just as—"

"Pierre," Max said, stifling a yawn.

"Oui, just as Pierre comes around the corner. 'Pierre, Pierre,' shout Jacques and Jean-Claude together. '*Ici! Vite! Vite!*'

"Pierre runs up to his panicking friends.

"'Up there in the field,' say Jacques and Jean-Claude in unison. 'A couple is making love.'

"Pierre breaks into a warm smile.

"'Zee birds,' he says. 'Zee bees, zee floweerz-z-z. *Amour* eez the reason we live.'

"'*Mais non, non*,' screams Jacques. '*Ecoutez*, Pierre. The woman, in the field, she is *dead!*'

"'*Sacre bleu*,' exclaims Pierre, just as—"

"Dr. Bernard," Max said. "And for God's sake, get on with it."

Stan was pretending to hang himself with Tracy's bikini top.

DG did his best to ignore them both. "Had another three characters to go but will wrap it up."

"Thank the stars," Stan said.

"Just as Dr. Bernard strolls up the lane. Jacques, Jean-Claude, and Pierre run up to him.

"'Dr. Bernard, Dr. Bernard,' they cry. 'Thank the Virgin Mary that you are here, Doctor.' They blurt out the story. 'In the field, Dr. Bernard. Behind the bushes, Dr. Bernard. A man and a woman, Dr. Bernard, they make *l'amour*, Dr. Bernard.'

"The doctor's face lights up instantly." DG was now sporting an enormous smile of his own. '*Ah, mes amis*,' says Dr. Bernard. '*L'amour* eez in the air, is eet not? It eez beautiful. It eeez a magical thing. Zee birds, zee bees, zee flowerz.'

"'*Mais non*, Doctor!' cry Jacques, Jean-Claude, and Pierre. 'Doctor, the woman in the field, *elle est mort*!'

"'*Mon dieu*,' cries Dr. Bernard. '*Attendez-vous ici*. I will go and look.'"

DG paused for effect and took the cigar back from Kylie. The four women were still gripped, hanging on his every word.

"Dr. Bernard sprints up the lane and disappears into the hedgerow," DG whispered, building the tension. "And one minute later, the doctor reappears and jogs back the short distance to where his anxious countrymen are standing.

"The doctor is smiling. 'My friends,' says Dr. Bernard, 'relax. There is nothing to worry about. The woman in the field, the woman that the man is making love to, she is not dead. *Non*, my friends she is...*English!*'"

All four women jumped at DG and plunged him to the bottom of the Jacuzzi. He and his golden smile slowly resurfaced a few moments later, the drenched Montecristo still trapped between his perfect teeth.

The obligatory foam fight then ensued, men versus women, which ended when Will had his spectacles knocked off. Hostilities had to be suspended while he searched for them. By the time they were located the mood had calmed.

Lisa was whispering into Will's ear.

Max unfortunately overheard, as he was sitting next to them.

"I'm going to show you exactly what English girls can do, Mr. Accountant Man," she said.

Will continued to stare straight forward, but his eyes were bulging. Obviously, Lisa wasn't holding his hand anymore.

CHAPTER 10

The helicopter pilot looked over his shoulder at the woman seated behind him. She hadn't said a single word since boarding. For two hours, she'd been staring blankly out of the window into the dark night.

"ETA is another two hours," the pilot said in a heavy Russian accent.

The woman acknowledged him with a slight dip of her head but continued to stare out into the darkness.

"As we briefed you before takeoff, Miss Rodriguez, you'll have to winch down with Yuri. It can be a difficult procedure at sea, but the wind is light tonight, so there will be no problems. Yuri and I have done this hundreds of times before. If you are hungry, there are sandwiches and drinks in the fridge behind you."

The woman dipped her head again but made no move to get up. The pilot returned to his controls.

"A cold fish, that one, Vladimir," his copilot whispered over the intercom.

"Da."

"But a very pretty fish," Yuri whispered again, grinning. "It'll be good to get up close and personal on the winch."

Vladimir punched him heavily on the arm.

Yuri jerked angrily but then restrained himself. "What?"

"Yuri, this isn't a joke," Vladimir said, glancing over his shoulder again to see if the woman had overheard. She hadn't moved. "Do you want our next trip to be to the bottom of the sea chained to a block of concrete?"

"I'm sorry, Vlad. You are right."

• • •

Maria Concepcion Victoria Rodriguez had overheard what Yuri had said, but it didn't bother her. She'd heard it all before many times. Four decades of equal-opportunities legislation for women had failed to stop man talk, as her mama used to call it, so she wasn't holding her breath with respect to these two.

Maria had something much more pressing on her mind.

She was twenty-five years old and from a city in Colombia called Medellin. She'd graduated from Stanford University with a degree in international law and now worked in her father's legal firm. She was already a lawyer, and she was going to be a good one. Amnesty International took up most of her free time.

Everything in Maria's life had always gone according to plan—school, family, friends, university, holidays, finding a job she loved. Her life had been a twenty-five-year-long fairy tale. But that had ended in the split second it took for a speeding truck to smash into her papa's car and crush him to pulp.

Maria's beloved papa was dead. And the safety cocoon he'd provided for her was gone. Her fairy tale had turned into a living nightmare.

She closed her eyes and pressed her forehead hard against the small round window. The glass was cold and covered in condensation, but she didn't notice. She was thinking yet again of the night two months ago when, unbelievably, things had gotten even worse.

That day had started so well. Maria had been feeling happy, a feeling she never thought to experience again. It had been four months since her papa's death. For a time, she'd begun to believe that her remaining years would be filled with only sadness and pain. But on that day, Carlo had asked her to marry him, and she had accepted.

He took her on the cable car up to the top of Mount Monserrate. Maria had been there numerous times before but never tired of the experience, as she'd told Carlo. The views from the top of the mountain overlooking Bogotá were breathtaking and never disappointed.

Carlo had seemed nervous and jumpy. She'd never seen him like that before; usually he was so confident. *Probably a work thing*, she'd thought.

He worked so many hours. They found a quiet place to sit away from the crowds and watched the sun set behind the mountains. A million city lights twinkled on the valley floor as darkness and rain came. They quickly nipped into the old church to await the next cable car.

The rain showed no signs of stopping.

Maria was wondering what they should do and turned around to ask what Carlo thought. To her surprise, she found him kneeling down behind her. He was holding up a small box.

Inside, resting on a cream leather cushion, was an engagement ring.

It was beautiful.

She held her breath.

The center stone was a sapphire. Even in the dim light it shone brightly out from inside the circle of diamonds surrounding it.

Maria knew what she wanted.

She loved Carlo. She always had, from the moment he'd come to her after her papa's death. He'd been a tower of strength. He'd been a rock for both Mama and her after Papa's accident. There was nothing to decide. She wanted to be his wife more than anything.

"Yes, yes, yes," she said, tears of joy flooding from her eyes.

Carlo jumped up in laughter, and they hugged and kissed and walked slowly through the pouring, warm rain back to the cable-car station.

Maria was eager to share the joyous news with Mama. Mama needed to share in her happiness.

Mama wept.

At first, Maria took her mother's tears for tears of joy, like her own from earlier that day, but it soon became clear that the droplets rolling over Mama's cheeks represented entirely different emotions. Despair, desperation, and fear were but three. Maria was confused and kept asking what was wrong, but Mama was inconsolable at the *happy* news, and then she began to shake and mumble incoherently. Maria helped her upstairs to lie down.

In the early hours, Mama came into her room and sat on the end of her bed. She was upright, in control, and not crying anymore.

Maria sat up. "Mama, what is it?" she asked anxiously.

"Maria, you must listen to me."

"But, Mama—"

"*Listen*, Maria, before my strength fails me."

Maria fell silent.

"I promised your papa never to tell you this, but now I must. He could never have foreseen this."

Mama took a deep breath and composed herself.

"Your papa was scared for our safety, you see, and for the safety of whomever I told. But Maria, he couldn't have known. I'm not frightened for myself, you understand. My life is over, but I am frightened for you."

"Mama, you're scaring me."

"Please, my darling, I have to finish," Mama said, raising her hand. "I've thought of nothing else but whether to tell you since Papa died. Tonight, I realized that I must tell you, however hard it is for me and for you. If I were you, then I would want to know."

Maria was still confused about Mama's reaction to her engagement. It was so unexpected, and this talk only added to her worry. She'd started to believe it was the grief over Papa's death, but now she wasn't so sure.

Mama continued. "The police told us that Papa's death was an accident, but it *wasn't*, Maria. I know it. Up until he was killed, Papa was working with the government on a secret plan to bring down the cartels, a plan that would bring the leaders of the Medellin drug cartel to justice."

"Papa died in an accident, Mama—a horrible accident but an accident. The police report is clear. Papa ran a red light, and the truck had no chance to stop. And, Mama, you know that the Medellín Cartel leaders were either jailed or killed over twenty years ago. Escobar's dead body was shown all over the TV news."

"*Listen* to me, Maria. The Medellín Cartel operated as many independent cells. It was always known that a number of these cells had remained undetected, and over the years some have grown and become separate cartels in their own right. The government prosecutors and Papa believed that the cartels were once again under one man's leadership, and they were closing in."

Maria listened. She'd heard stories of successors to Pablo Escobar since she was a child.

"Your papa was a very brave man. He knew full well that he would be killed if the cartels found out about what he was doing. He went to great lengths to keep his involvement secret, to protect himself and, of course, us. The government offered him twenty-four-hour police protection, but Papa refused. 'Anonymity and secrecy are our safest cover,' he said.

"A week before he died, Papa told me that the government's case had achieved a major breakthrough. A cartel lieutenant had fallen from grace and turned informant, exchanging immunity from prosecution for information. Papa thought they'd got them at last, but a corrupt lawyer was also working on the case, and the bastard passed over all of the intelligence to the cartels, including the names of those building the evidence. It was what your papa was always afraid of."

Dread's cold hands were beginning to squeeze Maria's throat. She knew that Mama was speaking the truth. She wanted to tell her to stop talking, not to say anything else, to stop now, before—

Mama continued. "The night before Papa died, he told me a secret that he'd never mentioned to anybody else, but one he could substantiate. He said that he was going to give me the evidence, just in case. He never said in case of what, but I knew what he meant. I was to deliver it anonymously to the office of the attorney general. Of course, Papa never got the chance to pass the evidence over to me.

"That night, Papa was more serious than I had ever seen him before. He even made me swear on the Bible in front of him.

"'Swear, Katarina,' he said. 'Swear you'll never tell a soul, not even Conchita.'"

Maria was rigid with fear. Hearing her father's pet name for her again made her feel physically sick. All of the pain of his death came back. She wanted to ease Mama's burden, but more than anything else in the world, she didn't want any more pain.

Mama had been a shadow of her former herself since the car crash. Some days, she'd not even risen from bed. She'd hidden away from family, friends, and work colleagues and even resisted telephone calls. Letters of condolence were still unopened on her dressing table, and the house curtains usually remained drawn until Maria returned from work.

Mama's health had worried Maria the most. Her mother's weight had plummeted. She looked pale and frail and gaunt. Initially, Maria had thought it was the natural process of grieving, but as the days extended into weeks and then months, she insisted that Dr. Tevez, the family doctor, visit twice a week. Mama's demeanor hadn't improved much, but at least Dr. Tevez had gotten her eating again, and the physical deterioration had stopped.

The Mama now sitting on the end of her bed was not frail. The old and tenacious Katarina Rodriguez had returned in full force. She was clearly steeled by her objective.

Maria was beginning to panic. She didn't want to know. Whatever it was, she couldn't face it.

"Mama, you shouldn't tell me. Papa couldn't have been clearer, could he? He obviously felt incredibly strongly that you alone should know his secret and *keep* it. So *please*, Mama, don't break your oath to him. *Please* don't."

"Papa is *dead*, Maria," Mama said, spitting the words through her teeth. "Taken from us by devils. *I* must now decide the best course of action to take. And it is *I* who must decide whether to stand by your papa's legacy or hide away behind fear. I will not give in to evil, and *I* have hidden away for too long, Maria. *I* have dishonored your papa's memory."

"No, Mama."

"I've been a fool, Maria, a weak, useless fool. I pretended that the reason for keeping silent was to secure our protection, but that way means that evil will prevail. You are your papa's and my jewel, my child, the most precious thing in our lives, and we both wanted you to live a beautiful life. It's all we ever wanted. But now I realize that merely *living* is not enough, my child, not enough for you, especially if it means living a lie."

"Mama, don't tell me," Maria screamed. She'd no idea what Mama was going to say, but she knew full well that she didn't want to hear it.

Mama moved along the bed and grabbed Maria's wrists. "Maria, your papa discovered evidence, corroborated by a defector before he, too, was killed, that proved all of the cartels were once again under one leadership. I'm so sorry, Maria; all I can do is say it. Papa told me that the supreme overlord of the Medellín Cartel is Andre Ortega. The Bogota Coffee Company is a front for his cocaine business."

For a moment, Maria was bemused, and then understanding smashed into her brain, followed by utter horror as she realised the possible ramifications. Her chest contracted, and bile poured into her mouth. She wrenched her hands free and spat down the front of her nightdress.

"No-o-o-!" she screamed. "No-o-o. Mama, you are mad. How can you say such things? Papa is…was wrong. That's insane. Carlo has helped us, Mama. He's helped you. If that was all true, then Carlo would know who killed P—"

Katarina Rodriguez shouted over her daughter's protests. "Papa said that Andre had been grooming Carlo to take over the business. He was astonished at how Andre had remained hidden from view and yet maintained control of a multibillion-dollar drug empire that distributes cocaine across half the United States and into parts of Europe."

"It's all lies, just lies," Maria screamed. "It's madness. You're a madwoman."

Katarina Rodriguez tried to sound as forceful as she could. "Papa said the informant had provided firsthand accounts of many killings. The cartel executes people for incompetence or for simply knowing too much. On occasion, whole families are wiped out as examples to others. Secrecy and loyalty are secured by the death penalty."

"Stop, Mama. Stop!"

Maria jumped out of bed and ran for the door. She needed to escape the mad woman's lies, but Mama caught her arm, her nails digging in and drawing blood. Maria fell heavily to the floor and knocked over the bedside table. The lamp fell to the floor and smashed. Maria thrashed, trying to break her mother's grip. She ripped her arm free just as her mother's full body weight came down on top of her. She was pinned to the floor.

"You *will* listen to me," Mama said.

Maria writhed and bucked and looked to one side, refusing to look her mama in the face. "It's lies, Mama, just lies. And you are mad. Carlo is a good man, and I love him." She twisted again in her mother's grasp and nearly unseated her.

Mama slapped her face. "Listen, Maria. You will listen to me."

Maria lay motionless on the floor, stunned by the strike. She looked blankly into her mother's face.

"Maria, do you think this is what I want to say? Do you think I want to say that Papa was murdered and that you, our precious daughter, are about to marry a man who knows his *killer*? Somebody that was perhaps even involved in his murder? What mother would want to say that? But

I *have* to tell you, Maria." Tears flowed down her mother's cheeks and splashed on Maria's face below. "What if, someday, you found out the truth? It could be years into the future, but what would you feel about me then? You'd never forgive me, Maria, and rightly so.

"This is all I've thought about, Maria. Should I tell you what Papa said or ignore it for both our safety? Eventually, I realized this was the wrong question. The right one is, which is the greater crime? Is it Andre Ortega's crime for being a drug lord, or is it mine for knowing that and still giving him my daughter?"

Mama was finished. She wearily stood and staggered out of the room, drained of all energy.

Maria lay frozen on the floor until morning.

Maria and Mama had never again spoken about what had been said that night. And Maria hadn't asked. The accusations hung heavily in the air, but both women were too weak and vulnerable to confront them. Mama had used her remaining strength to disclose what she thought Papa had said, and Maria had used hers to convince herself that either Papa was wrong or Mama was hallucinating in some way.

She'd told Dr. Tevez of Mama's mood swings, and he reassured her that it was the stress of grief. "It can do terrible things to the mind," the doctor had said.

And if Papa did have hard evidence, he could have handed it to Mama, she thought. *Yet he hadn't. And he did have time. So the evidence didn't exist. It was all a figment of Mama's disturbed mind. In addition, nobody else had come forward to accuse Andre.*

Colombia always had been a hotbed of malicious rumor and unfounded accusations. Jealousy about other people's wealth was commonplace, too. At the very worst, this was just more evidence of that. All Andre and Carlo were guilty of was having a successful business.

And she loved Carlo. He'd been patient and caring after Papa's death, and she totally believed in his innocence. She also passionately believed in justice, and Carlo hadn't been found guilty of anything, or even charged. She did consider giving him up for Mama's sake, but to deny that her and Carlo's love was true felt completely and utterly unjust. Therefore, she carried on with her plans to marry him. Initially, Mama tried to understand, but soon became withdrawn again.

In the end, Maria decided that marrying Carlo would be best for Mama, too. When she saw that her daughter was happily married, she would recognize Carlo as a fine son-in-law, and would also realize that Papa's accusations were false.

Consequently, Maria forged ahead with the wedding plans. And the hours needed to organize the happy event filled all her free time, which was good, as it stopped her thinking. With arrangements for the church, the reception, all of the guest accommodations, the flowers, the cars, and so on, not to mention the ever-expanding guest list, she never had more than a moment to spare. But in those infrequent moments, her mama's powerful words kept coming back to haunt her, and she knew they always would. Eventually, the tension grew too much, and one day she asked Carlo straight out when he came over for dinner. She'd just blurted it out.

"Do you and your father run the Medellín Cartel? Is he the supreme overlord?"

Carlo was thrown for a brief moment and then laughed. "Are you joking?"

Maria turned drip white. Her words had come out in a fit of anger fueled by the constant anxiety she felt. Carlo could see that she wasn't joking.

They were in Papa's small library, standing by the window, which looked out on a manicured lawn surrounded by large oak trees. The room was quiet and still, as if it understood that its master had passed on.

Nothing had been moved in the room. The impressive collection of leather-bound books were still in their place, Papa's papers were still neatly stacked on his old leather-inlaid desk, and the desk calendar still displayed January 28, the day he had died.

"The supreme overlord," Carlo said quietly. "Do you really think my father could be in such a position? A cartel leader? The cocaine world is a dangerous place, Maria, and that's why we've stayed in coffee. The cartels have affected us. We've had employees go missing and never return, and we have to pay 'protection,' but so do all Colombian businesses. It's the price of doing business in our country. It's wrong, but you either pay or go out of business. It's hard to produce coffee if your factories keep being burned down. And government officials can't stop it; half the time, they're on the cartel payrolls, too. But you know this, Maria. It's

commonplace, common knowledge. 'The supreme overlord,' my father…
It sounds like the title for some sort of intergalactic space ruler. 'Emperor
Zoltan, supreme overlord of the Seven Systems.'"

Carlo smiled. He took hold of Maria's hands and led her over to a
brown, leather sofa. They sat there for a moment in silence.

Maria was still as white as a sheet.

Carlo spoke slowly, looking straight into her eyes, never blinking.
"Maria, I love you. I work for my father and the Bogota Coffee Company.
You know this. I have never had any involvement in the drug trade, and
I never will. I fully understand your mama's grief and your grief, too."
He squeezed her hands. "I want to be a part of your family, Maria, not
destroy it." Tears filled his eyes. "How could you think such a terrible
thing of me?"

Maria looked down in shame.

"Maria, I didn't know your papa, but his death has broken my heart,
too, because it's given you such pain."

Maria placed the palm of her hand on his warm cheek. "Please forgive
me, Carlo." She wrapped her arms around him. She was crying softly. "I
don't believe what I said, I truly don't. It's just that Papa's death—"

Carlo kissed her on the forehead and wiped away her tears. "It's all
right, Maria. I do understand. It's been horrific for you both, but please
remember that I will always be here for you." Carlo paused. "Do…do you
still want to marry me?"

"Of course," said Maria, and she kissed him passionately.

● ● ●

A week later, Carlo had flown to Madrid on business. Maria had gone
back to the wedding preparations. She felt reassured. Her confidence was
returning. She was doing the right thing. She was sure. Mama was still
depressed and housebound, but she would come around by the time of
the ceremony. Maria was sure of that, too.

That was before she received the anonymous telephone call.

The man had called her at the office. He sounded extremely nervous.
He said that Vincente Rodriguez, her father, had helped him and his family when no one else would. Papa had always represented people who

couldn't afford to pay, so Maria wasn't surprised by the man's message of gratitude.

The caller continued. "I read in the newspaper that Vincente Rodriguez's daughter is to be married to Carlo Ortega, Andre Ortega's son. The Ortegas own the Bogota Coffee Company. You are Mr. Rodriguez's daughter?"

"Yes, I am, but—"

"And it's you who is getting married to Carlo Ortega?"

"Yes, but what—"

The man ignored her questions. "The Ortegas are dangerous men. They are not who they seem to be. Stay away from them."

"What do you mean?" Maria felt instantly sick, but the line was dead. The man had already hung up.

Maria boarded the next flight from Bogotá to Madrid—Carlo usually telephoned her every day but a call was no good to her; she needed to see Carlo's eyes again as he denied the accusation, and if she rang then he may talk her out of traveling too. There was no alternative—she must speak to him face to face—and she couldn't wait.

On arrival in Madrid sixteen hours later, she called Carlo's cell phone from outside the airport terminal—to arrange to meet him—but there was no reply. She tried again, and again—waited an hour and called again— still no reply—and then she called Carlo's helicopter pilot.

"We can't get through to him either," Vladimir said. "He must be at sea, away from a signal. We can take you?"

• • •

As Maria sat in the helicopter, she brought her cold hand up to her cheek, again feeling her mama's slap. It was the first and only time one of her parents had ever hit her.

"Miss Rodriguez," Vladimir said from the cockpit, "we'll be there in an hour."

CHAPTER 11

Max was alone on the flybridge. The other partygoers had finally turned in for what was left of the night.

DG, Kylie, and Dannii had departed first.

"There's two of them," DG had whispered. "So I'll need more time."

As cringey as ever, Max thought. *Not that cringey affected DG's pulling power.*

Stan and Tracy had been the next to leave. Apparently, Tracy was keen to watch *First Blood*. It was quite possibly the worst excuse Max had ever heard. "Lamentable," he'd said to Stan in passing.

That had left three in the hot tub.

Will and Lisa had just waited.

Half an hour went by in total silence.

It was excruciating.

Max pictured himself in the hot water as a slowly crinkling and swelling gooseberry.

Fortunately, Lisa's patience finally ran out. "Men," she said with a loud sigh, and then pulled Will from the tub. Will gave the impression of a condemned man being hauled off to the gallows. His face was screaming, "Help me, save me, save me, I'm innocent," but his legs aided his removal.

Max watched them disappear around the bridge superstructure on their way below decks. And then there was one. *And the little one said—*

"Ah, shut it," he said to himself.

The laughing, screaming, and perpetual talking and giggling through-out the night had tired out his ears. The quiet was welcome. He showered on deck and then toweled himself dry and redressed. The early morning air was somewhat cool, but a fresh *Conchita* crew polo shirt and some white trousers took the slight chill off.

He took a mini-stroll around the flybridge. The view out to sea was deep and dark—peaceful. He settled himself lazily in the captain's chair and relaxed, one bare foot resting on top of the dashboard, the other dangling loose.

He lit another cigar. The Montecristo tasted divine.

Max didn't smoke much—not at all, if he counted cigarettes and excluded the odd, classic Havana cigar. On average, he smoked two Montes a year as birthday and New Year's Eve treats, but this was his second of the evening. And it was good, really good. It was mellow and smooth and all the better without foam and soapsuds.

He inhaled deeply.

Cuba came to mind.

He envisioned hillsides of green tobacco plants ripening in the hot sun, and he could see Carmen-like local girls sitting around old ware-houses rolling the dried leaves on their olive-skinned thighs. It was prob-ably the world's greatest marketing strategy.

He peered out to sea again. The Mediterranean was black. Dawn was close, but there was no inkling of the sunrise just yet.

It was a serene moment.

Bliss.

It was a moment to cherish, but Max couldn't enjoy it. Something Dannii had said was really bothering him. It was after Stan had told a naff blond joke.

Stan had been mightily drunk, of course. He'd never have dared a blond joke at home; Tina would have skinned him alive. And he couldn't tell a joke at the best of times. But when he was drunk, unfortunately, he thought he could.

He couldn't.

"A blonde and a brunette jump off a building. Which one hits the floor first?" he'd said in one long slur.

Nobody bothered to answer.

"The brunette, of course," he'd said and hiccupped. "The blonde had to stop for directions."

Only Stan and Dannii laughed.

She'd then leaned over to Max. "People look at me and the girls and think 'dim,' Max," she'd whispered. "We know that, but I don't get it. Lisa has a chemistry degree, Kylie is studying law by correspondence course, Tracy essentially runs her dad's business as well as doing modeling work, and I'm between sales jobs—and all four of us are in a hot tub and drinking champagne on this beautiful yacht and enjoying life while they're stuck in boring offices doing spreadsheets. If people are so smart, then how come they can't see that? It's like they don't actually realize that *this is it*. That *this* time, right *now*, is *all* there actually is."

Max had felt embarrassed and humble. He still did.

Dannii was right, he thought. People—*him*, if he were to be specific— just didn't want to admit that truth, or their narrow-minded preconceptions. "Truth is true wisdom," his granddad had always said. So what was wisdom if it wasn't living life to the fullest? Not being restricted or controlled by other people's rules and beliefs took real courage and conviction, and clearly Dannii had both attributes in buckets.

Dannii was wise.

Max could hear his mum disagreeing. "Absolute rubbish," she'd say. "Stop daydreaming and get back to work. And when you get home, go through that list we made. I bet it's only half done. Lists are important, Max. You can enjoy yourself when you've ticked everything off and not before. I've never managed to finish my list, as I've told you before. But then again, I'm only seventy-two."

Mum lived her life through lists. They brought her order and discipline, and she'd insisted that Max make his own lists ever since he was a teen- ager—and Mum had plenty of additional items if he came up short. Do history homework. Polish shoes. Get a haircut. Tidy your room. Find Dad's pen. The current set of family lists were posted on the fridge. A Winston Churchill fridge magnet had secured Max's, while Margaret Thatcher and David Cameron fixed his mum's and dad's.

On the day Max moved into his new flat, Mum had been around to ensure the tradition continued.

"Hello, dear. I'm making a cuppa. I've brought around Winston. He's settling in on your fridge."

Mum hadn't mentioned anything about a list. But when Max had looked, he saw a familiar sheet of lined paper extending from under the great man's overcoat.

He'd run his finger down it.

Change the bedding. And make sure the pillows match.

Mum usually added a "helpful" comment.

Clean the dishes. Properly.

Clean the toilet. Properly. And get a loo brush.

Pay the electric bill.

Change the light bulb in the bedroom: 60 watt, low energy.

Reattach the towel rail.

Switch gas suppliers. South Western has a new, fixed-rate, two-year loyalty deal.

Max had sighed. He'd not even turned on the bloody cooker yet.

The list had continued.

Bleed the radiators. Find the bleeding radiator key.

Max had laughed. Mum would've meant that seriously; she never swore, and she didn't do jokes, not even of the bleeding-radiator-key variety.

At the bottom of the page had been "PTO."

Max had lifted Winston's feet a little and extracted the piece of paper.

Overleaf had been the final entry—his mother's fail-safe item. It was designed to ensure that her checklists—and everybody elses— were never ending. She added it to every list she ever made: Now make another list.

He'd said it aloud and sighed again.

Max's mum contended that everyone should have a checklist. And Max had come to believe that, too. Lists were efficient and helped people to remember things. But after what Dannii had said tonight, he realized an important point. It wasn't having a checklist that mattered but rather what was actually on it.

Dannii's list wouldn't mention reattaching the towel rail, bleeding the radiators, or finding the bleeding radiator key. If Max had to guess, Dannii's list would have only the following three entries:

1. Totally enjoy myself.
2. Do hair and nails.
3. Refer back to number one.

He needed to get himself a new checklist—or, rather, another new checklist. He'd had a go at making one a few weeks earlier, but the only entry he'd come up with was to swim underwater for two lengths of the local pool. That currently constituted his only goal in life, which, in retrospect was a bit limiting and, to say the least, odd.

Travel and working abroad came to mind.

His negative self chipped in.

You need money for that. And if you leave your job now, you'll be broke in a month and six rungs back down the career ladder. Do you really want to be starting all over again at thirty-two?

Dannii has no money. And no job security, either. Or even any idea what she's going to be doing next week. That's exactly what Dannii said she loved about her life: not knowing.

"Every day is exciting," she'd said. "I love waking up in the morning, and I leap out of bed, depending on who else is in it, of course."

She'd laughed merrily at that, as had Max.

He realized that worrying about money was just an excuse. It was his way of avoiding the fear of the unknown. And it was keeping him from excitement and the unexpected, both good and bad. It was keeping him from experience—from life. His current strategy was all about risk management, and it worked really well. Max managed risk, avoided problems, and consequently was bored rigid. Even on this amazing yacht, he was getting bored. *Let's face it. I'm sitting up here on my own and looking out to sea, trying to philosophize while my mates are having sex with gorgeous girls right below my feet.*

No, that's being unfair to myself—a bit. But I do need a change of mind-set.

He blew a smoke ring and watched it rise into the night. It captured twinkling stars inside the near-perfect ring, like glittering diamonds on a black velvet cloth. The ring continued to expand. Soon, thousands of stars were caught, and then millions, perhaps billions. The ring rose higher. Entire galaxies were encircled, an area of deep space millions of light years across. *Who knows how many alien civilizations are out there? Would the human race ever find out? Probably not. And maybe that's a good thing. We don't want some super technological lizard-like species coming to enslave us, or eat us. But what about all the amazing things we could learn too—incredible technology, incredible places, incredible beings, other ways to live, think, and exist.*

He continued watching the smoke ring's journey, strangely fascinated by the thoughts coming to mind. Eventually it faded away.

He yawned sleepily and switched on some late-night radio, and fell asleep.

An hour or so later he awoke.

Daylight was growing. He stretched his arms and legs and rubbed the side of his face. The leather stitching on the chair's arm, on which he'd rested his head, had pressed a groove across his left cheek. His back was stiff, and his shirt smelled of tobacco. Other than that, he felt surprisingly good, bearing in mind the amount of bourbon and champagne he'd drunk.

The champers, as DG called it, had run out in the middle of the night. There'd been a mild panic and talk of going ashore until Stan had discovered another ten cases in the galley.

Jack usually got drunk on three pints of lager and never touched wine or spirits, so all the booze was for his guests. This was a point in Jack's favor, as far as Stan was concerned, but DG insisted that Jack was just showing off again. DG was probably right—only the finest champagne for Jack North's friends. Max could hear Jack saying it. When would he ever learn?

At least he's buying his fair share of drinks now. Max remembered one time when Stan had kicked Jack up the backside in the Bull's Head car park; he'd been bending down to retie his shoelaces.

"You must think we were born yesterday, Jack. Strange how your shoelaces always come undone outside the pub. Get to the bar. It's your round. In fact, you're buying all night. And here's a tip, Northy. The next time you want to pull that old trick, don't wear slip-ons."

Max smiled and checked his watch. It was seven thirty, or six thirty in the United Kingdom. Back home, he'd be getting ready for work. He didn't bother with an alarm clock because he was always woken by footsteps in the flat above or the traffic at the busy crossroads below his bedroom window.

He closed his eyes.

It was so quiet.

So calm.

So beautifully still.

Apart from his own breathing, all he could hear was seawater lapping against the *Conchita*'s hull and the occasional flap of the Spanish flag flying on the stern.

A new sound entered his head.

It was a low, vibrating hum.

Mosquito.

He hated them. *Where is the bloody thing?*

He remembered hunting one on a holiday in Spain with Marcy. On her orders, he'd chased the bloodsucker all around the apartment and had despised the disgusting little bastards ever since. He'd never caught that one, either. A full hour of wild swings and swishes had produced only countless shoe marks all over the whitewashed walls. Covered in sweat, he'd given up the ghost. The mosquito was still at large, every now and then making an audible-but-invisible sortie. Marcy had wanted to sleep under the covers to avoid being bitten, but he'd complained about the heat and thrown them back again.

"Marcy there's only one, for God's sake," he'd said in a huff.

The following morning, he'd been pleased to report no bites and then spotted Marcy standing naked in front of the mirror. She was inspecting a line of red, swelling blotches that ran all the way from the middle of her back down to her right ankle.

"Oh," he'd said, remaining hidden beneath the sheets.

"It's all well doing that now, Max. Just look at me."

On the *Conchita*, the humming grew louder. He held his breath and listened harder. It wasn't a mosquito. The buzzing was too deep, and it was heavier somehow. Maybe it was a hair dryer. *One of the girls might be up.*

His eyes were drawn out to sea and up into the brightening sky. He saw a tiny, black dot high up and far off. He rubbed his eyes and searched for the binoculars, but he couldn't find them. The black dot remained visible. And it was growing bigger. The deep humming was louder, too.

The *Conchita*'s siren ripped up the new morning's silence. It was a horrible noise—shrill and vibrating, piercing and painful—but Max wasn't going below decks. *God knows what proceedings are still on going down there.*

Stan emerged first. He was half-dressed in shorts. "Fuck's sake. You've just ruined the end of *First Blood*. We'd better be under attack."

"We could be," Max said, pointing at the incoming helicopter. It was descending, still a good mile away. "Air-sea rescue?"

Stan didn't answer. He was staring hard at the approaching machine.

Will appeared. "What's going on?"

"Visitors," Max said.

"Police?" Will asked.

"More girls?" DG asked, up from the main deck. He was standing at the bottom of the stairs, watching, in a pair of faded Levi's. Kylie and Dannii were by his side in light-blue *Conchita* dressing gowns.

"Tell 'em I've already got more than I can handle," DG said, lovingly fondling Dannii's bottom.

"I'm not sure he has, Maxi," Kylie shouted. "But we're not sharing."

The two sisters looked at one another and giggled.

Lisa and Tracy climbed up onto the flybridge. They were also wearing *Conchita* dressing gowns. Lisa walked over to Will and took his hand, kissing him on the neck. Will looked immensely proud for a moment and then blushed.

"What the fuck?" Stan said.

Three hundred yards away, the helicopter suddenly plunged from the sky. A watery grave seemed inevitable. At high speed, a collision with the sea surface would be catastrophic. There'd be no survivors. Humans would be crushed before having the chance to drown.

Max didn't have the chance to cover his eyes.

And so he saw the huge machine implausibly pull up at the very last moment. It leveled out and skimmed the sea surface, still heading straight for the *Conchita*. It was no more than ten feet above the rippling water, its rotor blades leaving a cloud of white sea spray in its wake.

"It's going to ram us," Will screamed.

The strike would be midships at more than a hundred miles an hour.

This time, Max did cover his eyes but peeked through his fingers. There was no time for evasive action and nowhere to go. He was glued to the spot as a mass of green and yellow, glass and spinning metal, entirely filled his vision before it continued on and thundered over his head.

The noise was ear bursting. The vibrations in his feet and in the air around him were terrifying. For him, the whole world was shaking.

He ducked.

But the helicopter had already gone. The imminent, life-threatening danger was over. *Ducking must be an instinctive response. Something programmed into our brains from prehistoric times, a reaction that had once saved one of my ancestors, although not from helicopters.*

Just what the hell am I thinking about? Christ, the rubbish that goes through my head. He glanced around the deck.

It was full of squirming bodies, apart from Stan, who was still standing and scrutinizing. He'd never flinched at his impending death, and his eyes were still fixed on the sky.

Max stayed down. He was in a crouch but directed his gaze upward. He'd once heard of a guy being decapitated by a helicopter's rotor blades after a pleasure trip. It was a quick way to go but a rather messy clean-up. Apparently, the poor tourist's head had been superflicked toward the Colorado River while his unsuspecting right hand was still gripping a ten-dollar bill for the I've-had-the-trip-of-a-lifetime-to-the-Grand-Canyon photo, which, fortunately, wasn't just a headshot.

The helicopter of current concern was now banking steeply and high over the *Conchita*'s foredeck. It was like a giant, mutant, ninja mosquito. Camouflage green with multipaned, buglike glass windows at the front and short, stubby wings with a variety of intimidating cylinders hanging underneath.

It was still ascending. The momentum gained from its high-speed attack run was pushing it up an imaginary slope, as if it were going the wrong way up a ski jump. It paused at the summit, stopping dead in mid-air. The five-blade main rotor was still turning, as was the three-blade tail, and the two turbine engines were still producing power, proved by the incredible din, but it was all seemingly in vain. It reminded Max of those swinging boats at the fairgrounds, which pause at the top of the climb, and cause riders' loose change to fall out of their pockets.

After an eternity—in reality, about a second—the stationary helicopter rotated 180 degrees and slid gracefully back down its own path, ending in a rock-steady hover over the main deck and its still-confused and mostly crawling population.

All Max could hear were the rapid whirring chugging sounds coming from the rotor blades above him.

The downdraft from the blades was a hurricane-strength, and the deck had become one great vibration plate. Max always avoided those bloody-awful power plates at the local gym. He hated the feeling. They made his internal organs tickle. But there was no stepping off this one.

"What the fuck?" Stan shouted again, this time directly into Max's ear. It was the only way to make yourself heard. "It's a Russian Mil Mi-Twenty-Four gunship—armored transport with a heavy punch. And the guy flying it is military trained, for sure."

"What are those stick things?" Will shouted, pointing upward.

Stan looked incredulous but answered through a swirling gale of maps, cigar boxes, towels, crisp packets, and a dressing gown, which was Will's. Fortunately, Will was wearing his Roger Rabbit boxer shorts.

"Sweet Mary and Joseph," Stan said, "don't you lot know *anything*? The 'stick thing' pointing from the chin turret is a machine gun. It's a twelve point seven millimeter Yakushev-Borzov Gatling gun that can fire four to five thousand rounds a minute. Just to be clear, Will, that's the stick thing pointing directly at *you*. The other stick things beneath the wings are essentially antitank missiles, but, of course, they'll blow anything up, including big yachts!"

Will turned pale and swiftly moved a few feet to his left, pulling Lisa along with him.

"Stan, what do we do?" Max shouted while stamping down on Will's gown. It flapped wildly around his foot.

"Nothing to do," Stan said, "unless we chuck some empty champagne bottles at it."

"We could jump over the side," Will shouted, who had recovered his gown. "It's less than a mile to shore."

Max was up for that. He swam twice that far during most lunchtimes at work.

"Pointless, mate," Stan said. "We'd be sitting ducks. He'd machine-gun us before we got twenty yards. We'd have more bullet holes than a Tetley's tea bag has perforations."

Above them, the gunship's side door fell open. On land, it would provide a ramp for men and equipment to enter and exit. A man in military fatigues stepped into the black space and leaned out, tilting his head to survey the scene below. He was holding on to one of the side struts for support. His black helmet and tinted visor turned to the anxious audience almost directly below, but the man seemed more interested in the open deck area toward the stern. He disappeared inside the aircraft again.

"Maybe he's realized that we're not an aircraft carrier," DG shouted.

The helicopter slid smoothly back a few feet as if on a runner attached to the ceiling. It remained in a perfect hover closer to the stern.

"That's some flyer," Stan said.

The man reappeared in the doorway.

And then he jumped.

Kylie screamed. She was still screaming as two heavy boots landed softly on the deck.

Stan ran down the staircase and onto the main deck.

Max followed, even though he had no idea what he was going to do when he got there.

Life was becoming bizarre. Suddenly, the monotony of home, running a swimming pool, and drinking Stella Artois in the Bull's Head were appealing. *Better than being scared to bloody death; that's for sure.*

From the flybridge, it had seemed as if the soldier had just floated down. The rising sun was directly behind the helicopter, so it had obscured the winch wire. Max had shielded his eyes to try to see but saw only what looked like a black smudge descending.

The smudge was now a few feet from the stern rail and was busily unhooking carabiners and loosening straps, ignoring the group of bystanders who were fidgeting nervously nearby.

Max's eyes recovered from looking into the sun. And only then did he realize what the guy was doing. He wasn't unhooking himself; he was unhooking someone else—his passenger.

Two people had winched down.

The second guy was still hidden from view by the first guy's bulky body, as it must have been on the short descent. A second black helmet appeared as the winchman bent to release two carabiners attached to the smaller person's waist. Because of the noise, the strangers communicated between themselves by tapping on shoulders, legs, and helmets, probably some routine for checking the passenger for injuries. Two thumbs-up signals followed.

The winchman took two steps back and waved his arms above his head. Ten seconds later, he was clambering back into the helicopter, which was still in a controlled hover. It hadn't moved an inch. Five seconds after that, the steel side door was pulled up and shut, and then the huge, metal war machine dipped slightly forward and moved lazily off.

Eight confused, anxious, and still cowering bodies pulled their gazes away from the departing aircraft and toward the stranger who had been left behind.

"Typical Jack stunt, this," Will said. "He loves to show off."

"That's Jack?" DG asked.

"Not unless he's lost five stone," Max said.

"Plastic surgery?" DG asked.

"Could be, if they lengthened his legs six inches," Max said. "So I'm thinking not."

The stranger pulled off some thick, black, leather gloves and stuffed them into jacket side pockets. Small, olive-skinned hands were then placed on either side of an overly large tinted helmet. After a short struggle and a hefty tug, it came off.

Long, shiny black hair cascaded.

"It's like one of those shampoo commercials," DG said.

"Grow up, will you?" Stan said. He sounded intense. "This woman's just arrived courtesy of one of the cold war's most deadly weapons, DG, not a bloody Ziggy's taxi. This is serious shit."

Max hadn't heard the exchange. He was in a daze—star struck.

He'd already forgotten about the Russian gunship, the heavy machine guns, and the antitank missiles. He'd forgotten about nearly being decapitated, mosquitos, and everything else, too. All he could see and think about were emeralds—emerald-green eyes, to be exact. At this moment, they were filling his brain and leaving no room for anything else outside life support. They were the very same green eyes that had totally transfixed him the day before, except for one fundamental thing: these eyes were real human flesh and blood, not oil-based paint. The artist had done a good job—a great job—but had ultimately failed because the eyes staring straight at Max now were beyond compare, and certainly beyond the ability of a man to paint.

"Conchita," Max said.

The heavily breathing woman, and everybody else on deck, looked at him as if he were the one who had just dropped in from above. "Señor?" She sounded slightly alarmed.

"Conchita," Max said again. He just knew that the yacht was named after her.

The woman tilted her head slightly. The sunlight caught her eyes as she narrowed them. "My papa calls me Conchita, but everybody else calls me Maria. Señor, I don't know you, do I?"

Dannii whispered into her sister's ear. "How does he do that?"

"Do what?" Kylie said, not taking her eyes off Max or the new woman.

"You know," Dannii whispered. "Max knows the names of people he's never met before. He knew mine yesterday, and now he knows hers today. It's spooky."

Maria spoke again. She'd collected herself but still sounded slightly anxious and a little breathless. Her voice was a bit shaky.

"Who are you all?" she asked. She had a Spanish accent, but her English was excellent. Her feet were firmly planted on the deck, but her eyes were darting from left to right and back again. Occasionally, she glanced over toward the saloon.

Max stepped forward.

"There's nobody else onboard, Maria. There's just us." He held out his hand. It felt a bit formal, but he wasn't sure what else to do. "Let's start again," he said. "I'm Max West."

She looked down at his offered hand and then took it. Her handshake was surprisingly firm. *A business handshake*, thought Max. A good, firm handshake signaled confidence. Weak, limp, two-fingered, feeble efforts were one of his pet peeves, as were macho, knuckle-busting ones.

"Nice entrance, Maria. Very dramatic," he said, smiling and pointing to the now-empty sky above them. "We thought we were under attack."

Maria remained silent.

He tried again.

"We're Jack's friends."

Again, she said nothing.

"Jack North," Max said. "Ah, but you may not be aware that Jack was involved in a car crash yesterday. He's OK but unable to join us. We've been trying to contact him and Jules all day, but so far with no luck."

Maria looked as if she were in shock.

"Car crash?" She said.

Max chided himself. He was being thoughtless. News of the car crash must have knocked her for six. Maria hadn't known about it, and he'd just blurted it out. *I'm such an idiot.* The woman had expected to be greeted by Jack—her boyfriend? Instead, she was faced by strangers, and odd-looking strangers at that. Or maybe it wasn't the car accident at all. Maybe it was the sight of four semi-naked girls that had fazed her. She could have flown in to catch Jack out. If that were the case, then Jacky Boy was well and truly busted. "Done up like a kipper in a sleeping bag," as Max's mother would have said. No wonder the woman was shocked. She would assume that the car-crash story was a lie to protect Jack and that her boyfriend was hiding somewhere else onboard. And that would be why she kept peering over their heads and into the saloon, to see if Jack were lurking back there.

So what's freaking her, catching her boyfriend with his pants on the deck or the fact that he'd been injured in a car crash?

He'd no idea, so he gave up guessing.

What a waste of two seconds.

"Let me take your helmet, Maria," he said. "We'll go into the saloon for a drink. I need one. We can talk better in there. And Jack is OK, honestly. His assistant told us so."

"Amen to that, the drink bit," DG said. He took Kylie and Dannii's hands and led them into the saloon. Stan, Tracy, Will, and Lisa were on his heels.

Maria snapped out of her trance and followed them, handing her helmet to Max as she walked past him.

After a single step inside the saloon doors, she stopped. "The bastard," she said. She was visibly upset.

"It's her. It's her," Will said, jumping up from the sofa he'd just sat on. It was something of a eureka moment for him, and he was now pointing animatedly at the oil painting above the cocktail bar.

"Oh, for God's sake, Will," DG said, "are you on drugs, man? Wake up. Just how the hell do you run a business?"

Tracy, Kylie, Dannii, Lisa, and Stan, who were all seated around the quadrangle of leather sofas, turned their heads as one—first toward the portrait, and then to Maria and back again.

A wave of realization broke.

DG was incredulous. "You have got to be kidding," he said. "Can any of you remember your own names?"

Tracy wandered over to the bar for a closer look. "Oh yeah," she said. "I'd love a portrait like that myself one day. All I ever get are glamour shoots. You know, lift 'em up a bit, love. Open 'em a bit wider, love. That type of stuff. But that's classy."

Dannii turned to Maria. "Where was it painted, Maria?"

Maria's neck had flushed. She was embarrassed. "Here. Aboard the *Conchita,* only a few weeks ago."

She ran her fingers through her long hair, unconsciously reshaping it to the style in the painting. "A professional artist. It took an age, and it was a very boring process." Tears were in her eyes. "He said he would hang it himself in his cabin."

"The painter?" asked Dannii.

"No, my...my...boyfriend," said Maria.

She sat holding her head in her hands. "He's put it on display like a cheap centerfold," she said.

Tracy sat next to her and put her arms around her, trying to console. "That's not true, love. It's definitely not cheap, and I should know. I've never been a centerfold, either. That would be a promotion. I'm usually next to the advertisements at the back."

Maria wasn't listening. She was standing with Carlo in the old church on top of Mount Monserrate in Bogotá. She was reliving the moment he slipped the engagement ring on her finger and the kiss that followed. The beautiful ring was currently nestled at the bottom of her trouser pocket. She dragged herself back to the present.

"He said the portrait was so lifelike that it would drive him insane if other men could see it."

Tracy hugged her tighter. "That's men for you, love," she said. "They all have one thing in common."

Stan was interested. "What's that, love?"

Tracy smiled. "That you're all lying bastards." She blew him a kiss.

Stan looked hurt. "I'm not a liar."

"Give over," said Tracy. "You must think I was born under a blackberry bush, Stan. If you're not a liar, then I take it you'll be happy when I roll up at the bingo? Tina will be OK with that, will she?"

Stan looked mortified.

Tracy laughed.

"Don't worry yourself, Stanley. She won't hear it from me. I know the score. This is just a minibreak."

"That's not fair," Stan said.

"Cobblers," Tracy said. "You're a liar, Stan. Full stop. You told me that *Rambo III* was a better movie than *Rambo II*, too. That was another lie. *Rambo II* is a better plot and has a far superior screenplay. As a Rambo lover, you know this well, but you were buttering me up, as I'd said the action scenes in *Rambo III* were great. So there you are, my darling. You're a lying bastard, just like every other man on the planet—a lovable, lying bastard, but a great, big, lying bastard, nevertheless."

"Er...thanks," Stan said.

Max had seen the look on his friend's face before when Tina was sorting him out. It was a mixture of humiliation, injustice, and confusion. *Tina and Tracy. What a clash-of-the-titans matchup that would be. There'd be a clamor for ringside seats, but the back of the stadium would be a safer bet—less risk of having a nail clipper stuck in your eye.*

Awkward small talk then ensued while Lisa and Kylie went in search of food. They hoped that eating would calm everybody down. They arrived back from the galley a few minutes later with trays full of teas, coffees, crisps, pieces of carrot cake, and shortbread biscuits.

Lisa placed her tray carefully next to Will.

"Thank you, my darling," he said, adoringly.

Blimey, thought Max. *Lisa versus Jane wouldn't be a bad contest, either. Just what predicaments are we all getting into?*

"Look," Maria said. She'd gone from upset to frustrated. "You all seem to be very nice people, but who are you?"

Max had been thinking along the same lines. "OK, Maria," he said. "Obviously, Jack hasn't told you anything about us. He does like to surprise people—"

"Yeah, by pissing off and leaving. This is just like Blackpool," DG said.

"Aw, shut up DG, for fuck's sake," Stan said. "It's complicated enough as it is."

"Swearing in front of the ladies again, are we?" DG said, glaring.

"Guys!" Max said. "For Pete's sake. Come on. Let's sort this." He waited a moment for silence, which, thankfully, arrived. "Maria, I think the best thing to do is for me to lay out our story, and then you can fill in any missing bits from your angle. That OK?"

Maria nodded. "Yes, that sounds good, Max. Thank you. I promise not to interrupt."

For the next fifteen minutes, Max spoke about how the men all knew each other from school days, how Jack had inherited the burned-out mill and millions of pounds, the invitation to Majorca, Jack's car accident, the trip being canceled, the severe disappointment, the booze, the setting sail, the not knowing how to sail, the girls arriving—he didn't mention *secret entertainment*—and finally the amazement of seeing her winch down from a Russian helicopter gunship.

All five women listened intently. It was a surprising tale to them but hearing it outloud it was nearly as surprising for the men, too, and embarrassing.

Dannii slapped DG's face.

"Ow!" He held his face. "What was that for?"

Dannii was upset. "You set sail, DG, and the rest of you, too. You all knew your friend had been in a car accident and didn't know how he was. And you stole his yacht."

"Who does that?" Kylie asked, and she slapped DG's other cheek.

"Ow! Christ, it's not like that, girls."

"Sounds very much like it is," Lisa said, pulling her hand away from Will's. "I'm really disappointed in you, Will. I had you down as a better man than that."

Will was crestfallen.

"And don't think I'm not pissed off with you for stealing your friend's yacht, either," Tracy said, giving Stan a stare of daggers. "I thought you were all about friendship and looking after one another. It's all you kept going on about last night—honor and loyalty. Clearly, that's all bollocks. I'll remember not to rely on you lot, that's for sure."

Dannii's right. All the girls are. We have no excuses. "We know we've fucked up, girls, Maria," Max said. He didn't know what else to say. He felt like a total shit.

Stan had been awaiting a cuff from Tracy, which hadn't arrived—yet. He stood. "I'm going to get a bottle of bourbon," he said. "Give me a minute please, Maria. I've a feeling I'm not going to like this."

There was no bourbon left.

"Bugger," Stan said, holding up an empty bottle of Maker's Mark. "I'll nip below and find some more. Jack's got booze stored all over the place."

His shaven head disappeared down the staircase. Max turned toward Maria. *God, she's beautiful. Her eyes, her soft skin.* She'd opened her jacket, and he couldn't help notice the swell of her breasts.

Maria had kept her promise not to interrupt Max's explanation of who they were and how they'd come to be on the *Conchita*, but she was clearly exercised and desperate to speak. Her eyes had gotten wider and wider the longer Max's story had gone on, and she'd bitten her bottom lip. The indentations from her top teeth were still visible.

"Max?" she asked.

"Yes?"

"Are you listening?"

He felt stupid, as if his teacher had caught him daydreaming. But he didn't really want to listen. He didn't want to have it confirmed that Jack was her boyfriend.

"Yes."

"This is important. I need you to listen to me very carefully, Max. Do you understand?"

Bloody hell, he was back in kindergarten class.

"Yes, I'm listening."

Maria took a deep breath and spoke very slowly and very deliberately. "Max, all of you," she said, "the *Conchita* is not Jack North's yacht."

DG laughed. "Of course it's his yacht, love."

Maria shouted, and DG jumped in surprise, expecting another slap.

"*No* it isn't," she said. "It is *not* his yacht."

Nobody spoke.

"I'm sorry," Maria said. "Forgive my tone." She lowered her voice again. "But *please, please* listen to me." She was focusing on Max again, who finally seemed to be listening. "The *Conchita* is named after me, Max. You guessed that. And that's obviously my portrait above the bar. So I would know who owned her, wouldn't I? And until just now, I'd never even heard of Jack North. Or any of you. The helicopter crew tracked the *Conchita*'s beacon all throughout the night. We expected her to be in a Palma marina, but she was still easy to locate."

Max was nodding. He'd worked out that Jack probably didn't own the *Conchita* pretty much as soon as Maria had landed on deck and hadn't known him from Adam. The stupid chump had chartered the *Conchita* for the week and must have altered her name too. He was trying to hoodwink them all with more just-look-at-how-unbelievably-successful-I-am crap. Max had hoped that Jack was finished with the inflated ego rubbish, but apparently not.

"Jack's obviously charter—"

Maria cut him off. "No, Max. You're not listening. I don't know Jack North. And he didn't charter *Conchita*. She's not for hire. A Colombian businessman called Carlo Ortega owns the *Conchita*; he bought her two months ago. The *Conchita* is brand new, and he would never charter her out—ever. You people shouldn't be here. You need to leave immediately. You are all in great da—"

She suddenly stopped, but it was obvious what she had planned to say. "Carlo mustn't find you onboard. He"—she struggled for the right words—"I mean, you're on the wrong yacht, Max. And you need to go!"

Max's brain was disabled. This situation just didn't compute. He emitted a nervous laugh.

"Where's Jack's boat, then?" DG asked.

"How would I know?" Maria said. "I don't even know who Jack is. Where's your paperwork?"

Blank looks all round. "We haven't any," said Max. His mind had freed up a fraction. "Why would we have paperwork for a friend's yacht?"

"What I really don't understand is why someone told you to board the *Conchita*," Maria said.

Max looked down at his feet, hoping the deck would open up so that he could fall into the ocean beneath.

"Jules said we couldn't miss Jack's yacht," Will said. "It was the biggest in the marina."

Maria had a look of total incredulity on her face, which Max couldn't see, as he was still looking down.

"Oh my God," Dannii cried. "You didn't even know the name of the yacht you were supposed to be on. You just got on the biggest one, no questions asked, and then stole it."

Max couldn't speak.

"We're the world's greatest set of wankers," DG said.

"You'll find nobody disagreeing with you there, honey," Tracy said.

DG was shaking his head in disbelief. "Well, it beats getting lost on the way to Weston-super-Nightmare, that's for bloody sure. I'm off the hook for that one now. Christ."

Max realized some truths. Maria's boyfriend was a Colombian businessman millionaire who owned a superyacht, whereas in comparison he was the deputy manager of a swimming pool—and had nicked the aforesaid superyacht and, in the process, had proved himself to be nothing more than a complete idiot. Suddenly, he felt relaxed. There was nothing to play for. The game was over before the referee had blown the whistle to kick off. Maria was out of his league. But something else was worrying him now—even more than being branded a fool.

"Maria, you were about to say earlier that we were all in great danger. If this is Carlo's yacht and we have inadvertently stolen it, then that's not good, but don't you think you're overreacting?"

Maria fidgeted. "Well—"

She was drowned out by Kylie's shriek as Stan burst into the saloon.

"What the fuck has that tub-of-lard North landed us in?" he shouted, holding a black, L-shaped piece of metal out in front of him. "It's a fucking Uzi submachine gun, but this peashooter is nothing compared to the rest of the fucking arsenal down below. There are M16s, rocket launchers, grenades, and high explosives—enough to fight a small war."

"Jesus Christ," Max said.

CHAPTER 12

Sergeant Hernandez ushered Jack through the still-open cell door and pushed it shut. Ancient hinges screamed again, and a fresh dusting of rust sprinkled lightly to the dirty, stone floor.

Jack blinked.

He couldn't see properly. His eyes were unaccustomed to the darkness after the bright strip lights of the police station. He could only just pick out the portly sergeant, who was busily fumbling with the lock a few feet away from him, on the other side of the bars.

The sergeant had turned into a large, dark-gray blob by the time the key turned and the lock's corroded old tumblers rotated and unhappily slid the bolt home. A few seconds later, Jack heard a resounding *thunk* at the end of the corridor as the door separating the cells from the staircase leading up into the station slammed shut.

Then there was only silence and the foul smell of warm urine.

Not that Jack minded either; he was still elated. He slapped his naked thigh and guffawed. The gruff sound of his hoarse voice echoed off the damp, stone walls.

He laughed again.

It was just so funny.

Hi-fucking-larious.

Masa accused me of being a bloody drug lord. Me. Mr. Jack North. Can you fucking believe it? And not just any old drug lord, either, but the biggest of the big cheeses, el supremo of the supremos, the numero uno of the numero unos, the undisputed king of the biggest fucking drug cartel in the world, ever.

What a cock.

He chuckled again and rubbed his aching face. The various burns, bites, and scratches were sore, but his aching cheek muscles were what really hurt—from laughing.

Masa's preposterous accusations, combined with the utterly unadulterated and beautiful relief of discovering that it wasn't the mill fire they'd pulled him in for, provided a heady cocktail of comedy and salvation and had led to the riot of elation and laughter. Jack had lost it, big time. He'd howled with total abandon. Tears had been streaming over his sore cheeks, and the angrier Masa had become, the louder Jack had laughed.

Masa was a buffoon, a bowler-hatted man from the ministry. He was an incompetent, overconfident, egotistical prig. Jack had absolutely no idea what an *egotistical prig* was, but a frustrated magistrate had once called him one, and it had sounded pretty good—or pretty bad, depending on what the hell it meant.

Anyhow, what was undeniable was that Masa was a prize prick. He couldn't remember if Masa had said he was police, but he probably was. And in Jack's view, cops were trained over a long weekend at either the Inspector Clouseau School of Detectives or the Keystone Cops Academy. Cops the world over were thick and racist; everybody knew that—and Colombian cops would be no different—or at least that's what Jack thought.

However, there was something else about Masa. And it took one to know one. And because Jack *was* one, he knew. And it wasn't good.

Masa was a really nasty bastard.

Jack was gripping the cold bars. He squeezed them hard as fear began to stir once again in his empty belly. *Thank God for the European Union.*

Now, that was a sentence he'd never expected to think, but he meant it. Even though the Eurocrats were a set of wankers, they were also suddenly very reassuring. Europe had rules. He knew that from his continental business dealings. His so-called expert corporate lawyers and accountants had been spectacularly failing to get around Europe's bloody red tape for years.

"You can't sack a person for that, Mr. North."

"You must also employ these people, Mr. North."

"You can't sell goods to this country, Mr. North. It's a dictatorship, and the European Union has sanctions in place."

"You'll need a license from Brussels to ship goods through that port, Mr. North."

"Your delivery drivers can't drive that many hours in Europe without a break, Mr. North."

The European Union rulebook was endless, longer than the phone book's yellow pages and even more boring.

How is an honest businessman like me expected to make a living?

But right now, that didn't matter. Jack was sure it was the European Union's rules that were protecting him. If there were so many rules preventing businessmen like him from trading as he wanted to, then there were bound to be loads more European rules for all sorts of other stuff, too, such as policing, interrogation, and *torture.*

He wouldn't be going to Colombia for his holidays anytime soon; that was for damn sure, wherever the fuck it was. It wasn't in Europe, he was confident about that—pretty confident. It was near Brazil. Or was it Alaska or Greenland? *Oh, fuck it.* He didn't know where it was, but it wasn't in Europe. Geography wasn't his strongest suit. Miss Tindall, possibly the worst teacher of the whole sorry fucking bunch—and that was saying something—had seen to that. The fat-arsed cow could hardly find her way to the classroom they were in, although she knew where the tuck shop was, all right.

A shiver ran down his spine. *What would happen to me in Colombia?*

It wasn't worth thinking about, but he did, involuntarily. Evil had been burning brightly in Masa's small beady black eyes. The bastard wanted to cut him or worse, maybe electrify his balls or stub out a fag on the end of his nose or inside his ear. But he couldn't because Europe's rules were standing in his way. *Thank God for the European Union and its countless unelected, gravy-train-riding bureaucrats.*

He heard someone behind him speak.

"Señor, welcome back," Pedro said, getting up off the filthy bed.

Jack was startled. He'd forgotten about the smelly tramp.

"Sorry, señor."

Jack collected himself. "It's fine, Pedro. And the bed is yours; don't worry about that. The fleas have had enough bites out of me. They're not getting seconds."

The fleabites had been another unwelcome surprise. He'd not noticed them at all until he'd been ordered to remove his shirt. Now he was only too aware. The incessant itching saw to that. A quick count had identified ninety-seven small pink lumps covering the entirety of his upper chest and shoulders. He didn't bother counting the bites on his legs and feet; he couldn't see the bites on his back, as there was no mirror, and he was avoiding checking his groin because it didn't feel good at all down there, and if he knew, then that would be worse.

He wondered why the fleabites hadn't bothered him until just then, but then realized that the hot, stinging pains on the top of his head had dulled somewhat. The itching and the cold cell floor had come to the fore. His feet were freezing. The stone underfoot felt like hard ice, and it was wet, and covered in something brown and horrid.

Either mud or shite. So why don't I feel sick? The smell of shite usually makes me gip.

He sniffed tentatively.

The air stopped dead halfway up his nostrils.

His nose was bunged up.

That's why he hadn't noticed.

His mouth was dry.

He generated some spittle.

Bits of vomit were stuck down the sides of his mouth, with a big lump located behind his wisdom teeth—remnants of his introductory meeting with Masa.

His taste buds had stopped working, thankfully. Clearly, they were overwhelmed by the horrendous smells and tastes recently come their way. His tongue felt furry and numb.

Splat.

The globule of spit and mouth trash hit the very brick he was aiming at, and started to stretch out, descending slowly down to the cell floor.

That was better.

He felt cleaner.

He cleared his throat.

Splat.

Another globule hit the exact same spot.

Pedro had edged warily over to see what the smelly Englishman was doing. He was met with two trumpetlike snorts as Jack emptied first his left nostril and then his right.

Jack felt good.

His head was purged.

He breathed in deeply, reveling in the free-flowing air rushing through his sinuses.

And then he choked.

The stench!

He held his throat in panic. The fumes were overpowering. He couldn't breathe. More to the point, he didn't dare to do so.

I'm going to die.

The stink was horrendous: dog shite times ten. There was no breathable air, so he retched and coughed up more phlegm.

Splat.

"Better out than in," his mother used to say, usually just after she'd farted.

Mum wasn't a fancy-dinner party girl.

The foul smell in the cell was overpowering, as if something had died and was decaying—a dead skunk, maybe.

He pinched his nose, breathed, and gipped.

At least my head's clear. There must be some air mixed in with the hydrogen sulfide. That was the full extent of his chemistry knowledge.

He ran an index finger over his burned eyebrows. A long scab was forming. It went the whole length of his forehead with no break above the nose. It felt very sore, too, but it was sticky, which he assumed meant it was healing. The lack of a mirror in the cell was probably a good thing.

Pedro began throwing up.

"Bloody hell," said Jack. "Surely the smell's not too bad for you?"

Pedro was bent double. It wasn't the smell he reviled but rather the sight of thick globules of phlegm and bits of old vomit slowly sliding down the far cell wall—which his cellmate had freshly produced.

He retched again.

Jack couldn't stand other people being sick, but felt that he should at least offer his cellmate some support. He went over to see what he could do. The tramp took one look at the large, spotty, swollen, eyebrowless, burned, and dirty face approaching him and recoiled in horror.

Jack realized how bad he must look.

Won't be pulling any birds tonight.

He spotted his tattered, torn trousers at the head of the bed. Sergeant Hernandez must have left them there. *The world does have some decent people, after all.* He pulled them on and buttoned them up. The belt was gone, but they were still tight. He checked the pockets. All of his possessions were still there.

He had a Visa Gold card with a one-hundred-thousand-pound limit, a fifty-euro note, Max's letter of acceptance for the trip, and a half a box of orange and lime Tic Tac. Not exactly a Bear Grylls survival kit. The credit card and money were useless, for sure. He'd usually buy himself out of trouble, but that wasn't going to happen this time.

Weariness fell over him, and he plonked himself down on the cell's only chair, which was a three-legged, wooden stool. It was small but comfortable. A little mouse had been carved on one of the legs an inch below the seat.

Pedro was sitting opposite, on the floor, in the shadows, and was looking at him with extreme distaste.

Fucking tramp. Who's he to judge?

Jack let out a long sigh and closed his eyes. He imagined being in the surround shower in his six-bedroom hilltop villa. Sixteen nozzles, high pressure, steamy—just oh-so-fucking lovely.

The tramp was speaking.

"Señor? Have you any water?"

Jack's amazing shower vanished. "I've nothing, Pedro. There's no food or water for me."

A plastic bottle rolled up against his foot. Jack snatched it. "Thanks, Pedro."

The bottle was empty. He kicked the bottle away. "Very fucking funny."

"No, señor. Sorry, señor, but I have no water. The bottle is for you to piss in, in case you need to drink later. I do it sometimes because Sergeant Hernandez forgets that I'm here. Two days, on one occasion. I have my own bottle here." He held up a bottle that was three-quarters full of yellowish-green liquid.

"Jesu-u-us," Jack groaned. He'd no intention of drinking his own piss, but he did need a dump.

He spotted a hole the size of a dinner plate in the cell floor. *The toilet.* He'd not seen it before because it was partially covered by the end of the bed, which explained the smell of piss and crap he'd woken up to.

This place is a fucking dungeon.

Suddenly, he longed for England, beautiful Olde England. It was God's own country, the best place in the world. And all foreigners, such as Masa, knew it full well.

And the English legal system was the mother of all legal systems, too, including the European ones. Justice was available to all in England, as long as you had money, and he did. *And that's the way it should be, shouldn't it? The wealthy, like me, pay more taxes, create jobs for the poor people, and fund politicians, generally by giving out backhanders.*

The law was crucial to Jack's everyday way of life in England, good Olde England. On one occasion, he'd left his Bentley strewn across a couple of disabled parking bays in front of the Leeds Marriot. He'd been entertaining two women from the casino in the honeymoon suite. He'd awakened with a stinking hangover after a night of drink-induced impotence to find that his wallet was gone and three penalty parking notices were tucked under the Bentley's windscreen wipers. English justice came swiftly to the rescue. The wallet was a lost cause, too embarrassing to pursue, but all of the parking tickets were rescinded by Leeds City Council after Mr. Simon Rothchild Hartenshaw Brookstein, Jack's London legal eagle, pointed out to council bosses that Mr. North would be sacking ten employees, their council taxpayers, if they didn't.

And that was fair. Wasn't it? There must be some perks for being a successful entrepreneur. The parking tickets had been scrubbed, saving him seventy-five pounds, and although Rothchild's time had cost him more than five thousand pounds, it had been worth it. It was the principle.

Jack squatted awkwardly over the dark hole. He was well past the embarrassment of crapping in front of someone else.

The high stress and tension of the past few hours meant that he didn't have to push too hard.

He sighed with relief. "Pass me the bog roll, Pedro."

The tramp looked quizzical. "Que, señor?"

"The bloody toilet roll."

"Que?"

Jack was annoyed but tried to keep his temper. His thighs were beginning to ache. "You know, Pedro. *Servithios* paper."

"Que?"

"Servithios paper," he shouted, hoping that louder words may translate better. "For fuck's sake, Pedro." In exasperation, he made a rubbing motion.

"Ah-h-h," said the tramp, suddenly understanding. "No, señor. There is none of that."

Jack stared in disbelief. His legs were aching badly. "Well, that's just marvelous, Pedro. Just wait until I fill in the fucking customer survey."

"Que, señor?"

Jack could swear the old tramp was smiling. He looked to be biting his lip. *Dago bastard.* "Pedro," Jack said, sounding contrite.

"Yes, señor?"

"Do you understand any English?"

"Si, señor," Pedro said, smiling. "I do, yes."

"Well, *fuck off*, then."

Jack reached into his pocket and pulled out Max's letter and the fifty-euro note. *Just a two wiper, then.*

A moment later, he was finished. A fifty-euro arse wipe was the most expensive he'd ever had, but it was worth every cent. He sat back down on the stool, having given Pedro an exaggerated snarl, and consoled himself with a lime Tic Tac.

CHAPTER 13

"**S**o these are our options," Max said, "the ones I can think of, anyway."

He was standing with his back to the cocktail bar and addressing his audience, who were sitting around the saloon in the hot-tub pairings, and trio, of the previous night. Except Maria of course, who was perching on a bar stool next to him. The happy, carefree expressions of a few hours before had vanished forever. Replaced by the hard, fixed, lined faces that accompany tension and worry and a rapidly growing sense of fear.

"Option one," Max said. He was pretty much making it up as he went along, but somebody needed to say something. "We dock at the nearest marina, which is Andratx, and tie up and leave. We're gone. Andratx is half an hour's sail around the next headland."

He took a breath. "Now listen, everybody, and this is going to sound overly dramatic, but if we're being tracked, like Maria tracked us from the helicopter, then Carlo, or whoever else, could be waiting for us when we pull in to port."

Lisa looked shocked.

Will squeezed her hand.

"It'll be fine, Lisa," Max said, smiling. "I'm sure there'll be no problem, but as Jack Reacher says, 'Hope for the best, plan for the worst.' This is obviously just a monumental cock-up, but the facts may suggest to others that we took the *Conchita* deliberately, and some caution is required, even if it's unnecessary, as I'm sure it is."

"I think it is necessary, Max," Tracy said with a huff. "You idiots did take the *Conchita* deliberately, just buggered off out to sea without asking anyone, so what else is anybody supposed to think? Wankers, the lot of you, if you ask me."

Max couldn't help but agree to all she had said. "Well, in case that's true, we'll need to convince whoever that it truly was an accident, and if necessary, we'll have to admit the 'idiot-wanker' charge. My point is that Andratx is a small place, and therefore, it's unlikely there'll be much of a police presence, if the situation becomes a little difficult."

Clack.

Kylie and Tracy jumped in their seats, and all eyes flew toward Stan, who'd just rammed a magazine into the Uzi.

"It's got nine-millimeter ammo with a twenty-five-bullet magazine," he said, looking grim. "If Carlo or anybody else is stupid enough to cut up rough, then good luck to 'em."

"Jesus," Max said. "Go and put that bloody thing back down where you found it. You're scaring the girls." *And me.* "And rub it down for your fingerprints. Tina won't be thrilled at having to visit you in some Spanish jail every month for the next twenty years."

Tracy took off the thin wrap she was wearing and began rubbing down the Uzi, much to Stan's delight.

"Ooo, that's so good, baby," he said.

Tracy clipped him around the ear. "Silly sod," she said, unable to restrain a smile.

"Come on, Stan," Max said. "Be serious, for fuck's sake. We need your help."

"There's not much more serious than a fully loaded Uzi, Maxi," said Stan.

The clack of the Uzi being loaded had jolted Max. He'd heard the same sound a thousand times before in the movies. It was usually Arnie or Stallone— the goodies—who were locking and loading and blowing away the enemy, who, of course, were all baddies and deserved it. Coke, popcorn, excitement, and red mist—the ingredients for a fun night out at Showcase Cinemas, at least for all the action-movie fanatics.

The reality of a real weapon being made ready for use was totally different.

The long, thin magazine had crunched home. The sound was harsh and metallic. Max had winced. Thoughts of fingers being caught in the mechanism had come to mind, as well as ripped skin and snapped nails. A bit girly, but that's what he'd thought. And then there was the smell. No smell at the cinema—solvent and cinnamon, presumably gun oil. And the oil was important; the Uzi was a machine, an industrial product, a set of moving metal parts, designed and manufactured to fulfill a specific function—to kill.

Stan had laid the killing machine across his lap. One of his large hands was wrapped around the barrel. Max looked at the trigger. It looked innocuous; curved and about two inches long, enclosed in a metal hoop. It was hard to believe that with one purposeful pull of a forefinger, two seconds later, eight of the nine people in the saloon would be bleeding and dying or already dead.

The hairs on the back of Max's neck stood at attention. He'd labeled the events of the past couple of days as a comical farce, an *Only Fools and Horses*–type of plot where Del Boy and Rodney unscrew the wrong chandelier, or steal the wrong Reliant Robin, or maybe, even more ludicrously, the wrong bloody superyacht.

Pity it wasn't something ridiculous like that.

But it was.

And it wasn't.

Because this was deep shit.

How could this have happened?

Normal people like him and his mates made dumb mistakes sometimes— and caused problems for others. And on occasion they made totally stu-fucking-pendously-dumb mistakes, such as nicking the wrong superyacht. And rightly—and Max suspected usually—the *normal* superyacht owner would get pretty pissed off about it and might even prosecute. But normal superyacht owners didn't have Israeli made submachine guns or use fully armed Russian helicopter gunships for transport. Did they?

No, they fucking well didn't, he thought.

So whoever Carlo was, he wasn't a normal superyacht owner. He was therefore an *abnormal* superyacht owner.

No shit, Sherlock, Max thought.

There was a loud clink as Stan laid the Uzi down on the glass coffee table.

"Option two," Max said. "We use the dinghies and leave the *Conchita* right now; just up anchor and go. Ten minutes, and we're all on shore over there." He pointed toward a rocky outcrop. "From there, it's an easy climb to the main road and a taxi to the airport. We could be on a plane within an hour or so. A bit of luck, guys, and we hit the Bull's Head for last orders and a game of pool."

Will and DG both nodded.

"If you do that, I'll be able to cover for you," Maria said. "I've come here to see Carlo, so I'm staying onboard. I'll sail the *Conchita* back up to Palma myself and wait for him there."

"What would you tell him, Maria?" Will asked.

"I'll just keep it simple, Will, and as close to the truth as possible. I arrived, and a group of people I'd never seen before left, which is pretty much true."

Logical, if slightly odd, thought Max. But, more significantly, it would leave Maria alone on the yacht. He decided then and there that he couldn't do it. He wouldn't leave her. The truth was that he couldn't leave her. He felt scared, but however big a nightmare this Carlo was, the thought of abandoning Maria…

No, no, that wasn't it—she would be perfectly safe—who was he kidding? *I should be honest with myself, at least.* The truth was that he couldn't bear the thought of never seeing Maria again.

DG and Will were looking at him curiously.

"Option three," Max said. "We all power up to Palma. It's a good three-hour trip, but Palma has the biggest marina on the island, and we'll be inconspicuous with all the other big yachts. Majorcan police HQ will be based in Palma, too. If we see anything dodgy as we sail in, then we can call them. The cops will be with us in minutes. We could even stand off the quayside until they show up. If it's all clear, then we tie up, taxi to the airport, and away we go. And this way, we'll know that all the girls are safe, too, including you, Maria. It feels better than leaving you onboard alone."

"Safe until Carlo the arms dealer rocks up," Stan said. "Miss, if you don't mind me asking, just what the hell are you going to do when Carlo turns up?"

Stan didn't stand on ceremony. It was the question Max had been wondering about, too. It's what they were all thinking.

Maria remained silent but looked angry.

"Stan, which option is best?" Max asked, recognizing that Maria wasn't going to answer. "Have you any other ideas?"

Stan's forehead creased. "The first rule of warfare, Maxi, is to treat everybody you don't know as a dangerous enemy until proved otherwise."

"What if you've already shot them?" DG asked.

"Then they're not dangerous anymore," Stan said, looking grim. "It's better them than you, DG. I know you civilians don't work like that, as it's a bit unfriendly like, but it's preferable to being slotted the first time you turn your back. Therefore, option one is a definite no-no. I concur with your analysis, Max. Too risky. If we're being watched, and we should assume so, then there's likely to be a greeting party in Andratx. We'd be dead, and Carlo and his pals would be long gone before any serious cops turn up."

"You're being ridiculous," Will said. "Surely?"

Stan lightly kicked the Uzi barrel. It spun around on the table, scraping angrily against the glass.

The point was made.

"Option two is worse, an absolute death trap. If he is tracking our position, then he'll take us as we approach the shoreline. We wouldn't make it out of the dinghies. There would be no cover, no authorities, and no witnesses. Bloody suicide. Surprised you mentioned it, Maxi. So, option three, as you already know, is our best course of action. There's less chance of *contact* full stop."

"What do *slotted* and *contact* mean?" Lisa asked.

"Sorry, sweetheart," Stan said. "*Slotted* is common army talk for being shot dead, and *contact* means a shoot-out with the enemy, of which there's less chance in Palma because lots of people will be around. And as Max said, the authorities will be based there too. The risk in option three is that Palma is a few hours away, but I'd say it's our best option."

"Shot dead," Lisa whispered in shock.

"I thought you said it would all be fine, Max," Kylie said sharply, "that the situation might become a little difficult. That's not the same as being shot dead!"

"Stan's just being cautious. That's all," Max said, trying to calm her, although he felt far from calm himself. "It's what he's trained to do. Does anybody disagree with option three?"

"Well, I think I'd like to jump off right now," Tracy said. "But if you two think it's safer to go up to Palma, then let's get going."

Kylie, Dannii, and Lisa looked fearful, but all nodded.

"Maria?" Max asked.

"I agree. Palma is best. We'll be there by midafternoon." With that said, she slipped off her stool and, ignoring the room, walked out on deck.

"Option three and Palma it is," DG said, rising from his seat. "Let's have some drinks."

"Bring me one up top, DG," Will said. "I'll get us underway."

He and Lisa disappeared up the spiral staircase. A few seconds later, the engines fired up.

CHAPTER 14

Jack awoke with a start as Sergeant Hernandez unlocked the cell door. "Señor North, with me, please."

The sergeant somewhat apologetically snapped handcuffs over Jack's wrists and led him out of the cell and back up into the police station. The bright lights hurt Jack's eyes again, but at least he wasn't scared anymore because he was past caring. Through a squint, he could see that people were holding their noses and moving quickly out of his way. He wasn't bothered about that, either.

Outside interrogation room 1, his handcuffs were removed. The door was opened, and Jack stumbled inside.

Masa was nervously circling the small table. The huge captain was present, too, and still motionless. But he was watching from the far corner of the room.

"Sit down, please, Mr. North," Masa said, softly.

Jack shuffled around the table and sat down again on the grim, plastic chair. It was still grubby with sweat from his previous visit.

"Mr. North," said Masa, sounding friendly, "we got off on the wrong foot, I'm afraid. But it really would be to everybody's benefit, particularly your own, if you fully cooperated now."

Jack stared straight ahead, unresponsive.

Masa laid on the honey. "I can assure you, Jack, that this situation is giving me absolutely no pleasure at all." He smiled broadly. "It troubles me no end to see an Englishman in such a humiliating position."

Jack dipped his head to avoid the light shining down on him, but it wasn't only his eyes that were bothering him; his balls were itching like crazy. In his mind's eye, he could see thousands of sharp-teethed fleas running amok in his underpants.

Masa took the prisoner's head movement as acknowledgment. *The change of tactics is going well.* He'd underestimated this man the first time around, vastly, but he wouldn't be making the same mistake again. Jack North, if that really were his name, was obviously an expert in interrogation resistance, but this time it would be he, Alberto Masa, who was ready and in full control of his mind and emotions—and he would prevail. He'd used the time between sessions to work up a foolproof strategy to break the man. Of course, the task would have been easier back home. In Colombia, 240 volts and a beating usually did the trick. The threat of a second beating was seldom necessary, although on occasion a third was required, and one time a fourth. However, that man had turned out to be innocent.

But he wasn't in Bogotá now, and there was no point lamenting that fact. He would have to play by the American and European rules, which were soft, weak, and wasted precious time that they didn't have. He'd made the case for alternative methods. "This is a once-in-a-generation opportunity to strike at the very heart of the cartel leadership," he'd said, but the Europeans could talk only about human rights, and the Americans were still panicking over the CIA's secret rendition program. It was pathetic.

He'd argued with Colonel Quintero, his senior officer, about the need to use truth drugs at the very least, but apparently that was also an infringement of a suspect's legal rights. "What about the rights of the thousands of law-abiding Colombians killed by the cartel *sicarios*?" he'd asked, but Quintero had merely shrugged, while muttering something about his hands being tied.

And so there it was, the most important interrogation he'd ever undertaken, and he must succeed through the use of brainpower alone. It would be difficult. Tough. But as he'd told DEA Agent Clark earlier that day, "Twenty years of interrogation means I've seen them all—the madmen, the bad men, the clever men, and, worst of all, the mad, bad, clever men." Whichever category North fit into, he'd work out in due course.

And North had been a difficult problem to solve. Masa had puzzled long and hard while Jack was down in the cell. He thought the answer would never come, and then while he was signing an official paper, it just popped into his head.

And the answer was obvious.

Jack North was a tough nut on the inside, as well as on the outside, for sure. But first and foremost, he was an Englishman, and Englishmen were all the same—arrogant imperialists, all for queen and country, the need for fair play, and a love of that ludicrous game called cricket. These were the basic characteristics of the English—and North had displayed them already. So using them against him would be both simple and brilliant.

"The drug criminals have duped you, Mr. North. I can see that now, and I'm sorry I didn't see it before. Forgive me. So let's right this injustice. All the world knows that an Englishman is no pawn in a game for others to abuse, use, and disrespect."

Jack shook his head.

He obviously thinks it is an outrage too. Excellent.

Masa continued. "The British Empire ruled a third of the globe, Mr. North. Arguably, it was greater even than Imperial Rome, hence Great Britain. And your ancestors gave us Westminster Palace—the mother of all parliaments and western democracy, and built the world's greatest railways, and invented public health, and gave us the Beatles. Your nation and its subjects rightly command the respect of us all, Mr. North. Don't forget that."

Jack bared his teeth.

Masa was ecstatic. He'd hooked the prisoner and become his friend, a trusted ally—in less than two minutes. The pathetic fool was even smiling. A little bit of thought by a higher intelligence—his—and this stinking Englishman was drinking in every word, just as easily as if it were that horrendous, lukewarm beer they all drank in copious amounts. He smiled to himself, almost feeling sorry for the hapless fool.

All he had to do now was close.

"So, Mr. North. Help me put these foreigners away. Don't let them poke fun at England. What they've done is just not cricket. It's unfair, unjust, and they need to be held to account. So, please, tell me exactly what you know about the Medellín Cartel's business activities in Europe and exactly how you are involved, and I will do the rest. I'll make sure they pay for insulting you."

Masa fell silent. The moment of his triumph had arrived. He felt a surge of pride in his abilities—he had won. The next words to come from the English pig's mouth would be an admission of guilt.

And Jack was unable to contain himself any longer—but not in the way Masa was expecting.

"I'm sorry, Mr. Masa, but my balls are on fire," said Jack, thrusting both hands into his underpants and vigorously scratching and rubbing. He lifted his legs up off the chair to get right underneath. "Oh Christ, that feels so fucking good," he said. "Oh yeah, oh yeah. Oh fucking yeah."

It was a full five minutes before Jack had relieved every last itch. Finally, he sat back, rested his head on the top of the chair back, and grinned like a Cheshire cat on ecstasy.

His happy mood wasn't shared. Masa's left eye was twitching again, and saliva was running over the knuckles he was biting down on.

"You look a bit tense, mate," Jack said, offering his seat. "Would you like to sit down?"

The captain standing behind Jack shuffled around to the sidewall, slightly behind his boss, and began slowly shaking his head. He put a finger to his lips.

Jack didn't take the hint. "Come and sit down, Mr. Masa. Something's got you really worked up—"

Masa became hysterical. "You...you idiot! Didn't you hear anything I said? Anything?" He was squealing again.

Jack was truly nonplussed. The itch fest inside his underpants had been overwhelming and he'd heard very little of what the irate little man had said. "Got the bit about the British Empire. That's interesting to know. All we did in history was bloody pig iron. Oh, and you mentioned the meddling cartel again."

"Medellín! Medellín! Medellín! Medellín!" Masa screamed.

Jack suddenly understood that he might be spending a bit more time in the dungeon—like ten years. "Look, Mr. Masa. I am trying to help. Honestly. It's just that I'd never even heard of the meddl...Medellín Cartel, never mind how it operates. You've obviously had me under surveillance, so you know about my businesses and my personal life." He paused to think for a moment. "And I'd really appreciate it if you didn't tell Consuela about Tuesday and Friday nights at Lovebirds."

Masa was making huge efforts to control himself. "We're not going to tell anybody anything about you, Mr. North, not even that you're here. And that's the way it will stay until you cooperate—weeks, months, years, decades, centuries, and beyond eternity, if necessary."

That seemed excessive to Jack. "You can't do that. I've got rights," he shouted. "I'm European."

Jack was angry as well as scared. This wasn't fair, and he was an Englishman. That's one thing Masa was right about.

"Look at what you've done to me," Jack said, holding his arms aloft to emphasize his state. He was burned, sore, and bleeding, and his arms, chest, back, and legs were covered in swelling bite marks. "This is torture, and it's illegal. It's got to be. And that makes you a *torturer*. You're a torturer, Masa, and I've got the entire Human Rights Brigade on my side, for sure. You'll be tried for war crimes. They'll hang you like they did Hitler."

"Hitler shot himself, Mr. North."

"Well, whatever. I'm not saying another word until you get me a lawyer."

"Aha, so you do know something."

It was stalemate. Both men were dead beat, tired, and resigned to failure.

"Don't be a loon, man. Let me ring Jules, and then she can call Max."

"Who are Jules and Max? Associates? Accomplices?"

"Oh, give it up. Try 'friends,' although you won't have any. How can you possibly know all those details about me, where I lived, went to school, and my businesses, and yet know nothing about Jules and Max? Jules is my executive assistant, and Max is one of the guys I invited out to Majorca. They can both vouch for me."

"Do you really think we're that stupid, Mr. North?"

The answer to that is obvious, thought Jack.

Masa continued. "We're not stupid, Mr. North. The cartels are hard to break down due to their mastery of intelligence. The drug empires generate billions of dollars, and these criminal gangs can spend tens of millions of dollars to thwart our attempts to bring them to justice. They employ the best lawyers and use the best computer hackers to break into police and drug-enforcement administration systems to discover what evidence we have against them, as well as the names of informers and witnesses.

"Witnesses don't tend to last too long after that. The cartels wiretap phones, bug governmental offices, and drag anybody else they think may be useful off the street. If it's a beating or watching your daughter being gang raped, you usually talk. They've even bought taxicab companies to check on who's going to and from the airports and railway stations. Perhaps most damagingly, I'm sorry to say, there are countless police officers and even some judges on the drug producers' payroll. The cartels are the scourge of my country, Mr. North. But, unfortunately, they are also very, very clever—"

"But, Mr. Masa," Jack interrupted, "I'm not bright. I've no qualifications." He wasn't about to mention the *E* grade in information communications technology, as Masa may think he was some sort of superhacker. The silver star for the apple crumble didn't seem relevant, either.

"Maybe so," said Masa. His eye had stopped twitching. "But you see, the cartels use code words to initiate safety protocols in situations like the one you've found yourself in. The code word will be something innocuous like *cheeseburger*, which was actually a code being used until one of our undercover operatives discovered it—just before his death."

"But I don't know any code words, Mr. Masa. And even if I did I wouldn't say them, as you'd stick me back in that hole downstairs and throw away the key. It wouldn't be worth it."

"It would be worth it if your other option was a necktie."

"A necktie?"

"Yes, you heard me correctly, Mr. North. Colombian killers perfect signature cuts, a distinctive way of mutilating victims. It's a sign as to what awaits disloyalty. One infamous gang leaves its mark by slicing open a victim's neck before pushing his or her tongue down the throat and pulling it out through the slice. It creates a grotesque necktie. So, however repugnant the cells are downstairs, they would still be a more attractive proposition than a necktie. And there is my dilemma, Mr. North. If I let you call this Jules or your friend Max, then the telephone number itself could be a safety protocol that would instantly alert the cartels to your capture."

"Christ! Max is one of my school pals," Jack said, holding his throat. He didn't fancy a necktie. "I've known him since I was six years old. Max West of Gomersal, Cleckheaton, West Yorkshire. And there's DG, Will, and Stan, too. They're old schoolmates. Come on, Mr. Masa. Just how many other Colombian drug cartels have you come across being run out of Cleckheaton? Mum gets the *Spenborough Guardian* every Friday, and all I can remember are photographs of the mayor and advertisements for car boot sales, never any mention of global drug syndicates. You're being paranoid, Mr. Masa, if I may say so."

Masa seemed to be listening. He was worn down.

Jack continued. "Max and the others will be waiting for me in Porto Colom marina right now. And while they can't prove I'm not involved with this Medellín thing, at least they'll be as gobsmacked as me." He looked wistfully up at Masa, doing his best puppy-dog face. It always worked on Mum.

"You're lying."

Jack slumped forward and let his forehead hit the table with a thud.

Masa smiled. "But to humor you and anyone else here who has doubts"—he glanced toward the mirror—"let's call up your supposed school friend, Max West. Captain, please retrieve Mr. North's phone from the evidence store."

"But nobody took anything off me when I came in," said Jack. "Well, except for you taking my clothes."

"How would you know? You'd blacked out," Masa said.

"I know because all the stuff I had in my trouser pockets is still here."

Masa was incensed. "Captain!" he shouted.

The captain jumped to attention. "Sorry, sir. We thought the locals had done it."

"We are the professionals here, Captain Gonzales, not the local police who specialize in time-share fraud and handbag snatching."

"Sir! Understood, sir. Sorry, sir."

"I don't have my phone, anyway," Jack said. "It's in the car's glove box, and the locals can't be blamed for that, as they weren't even there. Max's number isn't in it, but Jules has it, which is why I want to ring her first."

The captain was doing his best to melt into the white wall as Masa gave him a you're-next-for-a-necktie look.

"Mr. North, are you trying to play me again? This Jules is a greater risk, as she works with you on the island. I agreed to let you call Max West, your *lifetime* friend, for whom you now expect me to believe you have no telephone number."

"Well, we haven't been talking since Blackp—Christ, this is madness. Jules is my executive assistant. She opens the post, arranges meetings, takes minutes, collates financial performance reports...actually, she does everything. She's brilliant."

"Well, it's nice to know you've realized the value of your executive assistant, Mr. North, as your value to me is diminishing by the second. I have no more time to waste on you. Another spell downstairs may help you remember something, perhaps even your *best friend's* phone number. Personally, I always carry a notebook with me. I recommend the practice of writing down important details, like your admission of running a brothel, for example."

Jack jumped up off his chair in a eureka moment, and then slumped heavily down again just as quickly.

"What is it?" Masa asked.

"Nothing," Jack said.

"Of course it was something. What?"

"I did have Max's number written down," Jack said.

"Well," Masa said, looking faintly interested, "where is it?"

Jack's forehead was placed squarely on the Formica tabletop—it felt hard and cool but not strong enough to kill himself against. *How can things keep getting worse?*

"Where is it?" Masa shouted.

"The letter's gone. Take me to the cell."

"Lying again."

"I'm not lying."

"So where is it? Show me. Or was it written in invisible ink? Perhaps eaten by a rat?"

Jack mumbled.

"I can't hear you, Mr. North."

Jack laughed. It was ridiculous. "If you must know, I wiped my hairy arse on it!"

CHAPTER 15

" Juliet. Harriet. Dinner is ready."

Jane was in a stinking mood; it had been a nightmare of a day. First, her much-anticipated tennis lesson with Franco, the new club coach, had been canceled due to rain. A lot of planning had gone into that lesson. She'd been tipped off by Celia, the club secretary, that Franco was from Milan and was totally gorgeous.

"He's young, tanned, and muscular, and he can service it up to me anytime," Celia had said.

Jane had reserved the first lesson at nine thirty that morning—a bottle of Chanel Number 5 for Celia had done the trick—she would have Franco until twelve thirty: three hours, the whole morning. The backhand needed a lot of work. The day before, she'd had a full-body tan, a paraffin facial, and a manicure, before buying a new tennis skirt and blouse, both tasteful but revealing. Sylvie from the salon had blow-dried her hair at eight o'clock. At nine, Jane was ready and very willing.

And then the lousy northern weather had ruined everything.

The north. Cold and crap.

To make matters worse, if that were possible, Samantha bloody Smith—the bitch from hell but also Jane's best friend and fiercest social competitor—had ended up with the first shot at Franco. The bloody northern rain had stopped in the afternoon, and the bloody northern sun had for once appeared. *The bloody north.* It couldn't even be relied on to rain consistently. Samantha would have had Franco's shorts off before he'd shouted, "New balls."

Incredibly, Jane's day had gone downhill from the disastrous morning. When she set off for home after having afternoon drinks at Charlotte's, the Freelander had run out of petrol. Her bloody useless husband hadn't filled the tank before buggering off on holiday. And, finally, to round off a thoroughly depressing twenty-four hours, Tamara from the beauty parlor had just rung, canceling tomorrow's body massage. Apparently, the masseuse's mother had been involved in a car crash in Warrington.

"But Tamara, why should that stop Sharon from coming in?" Jane had asked. *People just don't take their responsibilities seriously anymore*, she'd thought.

"Sharon's mother nearly died, Mrs. Bentley. She has a rare blood group. Sharon and her sister both gave two and a half pints of blood each and have been told to rest up for a few days. Sharon is drained, Mrs. Bentley, literally."

"Oh," Jane had said. "Tamara, it's just that I'm having an awful day."

Jane looked contemptuously across the kitchen table. In the middle, her daughters had constructed a twelve-high stack of empty Marks and Spencer ready-meal boxes. Family dinners. Delia Smith wouldn't have been impressed. But what was Jane supposed to do? Her bloody useless husband, Will, usually did all the cooking, and he'd buggered off for the whole week with his low-life friends. Jane had always despised them—*losers and thugs, the lot*—although that DG always gave her a funny feeling in the bottom of her stomach. It was his hips, so narrow, and his bum, so tight. *Yummy.* She had a quick peep whenever she picked Will up from that ghastly pub they all went to.

She pulled opened the fridge door and took out three more ready meals. Sicilian Chicken, Fisherman's Pie, and a Cumberland Sausage Casserole. *Prick the film four times and forty minutes in the oven. Easy enough.*

Will had stocked the fridge and left typed instructions for each day, but Jane had messed up on day one by allowing the girls to have different main courses and desserts, even though each product fed up to four people. It would mean two trips to Pizza Express at the end of the week.

The time on the large, round, imitation French railway-station clock on the wall above her head was six o'clock. Her parents would be here any minute. Jane and her mother would compare their respective men's countless flaws over drinks—as usual. In anticipation she poured herself another large sherry. González Byass, GB, mother called it, the product of one of Spain's most famous sherry bodegas. Mother said that GB was the only reason she hadn't strangled Jane's father years ago—poor Daddy.

The phone rang. It was Mother. She'd be delayed another thirty minutes because of a minor accident on the M1 just north of Sheffield.

Another woman's voice came over the phone.

"At the roundabout, take the third exit."

Jane heard a loud "tut."

"That's your father's other woman," her mother said. "Why he needs another woman to navigate, I really don't know. I'm quite capable of reading a map." She began to whisper but was loud enough for her husband to hear. "I think he fancies that woman, Jane. He calls her Elizabeth. It's unnatural, like ringing one of those zero-eight-nine-eight numbers."

Jane could hear her father go on the defensive.

"Oh no, Petal. It's just that if you're not with me, I might get lost. Elizabeth's just a backup."

"A backup? She doesn't sound a day over twenty-five. Dirty old man."

It was actually a bit of luck that Mother was delayed. Juliet and Harriet were harried into finishing most of the Sicilian Chicken. The girls were complaining that it was cold, and both wanted something else, but there wasn't time. The remains of the partly frozen meal, the unopened Cumberland Sausage Casserole and Fisherman's Pie, and the two sets of plastic plates, knives, and forks joined the other twelve empty boxes in the bottom of a refuse bag.

Jane pulled the bin-liner drawstring tight. After checking carefully around to ensure that nobody was watching, she dropped it into the neighbor's wheelie bin. Stage one was complete. Next, she emptied a Tupperware container full of potato and carrot peelings into the kitchen bin. The guinea-pig food—leftovers from Will's cooking—would do the trick. Mother always checked the bins.

"Up to your rooms, girls. Mummy has important work to do. And *don't* forget: I cooked tea again from scratch—potatoes, carrots, and fish—because your useless dad has left us all alone and gone sailing. Any remarks about M&S Sicilian Chicken, and you'll both be eating from Netto all next week."

Mother was a traditionalist at heart—home cooking, a spotless house, and a master at keeping her husband in check.

"Jane," she'd said after numerous glasses of GB at the wedding reception, "some mother-to-daughter advice. All that's required for a happy marriage is for you to manage the household, to cook and to fuck, unless, that is, he's not doing as he's told. He'll get the message soon enough."

Jane had been amazed. It was the one and only time she'd heard Mother swear.

From day one Will had done all of the cooking—Mother wouldn't approve—if she knew—and Mrs. Riggs came in twice a week to clean and iron. Mother didn't know that either, and she wasn't going to find out today. Mother's rules were useful but overly hard work, as all that was required to keep her husband in check was bedroom restrictions. Will would do anything to maintain his biweekly Sunday-night roll.

She topped up her sherry glass and sat heavily on the sofa, resting her stocking feet on the coffee table. She grimaced. Holes in both her stockings exposed her big toes. The nails were sticking right through. That was annoying. She'd have to change her tights before Mother arrived and also book in for a pedicure next week. She drank some sherry. *That's better. What's on the TV?* She picked up the remote and pressed the number one. BBC1 was the only decent channel. The local news program was just finishing up.

"And here is a summary of the Look North headlines," said the announcer.

Jane glanced out of the window.

No sign of Mother yet.

"The NHS in Yorkshire and Humberside is to cut ten thousand jobs over the next three years. Council tax is to rise by three percent for the second year running. And four men from Gomersal are tonight being hunted by Majorcan police after stealing a multimillion-pound yacht."

Jane spluttered GB down her white blouse; inadvertently switching channels to a debate about the efficiency of coastal-resort sewerage-outflow pipes, dropped the TV remote, and then spilled the remainder of the sherry between her legs as she groped to recover it. When she eventually got BBC1 back on again, it was the weather forecast.

What had she heard?

Four men had stolen a yacht? In Majorca?

Had Gomersal been mentioned?

She decided it hadn't been.

But why, then, was she asking herself if *Gomersal* had been mentioned, as surely the very fact that she was questioning herself about it must mean that Gomersal had been mentioned?

No that's rubbish. It was some other place that sounded like Gomersal—somewhere near Hull, perhaps. The people over there are always stealing things. Yes, that must be the case.

It must be. As the alternative scenario was that her imbecile of a husband had been brainwashed by his idiotic mates into becoming a fucking pirate.

Pirates. Don't be silly. Her mind was playing tricks. It was a ridiculous thought. The booze probably wasn't helping. She peered down to the end of the drive. Normality. Nothing but wide-open iron gates leading onto the main road. No reporters, no TV crews, and no police, and there was no traffic. Another ordinary, quiet afternoon, in the crappy north.

She felt a stickiness and discovered the large, wet patch of sherry across her crotch. *Oh my God, this just isn't fair.* She placed the empty glass on a side table and slumped back in the chair, closing her eyes. She was angry. This was entirely Will's fault for going away and leaving her to do absolutely everything. He'd be paying for this big time; that was for sure.

The front doorbell chimed, and the bell was immediately followed by an irritated *rat-a-tat-tat-tat-tat-tat*. The lion's-head door knocker must nearly be falling off.

Mother is so impatient.

The knocker sounded again, this time even louder. *Rat-a-tat-tat-tat-tat-tat.*

"Just use the bloody key I gave you, Mother," shouted Jane, as she hauled herself upright.

RAT-A-TAT-TAT-TAT-TAT-TAT.
RAT-A-TAT-TAT-TAT-TAT-TAT.
RAT-A-TAT-TAT-TAT-TAT-TAT.

"All right, all right," Jane said. "Hold your bloody horses, I'm coming." She walked quickly to the door and opened it. "Half an hour, I thought you—"

It wasn't Mother.

It was another woman—the angriest woman she'd ever seen. Instinctively, Jane took two steps back into the house, attempting to push the door shut as she did so. She failed due to the white stilettos standing on the threshold. The door bounced open again, and the angry woman stepped inside. Jane tensed, expecting an assault, which didn't materialize. The irate intruder, her face glowing bright red and her blond hair shaking with fury, marched straight toward the kitchen, and left her cowering behind the coat stand.

"I'm Tina," the woman snarled in passing.

Juliet heard the commotion from upstairs and came halfway down the stairs to investigate. She swiftly retreated as the blond storm entered. Two seconds later, her bedroom door slammed shut, and a chair back was heard jamming under the door handle.

Jane gathered herself and tentatively peeked into the kitchen. Tina was midway through an inspection of the household appliances. She disappeared from Jane's hall-based view as she pulled open the American walk-in fridge and then reappeared again as she opened up the dishwasher. One toast-crumbed dinner plate was inside. Tina clicked the door shut and pressed the start button. There was a whoosh of water, and the machine began to vibrate. Next in line was the double oven. Tina opened both doors and ran a bright-pink fingernail across the back of the glass, checking for dirt and grease. There was none. Mrs Riggs had done a thorough job.

Inspection complete, Tina perched on a breakfast stool and spun slowly around to face the hallway. She was still angry—very—in a cartoon steam would be venting from her ears—but her face wasn't quite so red, and her hair had stopped shaking.

Jane called in, softly but was ready to make a quick getaway. "Hello there? Er…Excuse me. Um…Tina, do I know you?"

The blond woman's fiery eyes spotted Jane's big toes, which were protruding from the holes in her tights. Jane gulped. Now it was her turn to be inspected.

Tina raised her gaze, pausing to take in the large, sticky, wet patch covering Jane's crotch and the sherry stains on the front of her blouse.

Worse humiliation was yet to come, as Tina's expression softened from hostility to pity—which as far as Jane was concerned was about as bad as it could possibly get. She blushed and twisted her hips toward the wall, as if she'd been caught nude by the window cleaner.

"Well, darling," Tina said, "we do have one thing in common, at least. It appears that our glorious menfolk have gone and stolen a yacht, and have then sodded off into the sunset. The question I have, Missy," she said—her voice rising to a painful shrill—"is exactly what do *you* know about it?"

Jane's knees wobbled, and she held on to the door frame for support.

CHAPTER 16

Captain Will headed the Conchita up the coast at top speed. But after twenty minutes or so, he throttled back. The Mediterranean Sea, which had been as flat as a millpond for the past two days, now had a covering of small, white-crested waves that were buffeting the luxury yacht and making for an uncomfortable ride.

"It'll add an hour to the trip," he shouted into the saloon. "But it's too choppy to carry on at full tilt without having the girls honking over the side, which will slow us down even more." He paused. "I'm glad we're going straight into Palma; I wouldn't want to get caught out at sea in that lot."

Max was sitting in the saloon and drinking an early-afternoon bourbon—another case of twelve bottles had turned up in the galley—in an effort to calm down and clear his head. He was facing the coastline and its high, imposing cliffs, which had been a constant feature for over half an hour. The *Conchita* was hugging the coastline in case of the need to make an emergency rush for shore, which seemed more and more ludicrous as time went by.

The near-vertical sandstone rock face was golden in the bright sunshine, the only greenery was sporadic, water-starved trees and some dried-out bushes that lined the summit. Consequently, the view out of Max's window consisted of 90 percent rock, topped off with an inch or two of blue sky—like a pint of Stella with a bright-blue head.

In a few hours, we'll be home and safe with some good stories for the Bull's Head crowd, thought Max—and, in his case, with some big regrets too.

Another gorgeous day. Shame we're all too busy running for our lives to enjoy it. He chided himself. *That's overdramatic.* Just like the emergency escape route to shore, but then the clack of the Uzi being armed sounded in his head, and he jumped out of his malaise.

He glanced behind him to see what Will was shouting about, expecting to see the narrow strip of blue sky on the landward side spread over the whole scene to starboard. He did a double take and swiveled sharply in his seat.

Jesus.

Out at sea, the scene was frightening. Biblical. A great storm was brewing in eerie silence. Smoke-black clouds the size of football stadiums were blooming and merging and expanding exponentially, fed relentlessly by some invisible and infinite resource. Very soon, the clouds would cover over the entire horizon. An orange, fiery glow radiated through the remaining patches of cloudless sky as the sun fought valiantly to keep its influence, but the growing darkness was winning.

What's that phrase Mum uses? Red sky at night, shepherd's delight. Red sky in the morning, a sailor's warning. Is it that way around? Once, he'd been sitting in the back of the family car on the way back from a day trip to Scarborough. Mum had pointed out the sunset. "Look, Maxi," she'd said. "Red sky at night, shepherd's delight. Lovely day for a picnic tomorrow." And it had been, too. On the strength of Mum's forecast, they'd gone to Harewood House Country Park for the day. It had been the hottest day of the summer.

Mum hadn't said anything about a red sky in the afternoon, although you didn't need to be qualified as a BBC weatherman or hear the shipping forecast to realize that the sinister event taking shape out at sea was most definitely a *warning,* and was in no way going to be a *delight.*

A dazzling flash lit up the sky. A billion electric light bulbs switched on and instantly off—bright light and then black dark. To the *Conchita's* port side was a beautiful Majorcan morning, with the promise of sunbathing, relaxation, and cocktails, yet a few miles off to starboard, the forces of Armageddon were mobilizing for an attack. It was a bizarre day.

The sooner we get to Palma, the better, Max thought. He wasn't too worried about the storm because it was still well out at sea and may not even be coming their way, but he could do without any other anxiety-provoking stuff going on in his head.

Maria came into the saloon and sat down on the sofa opposite. She'd changed out of her jumpsuit and was wearing tight, faded blue jeans; a plain, white T-shirt; and blue pumps. She'd tied her hair back and wore no makeup. Her only accessory was a simple leather bracelet. She looked spectacular.

It was the first time Max had been alone with her. DG, Kylie, and Dannii were down below in their cabin. Lisa was keeping Will company on the bridge, and Stan and Tracy were sitting arm in arm on the foredeck.

In some ways, Max was hoping to find that up close Maria had a zit or an odd-shaped freckle or that maybe one of her earlobes was slightly bigger than the other—something to confirm her as human rather than divine. He looked as hard as could while trying not to appear stalker-like or just plain sleazy, but he saw nothing. She was flawless. Perfect. Maybe she was divine—a mythical siren sent to lure poor, unsuspecting mortals like him onto the rocks. Maria's face would be the last thing he'd see before being smashed against cliffs and drowned. *Strangely reassuring. I could look at her for eternity and never get bored.*

Her portrait had taken his breath away, but it cheapened her. Maria didn't need to be half-dressed to grab people's attention. All she needed to do was be in the room, and suddenly life became fresh and exciting.

"Why are you here, Maria?" he asked, trying his best not to look at her thighs—and failing.

Maria was studying him too, her green eyes sparkling in the sunlight. *Who is this man, this Max West?* she thought. She'd met him only two hours ago, yet here she was, contemplating telling him everything. A voice spoke sharply in her head. It was Papa.

This is madness, Conchita. You know not to share secrets with strangers. Why would you take such a risk?

She replied as a young girl, her voice sounding small and weak. *Because I'm alone, Papa, and you are gone. I need somebody to trust, Papa.*

No, my beautiful daughter. You do not. It was naïveté and blind trust in Carlo that brought you to this dangerous place. Have you not learned anything?

Max could see that Maria was wrestling with some inner conflict. Christ, he'd plenty of personal experience with dilemmas himself, and he knew the signs: the staring eyes, the fidgeting, the forgetting of the thread of a conversation—generally, not being in the room. Worst of all was the sheer frustration at not being able to make a decision and move forward.

Whatever her dilemma, he could empathize. He reached out and took her hands. It seemed like the most natural thing in the world to do. Maria's fingers tensed, but she made no attempt to pull away.

Maria's consciousness reentered the room, and she relaxed. *She's obviously decided something*, thought Max.

Maria was determined. "It's a long and sad story, Max."

"Well, I've nowhere else to go. Can hardly walk to the shops." His outstretched forearms were beginning to ache, but there was no way he was letting go of her hands. "We've the whole journey back to Palma. That long enough?"

She smiled. "Yes, Max. That will be enough."

Why not? I've got to tell someone, and maybe this is the only chance I will get. Before Max could say anything else, Maria launched into her story.

"My full name is Maria Concepcion Victoria Rodriguez. Papa calls me Conchita—as I told you earlier. It's a pet name for Concepcion." She paused and flinched, recognizing that she'd used the present tense about her father. She didn't correct herself. "I'm a lawyer, Max. Papa is—was—too. He worked frequently with the governmental justice system. My mother runs a national charity that provides free education to street children, of which, unfortunately, there are many in Colombia.

"My beautiful parents have given me a love of the law and of how it can be used to help those in need. So, in my spare time, I work for Amnesty International. It's very rewarding work."

Christ, she's a saint, too. Then Max saw that she was crying. "Maria," he said, softly.

She freed a hand and wiped the tears away with her fingertips, but more tears swiftly followed.

"Tell me," Max said.

Maria closed her eyes and took a deep breath. "A few months ago, Papa..." She paused, keeping her eyes tightly shut. A tear rolled off her cheek and burst on the coffee table. "A few months ago, Papa was killed."

She bent her head forward and sobbed. Max gripped her hand tightly but said nothing; he didn't know what to say.

Maria composed herself again and raised her head. She was determined to carry on.

"I was studying at Stanford University at the time and, of course, went straight home to Mama. It was an awful time, truly the worst. All Mama and I could do was hold each other and cry. We cried for days on end, constantly. I thought we'd never stop.

"Papa's friends tried to find out what had happened. Nobody could believe it. Papa is..." She paused and let the sob pass. "Papa was such a careful driver. He used to say, 'Conchita, I must be the cheapest insurance risk in all of Colombia. Not a scratch in over forty years.'"

She smiled through her tears, remembering, and then her expression became grim again.

"Eventually, a café owner came forward. He had witnessed the whole event. Papa had stopped in the middle of a junction as the car directly in front of him unexpectedly braked. A speeding truck ran the red light and smashed straight into Papa's car—it was practically flattened. Papa didn't stand a chance. The truck driver ran off before the police arrived and was never found. The police think he was an illegal immigrant and was probably drunk.

"Mama and I were in despair. Life seemed so fragile, unfair, and so utterly pointless. I couldn't see how to carry on. That's when Carlo appeared. He knew of Papa, through work. Carlo visited every night, bringing cooked meals and the newspapers, and he would do the daily chores, even cleaning and ironing. He would stay for a couple of hours or so, whether Mama and I were up to speaking or not, and he would return the next day. He was an angel sent from God to help us, and I don't know what would have become of us without him.

I'll admit that the attention he gave me and Mama did feel strange. Carlo's father had invited our family over for dinner before Papa's death, and we hadn't attended, even though we were free. Papa made up an excuse. I put it down to a father protecting his little girl—apparently, Carlo did have a reputation with women—but I didn't really know. Carlo never showed that kind of interest in me, at least not at first. He was just caring and considerate."

Slimy bastard, thought Max.

"A few weeks after Papa's funeral, Carlo gently suggested I should return to work. He said my career would be a tribute to Papa's memory and that it would be a crime not to use all the experience and knowledge I'd gained from him. Carlo had really helped me through the grief, so I did go back."

Max knew what was coming next.

"A few months after Papa's death—"

Here we go, Max thought.

"—Carlo asked me out to dinner."

Surprise, surprise, Max thought. *So caring and considerate of him. My arse.*

Maria continued, unaware of Max's derision. "At first, it was platonic but over the next few weeks, I could tell that, for Carlo, it was much more."

Max's heart soared. *She doesn't feel the same way.*

"And I felt the same way," said Maria. "What girl wouldn't? Carlo is charming and funny and extremely handsome, and I already knew that he was good hearted. One afternoon, he asked me to marry him, and I said yes without hesitation."

Max felt a sharp pain in his stomach. It was worse than a mere punch. It was more like a body blow from a boxer with a long metal spike protruding from his glove.

Maria noticed his discomfort. "Are you OK, Max?"

"Uh, yeah. Indigestion. Please go on."

Tears welled in Maria's eyes again, but she carried on. "And then Mama told me that Papa had been murdered, and she accused Carlo of being involved in the drug trade."

Max stared at the beautiful vision in front of him but said nothing, and his face remained impassive. Bizarrely, the shock of finding out that Maria was engaged, though ebbing away, was still easily overpowering these new revelations of murder and serious criminality. Compared with everything else that had happened in the past twenty-four hours, murder and organized crime made perfect sense. Of course Maria's father's death was suspicious: another car blocks the road, a truck goes through a red light without slowing and plows straight into him, and the driver is never found. Max didn't need to be Sherlock Holmes to figure that one out. And as for

Carlo being in the drug trade—well, the guy had a superyacht tooled up like a battleship. *For God's sake, the girl is deluding herself. Why?*

"But I was sure Mama was wrong, so I carried on with my plans to marry Carlo."

"*What?*"

Maria wrenched her hand free of his, startled at the incredulity in his voice.

Max was startled, too, but for different reasons. He felt sure that Maria had left out huge portions of her story, but the crux was clear. Even though her own mother had accused her fiancé of being involved in the drug trade—and the arsenal below decks pretty much confirmed that—and even though Maria's father, very likely murdered, had clearly tried his level best to keep the aforesaid fiancé and his family away from her, she was still going to marry him.

Un-fucking-believable.

However gorgeous Maria is, she is also mentally deranged.

This is a waste of time.

He stood to leave, but Maria grabbed his arm.

"Please don't go, Max."

She looked desperate. He hesitated and then sat again.

"This all sounds strange," Maria said.

"You bet," Max said.

"Please let me explain."

He nodded. "OK."

"Mama's words kept coming back to haunt me. So, in the end, I confronted Carlo. I didn't know how to approach the subject, so I just asked him straight out."

"A bit of a shock for him I guess," Max said.

"It was. He laughed at first and then realized that I was serious. He sat with me and held my hands for a long time, just like you were doing before."

Max felt his face redden.

"He swore that his only business was the Bogota Coffee Company. He promised that he'd no involvement in the cocaine trade. I *believed* him, Max. It's impossible to be a successful businessman in Colombia without being accused of involvement in the cocaine trade. My country is riddled with suspicion and corruption because of cocaine, and to accuse somebody of earning money through drugs is an easy slur to make and one that's difficult to disprove."

"Do you still believe him?" Max asked the question sternly. "Come on, Maria. Wake up. This yacht is full of guns and bombs. You don't need an army and machine guns to produce coffee."

Maria was silent.

"Come on. What are you going to do if or when Carlo arrives?"

Maria was hesitant.

"Come on, Maria. What are you going to do?" Max asked again.

She knew Max wouldn't understand her answer. "I don't know for sure. But...but I have to know the truth, and then I have to marry him."

"What?"

Max jumped up again, but Maria caught his arm again. "You don't understand, Max."

"Too bloody right, I don't," he said, angrily. "How can you marry a man after finding out that he's a drug dealer or, more likely, a major manufacturer, looking at the cost of this lot?"

This time, Maria took his hands. "Please sit."

He sat. He didn't want to go, but this was just stupid. She was unfathomable, irrational, out of his reach, and, most likely, seriously bloody dangerous.

"My stupidity has brought me to this place, Max. Therefore, I must carry the burden, me alone. I will confront Carlo again. If he convinces me that guns and drugs are not his business, then I will marry him because I do love him. But if he has lied to me and does follow a life of violent crime, then I must still marry him anyway, as it's the only way to keep Mama safe."

Max finally understood. Maria had only just managed to cope with the turmoil of her father's death. She'd been broken and was in free fall. Carlo had caught her, put her back on her feet, and given her a reason to live: his love and her father's legacy. Her mother's accusations of murder and drugs threatened to take this safety net away from her again. This time, there'd be no one to catch her.

The Maria sitting in front of him now wasn't broken. She was deeply upset, of course, and fragile. But essentially, she was on an even keel— some people would even say calm. And that was really scary because it meant that Maria had resigned herself to her fate. She'd given up and accepted her lot—good, bad, or worse. He had been very wrong about her. He could see that now. Maria wasn't deluded or mad or dangerous at all. She did suspect Carlo, and she knew that something was very wrong, but she couldn't admit it to herself because that way led back to despair. She was trapped, just as surely as a bird in a cage, so the less she could prove about Carlo, the better, because it made ignoring the truth easier.

Max had another thought.

If Carlo is involved in organized drug crime, and if Maria's father was murdered, then what if the killing was drug related? Would Carlo have known about it?

He stopped himself from thinking any more, and he wasn't going to ask. He stood and went to refill his glass. *Might be a good idea to be consistently drunk from here on in*, he thought.

● ● ●

Max listened intently to Maria for another half an hour. He asked about the Colombian cocaine trade. It was interesting but frightening. Every now and then, he nodded to give the appearance of understanding. Occasionally, he'd throw in "Oh yes, I see that" or "Absolutely, I agree entirely."

He looked at ease, feigning a sense of calm, but on the inside, he was churning. If he'd been drinking milk instead of bourbon, it would have been mature cheddar long ago.

All Max knew about organized crime was from the movies and TV— *The Godfather, Reservoir Dogs, Goodfellas, The Sopranos, Boardwalk Empire*. All great and all violent. All exciting, too, with great characters, such as Tony Soprano and Nucky Thompson—mobsters and killers, both of them, but also strangely likable. Audiences wanted them to win, to evade the FBI and stay out of jail, and not to be shot dead. Soprano and Thompson were hardened criminals for sure, but they operated a code—usually only killing other bad guys and corrupt police—and they had a sense of humor and family values.

Colombian drug crime wasn't *The Sopranos* or *Boardwalk Empire*. Yes, there were assassinations, shootouts, and treachery in both, but unlike the TV shows, the drug gangs' violence was indiscriminate. There were no wry smiles and no good-hearted deeds. The drug cartels were led by cruel sadists, and their murderous deeds were brutal. Torture was commonplace, and kidnapping was an everyday occurrence, as was rape. Most of the so-called employees didn't even want to be involved, but they had no choice. It was either be a drug mule or work in the cocaine lab; otherwise, your whole family would be boiled alive—literally.

Only the cartel leadership—the really bad guys—and their trusted lieutenants really profited, and they did so on an unbelievable scale. They had lifestyles beyond the imagination. Personal jets, helicopters, mansions with huge grounds, wives, mistresses, servants, political power—essentially, whatever and whomever they wanted, they got. It was sick. They enjoyed millions and even billions of dollars while most of the Colombian population was half-starved.

But just who were these cartel guys? In Colombia, nobody seemed to know; even the bad guys themselves weren't totally sure. In the movies, bad guys were easy to spot. A purple jagged scar across a cheek would give a criminal away, or the barrel of a pump-action shotgun would stick out from under a long, black leather coat. Or else they'd be nasty to the waitress in the coffee shop or maybe push into the queue at the bank.

The top Colombian cartel guys weren't like that. They held family dinner parties. Cake and jelly for the kids, and laughs and games and smiles and singing. At the end of the evening, coats would be fetched, and there'd be hugs and kisses at the door as the host discreetly signaled to the car bomber. On the way home after a lovely time with your friends, as the wife is handing around the birthday cake, all lovingly wrapped in tissue napkins, you, your wife, and little Christiano and Sofia would be blown to kingdom come.

No way Tony or Nucky would do that.

Max had wanted to know about Maria's life, and now he did. He was kicking himself for asking. The faint hope he'd harbored of finding something in common with her was gone, as was the possibly of being able to help her and—the real reason—the chance to form some sort of relationship. The gulf between the brutal criminality Maria had described and his own boring, small-town suburban life was wider than the ocean waters separating Britain and South America.

His inner voice mocked him. *Wanting to save the damsel in distress? You stupid prick, Maxi. You're having a laugh. It's you who'll be needing her help, not the other way around.*

● ● ●

"Oh yes, I see," Max said calmly while picking a piece of fluff off his shirt.

Maria was impressed.

There was something solid about Max, something very reassuring.

He was a man at ease, both with himself and with the world. She'd deliberately been colorfully honest about the heinous crimes committed by the cartels. It brought home the frightening realities of her situation, but she also wanted Max to understand her predicament. Most people were shocked at the viciousness of the Colombian drug trade, but not this guy. He was taking it in his stride. Max had hidden depths, and she was happy with her decision to confide in him.

"I will help you, Maria," Max said, wondering if those words were coming from his mouth.

She was peering at him.

The two sparkling emeralds bore deeply. *She'll see past my pathetic façade. She will sense the trembling, panic-stricken fool cowering just behind a paper mask.* He held her gaze and even managed to produce a weak smile.

Maria was amazed. *How can he be so comfortable?* "Thank you, Max. After all I've told you about the cartels, I'm honored by your offer of support, but I can't accept. *If* Carlo is involved in drug crime, then I'd be risking the lives of you and all your friends, too. And for what? I can handle Carlo. He would never hurt me."

"Not while you're *his*, you mean."

He'd said it before he could stop himself.

Maria's face hardened. "I love him, Max. I've told you that my country is full of lies and conspiracy. The guns onboard the *Conchita* I don't understand, but it doesn't necessarily mean that Carlo is guilty—he may not even know about them."

Max had heard enough. "For God's sake Maria, of course he knows about them. It's his bloody yacht, as we've painfully discovered. And I'm pretty sure that Sunseeker doesn't do machine guns, bombs, and boxes of hand grenades, as standard, or even optional, extras."

"Innocent until proved otherwise," Maria said, defensively, angered by his mocking.

Before Max could reply, he heard Will shout from above. "Up here, everybody, at the double!"

• • •

Max answered Will's call.

Maria stayed below.

DG was the first to reach the flybridge, followed by Stan.

"This better be urgent, Skip," DG said. "You put me off my stroke." He was wearing a dressing gown and sweating profusely. He noticed the building storm. "Bloody hell, that looks nasty."

"Don't you ever get bored of shagging?" Stan asked.

Kylie and Dannii were standing together at the top of the stairs, fortunately just out of earshot.

"Stupid question, Stanley," DG said. "I treat every opportunity as if it might be my last. And on this occasion, that feels particularly apt."

"Well, I think that—"

"Guys, please!" Will said, exasperated. "We've had a distress call."

"I thought you said something about that last night," Max said. "And that it wasn't a problem."

"I did, but that was a different one," Will said. "At sea, distress calls are quite frequent. It's not usually anything serious, mostly running out of fuel or a sticky rudder, stuff like that. But it's the duty of the nearest boat to respond immediately and offer all available help. There's been a few distress calls, but none of the previous ones were anywhere near us. But now we've had another, and I'm pretty sure from the coordinates that it's that motor yacht over there." He pointed. "It's just over a mile away. Just there, see it?"

It was actually difficult to miss, as it was the only other vessel to be seen.

"Are you sure there are no other boats around?" Max asked.

"I checked the radar, Max. It's just them and us. It's our duty to respond."

"Like hell it is," Stan said, forcefully. "For all we know, it could be our pal Carlo wanting us to join him for afternoon tea and machine-gun practice, and look at that bloody storm. We're going to Palma as quick as we can. Somebody else will come for them. We've to sort out the girls and ourselves."

"There is nobody else," Will shouted.

Max was studying the radar. "Will's right, Stan," he said. "I'm not totally sure what I'm looking at, but there are only two green dots showing. Everyone else has already gone into port."

"And that's what we're fucking doing," Stan said, pushing Will away from the wheel and turning the *Conchita* to port and away from the other motor yacht.

"Stan, they could be out of fuel, or their engine may have packed up," Will said, pushing back as hard as he could but to no effect. It was like pushing a two-foot-thick brick wall.

Stan ignored him.

"Normally, it wouldn't be too bad," Will said. "But with that weather coming, they're in trouble."

"They could have kids onboard, Stan," DG said.

"That's right," Will said, seeing an opening. "What if it was your brother, Stan, and his two boys, your nephews? What would you do to the people who left them to get smashed up on the rocks?"

Stan was staring down at his feet.

"What are their names?" Will asked, turning the screw. "Gavin and... what's the other lad called? Is it Tim or Theo or—"

"Thomas! Thomas, for fuck's sake," Stan said.

Max and DG were smiling at each other. Stan was a sucker for kiddie guilt.

Stan ran a hand over his baldpate. "Bollocks, but we've got to be quick. Understand? If their boat's crocked, we bring 'em on here and leave theirs. We are not fucking towing them. They come onboard or else take their own chances."

Will nodded and took the wheel again, turning the *Conchita* back to starboard. Within a few minutes, they'd closed up to within four hundred yards of the seemingly lifeless vessel.

"See, Stan? They must be in trouble," Will shouted. "There's a guy on deck sending up a distress flare, although God knows why, as we're nearly to them."

Not so much up as straight at us, thought Max, suddenly aware of Will sprawling across the deck and the *Conchita* accelerating rapidly. Stan had thrown Will to one side and had retaken the wheel.

"What the hell?" Will said.

Max was desperately trying to stay on his feet as the superyacht banked hard to port in much the same way a jet fighter would in midair.

"Stan?" he yelled.

Military training had kicked ruthlessly in, and Stan was completely focused on the job at hand. He took the *Conchita* farther to port and rammed both engine throttles to maximum in one movement. The super-yacht's bow erupted from the sea as if she were trying to take off and swung around toward the shore, before crashing back through the water's surface.

The deck was a mass of screaming protests and flailing limbs. Kylie, Dannii, Tracy, and Lisa were all thrown violently off their feet. Initial screams of shock and surprise gave way to cries of pain, as knees, elbows, and heads all collided with each other.

Will scrambled underneath the captain's chair, the back of which both Max and DG were hanging on to for dear life.

"Stan?" Max shouted again.

This time, Stan answered. "That's no fucking flare!" he shouted over the roaring engines, while frantically urging the *Conchita* on. "Come on, come on, you fucking tug, move, move, move!"

Will caught hold of the chair leg and pulled himself to his feet. "It's a flare, you imbecile," he said, rubbing his cheek, which was tingling from the heat generated when he slid over the deck with his face pressed down into the teak.

Stan ignored him again. His focus was fixed firmly on the flying projectile, which had just roared past, thirty yards off the *Conchita*'s stern. It was a dark-green cylinder about a meter long with a yellow nose cone. At the back were four small tail fins around which a bright-orange glow radiated. The projectile's flight path was the cliff, about a mile away.

Will turned his head to follow it.

"Big flare!" DG shouted.

"That's no fucking flare," Stan said.

Will said nothing.

The "flare" met the sandstone cliffs—and detonated.

A flash of white light hurt watching eyes, before a low, rumbling, thunderclap rolled back out to sea. The air molecules around Max were resonating, and he could feel a pressure change inside his ears as a warm breeze blew through his hair. A plume of black smoke drifted up above the cliff tops.

There was a loud *crack*, and Max stared in utter amazement as a chunk of rock the size of a four bedroomed detached house broke away from the detonation site and tumbled to the sea. Over and over it turned before crashing into the blue swell, its entry point clearly marked by an explosion of white water that rose up from the depths like a great Icelandic geyser.

"*Shit*," said Will, DG, and Max in unison.

"Antitank missile," Stan shouted. "A Kornet, maybe. Russian. Has laser guidance, but it's fire-and-forget, and it's always difficult to hit a moving target, particularly one going from left to right. Fortunately, the guy shooting at us isn't an expert, although that's the first time I've seen someone just stick one on their shoulder. Usually they're mounted on a tripod or a vehicle."

There was no time for further analysis.

"Christ, there's another one coming!" Max shouted.

"I'm on it!" Stan shouted back.

This time, his actions were calmer, smoother, and more planned. And this time, Will didn't object. Far from it.

"Do something, Stan!" Will screamed. "Just fucking do something!"

Stan maintained a steady course. He appeared nonchalant, but Max could see that he was anything but. The fingers of both his hands were wrapped so tightly around the steering wheel that they'd gone completely white. And he was counting silently.

"Four, three, two—"

"Do something, Stan!" Will screamed again.

The missile was a hundred yards away. It was too late. The yellow nose cone was the size of a coffee mug saucer and getting larger by the microsecond. It was dead on target.

DG was frozen to the spot.

Max couldn't speak. *William Tell's son must have felt like this. An arrow heading straight toward him, between his eyes and up four inches, hopefully, to hit the apple sliding about on his trembling head.*

"One," Stan said, abruptly cutting both engines and spinning the wheel hard to starboard. The *Conchita* pitched horrendously and ground to a halt—it was the nearest thing to a handbrake turn at sea.

The missile passed twenty yards off the bow.

"Jesus H. Christ," DG said, watching the missile fly off toward the cliffs.

"Stay down, girls," Max said.

Will began to duck too, but Max pulled him back up. "Not you, Will. We need you to help keep lookout."

Dannii, Kylie, Tracy, and Lisa were all huddled together on the deck, nursing each other's bruises. They hadn't seen a thing and didn't want to. The fear in the men's eyes told them all they needed to know. Maria was still below, and there was no time to check on her.

"Forget that one, Maxi. It can't hurt us now," shouted Stan. "Keep your eyes peeled for whatever's next."

Max heard the second explosion, but didn't see it. He was concentrating on the motor yacht cruising parallel to them, about six or seven hundred yards away. A man, presumably the same one Will had seen on the foredeck a few moments ago, was still standing there, a tube resting on his shoulder. He was static and solid, like a bronze statue, just staring back across the blue void.

Max winced. The guy was enormous. It was easy to tell, even at this distance. It was the tube he was holding that gave it away: it seemed no bigger than a bicycle pump, yet the missiles flying overhead were at least three to four feet long.

"We're sitting ducks," Max shouted, keeping his gaze steady.

"We're penned in against the cliffs," Stan shouted. "It's no good; we're dead meat here. His aim is bound to improve soon."

"So what do we do?" DG shouted, coming to his senses. His dressing gown flapping madly in the breeze.

"We need space," said Stan. "We can outrun them, so we need open water."

The *Conchita's* powerful engines wound up again, and the familiar half-dome-shaped wake of boiling white water rose up as high as the stern rail. The great yacht surged forward and began to pull away from her pursuer. Five minutes later, the gap was more than a kilometer, and Stan moved over onto the same course.

"Smaller target if we are directly in front," he said.

Max hadn't taken his eyes off the dark figure. "He's not reloading, but he's not lowered the tube. I don't think he's going to fire again," he shouted.

"Is it the tube the missiles came from?" DG asked.

"One per tube, DG," said Stan. "But his mates could be unboxing another five Kornets as we speak. Only takes a few seconds to load and fire. It's our move. We've stolen a lead, but they'll sort themselves out soon enough."

"We're pulling farther ahead," said DG, feeling more hopeful. "We can beat them back to Palma."

Max wasn't so sure.

Stan confirmed his thoughts. "We can't outrun missiles, DG," he said. "We've been lucky twice."

Max was trying to think, which wasn't easy what with all the noise, constant buffeting, and abject terror. "What range do Kornets have?" he said.

"Three or four miles," said Stan.

Max looked behind him. The gap between the two yachts was maybe a kilometer and a half at most, not even a mile.

"Can we make Palma?" he asked.

"Sure," Stan said, "if we're not blown up."

"We're outrunning them," Will said.

"For now, Will," said Stan. "But it's a straight line up the coast. He has the best part of two hours to pick us off. He can just sit in behind us, ready himself, point, and fire. If he's got more missiles, well even that dumb fuck can't miss us forever. And before you say it, we can't go out to sea and come back in farther down the coast because they'll see us do it on the radar. They'll wait and intercept us on our way back in. We need space, three hundred sixty degrees to work in. What's that way, Maxi?" He pointed out to sea.

"A fucking hurricane," DG said.

"Landwise, you muppet," Stan said.

Max sat down in the captain's chair and tried to concentrate. The radar looked, well, like a radar, but how it operated was anybody's guess. The round screen was about the same size as an old vinyl 45, and anything it detected was showing up as green light. The Majorcan coastline was clearly defined, as were the *Conchita* and her pursuer, which were represented by two moving green dots. The rest of the screen was black—empty sea.

On the bottom edge of the radar screen was an oblong box displaying the range "+10 miles." And directly underneath that on the dashboard was a silver dial labeled "Range Adjuster."

Seems straight forward enough, Max thought. He turned the dial counterclockwise one click. The display changed to "+5 miles."

The coastline jumped toward him, and the two green dots separated. Which felt good. Instinctively, Max looked behind him again. The other motor yacht was still the same distance back, although maybe a touch farther away than it was a minute ago.

This time, he turned the dial four clicks clockwise to "+25 miles."

A long stretch of the south Majorcan coastline appeared, and the two green dots almost merged, which didn't feel so good. The rest of the screen was still black.

He turned the dial to "+55 miles."

To "+75 miles."

To "+110 miles."

The dial reached its limit as a familiar-shaped landmass emerged from the darkness.

"Ibiza," said Max. He recognized the island's shape from holiday brochures. "But it's a hundred miles away, four or five hours at this speed. And that's not allowing for hurricanes."

Max looked about him. It was three o'clock, and the weather was being spectacularly unfair. God or another supernatural was teasing them.

To port, it was still a beautiful day. Sunshine was reflecting off the sandstone cliffs and glinting on the choppy blue waters. On the beaches, sunglasses and sun cream would be the order of the day, an advisable precaution from the high ultraviolet light. However, out to starboard and the open sea, the swirling, black mass of angry, brooding clouds negated the need for sunscreen. All that was required in that direction were floodlights and a good prayer book.

Stan was smiling.

"What do you know that I don't?" said Max.

"I have clarity," Stan said. "It's death by explosion or death by drowning, Maxi. Take your pick. They'll get us eventually, up against the coast. So what's it to be?"

"I don't know, Stan. I'm scared shitless. I can't think straight."

"Stop it, Maxi," Stan said, cuffing Max on the back of the head. "This is definitely no time to shit yourself. If you do that, then you're dead already. So clear your head. You're cleverer than I am, and I need you to think. You can shit yourself when we're all safe again. But at that point, why would you give a flying fuck?"

To the astonishment of the terrified people around him, and most surprisingly to himself, Max started laughing. "You're right, Stan. Fuck it. So Palma's out. Even if we did make it back there, what's the chance of an unfriendly welcome? They can just radio ahead. We've no option."

For once in his life, Max felt absolutely sure. No dilemma, no positives and negatives to evaluate, no pros and cons to weigh up endlessly. No torturous mind wrestling, and no asking around for advice. There just wasn't time.

"Do it, Stan. Davy Jones's locker, here we come."

"Jesus H. Christ," DG said, slumping to one side as the *Conchita* turned starboard and headed out toward God's growing wrath.

Will couldn't speak; he was mortified.

• • •

Stan remained at the helm while Max did his best to navigate. DG and Will kept busy looking out to port and starboard, as it gave them something to do, while Kylie, Dannii, Tracy, and Lisa were still huddled together on the flybridge deck.

There was no sign of Maria.

Max couldn't understand what she was doing. Why hadn't she come back up top? She must have seen—and heard—what was going on. The explosions should have removed a few doubts about her precious Carlo; that's for sure. He checked the radar again. Ibiza seemed no closer. The other motor yacht had fallen well back; it was at least three miles off the *Conchita*'s stern. It seemed to have stopped.

"What do you think they're doing?" Max asked.

"Weighing up their options," Stan said. "I bet they still think we're going to make a run for Palma. Bottom line, though, is it makes no difference to us what they do. We're committed, and we can't go back. They'd easily spot us if we changed course."

The *Conchita* was gamely plowing on at speed, but it was an uncomfortable ride. It was almost impossible to stand upright without holding on to fixed chairs, the rails, or each other.

Daylight was going fast, and soon it would be dark. The choppy waves had gone, too, replaced by waves three to four feet high. A strengthening wind was blowing directly into their faces.

Maria finally appeared. She was wearing a red life jacket and carrying another eight, four over each arm. She passed them around after quickly demonstrating how they were to be fastened.

"Don't forget the whistle," DG said, trying to be humorous. He still hadn't recovered from the shock of seeing an antitank missile pass a few feet over his head.

Max placed a life jacket over his own head and tied it securely. "Thanks," he said, watching Maria's face. He could read nothing. She avoided his eyes and everyone else's. He could only imagine what was going through her mind, but she seemed to have found a purpose.

"Listen, please," she said, standing in the center of the flybridge. "The weather is going to get really bad."

"No shit, Kojak," DG said.

Maria ignored him. "You must stay in one place and hold on. Do not move around unless you absolutely have to. *Nobody* must go out on the foredeck. If anybody goes overboard, we'll never be able to recover them in these conditions."

"There's a boathook, Maria," Will said. "We could pull them in. It's clipped against the rail on the port side."

"Won't work, Will," said Maria. "In calm seas, it's difficult enough to pull somebody out of the water. But in these seas, it's impossible. The *Conchita* weighs one hundred thirty tons, and at slow speeds she'll be thrown around like a paper cup. It's not drowning that will kill you if you fall overboard, as you've a life vest on. It's being crushed by the hull or cut in half by the propellers. All we could realistically do is call in air-sea rescue or the coast guard, and that would be the safest option, also. So stay on the bridge or, preferably, go down below, as the weather is going to get much worse."

Maria disappeared below again but soon returned, this time with a large holdall. "This is wet-weather gear," she said. "There are waterproof jackets, trousers, sweaters, and hats."

DG immediately donned a bright-yellow, triangular hat, thinking it suited him. Kylie, Dannii, Tracy, and Lisa didn't agree, and all burst out laughing. He looked like some sort of eccentric admiral.

"Really mature," DG said. "You'd think we were on one of those adventure experience days. We're in deep shit, girls. That flare blew up half the fucking mountain back there, and it was meant for us."

"They know that, DG," Max said. "It's their way of coping."

"Well, I wish they'd get another—like being struck dumb with fear," he said, as Dannii gave him the finger.

"It will rain soon and get cold," Maria said. "Hypothermia will be a problem if we don't keep dry."

DG dragged the holdall over. "Come on, funny ladies. You heard the woman. Unless you've been training for just this very situation by wearing a bikini in the freezer overnight, you'd better choose a warmer outfit."

Tracy gave him a withering smile and selected a thick, woolly, red sweater and a red rain jacket. "If you don't mind me saying, darlin'," she said to Maria, "if it is your fella out there that's trying to blow us up, then you need to choose again. He's a real bad-un."

Dannii, Kylie, and Lisa, all nodded.

Maria said nothing as she pulled out some more jackets.

DG was incredulous.

"A *real bad-un*?" he said. "That's a little understated. He's more of a mass-murdering psychotic bastard, if you ask me."

● ● ●

"The bastards are definitely following," Max said.

Everyone had agreed on "the bastards" as the collective term for their pursuers.

"They're five miles back," Max said. "The radar's a total blank, apart from the two of us. We should reach Ibiza Town well before they do, or somewhere else on the coastline."

Maria was routing through the holdall. She was looking for another pair of wet-weather trousers for Kylie, as the previous pair didn't match her sister's.

"Maria," Max said, "what do you know about sailing in storms?"

She turned to face him. He felt that strange feeling in the bottom of his stomach again. Stop it, he told himself.

"Papa took me sailing when I was a young girl, in a dinghy. He only taught me the basics, but we went in all weathers. The *Conchita* is built to cope with heavy seas, but she will roll if the wind catches her side-on, as she stands higher out of the water than a sailing yacht. So we have to meet the waves head-on, not let them hit broadside. As the waves increase in size, we should slow down and aim the *Conchita*'s bow directly at them." Just then, a six-foot wave crashed into the port side. Maria was alarmed. "But not like that."

"What's happening?" Stan asked, belatedly trying to turn into the wave.

But it was too late. The superyacht started leaning heavily to starboard.

Kylie and Lisa both screamed as the deck became a slippery slope. Below decks, plates, glasses, vases, and everything else not secured crashed to the floor.

Soon the deck was so steep that it was impossible to stand without holding on to something. Once again, Max found himself hanging on to the captain's chair. He fell backward, his back pressing against the flybridge superstructure. Gravity held him in place, and he found himself staring upward into the black sky. *Jesus, we're going to capsize.*

The roll slowed to a long, drawn-out stop—an agelong pause. The *Conchita* was resting on the brink of oblivion, right on the watershed line. Max knew about watersheds from geography class. If a raindrop fell on one side of the watershed line, it ran one way down the mountain. If it fell to the other side, then it ran the other way. He never said it was rocket science.

Which side of the watershed line is Conchita *going to fall? Port and survival, or farther to starboard and—*

The superyacht whipped back the way she'd come and came briefly to an even keel before continuing to roll heavily over to port, but only half as far as the initial roll to starboard. Then she rolled back to starboard again, pausing a quarter of the way this time, before rolling back to port.

Max hung on to the captain's chair while watching Kylie and Dannii slide back and forth across the deck. His stomach was churning. It was how he used to be on the swinging boats at Blackpool Pleasure Beach. Finally, the *Conchita* steadied, and began moving forward again.

DG was ashen faced. "Thought we were done for, and that wave was a bloody tiddler compared to some of the others."

"I'm so sorry," Maria said.

Max didn't understand. "For what?" he asked, taking his hands off the chair. "You didn't cause that."

"For everything," she said. "I can't believe this is happening. Somebody is trying to kill you."

"And *you*, Maria," said Dannii. "That rocket thing wasn't going to be selective. It would have killed us all. Is it Carlo doing this?"

Maria was clearly confused. "I don't know, Dannii," she said. Her voice was weak and almost impossible to hear over the howling wind. She was desperately trying to make sense out of what was going on, but rational answers brought only pain.

She found her voice. "Do you want me to raise them on the radio?" she asked.

"Forget it," Stan said. "There's no negotiating to be done. We couldn't trust them, and I don't want to risk giving our identities away."

Maria nodded. "I understand." She whispered too softly for anybody to hear.

Maria had been holding on to the copilot's chair for support, but now she held her hands out for the wheel. "Stan. May I?" she said, more forcefully.

"Be my guest, love," Stan said, standing aside. "I've no bloody idea what I'm doing."

"That's not true," Maria said. "You saved all their lives." She thought about what she'd said and laid a hand on Stan's shoulder. "And you saved my life, too, Stan. Thank you."

Stan nodded sheepishly.

Maria took a firm grip of the wheel and steered slightly to port.

"We point the *Conchita*'s bow into the waves, and she will do the rest. See?" The superyacht cut through the top of an oncoming eight-foot wave.

A few minutes later, the rain arrived and reduced visibility to two hundred yards.

"They won't be shooting at us now, even if they get close," Stan said, "not that you could hit anything going up and down the way we are, even if you could see us in this rain."

"Doesn't rain imply the presence of drops?" DG asked. "There aren't any. It's just sheets of water. The gods are pissing on us."

"Kylie, do you think DG is religious?" asked Dannii. "I mean, he talks a lot about 'the gods.'"

Kylie, Dannii, and Lisa were huddled around DG's feet. They were holding each other's hands for extra comfort.

Kylie looked serious for a moment and then laughed. It was the first time in over two hours she'd not felt blind panic. "Good question, Sis," she said, smiling. "Is he religious? Well, he did shout, 'Jesus H. Christ!' last night, as he was coming in my mouth."

All three girls broke into hysterical laughter and started hugging each other.

Will was watching them with a sense of envy. "Strange what terror can do."

"That's females for you, Will," DG said. "The biggest mystery in the universe." He then noticed Will's colorless face. "Are you OK, Will? You look awful."

Will held his stomach. "My guts are churning, and my head's spinning. It was that pizza we had last night. I knew it was dodgy. I think I'm going to be—" He suddenly gipped into his hand.

"Aw, jeez," DG said, feeling sick himself. "Lie down on the floor, mate. That may settle you."

The *Conchita* was lurching up and down and from side to side in the heavy seas. Will prostrated himself beside the women. But after a minute or two, he climbed back to his feet and staggered down the stairs and onto the main deck. DG watched him cross slowly over to the stern, where he began vomiting over the rail and into the sea. The first long projectile was swiftly followed by three more in quick succession.

"Aw, the gods," DG said, keeping a watch on him. "Where is he getting it all from? That last lot must have sprayed out a good fifteen feet."

"Shut the fuck up, DG," Max shouted. "Go check he's OK."

"Sorry. It's OK. He's coming back."

A few moments later, Will clambered back to the bridge. Some color had returned to his cheeks. "Feel a bit better."

"We were checking the radar, Will," DG said. "We think you got the bastards with that last vomit missile."

"Fuck off," Will said.

The weather continued to deteriorate. Thunder crashed directly overhead, and thick, jagged bolts of lightning illuminated the great, black waves, which were rising higher and higher and taking on the form of shifting mountain ranges that blocked out the horizon. The wind was gale force, and driving rain battered the *Conchita's* superstructure and the exposed faces on deck.

Max felt the *Conchita* rising higher than before, right up onto the peak of a monumental wave. For a split second, he had a 360-degree view of the furious Mediterranean. The scene was terrifying, apocalyptic. He felt so small and vulnerable and helpless, a flower petal bobbing in the middle of a pan of bubbling milk, except the milk was black.

The *Conchita* plunged down the wave's far side. Maria spun the wheel hard to starboard to hit the next approaching wave head-on and then spun the wheel hard to port to meet another. It had been like this for over an hour. They'd made little progress toward Ibiza, a couple of miles at most. It would be days—weeks, at this rate—before they reached the island, if ever.

"I thought the Mediterranean was an inland lake for tourists on booze cruises," DG said. "Sunburn the only danger. This is the North Sea in January, and it's getting worse."

Another wave hit head-on. This time, one thousand gallons of seawater crashed over the bow and onto the foredeck. Two inflatable dinghies were ripped free, and both thumped into the flybridge roof before flying right over the main deck and into the sea.

"Christ," Max shouted. "If one of those waves hits broadside, we're sunk. We need to help Maria. DG, you take port side; Stan, starboard. I'll keep an eye on the radar and help on the wheel. Will, you don't look so good. Sit down."

Will had gone green.

More enormous waves appeared one after the other, but the lookout system worked well over the next hour. With the advance warning, Maria hit all the waves directly head-on. The yacht covered another five miles, too, and in the right direction, which Max deemed was good progress.

His confidence was growing. The *Conchita* could handle the waves, and she was moving forward, albeit slowly. Even the monstrous waves didn't seem quite as threatening.

"DG, where's Will?" he asked in a shout.

"Honking over the stern again," DG shouted back. "Poor sod. But don't worry. He's intertwined his arms and legs in the wires."

Before Max could look, Stan thumped his shoulder.

"Starboard!" Stan screamed. "Starboard! Starboard!"

Max had difficulty seeing through the driving rain. At first, he couldn't understand why Stan was so alarmed. If anything, the waves seemed smaller over on the starboard side, compared with most they'd already negotiated. But visibility was worse, as the cloud was lower. Then a frozen hand gripped his heart. The slate-gray curtain he could make out more clearly now wasn't a low cloud. It was a forty-foot-high wall of water that towered above the *Conchita* and was hurtling toward them.

It would hit them full-on broadside. They would be engulfed.

"Oh my God," DG said.

"It came from nowhere," Stan screamed. "I couldn't see it."

"Maria!" Max screamed.

Maria was spinning the wheel as fast as she could, but it was too late. The titanic wave was on them. It loomed over them like an invincible predator pausing for a moment to take in the joy of the kill.

And then the wave started to break.

Maria powered the starboard throttle up to maximum. "Hold on!" she screamed.

The flybridge's electric-sliding sunroof disintegrated as if it had been made of tissue paper, and the humans cowering underneath it were instantly submerged in seawater. Max gasped for air as saltwater filled his nostrils and windpipe. He coughed maniacally, instinctively wanting to hold his throat, but his conscious mind resisted the urge. He tightened his grip on the wheel and on Maria's waist, knowing that if he let go of either, one or both of them were dead.

The wave plowed on.

The *Conchita* was thrown heavily over to port and shoved unceremoniously along broadside, all the while slipping inexorably and terminally downward and toward the great wave's deep, sunken trough, which would be the superyacht's final resting place.

Only the tip of the wave had hit so far. The main crest was yet to fall, and it would have the force of a giant car crusher. The *Conchita* would be smashed to pieces.

Max spat out seawater and reinforced his grip on Maria's belt. She had a grim expression, and her fingers were locked on the wheel. She hadn't given up, and neither had he. She was struggling to turn the wheel to port and simultaneously throttle up both engines. Max helped her and heard the engines rev up behind him. It was a pitifully weak sound compared with the roar of the crashing waves, but the engines were working hard. He glanced behind him and saw that the black mountain of water rearing over them had begun to collapse. His heart was already pumping insanely fast, but it accelerated into what seemed to be one continuous beat. His throat contracted and curtailed his breath, but he forced his brain to ignore its impending extinction and concentrate on the next five seconds.

The *Conchita*'s bow was coming around. She was nearly running with the wave. There was a glimmer of hope. He gripped Maria's belt even tighter and closed his eyes. Surely, it would be too late. The wave's killer blow was already falling—he could sense it above and behind him. The turn was taking too long. It was agonizingly slow. Death was perched on his shoulder; time was up, life was up. And all they'd needed was just another few seconds.

He could feel the wave's cold breath on the back of his neck.

And then they were free.

The *Conchita* shot forward, finally released from the effort of making the turn. She was accelerating rapidly. The shadow cast by death was falling back, and the battered superyacht drove on still faster, powered more by the great wave chasing her than by her own screaming engines. But Max didn't care where the extra propulsion had come from.

Then, his hope died.

The inevitable had been only delayed.

Max saw it clearly.

The *Conchita*, pushed onward by the power of a million tons of rampaging seawater, was racing down the enormous wave's steep slope, but that clear freeway was about to end abruptly at the sea's equivalent of a brick wall.

The *Conchita*'s bow smashed into the bottom of the slope and plunged into the waiting trough—a yawning trench, a ready-made sea grave.

Max and Maria were thrown forward. Both crushed against the control panel. Others crashed into the bulkhead next to them, but he couldn't tell who they were because he couldn't turn his head. The pressure pushing him forward was too great. He felt as if he were going to drown. He couldn't breathe. His rib cage was about to explode. The bulky life jackets gave some protection, but the air had been forcibly pushed from his lungs, and he couldn't draw in any more.

The wave drove on; therefore, so did *Conchita*, deeper and deeper into the trench. The intense, excruciating pressure on bones, muscles, and soft tissue increased and doubled.

Max began to black out, enjoying the relief of losing consciousness, as the pains in his chest and back began to ease. Suddenly, he was airborne, floating serenely through the air and backward into space. He watched with a mixture of confusion and amazement as a lightning bolt streaked across the black sky.

Am I dying?

Then the *Conchita*'s bow erupted triumphantly from the sea, the entire front half of the superyacht rising totally clear of the water. As the *Conchita* hit the sea again, Max crashed wildly back to the deck.

He dragged himself back to his feet and breathed the sweet, salty air, ignoring the pains in his torso and spine.

Maria had beaten him back to the wheel. The captain's chair had held her in situ when the *Conchita* broke free. She was holding a hand across her eyes, protecting them as best she could from the driving rain, and was back on task, trying to pick out the next monster wave.

"I'm back on watch," Max said, gasping and looking around as he helped Stan back to his feet.

DG was back at his post, too. He was bruised from hitting his shoulder against a support pillar but otherwise OK. Tracy, Kylie, and Dannii had all crawled back to where they'd been sitting before the wave struck. They'd been lucky, too. They were just drenched, out of breath, and in shock.

Max tentatively straightened his back. There was no pain. It wasn't broken. He was OK, too. It was amazing that they were all OK. Bruised and battered, just like the *Conchita*, but all still seaworthy.

His heart missed a beat.

Oh God. Oh no.

"Will!" he shouted.

In panic, he looked back at the stern rail. Will had been sitting there, entwined in the wires. But he was there no longer. The rail was empty.

He scanned the rest of the deck.

Nothing.

Only windswept spray and bouncing rain.

Will had gone.

CHAPTER 17

Masa took a deep breath and tried to gather himself. He reached up to straighten his tie, but his fingers found only the bare nape of his neck. He remembered that his favorite tie was in the men's room waste bin, covered in vomit. *English pig.*

He stared at interrogation room 1's large mirror—imagining the men behind it laughing at his expense—and then, raising his sharp nose high into the air, strode out of the open door and into the adjoining room.

The room next door was dimly lit and hot. Three men were sitting at a long, narrow table that faced a one-way glass window and, of course, looked into interrogation room 1. Another man was sitting in the far corner, his chair against the wall.

Sergeant Hernandez from the local Majorcan police was at the far end of the table; Andres Chava, a handsome Spanish agent from Interpol, was seated in the middle; and Doug Clark, from the US Drug Enforcement Administration, was nearest the door.

Nobody was laughing.

The man in the corner must be the FBI agent that Clark told me about, thought Masa, glancing over. An idiot called Seymour Grant III. Ludicrous. Only the English aristocracy with their dukes and lords were worse. Apparently, Grant was the nephew of some FBI bigwig. Clearly, nepotism is a helpful feature of the American dream—for some.

"Seymour's had a difficult week, Alberto," said Clark. "I've said he can sit in as a favor to his uncle."

Masa could see what Clark meant. *Difficult, indeed.* Agent Grant was even difficult to look at. A plaster cast went from the top of his left shoulder down to his fingertips; he had two ripe-to-bursting black-and-blue eyes, and his nose was covered by some sort of plastic shield, under which black-and-yellow bruising had spread out across both cheeks. *Ouch.*

"Seymour," Clark said in a heavy New York accent. "Meet Albert Masa."

Grant acknowledged with his healthy arm. Masa ignored him.

"To the point," Clark said, doing his best to suppress a smile, "I'm not sure about North. He doesn't look like the new Don Pablo to me."

Masa looked insulted. "Oh, come on, Alberto. You have to admit Godfather North and the meddling cartel was pretty funny."

Masa didn't smile. "Escobar wasn't funny."

Masa was right on that score. Clark held up his hands in mock surrender. "OK, I guess we can all agree on that."

● ● ●

Doug Clark was in his midfifties. He was a bear of a guy. He stood six foot five, was big boned, and sported a full head of wavy gray hair. To his wife, he was cuddly and warm; to South American drug criminals everywhere, he was a worthy opponent. Clark had been a DEA agent for almost twenty-five years, and he'd spent most of that time in Colombia.

His first assignment had been the US-sponsored hunt for Pablo Emilio Escobar, known as Don Pablo to native Colombians.

Clark preferred to think of Don Pablo as Crazy Pablo, mainly because the gangster had owned a zoo. Elephants, giraffes, zebras, ostriches, and hippopotamuses had roamed freely around Crazy Pablo's ranch. Two decades later, to Clark's amazement, the hippopotamuses still did. Escobar also wore a new pair of sneakers every day, which Clark thought was mightily odd—he only owned one pair and had never taken them out of the box.

The first time Clark saw Pablo Escobar, he'd almost laughed. The guy looked like an old-style Mexican bandit. He could have been cast in *The Three Amigos* alongside Steve Martin and Chevy Chase.

But Crazy Pablo, as Masa had just said, wasn't funny. And the man was no fool, either. In 1989, *Forbes* magazine listed Escobar as the seventh-wealthiest man in the world with an estimated fortune of $9 billion, and Clark knew that was a severe underestimate.

The zoo was public relations. It made people smile. "Don Pablo is an animal lover, so the stories about murder are untrue," people used to say. "A man who looked after hippos can't be all that bad."

In Clark's view, Crazy Pablo wasn't bad; he was way past bad, about as far past bad as Hitler was.

Pablo Escobar could order the murder of anyone, anywhere, and at any time and he frequently did. His hit men were rewarded with bonuses for killing police, resulting in the violent deaths of over six hundred officers. Thousands of civilians and government officials were murdered, including over two hundred judges. Escobar's *sicarios* assassinated one Colombian presidential candidate, Luis Carlos Galán, and had tried to kill another, César Gaviria Trujillo, by blowing up a commercial airliner, Avianca flight 203. The plane crashed, killing 110 people. However, Gaviria wasn't on the flight, and he went on to become president of Colombia in 1990.

The drug cartels—in particular, Pablo Escobar's—turned Colombia into the murder capital of the world, a hellhole of violence, with 27,100 violent deaths in 1992 alone.

And when it came to nastiness, Crazy Pablo was an all-rounder—mass murderer, torturer, cocaine manufacturer and distributor, and pedophile too. Escobar had a penchant for teenage virgins, and he also owned a gynecologist's chair. The thought made Clark feel sick. The age of consent in Colombia was fourteen, and most of the girls Escobar abused were about that age, but that didn't matter to Clark.

Yet, twenty years on, and after all the pain and misery that the Medellín Cartel had caused, the city's poverty-stricken neighborhoods still pined for their Don Pablo. He was their hero, a modern-day Robin Hood. Most importantly, he was one of them—an uneducated local man who had become fabulously rich by crushing all those in the establishment who had opposed him. And he had used that extraordinary wealth to build football fields, churches, and houses for the ordinary people.

Clever Pablo!

Back in Washington, when the US secretary of state had asked Clark about Colombia, Clark had been frank. "Sir, it's the Wild West. Some *good*, a lot of really *bad,* and a big bucket load of seriously *ugly*—oh, and enough cocaine for the entire planet to get high."

"There must other trade going on?" the secretary had asked, slightly annoyed at the DEA agent's negativity.

Clark pondered for a moment. "Assassination is booming," he'd said. "Literally."

Colombia did have some high points, though. The women were stunning, for a start. Clark had married one, Lorena, a real beauty, although he only saw her twice a month because she lived in upstate New York, for safety reasons. Wives of DEA agents were a kidnap risk.

Clark's career goal was to rid Colombia of the drug-cartel scourge. He'd given himself five years, reassessed at ten years, and then twenty. It was an impossible task. If people could earn literally a thousand times more a day working in a jungle drug facility than they could farming food crops, then the results were a no-brainer.

Initially, the Colombian government and the US DEA had worked together and had achieved some great successes. A significant proportion of the supercartel leadership had been arrested or killed along with Don Pablo, and tons of cocaine had been confiscated. Street prices of the drug had increased fourfold in New York—a sure sign that the cartels were on the wane. But it didn't last.

A supercartel like the Medellín Cartel—and its major rival, the Cali Cartel—were large organizations employing hundreds, if not thousands, of people. Such cartels were drug-manufacturing supertankers and could be turned just as slowly. Therefore, law-enforcement resources could be easily targeted at the senior hierarchy—and they were. The supercartels were laid to rest, as was Crazy Pablo, but even before the bodies had cooled, so-called baby cartels sprang up to replace them.

The baby cartels were numerous and flexible. They were monstrous—like the many-headed hydra from Greek mythology; slice one head off, and watch in horror as another two grew. It was the classic cell-structure system used so successfully by the Irish Republican Army and Al Qaeda, and law enforcement agencies didn't have the capacity to respond.

The baby cartels thrived and multiplied. More cocaine than ever was produced, and street prices in New York went through the floor, which increased demand even further.

The only plus point was that these smaller gangs lacked the necessary business acumen to expand, particularly into new overseas markets, and the domestic murder rate dropped too. Killings were still rife, but they were almost always related to local turf wars, and rarely involved the public or government officials. The mass violence of the early nineties, when Pablo Escobar had declared war on the Colombian government, was over, but the cocaine trade was as lucrative as ever.

And now the cocaine trade was evolving again.

Someone had managed to unify the baby cartels—a supreme overlord. It sounded funny, but it wasn't. The cell structure remained in place for operational matters, but the local gangs were looking to a higher power for strategic leadership. They were like old English barons giving allegiance to an undisputed king.

And it was paying dividends. The supreme overlord had brought guile and expertise. Discipline. The petty squabbling had ceased; all of the cartels were concentrating on business and making money. Cocaine production had soared, and the excess supply was being used to develop export markets around the globe.

The age of the supercartel had returned. It was going to be Escobar all over again—except that it wasn't.

The new overlord clearly didn't possess Don Pablo's inflated ego and thus lacked his obsessive pursuit of fame and adoration. The new cocaine king was just as powerful as Escobar had been, and most likely was just as ruthless, but he was also focused on growing the business—and on remaining *anonymous*.

The Colombian government desperately wanted the supreme overlord neutralized, and quickly. They were terrified of escalating violence—because it would likely be aimed at them. Judges, police officers, and government officials were once again checking under their cars for explosives before setting off to work, and a fast-approaching motorbike was all it took to send politicians sprawling into the nearest shop to avoid a potential machine-gun attack.

Clark and Masa had headed up the search, and millions were spent on surveillance and data analysis, but to no avail. The new guy was a ghost. Clark and Masa argued about tactics daily and got exactly nowhere. Clark had even begun to doubt that a supreme overlord existed at all. Maybe he was just a myth—a drug Santa Claus?

And then a terrible thing happened.

Vincente Rodriguez was murdered. Ironically, the death gave Clark his first break.

That was how life could be in Colombia. Nothing was ever for free.

Vincente had been a lawyer working with the Colombian government to build a picture of the new supercartel's business model. Clark had met him a number of times at secret briefings and really liked him. The lawyer had been smooth, polished, and polite—in short, everything that Clark wasn't. The Bogotá police reported Vincente's death as a road-traffic accident, but Clark knew it goddamned wasn't. It was a cartel hit. It had all the hallmarks, and the national police were too scared to investigate, which as much proved it.

Clark reviewed the case file; one page containing two paragraphs—nothing useful—and sifted through the remains of Vincente's personal effects. His clothing and a leather briefcase had been pretty much incinerated in the fire caused by the explosion of the petrol tank. But a Moleskine paper diary, which must have been in Vincente's suit jacket on the backseat, had slipped out and under the driver's seat during the collision. It had miraculously survived, albeit it was severely charred.

Clark had studied it. The only oddity was that four dinner invitations, noted as "AOBCC Dinner," were in the paper version but didn't appear in Vincente's electronic diary.

It was probably nothing, but Clark followed it up, anyway.

Isobella, Vincente's secretary, thought that AOBCC stood for Andre Ortega, Bogota Coffee Company, because a representative of the company had called to inquire about Vincente's dietary requirements. Isobella had asked Vincente about the appointments, but he'd avoided answering.

"I thought it must be personal," Isobella said. "Although I did think it was a bit odd, as Vincente always told me about his personal engagements. He frequently worked late at the office, you see."

Even odder was that Andre Ortega denied any knowledge of the dinner engagements. He even denied knowing Vincente at all.

Maybe Isobella was wrong. Maybe AOBCC stood for something else.

Clark investigated the Bogota Coffee Company anyway. Nothing came up. The company was as clean as pure driven snow. Which was a red flag in itself, for most Bogotá businesses had at least some historical links to the criminal fraternity, even if it was just paying protection.

And then Andre Ortega's name cropped up again.

The desk sergeant pointed out to Clark that Vincente Rodriguez's daughter was about to marry, but it was to *whom* that surprised Clark. The engagement was announced in *El Tiempo*.

"Maria Rodriguez, daughter of Katarina and the late Vincente Rodriguez, is to marry Carlo Ortega, son of Andre and Camilla, owners of the Bogota Coffee Company."

Clark had never met Maria, but Vincente had talked endlessly about his "Conchita" in the few times they'd met. In fact, she was all he'd ever talked about, apart from the legal guff. And yet Vincente had never mentioned Maria's forthcoming engagement. The funeral had only been a few months ago, so Vincente must have vetted the lucky guy. That thought made Clark smile. The guy would have been grilled.

So why hadn't Vincente mentioned the happy news? And why had Andre Ortega denied knowing Vincente?

Clark checked the funeral-service videotape. It was always interesting to see who turned up at funerals—and even more interesting to see who was hiding in the trees.

The Ortega family wasn't there, either openly or looking from afar.

Did these two families know each other or not?

Could, two kids from Colombian high society date, fall in love, and get engaged without their fathers' knowledge.

Probably.

Two weeks later, a man, his wife, and their two teenage daughters had turned up in the Medellín River. They were handcuffed together. Apparently, the chain that had been locked around the mother's ankle and attached to a concrete block had slipped off. The bloated family had floated back to the surface. Again, no big deal in Colombia. It would be a major story in most cities around the world, no doubt, but it wasn't unheard of in Medellín, even post-Escobar. But it was very odd that nobody—not relatives, friends, or even the father's employer, the Bogota Coffee Company—had even reported them missing.

The Bogota Coffee Company, maybe not so pristine after all.

Clark put Andre Ortega under surveillance. Something smelled, but he wasn't all that excited.

And then he was. Very.

The DEA received intelligence from an undercover operative in London that a Russian crime syndicate was about to conclude a *major* Colombian cocaine-distribution deal. The operative wasn't aware of the exact details, but he did know that the contract was to be signed in Madrid in the next few weeks and, most significantly, would be signed *in person*. The deal was so big that the Russians had insisted that the Colombian leadership travel.

It has to be the supercartel. It has to be the supreme overlord. Surely.

Clark checked the airline passenger manifests every day. On the fifteenth day, he smashed his fists on his desk. There it was in small, black type:

Aerolineas Argentina, 24 July. Bogotá to Madrid—Mr. Carlo Ortega.

Was it really the Ortegas? Were they responsible for uniting the baby cartels? They had the resources; that was for sure. Had Vincente Rodriguez found out? Is that why he'd been killed? Or perhaps Vincente had been in league with the new supercartel. Is that why he'd kept the dinner reservations secret?

No, Clark couldn't believe that.

Vincente Rodriguez had loved Colombia; he'd loved the law; and, above all, he'd loved his Conchita. And he wouldn't marry Maria into the drug trade. No way.

The evidence against the Ortegas was circumstantial at best, most likely mere coincidences. But that didn't stop Clark's mind from buzzing.

He didn't believe in coincidences.

It was the Ortegas.

He knew it.

It was the goddamned Ortegas.

● ● ●

Masa continued. "Doug, Andres, we know that Jack North was talking to Carlo's men in the brothel, and he was driving along the same road as Carlo. That's more than coincidence. They were going to meet."

Doug Clark shrugged. "I'm not that sure. There were eighty-four men in Lovebirds, and North spoke to most of them, mainly bragging that he owned the joint. And Majorca's an island, Alberto. There aren't many roads to drive on."

Masa was incredulous. "Oh, come on, Doug. North is involved."

Clark remained relaxed. "Alberto, you've been questioning this guy for over two days, and he hasn't cracked. If North is involved, and I don't think he is, then he's small time. Carlo Ortega keeps all those but his most trusted men in the dark, so Jack North will be out of the loop. It's my guess that North is just unlucky—wrong place, wrong people, and wrong time. The only time he got lucky was inheriting a business, and my gut tells me that if he's done anything criminal, it has to do with that fire and not cocaine."

Masa was unable to hide his annoyance. "Just *how* unlucky can one man get?"

Clark leaned back in his chair and created an arch with his fingers. "I'm not convinced he's lying," he said. "And this interrogation is holding us up."

Masa turned up his nose. Clark knew it was pretty much pointless to argue with Alberto Masa when he was wound up. But Clark would get his main point across.

"Carlo Ortega is here for the taking," said Clark. "He's vulnerable, away from Colombia, away from his father, and away from the majority of his men. If the Ortegas do control the supercartel, then this is our chance—perhaps the only chance we'll ever get." He changed his tactic. "Alberto, this is your chance, too, to make history, to follow in Martinez's footsteps."

General Hugo Martinez was Alberto Masa's hero. A brave man, he was the police chief whom many in Colombia credited with finally bringing down Pablo Escobar.

Masa was having none of it. "North is the key."

Clark was not surprised. "I feel differently, Alberto. But the DEA will go along with what you say, for now."

Masa raised his eyebrows. "Are you saying you will disobey your orders?"

"No, I'm not, Alberto. But I do feel this operation is slipping away."

"You Americans and your feelings," Masa said, putting on a fake smile and trying to appear jocular. He had complete authority over the operation, but he needed Clark on his side, as the Americans provided all the surveillance hardware and most of the muscle. "It's facts and details that will lead us to Ortega, not *feelings*."

Clark shrugged again. He didn't say that the two of them might be interpreting the facts differently. Alberto was riding high on his Paso Fino stallion, so there was little point.

"The Englishman will lead us to Carlo Ortega," Masa said. "North was lying about his *best* friend's telephone number, he was lying about his alibi letter, and he didn't let on about meeting Carlo's men in the brothel—which we have on camera. He's a liar, and he's been caught. He knows more than he's letting on."

Clark was unimpressed. "Ever used a bare hand to wipe your ass, Alberto?"

Masa was appalled. "That's disgusting, Doug," he said, scrunching his face. "How's that meant to help?"

"It means just what the words say," Clark said.

Masa was defensive. "That letter never existed. I'd stake my career on it."

"You might be doing just that," said Clark. "The US government will go apeshit if we lose Ortega, might even rethink the aid budget."

That worried Masa. As much as the Colombian government didn't want American interference in their affairs, it did want the billions of dollars of international aid that funded everything from climate-change programs to Masa's own car.

"But why would North destroy his own alibi by using it as toilet paper? It doesn't make sense."

"It does if he was sitting on the john without paper and didn't know at that point the letter was his alibi," Clark said.

Masa was silent.

"We'll never know about the letter for sure," Sergeant Hernandez said. "North said he threw it into the sewer. We checked but found nothing."

"Aha," Masa said.

"Proves nothing," Sergeant Hernandez said. "It was a long shot, and a very smelly shot for the officer sent down to search. Chances are it was washed straight out to sea."

"If it was ever there," Masa said.

"True," said the sergeant.

"North wasn't filmed with Carlo's men in the brothel," said a voice from the back of the room.

It was FBI Special Agent Seymour Grant III.

"Seymour?" Clark said.

Grant explained. "Ortega's men were in Lovebirds at the time," he said, conscious that his face looked like a box of overripe plums.

"And?" Masa asked caustically.

Grant felt very uncomfortable, but was doing his best to contribute. He was jabbing a pencil underneath his cast but it just wasn't long enough to reach the itching skin up by his elbow—which was infuriating— and his whole body ached. However, his confidence—some would say great arrogance—was undiminished, as was his ambition. He was determined to use the calamitous events of the past few days to his personal advantage. Acute pain, bruises, and broken bones weren't going to get in the way of that.

As Uncle Owen had told him, "There's no bigger opportunity than an epic fuckup Seymour." And, boy, this was epic with a capital *E*.

Fortunately—very fortunately—only Grant himself knew the full truth of what had happened earlier that week in Santa Jerez. He now understood, of course, that it had been Carlo Ortega and his men inside the villa. *Pity that nobody told me so at the time. Might have stopped two FBI agents from becoming service martyrs.* He knew full well that Richards's and Johnson's deaths were squarely on his shoulders. *But, hey, shit happens. As long as nobody can pin the blame on me, then no damage has been done. Good result.* His operational report pinned all the responsibility for the disastrous mission on Richards. Obviously, Richards wasn't in a position to disagree.

Agent Johnson would have come in for severe criticism too, but, surprisingly, he'd been on Ortega's payroll all along—and so why would Johnson try to catch his own employer? Consequently, Grant thought it too risky to blame him. But it didn't matter, since Clark had shot the carrot-munching country bumpkin anyway. It had been the most dread-fully confusing of nights. The last thing Grant had seen before passing out was Agent Clark's gun barrel pointing at his chest, but fortunately he'd been mistaken about that, too. Clark had been targeting the Colombian standing behind him.

Uncle Owen had been thrilled. "You were courageous, Seymour—a credit to the FBI, an American hero," he'd said. "Didn't know you had it in you, boy, to be honest. Thought you'd run a mile at the first sign of trouble. But, hey, I'm pleased to have misjudged you."

Fucking charming, Grant had thought. *Some people had no faith.*

"Well?" Masa said harshly.

Grant could see just enough through his swollen eyes to notice that the stupid Colombian Masa was staring at him. "Carlo's men were in Lovebirds and not the brothel," said Seymour. "The brothel is upstairs." He knew this because he'd been to the brothel a year before—while holi-daying in Europe. He'd paid $200 for a Hungarian woman with massive breasts. It had been a major disappointment, mainly for her.

"So?" Masa said.

Grant stayed silent. Uncle Owen always said that if he didn't know what to say, then he should say nothing.

Andres Chava spoke. "Mr. Grant is saying that the nightclub is a lot bigger than the brothel, and the nightclub is where Carlo's men were, which is Doug's point, too. Much more likely that talking with North in there was coincidental."

"Exactly," Grant said.

Masa gave him a cold stare, but he seemed to accept the point. "Perhaps the FBI's finest would comment on yesterday's intelligence that the *package* would be departing from Porto Colom and not Palma, as originally planned."

Grant didn't have a clue, so he remained silent again.

"Agreed," Clark said. "And that's the strongest piece of evidence link-ing North to Carlo, but I still have difficulty buying it."

Chava was tapping his fingertips on the Formica tabletop. "Alberto," he said, "I have to agree with Doug. It's not illegal to own a yacht, forget a telephone number, or talk to people in a nightclub. We need to put everything into finding Ortega. We all agreed that the opportunity of catching Ortega and Rostov together was too good to miss, but miss them we did—and Ortega escaped to Majorca. Now we must widen the search, and to do that, we need more resources. We have to use the local police."

Chava took a deep breath. He expected an explosion.

And he got one.

Masa was incandescent.

"No! No! No! The only people who know the full details of this operation are the presidents of Colombia and the United States and the four of us in this room. And that's the way it must stay. The cartel has spies everywhere. Even the FBI has been infiltrated."

"I know, too," Grant said, "and Uncle Owen."

"What?" Masa asked.

"I told Seymour," Clark said. "Seemed appropriate, and I briefed Deputy Director Jefferson. But come on, Alberto; people are going to find out soon enough. We had a mass shootout at the Radisson yesterday, for God's sake—and somehow the news of a yacht being stolen has been reported in the UK."

Masa was calming down. He remembered that he had full authority over the hunt for Ortega. "It's too risky to involve others," he said, glaring at Grant. "I want one more crack at North. He's the key. I'll break him."

Clark wasn't surprised. His early optimism about capturing Carlo Ortega in the act had long since evaporated. He'd advised the US secretary of state that giving full authority to the Colombians was a mistake, but he'd been overruled—apparently, diplomatic relations were fragile.

"You have two hours, Alberto," he said. "Then we widen the search. Agreed? We have one dead motorist to account for already."

"And two dead Colombians," Chava said.

"And six Russians," Hernandez said.

"Russians don't count," Clark said. He looked at Masa. "So, do you agree, Alberto?"

"Only one civilian," Masa said. "Acceptable collateral damage, as you Americans would say."

"Tell that to his wife and daughter," Clark said.

Americans are pathetically sentimental, thought Masa. *Even those like Doug Clark, who've witnessed the drug cartels' cruelty firsthand.* Civilians would always be killed in the war on drugs. It was a certainty, and he was sure more would die here in Spain too, before the day was over.

"Alberto?" Clark asked.

"Yes. Agreed. Two hours, and then we mobilize." Masa left the room and called for his captain.

CHAPTER 18

"Will!" DG screamed.

The storm-filled night answered only with a howling gale.

"Will! Wi-i-ill!"

Max leaped down the stairs and onto the main deck. Maybe Will was hanging onto the stern rail out of sight from the bridge, or maybe he'd made it back into the saloon.

The driving rain was incessant. It was nearly impossible to see. Max held his hands out in front of his face and then pushed himself forward against the wailing wind to where DG was holding on to the side rail.

Apart from the two of them, the stern was empty. Max suddenly remembered the leather sofas and the sun loungers. They had gone, too. There was nothing to see but the rain and seawater being whipped across the deck.

"He might be in the saloon," Max shouted, and he staggered back to the double doors.

They were locked.

And there was nobody inside.

Will hadn't stood a chance. He'd been totally exposed and unsecure. Nobody could have held on. The wave would have swept him up and thrown him overboard as if he were a discarded wine cork.

How fucking stupid am I? Max felt nauseated. He was faint with grief at the knowledge that he could have stopped—no, make that *should have* stopped—Will from being in such a risky position. *Why did I let him go back there? What did it matter if he threw up on the flybridge? All that mattered was his safety.* He knew the answer only too well—because he was too busy cozying up to Maria.

Wanker.

He forced his way back over to DG. They both scanned the sea through bleary, rain-filled eyes. Intermittently, one of them would run from port to starboard and back again, hoping to catch a glimpse of Will's red life jacket. But there was nothing to see but tumultuous gray sea in every direction. It was a devastating scene, Mother Nature at her most powerful. Humans weren't meant to be there, and they definitely weren't welcome.

Max felt a hand on his arm.

It was Stan. "Can you see him?"

Max shook his head. "Don't even know which direction to look."

Stan peered into the night, moving from port to starboard and back again, just as Max and DG had done.

It was hopeless. The *Conchita* was being thrown around so much that Will could even be in front of them. They could easily have already run him down.

The propellers.

Oh God.

Max threw up on the deck.

"Did he have his life jacket on?" Stan asked. "Please tell me he did."

Max didn't recognize the expression on Stan's face, and then suddenly he realized that it was shock. "He did," he shouted. "Definitely. Maria helped him put it on."

Max grabbed DG and Stan and ushered them toward the flybridge staircase. There was no point searching from the main deck; visibility was too bad. Will was somewhere out there in a five-hundred-meter radius, and they'd have a better chance of spotting him higher up.

"The flybridge," Max shouted.

Maria was waiting at the top of the staircase. The blood had drained from her face. "I...I...I'm so sorry," she said. She was in shock, too.

They all peered out to sea again, but to no avail. There was nothing to see but the sea itself.

"It's my fault," Maria said, tears streaming down her face. "The *Conchita* wouldn't come around fast enough. She wouldn't turn. I...I don't know what to say."

She fell to her knees. Max dropped down beside her and wrapped his arms around her shaking shoulders. "It's not your fault, Maria," he said. "You were amazing."

He wasn't sure if she could hear him, but he carried on. "How you managed to run the *Conchita* with the wave was incredible. You saved us. And we know that." He looked up at the ring of frightened faces circling them and could sense agreement.

He pulled Maria to her feet. "Listen to me," he said. "Maria, all of you. We're not losing Will or anybody else. We'll get him back, and we'll all survive this."

They all wanted to believe.

"Will has a life jacket on, and the water's cold not freezing. He will survive. So we must focus and not let him down." His mind wanted to add *again* to the end of that sentence, but he didn't let it—this was no time to wallow in guilt; there'd be plenty of time for that later. "I'm going to radio the coast guard, and we push on to Ibiza to make sure a search is under-way. Ibiza Town is only four hours away, and the sooner we get there, the sooner we can help Will. OK?"

Nobody spoke.

"Stan?" he said.

Stan was still stunned. Fifteen guys from his regiment had been killed over the years, four of them friends he'd known since day one in the SAS. He'd been standing next to one, Lance Corporal Jake Wilson, when a Taliban sniper had shot him in the neck. And Stan had coped. It was his job to kill the enemy, and it was the enemy's job to kill him. War wasn't pretty or fair; he knew that and accepted it. Being killed for the country was a soldier's occupational hazard, a work-related risk, but Will wasn't a soldier—he was an accountant. The riskiest thing that Will ever did was put full-fat mayon-naise on his salad. Will resided in the *other* world, the "safe world," as Stan called it, a world without wars and bullets and without homemade bombs hidden in pipes. It was the world in which Tina lived. And Stan had believed that in the "safe world," all the people he loved—Tina, his mum and dad, and his friends, including Will—were safe when clearly, they weren't.

"Sergeant!" Max said.

Stan flinched. "We can't leave him, Max. It goes against everything I stand for."

Max understood. "I know, Stan. But the best thing we can do for Will is to make sure help gets here. We'll never locate him in this. And even if we do, we can't get him out of the water. We're more likely to kill him than save him. We have to go and get help."

Stan was unmoved.

"Stan, we have to go."

"Max is right," Maria said. "I know it's hard, but the best we can do for Will is to ensure that a search is underway."

"Stan?" Max asked.

Stan nodded and walked away.

"Right," Max said. "Everybody back to work. We can't help Will if we sink. DG, port watch. Stan will take starboard."

Maria slipped back behind the wheel. Her face was expressionless, and her eyes were blank, but Max knew what she was thinking—what they were all thinking.

Will is dead. He felt thudding next to his feet. It was Lisa pounding the deck with her fists. She was distraught.

"I love him!" she yelled.

Max put his hand on her arm, but she threw it off and spat in his face. "Bastard!"

Kylie and Dannii rushed past him and knelt beside her. Max looked away, salty tears mixing with the cold raindrops.

"You OK, Max?" DG asked. He'd seen what had happened.

Max nodded.

"It's not your fault, either," DG said.

Max couldn't look him in the eye but nodded again, keeping his gaze firmly on the radar screen.

"Two o'clock starboard," Stan called out.

Maria changed course and met the wave head-on.

It was another big wave but nothing like the monster that had taken Will. Seawater crashed over the bow rail.

"Nine o'clock," DG shouted.

Maria steered to port.

It carried on like this for the next two hours, with the waves continuing to reduce in significance. The mountainous peaks of the early hours of the morning had gone, transformed into bleak, rolling gray hills. The howling gale and pounding rain was on the wane too—giving way to strong winds and heavy showers.

Off the bow, a new day was dawning.

Ibiza Town was two hours away.

Max was standing behind Maria's left shoulder, pretending to know what he was doing, trying to hoodwink his own panicking mind, but fooling nobody, least of all himself. Occasionally, Maria's hair would blow into his face—he should've moved to one side, but he enjoyed the feeling. Then he felt dejected, as this would be the closest he would ever get to her. Then he felt guilty for feeling sorry for himself about a woman he'd met about five minutes ago, when a friend of nearly thirty years was drowning, or *had drowned*—and he was busy sailing off in the opposite direction.

The heavy white clouds parted, and the morning sun broke through.

Max shielded his eyes.

Yesterday, the sunshine had radiated optimism, but today it transmitted pain and hurt his eyes. The brightness betrayed a harsh reality: he would never feel good again. From this day forward until his death, it would be abject misery. How could it be anything else? Whenever it rained or he met up with Stan or DG in the Bull's Head, drove past the old school, saw a boat on TV or in a magazine, had a conversation at work or the hairdresser's about holidays, or a million other things, then his next thought would always be about Will's death and his own culpability.

What could he say to Juliet and Harriet?

He could hear the girls in his head. *Uncle Max, didn't you help Daddy?*

He could see their beautiful, distraught faces, waiting for his answer.

But what could he say?

The truth?

Well, girls, you see I fell for this beautiful girl. Maria is her name. She's great and clever, and you'd both really like her, and so I ignored your dad. We did have a quick look for him when he fell overboard, but we had to leave because the weather was really awful. We sailed to Ibiza and saved ourselves, and then I came straight home to tell you.

No George Medal for bravery, that was for sure.

He wouldn't go to jail. In the eyes of the law, he'd committed no crime. But in his own mind, he was guilty as sin.

He rechecked the radar. The innocuous blipping green dot—the cause of the fear driving them on—was eight miles off the stern and falling farther back. The *Conchita* was really gaining ground now, powering up and down the gentle slopes of the undulating swell, and increasing speed as the Mediterranean continued to flatten. The bastards were struggling out of the storm, but they were still doggedly in pursuit.

Max was more convinced than ever that it was Maria's fiancé behind them. In addition to being a multimillionaire and devilishly handsome, Maria told him that Carlo was also an experienced sailor, an Olympic-standard fencer, and a crack pistol shot.

Well, he bloody well would be, wouldn't he?

Apparently, the guy oozed natural talent and was a perfectionist, which was a powerful combination, but one that Max recognized was also taxing and stressful. The pursuit of excellence had driven him hard in his early teens, but somewhere on the road he'd pulled over into a lay-by and allowed mediocrity and an easy life to catch up.

"Carlo is very intelligent," Maria had told him. "As well as Spanish, he's fluent in Portuguese, Italian, French, and, of course, English."

"Of course he is," Max had replied, trying his best not to sound sarcastic but failing miserably. The guy was like some sort of superbeing. "Can he fly?" he'd asked.

"Not without a plane," Maria had said, smiling. "But sometimes he does appear out of thin air."

Carlo's mastered telepathic teleportation, he thought.

Yet something didn't quite stack up about Super Carlo. Max had been trying to pin his thoughts down for hours, but couldn't think straight. Now it came to him.

Why on earth would a multitalented, multilingual, multimillionaire superbeing, who was engaged to the most fabulous woman, attempt to blow up his own superyacht and with Maria on it?

The question did assume that Carlo was on the other yacht, but Max had got past assuming. It had to be Carlo.

The second part of the question was easy: somehow Carlo wasn't aware that Maria was onboard. It was also highly improbable he knew the Bull's Head Pool Team had nicked the *Conchita*. Otherwise, instead of launching antitank missiles and demolishing half the Majorcan coastline, he'd have taken a less aggressive approach and just told them all to get the fuck off his yacht. Much more efficient and naturally, they would all have complied. But—and it was a really big *but*—Carlo hadn't done that. He'd made absolutely no attempt to find out who was onboard before he fired. For a superintelligent, supertalented supercriminal, who, from what Maria had said, also prized his anonymity, that was a really dumb thing to do. He'd failed in his attempt to hit the *Conchita*, and the explosions would be heard for miles. Even sun-sleepy Majorcans would report missile detonations to the police, and someone must have heard or seen what happened, even with the storm brewing.

"Stan," Max said, "show me where you found the guns."

"Follow me," Stan said.

The lower deck was hot and noisy, and the floor was vibrating slightly. At the end of the narrow passageway was an oval-shaped wooden door. Stan opened it and the sound of the engines increased.

Max stooped and followed Stan inside. The two engines dominated the room. There were no moving parts to see, but the air prickled with energy.

"Beauties, aren't they?" Stan said. "Generate north of eight thousand horsepower. I don't think they're standard—they're souped-up."

Max placed a palm down on an engine block and felt the rhythmic pulsing vibrate through his bones. *Powerful engines. All very interesting but not what I need to know.* "Where are the *guns*?"

Max couldn't see an arsenal or the space for one, either. The engines were sitting side by side in the center of the room. The end wall was bare, except for an empty coat rack. One sidewall housed a large desk of dials and flashing lights, presumably the engine controls, and the wall behind Max was covered by five life-sized posters.

No guns!

However, the posters were worth a look.

Marilyn Monroe, Beyoncé, Scarlett Johansson, and Brigitte Bardot. Four amazing women either side of someone's clear favorite.

Max's, too.

Jennifer Aniston—dressed as Princess Leia. *Sensational. Truly sensational. Justin Theroux is such a lucky bastard.*

"Stan?"

"Beyoncé," Stan said, admiring the pop queen.

"Not the women—the guns. Where are the guns?"

"Oh. Right."

Stan unclipped a silver pen from its bracket on the control desk and walked over to where an incredibly glamorous Marilyn Monroe was stepping out of a New York taxi. As Max watched, fascinated, Stan pushed the tip of the pen into a small hole in the poster, where Marylyn's diamond earring should have been.

Stan swiveled the pen.

Click.

Something had unlocked.

Stan walked to his right, holding the pen as a handle, and the wall went along with him. Jennifer Aniston, Beyoncé, and half of Marilyn Monroe disappeared behind Scarlett Johansson and Brigitte Bardot—revealing the arsenal.

"Left to right," said Stan, tapping each weapon. "M16 assault rifles—standard US Army issue, although the Yanks are switching to M4 carbines for combat units—six of them, but there are spaces for eight. Here, we have two Minimis, Belgian-made light machine guns; again, one is out. So our pal Carlo could have a couple of M16s and a Minimi. Not pleasant. The Minimi fires over a thousand rounds a minute—not that the Belgians ever fire guns; they let us do that for them—but they sure can design them." He moved on. "Israeli Uzis—two of them—including the one I had earlier—designed by Uziel Gal—beautiful, simple, and deadly. The Uzi was one of the first weapons to use a telescoping bolt design, which allows the magazine to be housed in the pistol grip—makes for a shorter but better-balanced weapon."

Clearly, the Uzi was one of Stan's favorites.

"There's also a few handguns—Steyrs and SIG Sauers, mostly. The steel boxes contain ammo clips, mortar bombs, eight grenades, some phosphorous smoke screens, and a pile of HE. Oh, and there's a pack of detonators."

"HE?" Max asked.

"High explosive," Stan said, lifting what looked like a section of drainpipe. "And this is a Russian Kornet antitank missile. There are three. I didn't see them earlier on; I was too shocked at finding the Uzis and M16s instead of crates of San Miguel and bourbon. Kornets are serious ordnance—can disable a sixty-ton Abrams battle tank, as they did in the 2003 invasion of Iraq. Fortunately for us, the guy firing them yesterday wasn't too hot with the laser guidance. Otherwise, we'd be toast." He gently replaced the thick, green tube in its wooden slot.

"Last thing is the red box. Contains PE4—sorry, plastic explosive. Enough to sink Majorca. Want me to take you through the ammo?"

It was a dizzying array of firepower. Max didn't fully comprehend the scale of destruction that it could wreak, but it was horrific. "No need for that," Max said. "But tell me, how on earth did you guess to look behind the wall?"

Stan was confused. "Guess? I didn't guess. It's obvious. Stands out like a sore thumb. To create the recess meant pinching a good foot from this side of the room. So it's uneven."

To prove his point, he measured the room by walking toe to heel across the floor. Sure enough, the side they were standing on was narrower by a size 12 boot.

"I was hunting for booze," Stan said. "Reckoned old Jack would keep it well hidden from his guests, him being a stingy bastard. So as soon as I came in here and saw that pen, I thought 'aye, aye.' I mean, why else would anybody clip a pen on there?"

To have one handy, thought Max. *Perhaps note some power readings, tick a time sheet, play Sudoku, do a crossword, and many other things.*

Stan was inspecting a handgun.

Here was a guy who left school with a General Certificate of Secondary Education grade D in art and grade 1 in piano, and that was only because his mother bribed the piano teacher with tea and cakes after every Wednesday's lesson. *She needn't have bothered.* The music examiner was certain to pass her son, if only to make sure he never had to listen to Stan's excruciating rendition of "Greensleeves" ever again. The butterfly bun bribes were unnecessary.

Max refocused. "Stan, if you had something really valuable on this boat, something much more valuable than these weapons, something that must stay hidden, however hard anybody searched for it, then where would you put it?"

Stan looked down at the deck. "Under there. Depends how big we're talking, of course. If it were small, I'd seal it in a watertight bag and put it in the plumbing. If it were big, like this lot," he said, gesturing at the arsenal, "then it would have to be a purpose-built hidey-hole like this. Why?"

"Because there's *something else* on this boat; I'm sure of it. It's something so valuable that Carlo would rather destroy the *Conchita* and everybody onboard than risk it falling into the wrong person's hands—from his point of view, at least."

"What do you think it is?" Stan said.

"I've no idea. But it's here somewhere. I know it. It's the only thing that makes sense. And whatever it might be, it's the difference between life and death. Our lives. So I need you to find it."

Stan nodded. "I'm on it," he said and immediately started tapping the deck.

Max paused at the engine-room door.

Stan looked over.

"Stan," Max said, "I'm bloody glad you're on my side."

"Ditto, Maxi. Fucking ditto."

● ● ●

The island of Ibiza filled the horizon. Ibiza Town and its historic cathedral were clearly visible. Maria was still at the helm, and Max was focusing on the radar.

The bastards were fifteen miles back and appeared to have made it through the storm.

"We're twenty minutes out from the marinas. There're at least two big ones, and we've an hour's leeway," Max said. "I'll call the cops as soon as I get a signal, just in case there's an unfriendly welcoming party."

"What are you going to say?" DG asked.

"No big drama," Max said. "Just enough of a story to make them take me seriously and send someone down. Our main priorities are to drop the girls off and make sure there's a full search going on for Will."

Max had raised the coast guard on the ship-to-shore radio earlier. Thirty minutes before, they'd spotted an orange helicopter heading out to sea.

"Bringing the plods down to us is the right thing to do," DG said. "They'll think we're a right set of wankers, buggering off on the wrong yacht, but that's better than joining the unembarrassed dead. Do you think that chopper will find Will?"

DG's tone betrayed his pessimism. Max felt the same, but didn't answer.

A signal bar appeared on his mobile phone. He immediately dialed the local police. On the fourth ring, it was picked up by a police operator, who, fortunately, spoke good English. *Some luck at last.* Max quickly explained how he and his friends had found a handgun aboard their charter yacht. The operator agreed to send someone down to the quayside to recover it.

"But there're loads of guns," DG said.

"Why mention them?" Max said. "One's enough to get a bit of security at the dock—we don't need the Spanish army."

"You sure?" DG said.

Max didn't answer.

They were approaching the harbor wall. Maria throttled back to three knots. The *Conchita*'s bow nestled softly into the water. Moments later, they slipped through the concrete opening and into a huge man-made lagoon.

The *Conchita* was the only craft moving. Max felt horribly conspicuous, as if he were walking out alone into the middle of a vast, empty stadium. There were no waves in the lagoon. The water was flat and black, like tarmac. After the swirling seas, it looked solid enough to stand on.

The Marina Botafoch entrance was ahead to starboard about a kilometer away, which was a long way at three knots when the killers pursuing you were doing nearer to twenty.

Maria wouldn't increase speed. "The enclosed space is dangerous for *Conchita*," she said.

Max couldn't see why. Still, they had some time. He anxiously scanned the harbor, imagining that speedboats bristling with gunmen were about to burst out from behind the half-loaded container ship moored by a large warehouse. But the only movement came from the water rippling around the *Conchita*, and the only sound came from the groaning ropes holding the container ship in check.

He rechecked the radar. The green blip was much closer. "Maria."

She recognized the alarm in his voice.

The *Conchita's* engines picked up to five knots.

It was still painful going.

As the Marina Botafoch came into full view, the *Conchita* slowed again and crawled in through the open metal gates. *Thank God*, Max thought. Now all they had to do was tie up.

Or so he thought.

There was a problem.

DG summed it up. "There's not space for a fucking canoe. It's full. Packed solid. Worse than parking at United. It's the weather. Everybody is in, and you can't exactly blame 'em."

They crept slowly up and down the long rows of yachts.

Four rows. No spaces.

Five rows. No spaces.

The green blip was three miles from the harbor and closing in rapidly.

Six rows.

Still nothing.

Saturday mornings in the Tesco car park, Max thought. Except at least there, he could pull up in the middle of an aisle and wait for somebody to leave. After a minute or two, a shopper would appear with a trolley full of provisions, and car-park chicken—the early-weekend game of necessity rather than choice in Cleckheaton—would begin. Other frustrated waiting drivers—ignoring the first in line principle—were also ready to pounce. Max usually won these encounters on account of his Vauxhall Astra being a heap of junk. Another dent would probably straighten out an old one.

However, this wasn't Tesco, and they'd could wait for somebody to leave. It could be days before anybody turned up.

They had minutes.

Stan appeared on the bridge. "Found nothing so far, Maxi. But I've still to check under the front cabins. I've come up for air. It's sweltering down there. Last bit will take me another twenty minutes."

"What are you doing down there, Stan?" DG asked.

"We've not time, Stan," Max said.

Stan looked around. "Bollocks," he said, ignoring DG's question. "I'll go up front and have a look over the far side." He picked up the binoculars and raced down the stairs to the main deck.

The results didn't improve; the marina was full.

Ten minutes later, they'd checked out the Nueva Marina with the same outcome.

"Crammed," DG said. "Not room for a matchbox. There's no sign of the cops, either," he said, looking nervously toward the harbor entrance. "They're going to catch us in here."

Max rechecked the radar. The width of his thumb separated the green blips. "They're still twenty minutes away. We'll tie up against another yacht. Double park."

"Fucking hell, Max," DG said. "I wish you'd told me that before. Oh God..."

Max followed DG's gaze. Stan was up by the bow, flapping his arms wildly, desperately trying to get their attention, and pointing to an area on the quayside a few hundred yards away.

"Back," he was shouting.

"Shit. Carlo must have men here," Max said in dismay.

"They're standing in front of the marina yacht club. I can see them," DG said, alarmed. "Turn us around, Max. We need to get out of here."

Max wasn't sure. "Not yet, DG. They can't hurt us from over there. I'm going to call the police again."

Stan was doing odd, circular motions with his hands. Then in frustration at not being understood gave up and began running back to the flybridge.

"Stan's saying to go,'" DG said. "Max, they might have another fucking rocket."

Stan vaulted onto the flybridge. He was in a panic. "Turn us around, Max. We've got to get going!"

"I'm ringing the cops," Max said. "Calm down, for fuck's sake. They're not going to fire at us in the marina, even I know that. And it's safer inside here than it will be in the main harbor or out at sea."

"You don't understand, Max." Stan's face was ruby red; he was blowing hard and was desperate. "Max, I couldn't care less about Carlo. We've got to go *now*."

Max didn't understand, and Stan was panicking him now. "Jesus, if you start cracking up, Stan, then what chance have the rest of us got? I've just checked the radar, and the bastards are still twenty minutes away. There's nobody on the quayside by the main road, and that's where the cops will arrive. We've got time to moor up and follow through with the plan, even if Carlo's goons are over there."

"I've just told you I'm not bothered about Carlo or his men," Stan said. "It's *them* I'm bothered about. See for yourself, over there." He handed Max the binoculars.

Max was confounded but took them and looked over to where Stan was pointing again. A sign came into view. The image was blurry. He refocused.

CLUB NAUTICO IBIZA

He moved his view slowly to the right. A face filled the entire round frame.

He jumped back in shock and banged his head against DG's nose.

"Ow," DG said.

"Jesus," said Max. "Is that—"

"Yes," Stan whimpered.

Max looked again, zooming out a little—less scary that way. It was Tina, right enough. She was staring right down the lens—very disturbing. *What the hell is she doing here?*

Stan was sobbing.

Tina's expression was a picture of discontentment—snarling would be a better description. Her blond head was bobbing up and down, her hands were placed squarely on her hips, and a silver diamante-encrusted high heel was vigorously tapping the concrete path. *Tina's not happy, not happy at all.*

"Stan, listen," Max said. "If we moor up quickly, you can be well away by the time Tina gets over here. I'll square it with her, somehow." He didn't sound very convincing.

"Look again," Stan said, mid-sob.

"What?"

"Look again!"

Max re-raised the binoculars, pinpointed Tina, and zoomed out some more. His stomach squeezed down to the size of an egg. "Jane!"

There stood the wife of Will, their best mate, the guy they'd just abandoned, alone, in the middle of the Mediterranean.

"Jesus," Max said.

"You're not finished," Stan said. "Look to the right."

"Eh?"

Max scanned right. It couldn't get any worse. *Tina and Jane. The most terrifying woman in the world, and Will's widow.* He glimpsed something to Jane's left.

It was a fluffy green hat.

His mouth opened, but no sound came out. There was only one fluffy, green hat like that in the entire world.

"Mum!"

DG was swinging his arms about in disbelief. "Fuck me. If this wasn't just total shite, it would be hilarious. I mean, is it teatime, Max? Mum come to call you in? Go on, then; off you trot. At least you'll avoid being murdered."

"Oh, shut the fuck up," Max said.

DG was seriously pissed off. "I just feel left out, boys. My mum's not come to collect me."

Max handed him the binoculars. "Somebody has."

"Eh?"

DG took the binoculars and focused in on the quayside. It took him a moment to see what Max was talking about.

"It can't be."

"It is," Max said.

"It can't be," DG said again.

"It is."

"But what's Mr. Fucking Patel doing here?"

"Maybe that Ford Focus you were telling me about got returned," Max said. "How the hell do I know?"

DG was at a loss for words.

Stan began to plead. "Please say we don't have to tie up, Max. I'd rather take my chances with those bastards chasing us. Tina will kill me for sure."

Max was thinking. Nothing useful came to mind.

Stan tried to strengthen his argument. "Tina might kill you as well, Max, and DG, and Will." He then remembered that Will was probably dead already, but his anxiety over Tina drove him on. "It's bad enough having stolen this bloody yacht, but she'll castrate me with her nail scissors over the women."

The last time Max had seen Tracy, she'd been prostrate on a sofa, wearing one of Stan's T-shirts, and a pair of skimpy knickers, on the back of which Stan had written "SAS PROPERTY".

"Please, Max," Stan said. "Think of another plan, one that involves going back out to sea."

"We can't tie up," DG said.

"I agree entirely," Stan said.

"Shut up, Stan. Why not, DG?" Max said.

"Because of Jane, more than anything else. What would we say to her? We abandoned her husband at sea. And if that's not bad enough, there's a six-foot redhead downstairs that's constantly screaming his name. That would kill Jane, and Tina would kill Stan and you and me."

And there are still no cops in sight, thought Max.

"Maria, we're not landing. We're going," he said.

"Good decision," Stan said, slapping him on the back.

Maria was bemused. "Are you sure, Max, after all we've been through to reach here?"

"Maria, that's Will's wife over on the quay, along with Stan's girlfriend, my mother, and—even more bizarrely—DG's boss. I don't know what the hell they're doing here, but we can't tell Jane that we left Will for de—"

"But it was impossible to find him in the storm," Maria said.

"I know, but she'll never hear our explanation, and Lord knows how we could explain Lisa."

Right on cue, Lisa began howling.

A moment later, the *Conchita*'s engines powered up, and the yacht sped out of the marina and toward the harbor entrance.

This time, they ignored the signposted speed limit of three knots.

CHAPTER 19

Pedro greeted Jack. "Welcome back, señor."

Jack didn't respond. He was exhausted, sick of talking, and not about to converse with a tramp.

Pedro was unfazed. "I'm well, señor, in case you were wondering."

"I wasn't."

Pedro ignored the remark. "Señor Jack, you don't look so good. Have a drink." He held out a plastic bottle.

"I'll drink my own piss first, if that's OK with you, Pedro. Not that I can fucking go."

"No, señor. It's only water, I assure you."

Jack grabbed the bottle and drank greedily. The water was warm and slightly tangy, but still refreshing. He finished the bottle.

"Although I did piss in the bottle yesterday," Pedro said, as an afterthought.

Marvelous, thought Jack, but he was past caring. The water had tasted divine, whoever's piss was in it.

"I'm sorry, Pedro. I finished the lot."

"Don't worry, señor," Pedro said, smiling. "You must have really needed it. And don't worry; they'll soon let you go. They can't keep you down here forever—unless, like me, you want to stay."

"It might be better if I did, Pedro. I've made a right dog's breakfast of things."

"You make breakfast for a dog?"

"No, no. I mean I've messed up. I did the dirty on some very good people, Pedro. There'll be nobody waiting outside for me."

"Señor?"

Jack sighed. He was beat. "I've lost my best mates, and I've cheated on the only woman who ever loved me—except my mother, that is, and she doesn't count because she has to love me. I'm a waster, Pedro, a dirty, fucking stupid, foolish waster, and I deserve all this."

Pedro was laughing. "Señor Jack, if you are a fool, then how big a fool must I be? I must be the biggest fool in all Majorca—all Spain, maybe." He sat down opposite Jack. "Please tell me about your amigos."

Jack sat heavily on the cell floor, too, and leaned back against the damp wall. "What the fuck, Pedro? Who else am I going to tell?"

For the next hour, he talked about Max, Stan, DG, and Will, and about how they'd been seated next to each other on the first day of school. Will cried as his mum waved good-bye through the classroom window, and he'd not stopped weeping until Miss Ainsworth emptied out a huge jigsaw puzzle on the table. The puzzle had been a scene depicting a Roman chariot race, like the one in *Ben-Hur*, which was Jack's favorite film. The puzzle took all morning to complete. When they finished it, all five boys had become friends.

Young Jack loved school. Until then, he had had no friends. Then, in just one morning, he had made the best four friends ever. And although over the years he'd fallen out of love with school, exams, and teachers, he'd kept his friendships. He also loved being a member of the Bulls Head Pool Team and treasured the annual trips.

And then he had messed it all up.

They were in Blackpool on the last night of one of their best-ever trips. Amazingly, Jack had earlier scored with a local hairdresser called Simone, and the happy five men were staggering back to the digs when a group of twenty locals rounded the corner and stood in their path.

"Which one of you bastards fucked Simone?" asked a big, burly skinhead with a red tattoo of "Simone Forever" running down his forearm.

"Come on, lads. We're just going home," Max said. "We don't know Simone, and we don't want any trouble."

"It was him, Gripper," said a girl with bright-pink hair and a bone-shaped piercing through her nose. "He took advantage of me when I was drunk." She pointed straight at Jack.

This was partially true. Jack had met Simone earlier that evening, but he hadn't known her name until just then. She'd been in front of him at the bar—ordering four Smirnoff vodkas—two for her and two for her mate. But when she received the bill, she was five pounds light. Having queued for ten minutes to get served, she was keen not to lose the booze.

She'd turned to Jack. "Hey, ugly."

Jack had looked behind him, but there was nobody there.

"Yeah, you," she'd said. "Give me five quid, and I'll give you a blow job."

Jack had dug quickly into his pocket. "Only got tenners," he'd said, pulling one off his wad.

Simone had snatched it from him. "I'll make it a good one."

After depositing the drinks with her electric-blue-haired friend for safekeeping, Simone led Jack outside and behind some wheelie bins. Forty-five seconds later, Jack was standing on his own, with his trousers around his ankles, as two elderly women in cleaner's outfits rounded the corner for an unauthorized fag break.

The women had laughed raucously.

"Want another one, love?" one of them had said. She had curlers in her hair. "I could take my teeth out."

"Give over, Hilda," her colleague had said. "Can't you see the lad's in shock? Must have been his first blowy—that, or she bit it."

Gripper grabbed Max's collar and was about to punch him when Stan's right fist smashed into his nose. It was a fierce blow. The skinhead went down like sack of potatoes as the rest of his gang piled in. DG and Will joined the fracas, which ended as fast as it had started when Stan threatened to break off Gripper's arm.

By then, Jack had gone.

The scrap had scared him. He'd felt pretty much the same during clashes with the grammar school, but somehow, had managed to overcome his fear then—he once even landed a couple of blows on a swotty-looking kid before a rugby type had kicked him in the balls and stamped on his fingers. Jack had crawled off into some bushes in agony and thrown up. For weeks afterward, he was unable to masturbate and regularly woke up cupping his testicles and whimpering.

As the mob came forward that night in Blackpool, Jack's balls had literally retracted in fright. The next thing he knew, he was running. He ran faster and farther than he'd ever run before, and he didn't stop until he was a good couple of miles up the promenade. Eventually, exhausted, he stopped and leaned against the seawall for support. Tears of shame rolled off his face and splashed onto the weathered concrete by his feet. That night, he slept in the railway station waiting room. He caught the first train home in the morning.

He couldn't face his four friends. For the next two years, he avoided all contact. Max had left countless messages on his phone. And on at least four occasions, Jack knew that Max, DG, and Will had called in at the mill. He once watched Max and DG from his office window, as they stood outside the main entrance in the rain. He wanted to go to them—but he couldn't. Eventually, he asked his secretary to tell them he was busy.

Jack had needed a new start and settled on Majorca, away from his embarrassment and shame, and away from the worry of bumping into Max and the others. And Majorca was where he met Consuela, his housekeeper. For the first few months, Jack had ordered her about as he did everybody else. Then, unprompted, and after washing the dishes one night, Consuela sat down next to him in the lounge and started watching television. Jack was outraged—the audacity of the woman—but he said nothing. Consuela did the same on the next night, and the next, and the next, and Jack still said nothing. On the fifth occasion, much to his surprise, he broke the silence.

"Cup of tea, Consuela?" he asked, and then watched as she got up to put the kettle on. They talked over tea. The conversation was a bit stilted, with Consuela talking about her life as best as she could in patchy English. But as the night wore on, Jack opened up, too. It turned out that Consuela was the local mayor's daughter, but she had had a falling-out with her father after marrying a local plumber. Apparently, the husband wasn't good enough. Consuela had a son and a daughter, and both of them were studying in Madrid. Unfortunately, the husband had died of cancer two years earlier and had left his wife with nothing but debt.

A month on from their first cuppa, Consuela and Jack had awakened together with sunshine streaming through the window. It was the happiest Jack could ever remember feeling. He felt at ease with Consuela and even told her about Max, DG, Stan, Will, and the Blackpool Incident. She gently persuaded him over the next few months to get back in touch, and Jack had finally plucked up the courage, asking Jules to write to Max. Much to his shock, the invitation had been accepted. And although a great part of him was fearful over Stan's reaction, another part of him was hopeful of reconciliation.

Jack had heard Stan's voice in his sleep for years. "It's the ultimate code, men," Stan would declare. "If one of us fights, then we *all* fight. If one of us is captured, then we *all* go back, whatever the risk, whatever the odds. There is no more powerful feeling than knowing your mates will *always* return."

In Blackpool, Jack had run. He'd abandoned his friends in their time of need, and he'd not returned—he'd deserted. Then taken the train home. He'd left and hadn't even tried to find out if they were OK. He'd broken the *ultimate code*. In Stan's eyes, that meant he would forever be the lowest of the low.

A coward.

Jack sighed again. "So there you have it, Pedro. I deserve to rot in here, not for what those bloody idiots up there think I've done, as that's complete bollocks, but for being a total loser."

Pedro had been listening intently. "Señor Jack. You are too hard on yourself. And you should have more faith in your amigos. If these men are half the men you say they are, then they will still be there for you. Didn't you say they never stopped calling, and doesn't this Stan believe in his own ultimate code?"

"What do you mean?"

"Well, if this Stan believes in his own code, then he must return for you. Mustn't he?"

"Yes, but—"

"Señor. Would you continue to call on somebody, wait in the rain for him, fly out to Majorca to visit him, if you didn't actually want to see him?"

There were footsteps in the passage.

CHAPTER 20

The *Conchita* was traveling fast and east along Ibiza's parched coastline.

"Bastards are right on our tail," Stan said, watching the radar. He was still traumatized from seeing Tina standing on the quayside. Occasionally, he'd glance back toward Ibiza Town and grimace. "Another few minutes, and they'd have caught us inside the harbor. I think I can just see them with my eyes. We look to be pulling away."

"Go and finish your search, Stan, while there's time," Max said.

Stan disappeared below decks. He was happy to be out of sight and have a distraction—even though Tina was long gone.

DG reappeared on the flybridge. He'd been down to explain to the girls why the plan had changed. "Interesting one, that Tracy," he said. "Wasn't worried about anything. Said Stan would protect her, whatever happened."

"Not if Tina sticks a carving knife through his heart, he won't," Max said.

The girls had unanimously decided not to leave the yacht without police protection, and they had fully understood the dilemma over Jane. On one hand, a wife had the right to know that her husband was dead; on the other hand, how could they explain abandoning Will at sea? The four women could hardly believe what had happened themselves, so what were the chances of Jane understanding? They also recognized that their presence onboard somewhat complicated matters. DG had insisted that the extra time would also be useful for thinking through their actions.

"That would make perfect sense," Tracy said, "if we weren't being hunted by a pack of murderers."

The women's conclusion was a reluctant acceptance of the decision to flee, but their take-home message was clear, too: they didn't want to die.

Max contacted the coast guard again and received news that the search for Will had been underway for over four hours. So far, no sightings had been reported. The search would continue all day until dark and then restart the following morning, depending on weather conditions, which were forecast to deteriorate. The officer promised to radio him back if there were any developments.

"We've got to tie up, DG, and get the girls and ourselves off this bloody thing," Max said. "But it needs to be somewhere we won't get machine-gunned running up the beach, and somewhere we can get away from and get transport to the airport."

And that was the problem. If they anchored somewhere deserted and used the remaining dinghy to go ashore, even out of sight of their pursuers, then the bastards would see them pull in on their radar, and theoretically could have men there to greet them in minutes.

"Do you think we're blowing this out of all proportion?" DG asked.

"What?"

"You know, Carlo killing us, machine guns firing like it's D-Day in Normandy. Are we imagining it all?"

"We didn't imagine those missiles or the bloody great holes they blasted in the cliffs."

As if to highlight their doubts, a red van came into view on a piece of coastal road. Was it a local builder on his way to a roofing job? Or a group of heavily armed men shadowing their every move? Max had a vision of the back doors opening up to reveal a heavy machine gun mounted on a tripod. Perhaps DG was right, in part—too much imagination—but a populated area would be a safer jumping-off point. Preferably a town with a police station. He studied the map again, moving his finger slowly along the coastline.

"Roca Llisa." It was a town, or at least a big village, a few miles farther up the coast.

"Same plan, DG," he said. "We call the cops before we pull in, and hopefully this time they'll show up. Agree?"

DG gave a sullen nod.

He looks exhausted. Max knew exactly how DG felt. Two days of partying had been followed by two days of incredible stress and anguish—that showed no sign of abating. Max had slept for just two or three hours in the last forty-eight, and neither his mind nor his body could take much more. Adrenaline and the thought of reaching Ibiza Town had been the only things keeping him going. *Reach Ibiza Town, and then I'm done. Just reach Ibiza Town, and everything will be all right.* He knew he was kidding himself, but ignoring the horrendous situation was the only way he could operate. *Reach Ibiza Town, get the girls to safety, ensure Will is found, and we can all go home—and sleep.*

But Ibiza Town had come and gone. They'd never even stepped ashore. He'd been hopelessly optimistic—naïve in the extreme—just as DG had been with his wishful thinking that they were imagining the whole thing.

Max's plan had failed, and there was no plan B.

A voice in his head mocked him. *Your so-called plan failed because your mum showed up. Funny, if it wasn't pathetic. It's teatime, little Maxi. Chicken nuggets and jelly—your favorite. Jesus Christ, man, what the hell are you playing at? You've no right to risk other people's lives with your harebrained thinking. Stan should be in charge. He's a real leader. A real soldier. SAS. He's fought in real wars with real bullets and used tried-and-tested military tactics. If necessary, he knows how to kill. Whereas you—well, what can I say?—you're deputy manager of Spenborough Swimming Pool, for God's sake. Very helpful. What are you going to do when those gangsters turn up and start shooting—teach them breaststroke?*

Max knew the voice was right, but Stan had always looked to him for leadership. That was fair enough when discussing pool-team tactics or what to buy Tina for Christmas, but this was different. Warfare was Stan's domain. *He should lead.* Max's stomach churned. He felt drained, beaten, and downright foolish.

Kylie, Dannii, Lisa, and Tracy appeared, carrying trays of food.

"Cheese-and-ham sandwiches," Tracy said. "Packets of crisps, too, and chocolates and bottles of beer." She looked behind at the distant-but-visible motor yacht but didn't mention it. "And this is for dessert," she said, triumphantly holding up a bottle of bourbon.

It reminded Max of the party. *Could that only have been two days ago? Yesterday really.* It was unbelievable. He forced a smile and picked a cheese-and-ham sandwich from Kylie's tray. He'd no appetite but took a token bite to be polite. The girls had made the effort. *Bizarre how you behave under stress*, he thought. He stopped midchew, his mouth watering ridiculously. Food had never tasted so good. He greedily wolfed the sandwich and grabbed another two from the tray. He didn't even like cheese and ham.

"Hungry boy," Kylie said, smiling.

It was the first nonalcoholic thing Max had put into his body, other than Montecristo cigar smoke, in nearly twenty-four hours. His stomach immediately settled, clearly very grateful, and a boost of energy suddenly lifted his spirits. He stretched his back muscles as a wave of positivity eliminated his negative thoughts.

Come on, Maxi, he told himself. *Stop moping and get on the fuck on with it.* "Thank you, girls. Thank you so much." He hugged Kylie, who blushed.

"They're only cheese-and-ham sandwiches," Tracy said, who bit into one herself, trying to see what all the fuss was about.

Max surveyed the flybridge and the people on it. *We've achieved so much together*, he thought. *Survived.* Everybody else was living through the same nightmare as he was, and they were playing their parts. No one was giving up. The girls could have gone ashore in Ibiza Town, could have demanded to go, but they hadn't. They hardly knew Will, and had never met Jane, yet they had put their lives at risk again. And now they were making cheese-and-ham sandwiches. It was awesome.

A huge smile spread across his face.

He heard a crackle from the radio speaker.

"*Conchita*," said a voice. "Come in, *Conchita*."

"Search and Rescue?" asked DG.

Max grabbed the receiver and pressed the transmit button. "This is *Conchita*," said Max, his heart pounding.

"*Conchita*. Somebody wishes to talk to you."

There was a pause.

And then.

"Max, it's me. It's Will. I'm OK, guys, I'm OK. Stan, DG, I'm OK."

Lisa dropped her tray and fell to her knees, sobbing. Max and DG instinctively raised their arms to the sky and cried out in euphoria.

The relief was indescribable. Max felt faint and staggered over to the rail for support. He quietly thanked God, Search and Rescue, Mother Teresa, and anybody else he could think of. Jesus Christ, he'd been so fucking lucky. Juliet's and Harriet's angelic faces popped into his head. Their tearstained cheeks at the loss of their father had disappeared, replaced by crinkles of laughter and cries of jubilation as they greeted Will on his return.

"Thank you!" Max shouted into the sky.

The embraces and shouts of joy were still in full flow when Max suddenly realized that they hadn't acknowledged Will—he still didn't know he'd been heard. Max picked up the receiver to speak again—as another man's voice came through.

"We know you are listening, Max."

The voice was articulate.

Maria let out a small scream and held a hand to her mouth.

The voice continued. "As Will said, he is OK. For now. However, let me be very clear. It is very important for Will that the *Conchita* is returned to me immediately. Do you understand, Max?"

Maria reached over to grab the receiver, but Max pulled it away. "No," he said, shaking his head.

"But I can help you," Maria said. "All of you. We know it's Carlo now, so I can explain everything to him and ask him to put you ashore."

Max's grip was almost crushing the receiver. His knuckles were white. *This must be what it feels like to be given the all clear from cancer, and then take a phone call at a celebration dinner later that night telling you there's been a terrible mistake, and you've actually only a month to live— we're very sorry—hope you have a good evening—good-bye.*

Max's brain was still recovering from the shock. He tried to think aloud. "Maria, maybe you shouldn't let Carlo know you're here. Not yet."

Maria was confused. "But my presence will protect you," she said.

Max was working his thoughts out—sort of. "I know you don't want to hear this Maria, but Carlo just threatened Will. And we know for certain now that it was Carlo that fired the missiles. So whatever you say to him, and whatever assurances he gives you in return—we can't believe him.

Your presence here may well protect us for a while, but what happens after you leave? I just think that if Carlo doesn't know you're here, then maybe you should keep it that way, at least until we know what he's going to do—and it may put you in a better position to help us get safely away, including Will. But it's up to you."

He passed the receiver over to Maria. She took it. She was staring into his eyes, judging him, and questioning herself. She depressed the transmit button, but said nothing—and then handed the receiver back.

The radio sounded again.

"I know you can hear me, Max. Acknowledge."

Max responded. "Why are you threatening Will? We took the *Conchita* by mistake. We honestly thought it was our friend's yacht."

The voice was stern and unsympathetic. "So Will has told me, but how can I trust a man that abandons his friend at sea. Will for the *Conchita*. Start sailing over to us."

Max responded again. "I need some time. I have to talk to my friends."

"Ten minutes" was the terse reply. 'Then I want to see the *Conchita* moving toward us. I do hope for Will's sake that you don't abandon him a second time."

Silence.

"What the fuck?" DG said. "We need to call the cops."

"We can't," Max said. "It's too risky for Will. You heard him. It was a pretty undisguised threat."

"Jesus H. Christ, it's actually getting worse," DG said, thumping his fist against what remained of the flybridge roof.

"It isn't," Max said. "Two minutes ago, I'd have settled for this. Will is alive and safe. It's a miracle they picked him up."

DG wasn't as satisfied. "Define what you mean by *safe*," he said. "In my book, drowning or a bullet in the head leads to the same outcome. Progress is not what I'm feeling."

Lisa, who was trying to make sense of her own emotional roller coaster, was the next to speak. "Maria, how come Carlo isn't trying to blow us up anymore?"

Maria didn't answer. She was sitting in the captain's chair, looking far out to sea, perhaps trying to understand what the unfolding events meant for her.

Max answered. "Because Will told him who we are, Lisa."

"He's also got control of us now," DG said. "All we can do is trust him and do whatever he says."

"We can't trust him," Max said. "But we do need some cards, something to bargain with."

"We could exchange these," Stan said, coming up the staircase. He'd heard Carlo's ultimatum. He was holding two pieces of plastic piping.

"Not sure Carlo will go for that, Stan," DG said, "unless he's fitting a sink."

Stan gave him a derisory look and tipped the pipes. There was a rustling sound, before hundreds of small glass fragments spilled onto the deck and started bouncing around their feet.

"He won't go for broken glass, either, you dummy," DG said.

Dannii knelt down, a look of wonder on her face.

"Careful, babe," DG said. "Don't cut yourself."

"Diamonds!" Dannii whispered.

"What?" DG asked.

"Diamonds," she said again but louder. "Diamonds."

Danii was in a trance.

She gathered two handfuls of the sparkling stones and lifted them above her head, letting them slip through her fingers, glorying in the feel as they ran through her hair and over her skin.

"Diamonds!"

Kylie, Tracy, and Lisa joined in the fun, crawling around on all fours and frantically picking up as many jewels as they could. The men looked on, bewildered.

"We're rich," Dannii cried. "We're millionaires! Zillionaires! We're rich!"

"Easy, babe," DG said, trying to calm her. "They're not ours."

It was Dannii's turn to give him a derisory look. "I'm not soft, DG. I do know that. It's just that I've always dreamed of saying that, so don't spoil it for me." With that, she started screaming again. "We're rich! Rich! Rich! Rich! As rich as Queen Elizabeth! Richer than Simon Cowell!"

"Christ," Max said. "Where did you find them, Stan? And why did you just dump them on the bloody deck?"

Stan looked sheepish. "Fake piping under the master stateroom. Sorry about the drama. Was just happy about Will," he said.

"I suppose it'll take their minds off the rest of it." Max glanced at the four women. They had stopped screaming, for now, and were diligently counting the shining stones. "So the situation's changed again. Will's alive, and Jane's waiting for him on the quayside at Ibiza Town, and we've got millions in diamonds. So how do we best get him back?"

"How do we get him back without all being killed in the process, you mean," Stan said.

"By either Carlo or Tina," DG said, not very helpfully.

"We need a new plan in seven minutes," Max said. "Girls, up you get. The diamonds will wait a minute. We need your input."

The women reluctantly stood and as a group they crowded around the map and discussed what they should do. When the ten-minute deadline arrived they had the beginnings of a plan—but implementation would be on the hoof.

Max picked up the microphone once more. "That'll have to do."

"What if Carlo won't accept?" Maria asked urgently.

Max was surprised at hearing her voice; Maria had been the only one not to contribute to the discussion. *She's scared, but she's keeping it together.* "He *will* accept, Maria," Max said. "Carlo wants this over as much as we do." He pushed the small, red button and spoke out into space. "This is Max."

The voice Maria had recognized as Carlo's immediately replied. "Slow down and sail *Conchita* over to us."

"There are some things to sort out before we do that," Max said, as calmly as he could.

Carlo became irritated. "You are not in any position to make demands, and neither is Will. So sail the *Conchita* over to us."

Max replied, "That's not going to happen. And cut the threats." He was working hard to remain calm inside. He'd be no use to Will scatter-brained and jumpy. He needed to think on his feet. "You want this to be over, too," he said. "Who are you, and why are you doing this?"

The reply was abrupt. "You know what I want. The *Conchita*."

"All you had to do was ask," Max said.

There was a pause. "I'm asking now!"

"Bit late," said Max. "Maybe if you hadn't kidnapped Will."

"I saved Will. You left him for dead!"

Max had to concede that point. "The missiles haven't built up much trust, either."

After another pause, Carlo was more conciliatory. "Call me Amigo."

Yeah, right. Max could almost hear Carlo smirking. *Arrogant fucker.*

"I can see your point, Max," Carlo continued. "But try to see it from my point of view. You have provoked this situation by stealing the *Conchita*, involving yourself in my business, and causing me to steal another yacht. Ironically, the *Infamous Five*, according to the logbook, is owned by a Mr. Jack North, the friend you were supposedly coming to meet."

"Did he say the *Infamous Five*?" asked Stan.

Max nodded. "He did."

Stan was confused. "But that's what our gang was called at school. Why would Jack do that? He hates us."

"I've told you for years that he doesn't," Max said.

"But—"

"There's no time for this now, Stan."

Max spoke into the receiver again. "I want to hear Will." He couldn't bring himself to say *Amigo,* and had to keep reminding himself not to say Carlo's real name either—he didn't want to accidentally let on they knew who he was.

"You've already heard from him."

"Put him on again. Please."

A few seconds later, Will's familiar voice came back over the waves. "I'm OK," he said, sounding nervous and jittery. "Amigo wants to exchange me for the yacht. Strange he chose Amigo; it's my favorite film, but *A Hard Day's Night* would be more appropriate. I've told him that this is a major cock-up." Will's voice descended into a whisper. "He's promised to let us go—us and the girls—but he's not playing games, Maxi. He really means it."

Will's voice trailed away, and Carlo came back on. "You've heard Will. Now please come over and collect him."

Max took a deep breath. "We'll meet you at Cabrera Island. It's three or four hours from here, but there's protected water, so the exchange will be easier. We're not sailors, and this swell is too great." He paused for a moment but didn't release the button, not allowing a reply. "Amigo, this is not up for discussion. Cabrera Island." He hated uttering *Amigo.*

A *friend* was the last thing this guy was to him, but any way of softening his enemy's thoughts would do. He released the button.

There was a long, static-filled pause.

A minute went by.

He's calculating, thought Max.

Finally, a response came through. "Cabrera is acceptable. No tricks, or Will's children will never forgive you."

Click.

Silence.

Max looked around at the group. "He doesn't know about Maria," he said. "And I'm pretty sure he doesn't know we've found the weapons or the diamonds, either. We know a bit more, too. There are four of them, all armed to the teeth, and the *Infamous Five* is Jack's, no doubt about that. Stan, talk us through Cabrera."

Stan bent over the large map and placed a stubby finger on Cabrera. Everybody but Maria looked on.

"As we discussed a few moments ago, there are a group of tiny islands about thirty miles from here. Cabrera is the largest, and is a near-complete ring of low-lying hills that have created a lake out at sea. Cabrera Sound. A narrow inlet provides the only access, and so there's only one way in, and also only one way out. According to the tourist guidebook, it's a nature reserve that attracts visitors in the summer. But there's no accommodation, and you need a permit to moor overnight. What with the storm, it's unlikely anybody else will be there, which is both good news and bad. The best thing about Cabrera Island is that Carlo can't bring in reinforcements by road; therefore, we can't be ambushed on arrival. Belt and braces, we could exchange Will for the *Conchita* on the sound itself or on the island, which means that if Carlo wants to cover both possibilities, he'll have to split his force of four. The bad news is the helicopter gunship; it worries the shit out of me. If that's around, we're stuffed."

"We also know that Carlo is impetuous," Max said.

"How does that help?" Stan asked.

"I'm not sure yet, to be honest, but it's a weakness. Carlo doesn't plan, he just acts."

"Brilliant," DG said. "You mean the guy shoots first and asks questions later. Very reassuring—in an he's-already-shot-me kind of way. Helpful."

"OK," Max said. "I know it sounds limp, but we actually know more about Carlo than he knows about us."

"Unless Will told him," Stan said.

"He won't mention the SAS or that we know who Carlo is. My guess is that until Carlo has more information, he'll regard us all as a threat, which is helpful to know. He's trigger-happy, which is scary, but he might continue to overestimate us. He's impulsive. But for a supposedly intelligent bloke, he seems to miss the obvious."

"Like what?" DG asked.

Max was getting irritated. "Like he could have just sailed up to the *Conchita* yesterday afternoon and told us to get the fuck off his boat."

"Fair point," DG said.

"How do you know there are four of them?" Maria asked.

"I can answer that," DG said, turning toward her. "Clever lad, our Will. His favorite film is *The Three Amigos*, but Will said *A Hard Day's Night* would be more appropriate. You see, the Beatles star in *A Hard Day's Night*, and they were the Fab Four, and so there are four. See?"

● ● ●

Three and a half hours later, Cabrera came into view. Carlo had already arrived. Max had watched the radar with mounting mistrust as the *Infamous Five*—a mile or so to the west—had increased speed and forged ahead of them, but there seemed no point in racing—or so he thought.

From the description of Cabrera in the tourist guide, Max was expecting to see shallow hills. Instead imposing jagged stone cliffs rose vertically from the sea. The heavy dark-blue swell was crashing rhythmically and powerfully into the wet rock face, and white froth was shooting up into the air, lacing the atmosphere with salt.

Cabrera is magnificent, he thought. Magical. A mythical island fortress with impregnable walls, perhaps guarding secrets and legends from a long-forgotten age.

The cliff face was unbroken. There was no way in.

"Where's the inlet?" Stan asked.

"Should be right here," DG said, checking the map again.

There was nothing to see—nothing that looked like an inlet, anyway. Just solid rock and an entrance to an underwater cave, which appeared and disappeared as the waves crashed in and out.

Max was beginning to think they were in the wrong place.

"There," DG said.

"Where?" Max said, who was looking at exactly the same spot but could see nothing but solid cliff face.

"Look hard," DG said. "Farther on from the cave there's a line. Two different-colored rock faces."

Max followed DG's outstretched finger. Sure enough, there was a line—like one drawn by a giant, brown felt-tip pen. It was jagged and ran all the way from the top of the cliff to the sea below. As Max peered closer, he saw that the line was becoming wider. *This is crazy. It's as if the cliff face is splitting apart like two gigantic, stone doors slowly creaking open.* He shivered. *What if Cabrera is magical? What if the cliffs close in behind us?*

The mouth of the inlet came fully into view.

"It's like a Norwegian fjord," said DG. "The entrance is almost impossible to see until you are directly opposite."

Max chided himself. *My stupid imagination. Gigantic stone doors! As if there's not enough to worry about already.*

Maria skillfully lined the *Conchita* up with the cutting. A few minutes later, they slipped slowly inside. There was only six feet of clearance on each side, but fortunately, the swell had diminished. Stan and DG were nervously surveying the cliff summits, expecting deadly boulders to fall at any moment. But not much could be done even if there were such an avalanche, as the only way was forward. There was no room to turn the *Conchita* about.

"Can't we go any quicker? We're sitting ducks," Stan said. "This is the best place for an ambush I've ever seen, and Carlo has been here for over twenty minutes. He's had plenty of time to get his men up on top."

"If that was his intention, we'd be at the bottom already," said Max, not even bothering to look up. He spoke in a whisper, aware that his voice was echoing around the cliffs.

The *Conchita* moved slowly on. The inlet began to curve gently left and, to everyone's horror, was narrowing too. The 360-degree view was dark-brown rock. Forward, behind, and to each side—vertical, rugged, cliff face.

Finally, the long bend ran out, and the inlet widened again.

"Cabrera Sound straight ahead," DG said.

"Thank God," Stan said. "I thought we were going to get stuck."

"Might be better if we had," DG said under his breath.

The cliffs were giving way to gentle hills. And a few minutes later, the *Conchita* emerged out of the inlet and into a large sea lake. Cabrera Sound. The waters inside were flat and crystal clear creating an enormous mirror, which reflected a perfect image of the surrounding hills. On a different day, the calmness and serenity on the sound would have been idyllic, but today it felt darkly disturbing.

There were no other yachts in view, and the only movement came from a solitary eagle soaring high above the barren hills.

"Where are the bastards? And is that a house?" DG asked. He pointed to a small stone building halfway up the hillside on the port side.

"They're just around that spur," Stan said, remembering some geography. "They'll come into view any second. And that's a café," he said. "It's usually open seven days a week but won't be opening today, on account of the storm."

"I wasn't angling for a fry-up," DG said, sounding annoyed.

"I wasn't trying to be funny," Stan said.

"Good, 'cause you weren't." DG looked tense and weary.

"It's just the bastards and us," Stan said.

The *Conchita* cleared the spur, which jutted out into the lake. And suddenly, there she was: the *Infamous Five.*

White and gleaming, with dark-blue stripes running along the hull, she was half the size of the *Conchita* and lying motionless, just as she had been the first time Max saw her—during the fake distress call—and before firing missiles.

Max felt unnerved and gloomy. Seeing the *Infamous Five* up close confirmed the current situation as real—truly scary, and deadly—not just the product of an overactive imagination, after all. For twenty-four hours, the enemy had been no more than a small, flashing green dot on the radar, harmless and distant. But no longer.

The *Infamous Five* was sitting quietly on her own mirror image. There was no skull-and-crossbones flag flying from the yardarm, and as yet no more missiles erupting from the foredeck. Yet the only feeling in Max's chest was dread.

He had been wondering whether a few drenched campers might be hiding out in the lee of the hills, as bystanders may subdue any trigger-happy tendencies, but there was nobody to see. Not even a flock of sheep or a band of mountain goats—just rocks, boulders, stones, mud, and bushy scrub.

Good for public safety, I guess. Max pulled his thoughts back to the job at hand. *The exchange. The Conchita for Will. God. Who am I kidding? Idiot. What do I know about exchanges? Well, apart from remembering to take the receipt as proof of purchase.*

Maria cut the engines, and the world became silent. The *Conchita* drifted to a stop. The *Infamous Five* was still lifeless, three hundred meters away.

DG released the anchor chains. A crescendo of rough metal grinding over rough metal resounded excruciatingly around the hills as both anchors plunged into the sea and sank quickly into the sandy seabed. The superyacht paused and held on the tensing chains—and as the echoing, metallic clanging died away, the deathly silence returned.

"To the swimming platform," Max shouted, startling himself with the loudness of his voice. For a moment, he worried that those aboard the *Infamous Five* had heard him, and he looked anxiously across the water. But there was no movement.

He looked down onto the main deck and watched as Stan helped Kylie, Dannii, Tracy, and Lisa—all wearing rain jackets and hoodies—into the inflatable. Stan glanced up at him, expressionless, before jumping in himself and ripping the engine cord. The outboard motor burst into life, and the dinghy immediately sped away toward shore.

The radio crackled into life. "I said no tricks. Will is going to pay for your foolishness."

Carlo wasn't amused.

DG and Maria were standing next to Max as he quickly responded. "We're taking the girls ashore. They can wait over on the island. Now we only have to make one trip over to you in order to make the exchange. We'll pick the girls up when you've left Cabrera."

Max waited for a response, but then realized he was still pressing down the transmit button. He decided to carry on.

"When the inflatable returns, we'll come over to you, approaching from your port side. Simultaneously you can leave from starboard and come over to the *Conchita*. This way, we never have to meet. Leave Will on the *Infamous Five*."

Max held his breath and released the button.

There was silence.

Come on, you bastard. He noticed his index finger was furiously tapping the radio receiver.

"That's a good idea, Max."

Carlo sounded relaxed, in control. "But, unfortunately, we lost our inflatables in the storm. We'll need to use your inflatable to make our way across to the *Conchita*, unless, of course, we bring both yachts together."

"We're not doing that," DG said. "Are we?"

"No, we're not," Max said.

In either of Carlo's scenarios, they'd be bigger sitting ducks than they were when they came in through the inlet. Carlo would have them at point-blank range; he could take them out whenever he felt like it. *Crawling up a beach under machine-gun fire sounds better. Christ. But how else can we get Will back?* There was nothing for it. He would have to trust Carlo to some degree.

"You said Carlo probably wouldn't go for our exchange scenario, anyway," DG said.

"I know," Max said, but he wasn't really listening.

"And you said we couldn't trust him, didn't you?" DG asked.

Max ignored the question. He had no answer. Not a decent one anyway. He'd analyzed and reanalyzed the situation. It was impossible. Every scenario relied on Carlo keeping his word and handing over Will unharmed. The only way to be totally safe was to abandon his friend again, and that wasn't an option. The bottom line was that Carlo was in the driver's seat, and they were all merely passengers on his bus.

Stan throttled back and the dinghy pulled up alongside the swimming platform. He bounded up to the flybridge. "What'd he say?"

"Are the girls OK?" Max asked.

"Yeah. They're hidden in a little culvert just behind the beach."

"That's good." Max fidgeted uncomfortably. "Stan, I want you to take DG and Maria over there, too, and then I need you to stay on the island to protect everybody. I'm staying here."

Stan's expression turned grim. "That's not the plan, not what we agreed."

"And I'm not leaving, either," Maria said sternly. "I'm staying here, Max. I've told you that time and time again."

Max was exasperated. "Maria, for Christ's sake. Carlo's obviously not the guy you think he is. He's tried to kill us all already, and he's kidnapped Will. How much more fucking proof do you need?"

"He tried to kill you, not me," Maria said with venom. She almost spat the words out. "He doesn't even know I'm here."

How could she say and think that? "All I'm trying to do is protect—"

Maria prodded him hard in the chest. Her green eyes were flaming. "Cut the hero bullshit, Max. Carlo loves me. I know he does, and I…I love him, too."

Max was stunned. Her finger may as well have been a red-hot poker. Tears of frustration welled in his eyes, but he managed to hold them at bay. He didn't understand. *How could she say that to me after all that has happened? And how could she still love Carlo after all she's learned about him?* Pins and needles spread across his chest, and his brain was hurting. It was overheating from endless circular and fruitless analysis. *How could she? How could she? It just didn't compute. How could she still love him?*

He fought to distance himself from his mind, to keep control. He let his head fall backward on his neck and looked up into the endless blue.

The sky was completely clear. Not a cloud in sight. One dark dot—the eagle—was directly overhead, alone and so so high. It was gliding easily over the roof of the world.

It's too late, Max thought.

The die was cast, whoever had cast it.

He calmed, knowing what he had to do.

"Stan," he said, ignoring Maria, "take DG to shore. We can't trust this murdering bastard."

"Max, I'm not leaving you. You need me," Stan said stubbornly.

"You're right, Stan. I do need you. In fact, I need you now more than I've ever needed you before, but most of all I *need* you to trust me."

"What's your plan?" Stan asked, suspicious.

"Stan!"

Stan stayed put. "What's your plan?" he said harshly.

"Have I ever let you down, my friend?"

Stan remained where he was but fidgeted uncomfortably.

"Well, have I?"

"No, but—"

"So *please*, Stan. There's no time for debate. It's the only way I can think of to get Will back alive. I can't live with his death, and neither can you. Trust me, Stan. I know what I'm doing."

Max was lying—he didn't know what he was doing—and it wasn't all about Will either. The original thinking was that if Carlo didn't agree to exchange Will for the *Conchita* without actually meeting, then they'd all go over to the island and hide out there—and hopefully Carlo would leave Will unarmed, reclaim his superyacht, and sail away—or as DG had put it, "hopefully he'll just fuck off." Max had thought that when push came to shove Maria would elect to come over to the island too—after all she knew Carlo was a criminal now for sure—but she'd refused. If Max left now he may never see her again—and whilst he couldn't contemplate the thought of Will dying, he couldn't contemplate the thought of never seeing Maria again either.

Stan stared into his best friend's eyes.

Max stared back, hoping his confident pretense would hold out.

Apparently, Stan was satisfied. He spun around on the spot and ran back down the stairs to where the dinghy was bobbing about at the stern.

It was DG's turn to stare. "You have got to be fucking joking, Maxi. Admit it. You've no idea what you're going to do. And none of this shit is going to make any difference to Will. That bastard over there is either going to kill him or let him loose, and there's sweet fuck all that you—or any of us, for that matter—can do about that. I know you, Max, better than anyone, and this isn't just about Will. It's about her too." He glanced over at Maria and then back at Max. "And I'm telling you, mate, she's not worth dying for."

Maria's mouth was half-open in shock.

DG continued his rant. "She's hooked on this gangster's line good and proper, Max, whatever the murdering fuck has done."

"I don't want anyone to be hurt," Maria said, finding her voice.

"Too fucking late for that, darling," DG said curtly, "and too late to play 'little Miss Innocent' too."

DG placed his hands on Max's shoulders, calming a little, and trying to reason with his friend. "It's just neurochemicals, Max—phenylethylamine, norepinephrine, and dopamine."

Max thought he'd misheard. "What the hell are you talking about?"

"Lisa told me. Neurochemicals. She has a degree in chemistry. Bright girl. She said that's what I'm addicted to, and I think she's right. The chemicals create the spark that I think is love, but it isn't. It's just fucking chemicals. So come on, please, Max. Let the neurochemicals go, and let her go, and come over to the island. We need to stick together."

"I can't," Max said. "I need to see this through. Please, DG. I have to do it."

"No, you don't," DG said. "No more than the rest of us do. There's no point to staying. There's just as much chance of getting Will back whether we stay or go. She wants to stay, and she won't come to harm, so leave her. Carlo the Murderer loves her, and he's welcome to her. Come on, we're going."

DG grabbed Max's arm and pulled him toward the steps. Max held firm, but DG slapped him on the cheek. The blow took Max by surprise and knocked him off his feet. He swung a fist wildly in return, but DG had already moved quickly to one side, and the punch flew harmlessly past his right ear. Max was off balance again and struggling to remain upright, as DG wrapped both his arms tightly around him in a human straitjacket.

"Listen!" DG shouted. "Listen!"

Max struggled, and DG released him.

"Get off," Max said.

"OK," DG said. "OK. I'm not going to tell you what to do. The world has gone fucking mad, and maybe I don't know shite anymore, but there will be another girl. This gangster's moll is not the only one, Maxi. So please, wake up. You're going to die here, *really fucking die*, and for what? A fairy tale? A fantasy. It's all in your head. She's as real as Cinderella or Ariel. She doesn't exist. She doesn't love you, Maxi, and she never will because she loves that fucking wanker over there, the one that's holding Will hostage. So what does all that say about her?"

DG turned to face Maria. "Yes, that's right, darling. You've only known Max for a couple of days, but after all that's happened, can't you see that my friend is worth ten thousand of that piece-of-shit of yours? Whether he admits it or not, I know he's doing this for *you* as much for Will, and you don't even realize. Well, now you fucking well do."

Maria was horrified.

"I have to see this through, DG," Max whispered. "I'm sorry."

"I know," DG said. He kissed Max on the forehead. "I know you do. I love you, man." And with that, he turned and ran down the steps to join Stan.

As the dinghy outboard started up, Maria turned to Max. "Is that true?"

"Which bit?"

"You know," Maria said urgently. "Please go, Max. There is still time to lea—"

"Get yourself out of sight in the saloon," Max said, unable to meet her gaze. "At least you can do that for me."

At that moment, the radio crackled to life again.

CHAPTER 21

Jack was back in interrogation room 1.

"Mr. North, my colleagues are beginning to doubt my opinion of your guilt," Masa said. He glanced over at the mirror to where he thought Andres Chava from Interpol was sitting. "However, I have more experience in dealing with hardened criminals—devious, resourceful criminals that would gladly sacrifice members of their own family without a second's thought."

Masa stood proudly to his full height, which Jack estimated was about five foot three.

Smug, short arse, thought Jack. A laptop computer was sitting on the Formica table. Its screen was open but facing Masa, away from Jack.

"Additional information has come to light, Mr. North, CCTV footage, and it proves you've been lying."

Jack gulped. *CCTV footage. The mill fire. Oh God!*

Masa raised an index finger and swooped it flamboyantly down on the Enter key, and then spun the laptop around.

Jack looked. It was CCTV footage, but not of the mill. *Thank God.*

"This is from a security camera in Porto Colom," Masa said. "Do you recognize any of these men?"

The picture was clear and in color, much better than the grainy, black-and-white images he remembered seeing on *Crimewatch*. Four men came into view, their backs toward the camera. They walked quickly along the marina quayside. One of them turned as he reached the Porto Colom Yacht Club sign. He was a stocky, shaven-headed guy.

Jack jumped upright. "Stan! Yes, yes, it's them. I told you they'd be there, Mr. Masa. That's Stan Longbottom, and the others are Max, DG, and Will. They're going to my yacht. You've got to believe me now."

He sat back in his chair and chuckled, feeling relaxed. But what happened next was a shock. "Not *that* yacht!" he yelled at the monitor. "You dickheads!"

He watched in disbelief as DG crossed over the wrong gangplank, onto the wrong yacht. The other three men swiftly followed. It was ridiculous.

What's going on? Did they go sailing with somebody else? Did they ditch my invitation? They must have—those bastards!

He hoped to see his four old school chums recognize their mistake and cross back over to the quayside, but they didn't. A few moments later, they disappeared from view.

"They're going sailing with somebody else," he said, incredulously.

Masa was smirking.

"Mr. North, give me some respect, please. Your school-reunion story was a good cover, but you've been found out. Modern technology proves you are a liar. As I said earlier, I've known men like you to sacrifice their own brothers to the cartels, so a bunch of old school friends against whom you hold a grudge is no big loss. As you English sometimes say, you killed two birds with one stone."

"Eh?" said Jack, not comprehending.

"Admit it," Masa said. "Your 'friends' are mules."

"Mules? Like donkeys, you mean?"

Masa's patience was wearing thin again. "Your school friends are drug mules, Mr. North. You hired them to take contraband into the UK."

"Eh?"

"Do they realize the danger they're in? The risks they're running? A few thousand euros for carrying a small package in their suitcase. Easy money. Did you mention the thirty-five-year jail sentence?"

Jack was still stunned. He'd just realized that Max and the others weren't going sailing with somebody else. "They got on the wrong fucking yacht," he said to himself more so than to Masa. Then he was distracted as Masa restarted the video footage.

Porto Colom marina came back into view, and Jack saw a man wearing a black suit striding purposefully along the walkway. Three other men in black overalls and black baseball caps followed. Two were carrying what looked like ski bags, and a third—an enormous man who was at least seven feet tall and with a muscular frame to match—had a coffin-like box over each shoulder.

Gloom set in.

Jack knew where they were headed. *Where else would they be going on a fucked up day like this?*

His hopes rose as the four men paused momentarily at the vacant slot left by the departed yacht, which Jack's idiotic schoolmates had obviously taken. But those hopes were quickly squashed as the man in the black suit stepped over the *Infamous Five's* gangplank. His colleagues followed.

"Take me back to Pedro," Jack whispered. "He's the only sane person left in this fucked-up world."

Masa was beaming. "Twenty minutes later, your motor yacht departed, Mr. North. It was your yacht, yes?"

"You know it was. But I'm telling you, I've never seen those men before. Although there was a gorilla like that guy at the back in Lovebirds. He scared the girls. Now, you'll probably not be remotely interested in this, Mr. Masa, but those men just stole my yacht. Why don't you just arrest them and see who the fuckers are? And get my yacht back."

The laptop was still running, and the huge man reappeared. He stepped over the gangplank in one enormous stride, and peered straight into the CCTV camera as he lumbered along the quayside.

"It is him!" Jack shouted.

"Who?" Masa asked.

"Him. The guy I just told you about. He came into the club with two other thugs, and we threw 'em out for getting too heavy with girls. It took ten of my staff to throw that monster out."

Masa let out a deep breath and raised his arms in triumph. "Finally, you admit involvement with the cartels." He was looking directly at the mirror again, smug self-righteousness written all over his face. "You've been a tough nut to crack, Mr. North. But I knew we'd get there in the end."

Jack lifted his gaze from the laptop after watching the huge man reboard with another two large boxes. He stood. "There's only one of us who is cracked around here, Masa, and it's not me!" he shouted, slamming his fists down on the table.

It bounced under the force.

Masa stepped back in alarm. "Restrain him, Captain," he squealed, just as the door opened.

Doug Clark entered. "No need for that, Captain Pique."

Jack banged on the table again.

"Mr. North!" Clark said.

Jack stopped in his tracks. Clark's commanding voice blew away the red mist that was firing his thoughts. He'd been about to punch Masa, which was probably a bad decision, though it would have been enjoyable. The urge to want to fight had surprised Jack, he was usually terrified of violence—or rather the possibility of being hit back—never mind being machine-gunned.

He sat again and calmed himself.

Clark addressed Masa. "Andres and I have just studied Lieutenant Torres's report, and we're in agreement. Torres concludes that Mr. North is of low intelligence, both intellectually and emotionally. He hasn't the mental agility to lie to us. Torres believes that, at worst, North is a pawn in Ortega's organization, very likely expendable, and most likely an unwitting accomplice."

Jack was listening. "Would you pass on my sincere thanks to Lieutenant Torres for the confidence boost?" he asked sarcastically. "I am actually here, you know, whoever you are."

Clark laughed. "Sorry, Mr. North. My name is Doug Clark. I'm an agent with the US Drug Enforcement Administration. This is Alberto—"

"I know who he is," Jack said.

"Of course you do," Clark said.

Jack continued. "It's polite to wait until someone has left the room before calling them names. And in addition, Mr. Clark, even a person of low intelligence, both intellectually and emotionally, knows an assessment done by someone they've never actually met can't be up to much."

Clark smiled. "Lieutenant Torres knows you well. And here he is."

Two men were standing behind Clark. One was a tall good-looking man in a suit, and the other was of medium height and wearing full police uniform. Clark beckoned the uniformed officer forward.

"Lieutenant Torres," said Clark, introducing him to Jack.

Torres was immaculate. A dark-blue slim-fitting jacket hugged to perfection, and the creases on each trouser leg could have been used as a ruler. Gold braid covered the brim of his hat, and his brass belt buckle dazzled in the bright electric light.

"Never seen him before in my life," Jack said confidently.

"Lieutenant Torres is a criminal psychologist," Clark said.

"So what?" Jack was growing irritated. "I've seen *CSI: Miami*. He's comparing me to a random prolife. Probably deduced all that bullshit from one of my old school history essays. Well, if he did, he needs to think again, as Mum wrote them all." He laughed. "Mum was shite at history."

"Lieutenant Torres does know you well," said Clark, smiling again. "Lieutenant?"

Lieutenant Torres removed his hat.

Jack looked on, puzzled. He'd never met Torres. Had he? *Surely, I'd remember him.* For some reason, however, a small part of his brain wasn't totally convinced. It reminded him of the time he'd seen a woman at the fish counter in Tesco's. He knew that he knew her, but he couldn't work out from where. Eventually, he'd decided that she must be a machinist at the mill. Then, he'd been watching *Coronation Street* with his mum, and the woman had walked into the fictional Rovers Return. But this Torres guy had never been in Coronation Street—for definite.

"Hello, Mr. North," said the lieutenant in perfect Old Etonian. "My father was the Spanish ambassador to your country, and so I know London very well, but not so much the north of England. I will roughen up my accent a little for you."

The lieutenant grimaced slightly and spoke again. "Señor Jack, you make breakfast for a dog?"

Jack's mouth fell open. "Pe-Pedro?"

"Si, señor," the lieutenant said, unable to contain his glee. "Si, Señor Jack. I am Pedro."

Jack couldn't get his head around it. "But, Pedro, how did you get out?"

This time, both Clark and Chava laughed.

Masa didn't.

"Alberto, do you still believe this man is a master criminal?" Chava asked.

Masa's temper got the better of him. He began wagging his finger crazily and stuttering in his effort to release a volley of accusations about the incompetence of everybody but himself.

Clark butted in. "Come on, Alberto. Take a chill pill. This guy's not worth it. He's a nobody."

"Cheers again," Jack said.

"Sorry, Mr. North," Clark said, glancing sideways. "But I'm talking about serious organized crime here."

The American continued. "Alberto, the upshot is that I'm widening the search for Carlo; otherwise, it'll be too late. Are you with me? I really don't want to go over your head."

Masa was silent.

"Alberto, let's do this together," Chava said.

"Come on, Alberto," Clark said.

Masa had calmed a little, and his belief in Jack's guilt was wavering, too. He nodded assent. He wanted Ortega as much as anybody did. Then he spotted the English pig winking at him again and made a grab for Jack's throat. Luckily, Chava caught him midlaunch and hustled him quickly from the room.

Jack was howling with laughter until the huge captain slapped the top of his head. "Oy," Jack said. "You can't do that. I wish to make a complaint, Agent Clark. He just assaulted me."

"Did he?" Clark asked, feigning surprise. "I never saw anything." And he slapped Jack over the head again for good measure, much to the captain's amusement.

CHAPTER 22

Max picked up the radio handset.

"This is Max," he said.

The responder was annoyed.

"You are provoking me—a stupid thing to do," Carlo said. "Now, sail over to me immediately or el—"

Max cut him off.

The hum of the outboard motor powering Stan and DG over to the island became the only sound. Max waited a few seconds and then clicked on the receiver.

"Forget the threats," he said. "There's only me onboard, and I've no dinghy. Everybody else is over on the island. So you'll need to bring Will over here. And cut the bullshit. I know you've still got a dinghy. We'll use it to cross to the *Infamous Five* after the exchange. Our friends can rejoin us there."

The response was terse. "That's not what we agreed."

"Correct," Max said. "We didn't. But I'm fucked if I'm swimming over."

Click. Max switched off the radio set and picked up yesterday's Montecristo—he'd found it dry and unbroken in his waterproof jacket pocket. A good couple of inches remained. He lit it and remembered being alone after the party, when the smoke ring rose slowly toward DG's gods. It had contained his new list—new goals for a new life, a fresh start.

He didn't remember asking for this lot.

He inhaled and thought about what DG had just said. His friend was right about him having no plan. In fact, it was worse than that. He had absolutely no idea whatsoever about what he was going to do when Carlo arrived. *Except probably die.*

But DG was wrong to make out his principal motivation for staying onboard was Maria. He did want her, of course he did, more than he thought was possible, even though it was futile. But what truly drove him on were thoughts of Juliet and Harriet, Will's two daughters. He kept imagining waking in the morning and having a moment of ignorant bliss before the girls' tearstained faces flashed before his eyes. If Will died that was the vision he'd see every day for the rest of his life, and he couldn't live like that. *Daddy's never coming home, girls,* Jane was saying in his thoughts. *And Uncle Max has come by to tell you exactly why not.*

Maria popped into his head. The Maria in the portrait. Dazzling green eyes, long black hair laying across smooth, olive-skinned shoulders—and suddenly Max wasn't so sure that Juliet and Harriet were the main reasons for staying.

Christ, maybe DG is right. What does that say about me? Am I doing this to show her that all men aren't like Carlo? And then what? Die? Great.

Max knew that what DG had said about Maria was true. She was in love with a gangster. And she fully understood what Carlo was, too.

And not just a gangster, but the gangster who might well be about to kill me.

He was being overdramatic again, but then remembered the missiles and the guns. Paranoia and a vivid imagination weren't destabilizing his sanity; real life was.

So who am I doing this for? Myself? Juliet and Harriet? Maria? Will?

He didn't know, so he gave up trying to work it out.

There were sounds of activity on the *Infamous Five.*

Max's neck cricked painfully as his head snapped around to see what was happening, but he still couldn't detect any movement. Suddenly he felt cold, really cold. It was a beautiful warm day, but he was freezing. This must be what people meant by the icy hand of death. He tried to think of home. A book he'd read one summer said that distracting the mind helped manage fear. Keep the mind busy with something else.

He took another drag on the Montecristo, and another, and felt light-headed. A photo of a gravestone popped into his head. His. Cheery. A slab of dull-gray marble with the following epitaph:

Here lies Max West. He found the One—and then died.

Jesus. That sums it up pretty well.

The Montecristo was tasting all the better for knowing the danger of lung cancer was irrelevant. It wasn't going to kill him this afternoon.

He savored the warm smoke. "Shit, that is so good."

The *Infamous Five* was drifting on her anchor chain. Her stern was coming around and nearly facing the *Conchita*. Max could see that two dinghies had been laid in the water.

Lying bastard.

Max checked on Stan and DG's progress. They had reached shore and were lugging heavy bags up the beach. Kylie and Tracy were pulling the dinghy out of the surf. They were safe.

Good.

His thoughts returned to Carlo. Maybe the guy did love Maria. Just because he was a mass-murdering, psychotic bastard—according to DG—didn't mean he wasn't capable of falling in love or of being compassionate. Maria said Carlo had comforted her and her mama for months on end. Was that all a ruse? He didn't think so. The chances were that Carlo really had fallen in love with Maria and that he didn't know that she was aboard the *Conchita*.

Max smiled, hearing another DG retort in his head.

"And if that's the case, maybe we're being a bit too hard on old Carlo. Maybe he's not such a bad a sport, after all, as he was only wanting to blow up every fucker apart from Miss Colombia!"

He pulled heavily on the Montecristo, which was nearly done—leaned back and blew the smoke upwards. The distraction technique was working pretty well, although panic was just a misjudged thought away.

Where was I? Oh yeah. Carlo is an evil bastard but probably loves Maria. And therefore he wouldn't have fired antitank missiles at his own yacht if he'd known his fiancée was aboard.

But he did fire. And there was that question again, the one that had been dogging him every minute or so for the past twenty-four hours. Even though Carlo didn't know Maria was onboard, *still why did he fire?*

The bulging leather bag containing the diamonds was sitting on the table beside him—riches beyond his comprehension. He remembered Dannii's seamless transition from good-time party girl to diamond expert and then to ecstatic lottery winner, all in the time it took for the precious gems to slide from the end of the pipe and start bouncing around the deck. Dannii's estimate was twenty million pounds plus, which yet again brought him back to *the* question that he couldn't answer.

He spoke it aloud in a cloud of cigar smoke. "Why would Carlo want to destroy the *Conchita*?"

The antitank missiles would alert the authorities to his presence, cost him twenty million pounds in diamonds, and a superyacht, and a military arsenal, and God knows what else.

He'd said it without thinking. "And God knows what else."

It was obvious. There had to be something else undiscovered aboard the *Conchita*—something even more valuable than millions in diamonds. Otherwise why would Carlo still be prepared to destroy the Conchita. He would clearly go to any lengths to ensure nobody else got their hands on it.

But what was it?

He'd no idea.

And surely Stan would have found it. He'd scoured the *Conchita* from top to bottom and taken most of her apart.

Max tried to put himself into Carlo's shoes, which wasn't easy to do. *If I was a superintelligent, multilingual international drug lord who's also an Olympic-standard fencer, a billionaire, and a murderer, then what would I value over anything else?* Two ideas came to mind.

Maria.

But Carlo was already engaged to her.

An Olympic gold medal.

Ridiculous.

Think again.

But he never got the chance. His heart missed a beat. Four men were standing on the stern of the *Infamous Five* and were staring across the still water at him. Max stared back. He wasn't being macho; he was just unable to look away.

Two of the men were carrying a sack. It seemed heavy. They tossed it carelessly into one of the dinghies and climbed in after it. A third man stepped into the other dinghy, and the fourth passed him two machine guns and stepped in, too. A few moments later, both outboard motors burst into life. One dinghy began making the short journey over to the *Conchita*, and the other went speeding off toward the island, until its high-pitched motor coughed, spluttered, and cut out.

Max shivered. Ready or not, it was time to face the music. He flicked the stub of the smoldering Montecristo and watched it tumble into the sea. It plopped noiselessly into the water, and floated, causing small circular ripples. It reminded Max of the rock slab blasted from the cliff by the antitank missile, albeit on an altogether less impressive scale.

A minute later, Max walked onto the main deck just as the dinghy arrived at the swimming platform.

One man began tying on while the other raced toward him. Max flinched at the man's pounding steps, but it was only when the heavyweight stomping ceased that he fully recognized the enormousness of what was facing him. The man in front of him was a giant—an ogre, a grotesque, comic-book rogue—seven feet tall, with large, ugly warts on his face, and muscles so big that they were bulging out of his clothing. He was wearing black military fatigues and two ammunition belts crossed over his chest. His black boots were just massive and planted in a stabilizing, solid stance.

Ordinarily, Max would have laughed. *Great, fancy dress outfit.* Except this oversized cartoon villain was pointing a Minimi machine gun at his chest—Max recognized the model from Stan's tutorial—and it wasn't a fake accessory from the fancy dress shop.

In the engine room's secret compartment, the Minimi had appeared unwieldy and weighty. But in this man's hands, which were the size of frying pans, it looked like a toy. Max noticed three black boxes attached to the man's waist belt and remembered Stan pointing them out in the engine room.

"Ammunition. Two hundred rounds in each box," Stan had said.

Jesus Christ. How many times is he going to shoot me?

The ogre could sense Max's growing fear and smiled, exposing an irregular set of crooked, nicotine-stained teeth.

The second man came on deck. A bigger contrast between two individuals, there couldn't be. *An ogre and a city slicker.* This guy had the relaxed air of a top banker taking a mid-afternoon stroll around the city park before returning to his penthouse office for a meeting with his personal tailor. He was immaculate. A crisp, white, open-necked shirt, and not a black hair out of place.

It was Carlo for sure.

He was considering his prisoner. Max returned the examination and spotted white, powdery residue on Carlo's ankle boots. Salt. From the raging sea. *Not such a pleasant crossing for you either, then.*

A third man stumbled up onto the deck. An old sack was over his head, so he couldn't see, and his hands were tied behind his back. He must have been inside the larger sack, which Max had seen thrown into the dinghy. The man edged gingerly forward. He was making good but slow progress until the ogre got bored and shoved him in the back. Max stepped forward and caught the man as he fell headfirst toward the deck.

"I've got you, Will," said Max.

The man whimpered.

Carlo pulled a gun from behind his back.

"Miguel, search the yacht. I'll cover these two."

"Si, Carlo."

The ogre disappeared into the saloon.

He would find Maria.

Two long minutes ticked by.

Max's brain was running two scenarios. One, Maria would scream as she was dragged out on deck. Two, Maria would whoop with delight as she joyfully skipped through the saloon doors and into Carlo's welcoming arms.

Neither prospect was good.

Miguel reappeared. He was alone.

"Just him, Carlo."

"Good." Carlo lowered his gun. "Remove the bag and the tape."

The ogre unceremoniously ripped the sack off Will's head. Will blinked madly in the bright sunshine, desperately trying to see where Max was. He couldn't speak, his mouth was taped closed, with tape wrapped tightly right around his head. The ogre pulled a large hunting knife from a sheath on the outside of his leg above his ankle and used it to slice through both the tape and the skin on the back of Will's skull. Blood spewed down Will's white polo shirt as the tape and chunks of brown hair were pulled away.

Will screamed.

"Jesus Christ," Max shouted, trying to hold him upright.

Will was shaking with pain and fear, but suddenly, a higher purpose took hold. "Max, he's going to kill all of us," he blurted out, not expecting to be given the chance to say much more. "There are two men going over to the island with orders to kill everybody there. We're done for, Max, and it's all my fault for falling overboard."

Max put his hand on Will's cheek as Carlo raised his gun.

"It's OK, Will," Max said, looking past him at Carlo. "I know what he intends to do, and falling overboard made no difference to that."

He heard a small noise from the saloon behind him. For another heart-stopping moment, Max thought that Carlo and Miguel had heard it, too. But neither man's demeanor changed.

Will slumped to the deck and held on to Max's legs.

"So, you must be Max," Carlo said.

"And you are Carlo, according to that dog of yours. Carlo who?"

The aggrieved ogre took a step forward, but a lazily raised hand from his boss stopped him in his tracks.

"Who I am is of no importance, Max. I will soon be gone, but I do apologize for Miguel's actions. He has many fine qualities, but alas, finesse is not one of them." He smiled warmly at his employee, who, in turn, displayed his unhealthy front teeth.

Drips of sweat were running down Max's back, and he could feel an artery in his neck pulsating alarmingly. He thought he might be about to have a heart attack, but was desperately trying to keep his wits about him. The stomach acid in his throat and the scolding heartburn weren't helping. It was difficult to talk and swallow saliva at the same time. He slowed his breathing, but he could sense panic was sitting on his shoulder.

"I thought that even murderers had a code, at least a sense of honor," he said and coughed slightly. "You've not even the decency to explain why you're about to butcher innocent people over nothing more than a stupid misunderstanding."

He was about to cough again but resisted and swallowed hard. He was determined to wait calmly for a reply.

Carlo shrugged and surveyed the surrounding hills. He was searching for any signs of a threat and was listening hard too. He walked over to the port side and then to starboard, leaning right over the side of the *Conchita*, as if he were checking to see if pirates were climbing up the anchor chains. Satisfied none were, he turned to face Max.

"It's a shame we won't get to know each other," Carlo said. "However, I am a man of honor." He looked out to sea, as if some of the thoughts he was harboring were of a place far away. "You know of Colombia?"

"Of course," Max said.

"Most Europeans think it's in Africa," Carlo said, almost absentmindedly.

"No, they don't," said Max. "Most know it's in South America."

Carlo continued. "We live on the same planet, Max. But we might as well live in different galaxies." He looked distant—and maybe even sad. "We have totally different lives."

"We're both here now," Max said. "So the world can't be that big."

"Indeed so," Carlo said. "And that's why it's a big problem. Our worlds and lives have collided."

"What are you talking about?"

Carlo ignored his question. "Two of my brothers died this week."

Max assumed that Carlo was talking about two of his employees. Maria hadn't mentioned brothers or sisters. Surely, if members of Carlo's own family had been killed, then he'd be a bit more upset than he appeared now. Plus, wouldn't he be at home, grieving with his family, instead of chasing a bunch of idiots across the Mediterranean?

"Did they drown on the crossing?"

Carlo shook his head. "I can't take chances, Max. Business failure isn't bankruptcy for me; it's death."

Max heard another noise from behind him—from inside the saloon. It was a knock, as if someone had stretched out their legs and banged into something.

Again, nobody else heard.

"How can we possibly pose a problem to your business, for God's sake?" asked Max. "Come on, Carlo. We'd never even heard of you until just now. And we don't even know what your business is."

Carlo became stern. Max could see the steel in the man—feel the coldness.

"How do I know that?" Carlo asked. "I have to assume you're a threat because I don't know who you are. How do I know that Max is even your real name? Are you working with the Drug Enforcement Administration? Are you a spy? Who are your colleagues? Fellow agents? Interpol? Colombian government officials? I don't know. You could be anybody, Max. The police, a mercenary, an investigative journalist—they've caused me some trouble in the past. My family has survived this long only by eliminating risk when we see it, the minute we see it. Our rivals—business competitors, if you will—eagerly wait to take our place. They stand with daggers drawn, and if I were to show weakness and hesitate, then they would strike. And I would do the same to them. Indeed, I have done so many times."

Max just listened. It was about as close to a confession as Carlo could get without saying he ran a drug business.

Carlo continued. "If ordinary people like you make a mistake at work, you're sent on a training course. But in my business, mistakes mean death. Two of my men were killed this week as I said, and it's my responsibility to make sure their deaths are the last on this ill-fated trip. I can't take chances. You and your stupid friends shouldn't be here."

"So the truth means nothing?" Max asked.

Carlo laughed. The sadness is his eyes was long gone. "So naïve. What is the truth? Innocent and guilty are killed every day all over the world, but who decides who are the innocent and who are the guilty? Terrorist or freedom fighter? The British government has slaughtered thousands in the so-called war against terror, and yet other British politicians argue the Iraq War was illegal and about nothing more than securing Arabian oil."

Max was standing perfectly still. On one level, somewhere far away at the back of his brain, he was curious and genuinely interested to know how a murderer could justify his crimes. Yet on a more practical level, he was worried that if he tried to move his legs, he would fall over. They felt like jelly. He knew it didn't matter how strong his arguments for not being killed were. He could have a personal note of excuse written by Jesus, and still this self-righteous bastard would kill both him and Will. However, he needed more time. He desperately wanted to live—he had to prolong this drama for as long as possible and hope for a miracle.

In response to Carlo, he wanted to say what DG would have said. *"I'm not sure other people will make the link between the war against Assad and ISIS and you, Carlo, i.e. murdering folk that took the wrong booze cruise."* But he didn't. "We know nothing of your business, Carlo.

Colombia is thousands of miles from here. This is madness, and you know it is. So, please, just let us go."

Will had passed out and slumped forward. Considering the blood loss, dehydration, and stress, this was not surprising. He became conscious again and looked soulfully into Max's face, choosing not to see whatever was happening behind him.

Carlo was speaking again. "You are unlucky. I usually work through intermediaries, but on rare occasion I need to oversee operations personally, as is the case here. This transaction has not gone well. There have been unforeseen complications, and I must mop up quickly and return home."

Max was deciphering "mop up," when Carlo smiled. "Fortunately, a more pleasant transaction awaits in Bogotá."

Max knew what Carlo was talking about. *The wedding. Carlo and Maria. Mr. and Mrs. Gangster. Maria wouldn't be too happy being classified as a "pleasant transaction." Although that did sound better than being an "unforeseen complication."*

His thoughts went back to Maria. *Is she listening in the saloon, or has she gone below decks until the dirty work is over?* "I'm guessing it's not bananas you export to Europe," he said.

"Coffee, actually." Carlo smiled again. "But if that's all we were selling, then I wouldn't need Miguel's expertise."

The ogre grunted and displayed his brown teeth again.

"I'm sorry, Max. Our time is up," Carlo said as if he were finishing off a staff meeting.

Max realized that Carlo was only referring to his and Will's time. "Are your wife and kids waiting in Bogotá?" Max asked forcefully. "You see, Carlo, Will wants to go home to his wife and daughters." He was still holding on to Will's blood-soaked collar to stop him from slumping forward again. "His wife is called Jane. She's waiting for him right now in Ibiza Town. We saw her standing on the quay."

Will looked up at Max, forgetting his pains. "Jane is here?" he asked in a whimper.

Max carried on. "Will has two daughters. Juliet is eight, and Harriet is six. It was Juliet's birthday last month. She got a bike, which Will promised to show her how to ride. We didn't see the girls on the quay, so they're probably waiting at home. I'd love to hear you justify to your wife that you murdered a father of two on the million-to-one chance he was some kind of undercover CIA operative. Christ, man, you're sick. You've watched too many movies, and your wife is sick, too, if she buys all your bullshit."

Max listened for any noises behind him, a signal that maybe Maria was coming to his rescue.

He heard nothing but silence.

Carlo was unmoved. "Over the years, many have pleaded for their lives and the lives of their families. I've witnessed acts of immense courage, with parents offering themselves in exchange for wayward offspring. It doesn't work. Disloyalty and incompetence are cancerous, and they must be cut out before they destroy us all. Even my father and his associates have had to sacrifice untrustworthy family members over the years, as to do otherwise would show favoritism and, therefore, vulnerability. Loyalty is everything. I am not married yet Max, but soon will be to an amazing woman. She lives in your world of ideals and dreams, and I'm glad she does. But as I love Maria, she also loves me, and in time she'll adjust to the life I have to lead."

"I'm sure she will," Max said. "After all, what she doesn't know can't hurt her, and I hazard to guess the lifestyle you can give her means she'll conveniently ignore all of your murdering exploits. I'm sure Maria will be very proud of her husband."

Carlo laughed. "Very good. It's a shame you will never know Maria; otherwise, you wouldn't say that. I keep my world secret from her not because I don't trust her, or because I worry she couldn't cope with knowing, but because she is my sanctuary and my joy. The luxury of everyday living is denied me, but Maria gives me respite and peace. She keeps me sane."

The outboard motor on the dinghy taking Carlo's other two men over to the island fired up again, and Carlo walked over to the rail and waved. One of the men saw him and signaled a thumbs-up just as the engine coughed and cut out again. This time, the men didn't bother attempting to restart it but, rather, began paddling toward shore.

Carlo turned back to Max.

"Max, I have learned to accept myself and what I must do to protect my family. I box off my personal life, as it's the only way I can hope to enjoy it. My way of living has compensations, but it isn't ideal. I really don't want to kill you and your friends, but I have to. It's as simple as that. Nothing personal, just business. That's all."

"And you call me naïve," Max said, not hiding the utter contempt in his voice. "Of course killing somebody is personal. Just how much more personal can you get? And you can box off murdering us as much as you like, but all those boxes are still contained in your *own* miserable head. You and only you are responsible. 'Businessman'? Don't make me laugh. All you are is nothing but a dirty, stinking murderer."

Carlo shrugged.

Max kept talking. "What's your justification for killing the six people over on the island?"

Carlo was in business mode. "My men will kill your friends and then enjoy the women—first. I think they deserve a reward for their efforts last night. No doubt, you and your friends already sampled them. Good-bye, Max."

Carlo turned to leave.

It was the moment the ogre had been waiting for. His black eyes were sparkling. He enjoyed nothing better than eliminating Carlo's risks, and he was itching to shoot up this little shit.

Max was looking right down the barrel. *This is it. One more second, and I'll be dead and gone.*

He didn't want to die, he never really believed he would—not today—but now he was going to.

Maria bolted from the saloon. She was running wild, a look of total madness on her face. She skidded to a stop directly in front of Max and directly in line between him and the Minimi, as Miguel's finger began pulling the trigger.

"Stop, Carlo. Stop!" she was shouting.

Miguel wrenched the already-firing gun skyward and away to his right. A line of heavy bullets ripped the air next to Max's ear, smashed through the saloon windows, and blasted part of the flybridge superstructure clean away.

The giant man had recognized Maria even before she'd cried out Carlo's name, even though he'd never met her. Otherwise, it would have been too late.

Maria edged slowly backward, her arms outstretched toward the smoking machine gun in a protective gesture, until her leg knocked into Will's head. "Carlo, stop this. These people have done nothing, and they know nothing of you."

Carlo had frozen in horror. He'd been leaving but had only taken a few steps away. His calm exterior had been shattered. He'd thought he and Miguel were under attack from an unidentified member of Max's crew—someone who'd been hidden out below decks—and he'd raised his own gun to fire. He was still aiming at Maria's head now. A vision of himself pulling the trigger and blowing a hole in her skull flashed before his eyes.

"Maria?" he whispered, lowering his gun.

The last time he'd seen her was at El Dorado International Airport in Bogotá, when she'd seen him off on the flight to Madrid. He'd last spoken to her a couple of days ago, telling her he'd be home earlier than scheduled—being confident he'd evade the authorities in Spain. And everything back home had seemed fine too. He remembered that Maria sounded happy, and was arranging their wedding—and was in Colombia—so how could she be here?

He was still questioning his eyes.

Then he strode forward and threw his arms around his trembling fiancée. The Sig Sauer P226 nine-millimeter still in his hand.

"Maria, my love. How is this possible?"

He closed his eyes and thanked God above for stopping him open fire. When he opened them again, he was looking straight at Max, and realization dawned. Maria had heard everything—his double life, the Ortega family's involvement in the drug trade, and the executions, and worst of all, she had witnessed his cold-blooded intent to kill all of these people, including the father of two young daughters currently bleeding all over the deck. The illusion of being a coffee producer was well and truly at an end. And this idiotic fool was responsible.

Max knew that he was doomed. He'd seen Carlo's expression change from one of shock at seeing Maria, to utter confusion as to how she got there, and finally to pure hatred—as he fully understood the implications.

Maria didn't return Carlo's embrace. She waited for Carlo to release his grip and then pushed him away. Her eyes were red and puffy from silently weeping in her hiding place behind the saloon-door curtains. Miguel had used his machine-gun barrel to pull the material to one side—when he'd searched inside—but he'd been looking for armed men with guns at the ready. He failed to spot Maria, who was lain prostrate on the floor and was partially hidden by a side table.

She mustered some strength. "These people cannot hurt you, Carlo. They know nothing of you."

Before Carlo could answer, Maria's face screwed up in further anguish.

"What is it, my love?" Carlo asked, grabbing her arm.

Maria ripped it away and stared at him. "Who killed Papa?" she said, stumbling backward. She tripped over Will's foot and fell to the deck.

Carlo rushed forward and tried to lift her, but she was limp. She slumped back down again and curled into a ball.

"Maria," said Carlo. "You don't know what you heard. Please talk to me." He pulled her up into a sitting position. She opened her eyes and sat cross-legged, her head in her hands. Carlo knelt by her.

"I love you, Maria, and your mama, and I would have loved your papa, too. Please, darling. Look at me."

Maria's voice was a whisper. "You didn't even know me or Mama until after Papa was killed."

"I swear to you, Maria. I swear I could never hurt you or your family."

Maria lifted her head and looked into his face. "I just heard you say that it was necessary to sacrifice untrustworthy family members. Papa was working with the government to bring down the cartels. He could have destroyed your entire business, everything your father and...and *you*, Carlo, have built. What better reason could you have to kill him?" She buried her head in her hands again.

Carlo was desperate. "No, no, no. I swear, Maria."

Max knew that Maria had been hanging on to the faint chance that Carlo really was a legitimate businessman, however unlikely that prospect seemed. But now all her hopes had been swept away. She was exhausted both mentally and physically—her body like that of a battery-operated doll that had just been switched off.

The lies she'd told herself had helped her to cope. It had been hell after Papa's death. But with Carlo, she'd begun to move on with her life and leave the seemingly depthless grief behind. Now, the stinging pain of his killing was back with a vengeance, and Papa was dying all over again.

Her childish dreams of living happily ever after were ashes, just as her father's body was. And it was murder. She knew that for certain now.

Carlo stood with Maria sitting at his feet. He realized that further talk at the moment was futile.

Max bent down to comfort her but stopped at Miguel's loud grunt.

Carlo stared at him. "Were you coming to help Maria?"

Max realized his mistake.

"When did Maria arrive on the yacht?" said Carlo. "And how did she get here?"

Max could hardly believe that Maria had only appeared yesterday morning, but he said nothing.

Carlo answered his own questions. "Of course. Vladimir. She flew out to the *Conchita* from Madrid. And that can't have been much before yesterday," he said, realization dawning. "I telephoned her in Colombia the day before that."

Max was guessing what Carlo was about to do.

He was right.

"You fool," Carlo shouted, and he punched Max violently on the cheek.

Max's head whipped around as if it were on a turntable. It was his left cheek again, the same one DG had slapped earlier, but this time it felt like the bone had been smashed. He managed to keep his feet and stood straight, expecting another blow.

None came.

The pleading-and-caring Carlo of a few seconds ago had disappeared. Now his tone was caustic.

"This is why I have to be the man I am. Your sentimentality has got you killed, Max. For a moment, I thought you were clever, but you're just like all the other fools I've killed. You're going to die because of a woman you met yesterday—a woman who is in love with another man, who will be married next month, and who will have forgotten about you next week. All your death will truly achieve is to bring Maria and me closer, as you have forced me to share all my life with her."

Max was feeling downright stupid. What Carlo had just said was exactly what DG had warned him about—and he'd not listened. Understanding his own foolishness hurt more than the punch had done. He glanced down at Maria, who was still sitting on the deck. *Jesus, I'm such a joke. I'm going to die over a teenage fantasy, a wet dream.*

He'd wasted his life. He would never have a wife, children, or grand-children, or any more memorable adventures. Of all the opportunities he'd had to take a stand, he'd chosen this one. *Talk about being a loser.*

His inner voice was angry but sanguine. *Don't worry, dickhead. You won't be making this mistake again. Ever!*

Maria raised her head and looked up at him. His heart lifted.

Carlo punched again, this time knocking Max clean off his feet. His head banged hard into the teak decking and he blacked out for a moment.

When he came around Carlo was standing over him.

"I have no pity for you, Max, only embarrassment that I ever took you seriously."

Max rolled away and staggered to his feet as Carlo pulled Maria to hers too.

"You will watch, Maria," said Carlo, physically turning her head around to face Max and Will.

"Maria should honor your sacrifices. And Max, you can die knowing that Maria is with me."

"Please, Carlo, no," said Maria. "Please don't kill them. I am to be your wife, Carlo, so please don't kill them."

But Carlo wasn't listening. He was cold and stern and determined to finish what needed to be done. "You will be family, Maria. And as you've discovered today, this is not the only time I've killed to keep my family safe, nor will it be the last.

"Miguel," he said, summoning the once again grinning ogre.

CHAPTER 23

"Wait," Max said in alarm, reaching his hands out toward Miguel's machine gun, as Maria had done earlier. "Shooting us will be bad for business Carlo, I promise you. Maybe even catastrophic."

Carlo was dismissive. Men would say anything when they were about to die. "Really?"

Max glanced toward the saloon. "Go see for yourself."

The color instantly drained from Carlo's face. He let go of Maria's hand and dashed into the saloon.

Max took a firmer grip on Will's collar, his fingers inadvertently squeezing blood from the blood-soaked material.

A moment of breathless silence was broken by a howl of fury and the sound of much breaking glass. Vases and ornaments were smashing into the mirrored cocktail bar.

Carlo reappeared. Fire was burning in his eyes. Letting out an animalistic roar he ran at the object of his fury—Max—swinging the Sig Sauer with as much force as he could muster. Max had no chance of avoiding the blow. The pistol slammed into the right side of his skull with a sickening crack. His legs crumpled, and he collapsed to his knees, clutching his head, as his own and Maria's screams filled his ears. He never saw Carlo's right boot smash into his ribs, but the impact kicked the breath from his lungs. He doubled up and vomited. His vision turned black. He couldn't see, and he couldn't breathe.

Have I been shot through the head? It was either that or a knitting needle had been pushed into his temple, behind both eyes, and out the other side. But he could still feel pain—that was for sure—and think and hear. Maria was yelling at Carlo to stop. *I wouldn't know that if my brain had a hole in it.* He lifted a hand to explore the side of his head. Warm liquid was running freely from a gaping cut, but there were no bone fragments. His vision lightened to dark gray—a swirling fog—in which familiar shadows were dancing.

"Are you OK, Max?"

It was Will. He was whispering anxiously into his ear.

Max couldn't respond. His mouth wouldn't work.

Another hand pressed down on his shoulder. He readied for another blow or worse. But nothing came.

It was Maria. "Carlo, if I mean anything to you, then let him be," she said, standing over Max.

"Out of the way, Maria. You don't understand." Carlo was still in a rage, and he pushed her roughly away. Maria stumbled backward, leaving Max unprotected, and Carlo took advantage of the opportunity and placed the barrel of his gun against Max's forehead.

"No, Carlo. Please, no," Maria pleaded through her tears. She knew that if he shot this man dead, there was no way back for him—or her.

Carlo ignored the pleas and pushed the barrel forward, forcing Max's head backward—compelling him to look into his assassin's eyes.

"I underestimated you," Carlo said through gritted teeth. "I won't make that mistake again, believe me. Now, give me back what is mine, or I will splash your brains all over the deck."

Max's blurry vision; the acute, stabbing pain behind his eyes; and the amount of blood dripping down his shirtfront had sent his mind into meltdown. His brain was demanding that all conscious attention be placed on physical injuries and the need to seek emergency medical treatment, and fast—but another part of him knew that this wasn't an option. His subconscious intervened. Fractured skull and possible brain damage was to be put aside, rational thought was necessary to survive—accident and emergency departments weren't much use if half your head was missing.

Max tried to focus his swimming eyes. The periphery of Carlo's face emerged out of the gloom, but the center of his face was totally black, a splotch of ink covering the middle of a photograph, a black puddle. His central vision had been destroyed? He dismissed the thought, and concentrated harder, ignoring the throbbing pain inside his left ear. The ink splotch moved to where Carlo's mouth should have been. Two knuckles directly below it. *How is that possible*? He became aware of another pain. Something was pressing hard against his forehead and it hurt—a lot. *What is happening?*

He moved his head slightly. The right half of Carlo's face appeared. The black splotch had moved. Sunshine glinted off black metal. Gun metal. He understood. The ink splotch was a gun, the pain in the middle of his forehead was being caused by the gun's muzzle digging into his skin, and the two knuckles being where Carlo's mouth should be, were, in fact knuckles, and part of Carlo's fingers, which were wrapped tightly around the trigger.

He heard DG's voice in his head. *"He'll still miss your pea-sized brain."*

"Not now, DG."

Carlo heard him. "What?"

Max closed his eyes and forced himself to concentrate—forced himself to regain clarity. He ignored the bolts of pain and the blood dripping to the deck. When he opened his eyes again, he felt totally different. He focused again on the gun sticking into his forehead, and then moved his gaze slowly along the barrel to where Carlo's fingers were obscuring the trigger. His right eye was weeping from the pressure building up behind it, but he refused to acknowledge the appalling sensation. He willed his eyes on—a hand, a wrist, a white cuff, a white-shirted arm, a white-shirted shoulder, an open collar, black chest hair, a tanned neck, and, finally, an expression of hatred.

Carlo loathed him, that was plain to see, but there was something other than anger in his expression: doubt.

Max was tapping into energy reserves embedded so deeply within himself that even he hadn't known they existed. He reached down with a hand and felt for the deck, keeping his eyes glued onto his assailant's faltering stare. His fingers touched the smooth grooves in the teak, and he opened his palm, pressing down to steady himself. He felt stable.

Now he would stand.

Carlo forced the cold muzzle harder against his head.

Max was numb to any more pain. He would stand. His aching leg muscles, depleted by blood loss and trauma, began to work and kept on working. He would stand. He would do this. The muzzle cut the skin on his forehead but Max redoubled his efforts and made it up off his knees. He was more determined to stand upright than he had ever been to do anything in his life.

As he made it to his feet, Maria gasped and held a hand to her mouth.

Max smiled, still staring into Carlo's flittering eyes; the muzzle of the Sig Sauer P226 still rammed against his forehead. Was there a bullet with his name on it a few inches from his brain? He remembered Stan telling him that after a gun's trigger was pulled the firing pin hammered home and exploded the propellant in the bullet casing, creating a relatively large quantity of gas very quickly, which in accordance with Newton's third law of motion—"action and reaction"— sends the dangerous bit —the bullet—down the gun barrel at three hundred meters per second—so six inches wouldn't leave time to read the paper that was for sure—but it didn't matter. Max felt invincible. A power of incredible intensity was running through each and every cell in his body.

"Go on, then, you son of a bitch," he said.

Carlo blinked. The gun shaking slightly in his grip; indecision was written all over his face.

"Shoot," Max said. "It's what you wanted to do. What are you waiting for? Or are you wondering what my good friend Stan over on the island will do with your secret if you harm anybody else? I'll save some time and tell you. He'll make sure it reaches the US Drug Enforcement Administration, the FBI, and every other police authority he can think of."

Carlo held his gun steady for a moment then pulled it away from Max's head, placing it instead against Will's blood-matted hair.

"Tell your friend Stan to come back. Otherwise, Will dies."

Max suddenly felt faint. The adrenaline was beginning to wear off. "Go to hell, Carlo," he said. "Aren't you listening? If anybody else dies, then the DEA gets a parcel."

Carlo pulled the gun away from Will's head too, and tucked it behind his back. He gathered his thoughts, looking across at the island. "Franco and Diego are about to kill your friends," said Carlo. "When they do, I will recover the item from Stan's dead body. After that, you can watch as

Miguel cuts open Will's throat, and then you can feel the cold blade for yourself."

Max laughed; he couldn't help it. He'd realized that the guy standing in front of him, even with a gun, was no better or stronger than he was. And he'd realized that his gun-toting men, Franco and Carlo, were no better or stronger than his friends either, particularly Stan—or so he hoped—because if Franco and Diego succeeded, then they were all dead.

Carlo, Miguel, Will, and Maria, were all looking at him as if he were crazy.

"You find the death of your friends funny?" Carlo asked.

Franco and Diego had paddled to the shoreline. They jumped into the surf a few yards from dry sand, but the sea was still two or three feet deep, and they were struggling to keep the heavily laden boat stable while moving it slowly forward. The beach was deserted. A long, sweeping arc of fine sand running a half a mile in each direction, but only fifty yards or so deep. It was bordered by a line of thick, black bushes. Behind them was dusty, barren scrub that rose gently up into Cabrera's hills.

A lone figure emerged from between two large clumps of bush. A stocky silhouette against the pale landscape. Stan was out of sight of Franco and Diego, just along the beach, but was clearly visible to those aboard the *Conchita*.

"Who's that?" asked Carlo.

Sun glinted off the man's baldpate.

Max didn't reply. He'd stopped laughing and was biting his nails.

Franco and Diego were out of the surf and starting to pull the dinghy up the beach. The lone figure disappeared.

Good, thought Max. *Stan'll get everybody away to safety. There'll be plenty of places to hide out in the hills.*

Carlo had calmed too. Franco and Diego were two of his best men; the situation was nearly under control.

Stan re-emerged, this time from the bushes directly behind the two men on the beach.

Carlo stiffened.

As did Max.

The next twenty seconds were a blur to them both—and are best described as separate actions.

Stan took two long strides down the beach, and stopped, widening his stance and digging his boots into the sand, to create a firm base.

Carlo fired his Sig Sauer into the air twice—in warning.

Franco and Diego looked across at the *Conchita*, and smiled, assuming two hostlies had just been dispatched.

Stan raised his arms.

Miguel fired a burst of machine-gun fire.

Franco and Diego looked across the water again, this time in confusion—then realized the gunfire was a warning of danger.

An orange flame erupted from the rear of the tube resting on Stan's right shoulder.

Miguel fired again.

Franco and Diego turned around in panic to see a man—and a missile erupting from the launch tube mounted on his shoulder.

Franco went for his M16.

The Kornet missile efficiently completed its short journey and struck the dinghy's outboard motor, exploding with an air-splitting crack fifty times louder than the machine-gun fire.

The dinghy and everything in a twenty yard radius—including Franco and Diego—was consumed by a fireball which almost instantly transformed into a thick black cloud, out of which rose a cluster of dark objects—up and up they went.

Max wondered what they were.

The objects splashed into the sea.

Max understood. *Jesus! Body parts!*

More splashes.

Silence.

Stan was alone on the beach, still standing absolutely rock steady. Then, satisfied that the job was done, he put the empty missile tube under his arm and turned away, disappearing behind the same bushes he'd emerged from only twenty seconds before.

Carlo was staring across at the now empty beach in disbelief. "Who was that?"

"That was my plumber," said Max.

"Plumber?" Carlo said, not understanding.

Max didn't elaborate. His temple began to throb again and he winced. The vision in his left eye was dimming again. But this was no time to stop. "Carlo, this yacht, the guns in the engine room, and the diamonds are all going to be handed over to the police."

Carlo's eyes widened.

"Yes, that's right. We know about the armory and the diamonds," said Max. "The police will get everything—we're not thieves—everything *except* what Stan is keeping safe. And it will stay that way unless you harm any of us—either now or in the future."

He paused for a moment. He wasn't waiting for a reply so much as he was making sure that he hadn't forgotten anything. Carlo was still looking over to where his two men had last been alive.

"Do you hear me?" Max said, forcefully. "Do you agree?"

Carlo gave the faintest of nods.

"That's good," Max said. "Now, get your sorry ass off the *Conchita*." He looked over at Miguel. "And take this murdering piece of shit with you."

Carlo looked at Maria, and realized this wasn't the time or place to seek reconciliation. She was kneeling on the deck comforting Will, and was unable to meet his gaze.

"Miguel," Carlo said, almost in a whisper.

Miguel grunted acknowledgment. He was peering at a spot a hundred meters offshore, where pieces of his two brothers were bobbing up and down in the sea.

Carlo found his voice. "Miguel, back to the other boat. Now is not the time." He reached down and grabbed Maria's arm.

Max stepped forward and laid a hand gently on Maria's shoulder. "She's staying, Carlo."

Carlo didn't react as Max anticipated. He let go of Maria's arm, and she sank back to the deck. "Maria's to be my wife," he said, as if feeling the need to explain himself.

Max thought he understood. "She's in shock, Carlo. Look at her. The last thing Maria needs right now is to be on the run from the law."

Carlo seemed to agree. He knelt and pulled Maria to him; she didn't resist but neither reciprocated.

"I'll take her to Palma," Max said. "Where Maria goes from there is her business. If it's not to you, and you truly love her Carlo, then you'll let her

go. But just in case you get confused by your business-comes-first principles, then you need to know that the insurance policy covers her, too. If
anything happens to Maria, the DEA gets a parcel."

Carlo ran his fingers through Maria's long, black hair. He spoke softly.
"Maria, I swear on my life and on my love for you that I had nothing to do
with your papa's death. Please, please believe me. It is the truth."

He took one of Maria's hands and placed it on his chest. "Search my
heart, my darling. I love you, Maria. And if you love me, too, then we can
still be together."

He kissed her softly on the cheek and stood. "Miguel, we go." And
without even glancing in Max's direction, Carlo turned and disappeared
down the stairway to the main deck—on his way to the dinghy moored at
the swimming platform.

Max couldn't believe it: Carlo was going.

*It's over. Will's safe. I'm safe. Stan, DG, and the girls are all safe.
Maria's safe. Talk about a good result—except maybe for the fractured
skull and losing my eyesight, of course.* It was black joke but he was laughing inside. His body was wrecked, but he was feeling lucky—lucky to be
alive.

Miguel, the ogre, re-slung the Minimi over his shoulder and made
to leave, too. His loyalty toward Carlo had always been unwavering. He
loved Carlo like a brother. He took two steps and then hesitated. *But who
is this man?* Miguel thought. *This Englishman. Max. And why didn't Carlo
kill him?*

Miguel's father had been one of Andre Ortega's sicarios—a cold-
blooded killer, and an even colder parent. His three sons, of which Miguel
was the youngest, weren't the slightest bit sorry when their father was
shot dead by Colombian police, but they were devastated that Mama was
killed, too. The two offending police officers were stabbed to death after
watching their wives meet the same fate.

Andre took the three boys in and provided food, housing, money, weapons training, and targets. Franco, Diego, and Miguel proved themselves to
be exceptional killers—a hereditary talent—the only thing of use their father
had given them. Over the next two decades, the brothers tortured and murdered mercilessly to protect the Ortega family's drug empire, and they were
rewarded handsomely for their efforts. They became Carlo Ortega's most

trusted lieutenants. Were his personal protection. And in all those years of service, Miguel had never seen Carlo outmaneuvered—not once. But of course this wasn't the only reason Miguel's blood was about to boil over.

Franco and Diego, his brothers, were dead. They'd been blown to smithereens right before his eyes. He'd just noticed Diego's smoldering, headless torso floating chest up only forty yards off the port bow, and Franco had met the same destructive fate. And what had Carlo done to exact revenge? Nothing but whisper into the ugly bitch's ear.

How little Carlo valued my brothers, Miguel thought. Then realized a painful truth—how little Carlo must value him also.

Miguel, as DG would say, wasn't the brightest bulb in the chandelier, and his primitive thought processes were having difficulty processing the events of the past few minutes. However, the primitive brain itself, including Miguel's, doesn't need to think, analyse, and weigh up options: it is programmed to *act* on gut feel—to use the current emotion—which in Miguel's case was *blind rage*.

Miguel acted.

Roaring like a great, wounded bear he ran at Max, grabbing him by the waist and lifting him clean off his feet. Without slowing, the huge man strode over to the rail and with the strength and style of an Olympic shot-putter, launched his victim over the side.

Max, still dazed from Carlo's earlier blow and euphoric after seeing Carlo leave, was off-guard, and taken completely by surprise. His vision was returning, but it wasn't clear, and being unsteady on his feet made it easier for Miguel to pick him up and hurl him—that and the fact that Miguel was seven feet tall and built like a brick built shit house.

Wind rushed by his ears as he plummeted haplessly toward the crystal waters below. The shock of this appalling event—in the continuing series of appalling events—hadn't totally set in when an *even more* appalling event took place: Miguel came tumbling in after him—the enormous man's momentum carrying him over the side too.

As Max's spine smacked into the sea surface, he closed his eyes and folded his arms across his chest. There was no way to avoid the arm-flapping double-decker bus that was about to land squarely on top of him.

Miguel landed—crashed—and both men plunged underwater. Arms as strong as tree branches wrapped around Max's body—trapping him in a viselike grip. Escape was impossible—Harry Houdini, the great escapologist, would have accepted defeat.

The bizarre coupling sank rapidly to the seabed thirty feet below and settled down into the white, sandy, bottom.

Max lay completely still; wearing a human straitjacket, he could do little else. He was still on his back, looking up toward the surface, as a million chaotic air bubbles pinpointed the spot he and Miguel had entered the water. Not the neatest entry—Tom Daley, the Olympic diver, had nothing to worry about, that was for sure.

His eyes were drawn to the *Conchita*'s white hull, where reflected sunlight danced to the tune of the disturbed waters. *Christ, after all this, I'm going to drown.*

He turned his face instinctively to one side as Miguel's massive fist pounded into his cheek.

As a kid, he'd wondered whether it was possible to punch effectively underwater. The answer was yes. The blow was excruciating. Fortunately, it was on the side opposite to his gashed temple.

Another blow came, but this time Max was ready for it and nuzzled his head into Miguel's armpit—not something he'd have normally chosen to do. The punch glanced painfully off his ear and drilled into the sand, causing his underwater assailant to lose balance and roll over. Max took his chance and slid out from underneath his attacker, and kicked for the surface, but Miguel's free hand caught hold of his heel and dragged him back.

Somehow, Miguel had managed to stand upright, and was holding Max in place on the seabed with a huge black-booted foot centered on his chest. All Max could do was watch as his about-to-be murderer began to unsling the Minimi.

Jesus, he's going to shoot me. Do guns work underwater? Why doesn't he just stab me?

The hunting knife—the one used to brutally cut the tape from Will's head—was still strapped to Miguel's right leg—Max could see the outline of the handle through the giant's trousers.

Realization dawned. The huge man wasn't trying to shoot him; he was trying to rid himself of the Minimi's weight. The gun, the ammunition packs, and the grenades would weigh tens of kilos, and that's why Miguel was able to stand on the seabed. He was a human anchor. Unless he could jettison most of that weight, he wouldn't be swimming back to the surface—he'd need to be winched.

All well and good, but you'll have drowned, too. That was Max's negative alter ego.

No, he bloody well won't was his positive response.

Max's mind had flashed back a year. He was sitting at his kitchen table, trying to compile a list of life goals. It had been a depressing experience. After an entire evening of brain ache, the final list stood at one item. One miserable, single entry. He remembered just how pathetic he'd felt.

<u>Life Goals-Max West</u>
1. To swim underwater for two lengths of Spenborough Pool.
2.

But he'd actually given it a go.

Two months of lung-busting effort, three times a week, and he'd stretched out his fingers to touch the far end of the pool. One length. Fifty meters. He'd surfaced not so much elated but rather red-faced and desperate for air. He was halfway. Doubling it and avoiding a cardiac arrest was beyond him.

Then, during a lunch break, he'd been casually flicking through a magazine left by a member of the Yorkshire County Swimming Squad. There was a feature on a New Zealander called Dave Mullins, who'd just swum underwater for over two hundred meters, holding his breath for an incredible four minutes. Suddenly, swimming a hundred meters didn't seem so impossible anymore. If Dave Mullins could do two hundred meters, then surely he could do half of that.

Three months later, Max stretched out his fingers again, and surfaced exhausted with a red face again, but this time with exhilaration, too.

One hundred meters.

There was nobody to applaud, but the achievement felt so good he gave himself a stretch target: one hundred fifty meters.

The day before leaving for Palma, he was within ten meters of that goal—a hundred and forty meters. Holding his breath for three minutes and ten seconds.

Max twisted. Enough to distract Miguel but not enough to invite another punch, hopefully. He had a full minute of air left, but knew that Miguel didn't. The sudden movement caused Miguel's huge left boot to slip off his chest, but it immediately stamped down on his shoulder. Max was still pinned to the seabed, but that didn't matter anymore. Miguel bent down to strike him again but thought better of it and slid his boot back onto Max's chest. More precious seconds had elapsed, and more precious oxygen, had been wasted. Max twisted again, but this time Miguel was ready. He pressed his boot down harder, all the while pulling more urgently at the Minimi's shoulder strap.

Ten seconds later, Miguel was beginning to panic. The machine gun was stuck fast. It wouldn't come off. He needed to cut the strap. Suddenly he remembered his hunting knife and grabbed for it in triumph, but the sheath was empty—the knife was gone. Max had reached for it a few seconds earlier and had slipped it under the sand. Miguel's salvation was only a few inches from his right boot but he couldn't see it.

Miguel became frantic. He reached back over his shoulder and began yanking at the Minimi's barrel—it was a final desperate act. And it was futile, as the machine gun's strap had caught between two bullets on the ammunition belts—and pulling at the barrel only caused the strap to tighten further.

The Minimi wouldn't move, and Miguel's rational thoughts—and there weren't many—were close to being overruled by the need for air.

The downward pressure on Max's shoulder eased, but he remained motionless, watching with both horror and relief at the sickening event unfolding directly above him.

The muscles in Miguel's neck were straining, and the huge man's eyes were bulging. He was valiantly fighting his lungs' burning desire to inhale, but he was about to lose. Tiny bubbles, the last of his precious air, were escaping in a steady stream through the gaps in his clenched teeth. They raced upward.

The bubbles stopped. Miguel's lungs were empty, deflated.

Max knew the brain would resist the need to breathe underwater; eventually, however, the physical necessity for oxygenated blood would overcome rational thought.

Miguel's mouth opened wide, and he breathed in. The muscles defied for so long were let loose, and they took full advantage, sucking in hungrily. One second, the huge man was pulling wildly at the Minimi; the next, he was swaying gently to and fro in the currents of his own making, his chest full of crystal-clear seawater.

Max lifted the boot off his chest. It still had some weight because of the heavy body and armaments, but it moved easily enough. Free from constraint, the buoyancy left in his own lungs lifted him slowly off the seabed.

You'll never know Davy Mullins, but thankyou.

Miguel's body was still standing upright. Blank, lifeless eyes stared into the watery void. He looked like the statue of a warrior from some submerged and lost civilization.

Max had another half minute of air left when he broke the surface a few yards from where he'd fallen in. Fresh air never tasted so good. Will was there to greet him.

"It's Max, it's Max, it's Max," Will said, clearly elated, while anxiously searching the sea around his friend.

Max grabbed the life ring Will had dropped. "Where's Carlo?" he gasped.

"Gone," Will said. "Where's Miguel?"

Max kicked his feet and made it around to the stern, where he crawled up onto the partially submerged platform. He lay still, suddenly more exhausted than he'd ever been in his life. He didn't have the energy to move another muscle. Blood was leaking into the water from the side of his head.

"Miguel?" Will asked again.

Max didn't hear him. He was unconscious. He came around a few minutes later on a sun lounger. Will and Maria were staring at him. Will kept slapping his cheek.

"Will, please stop. I've been slapped enough today."

"You've got to stay awake, Max," Will said. "I don't know why, but it's important."

Maria was checking Max's injuries. He felt so very tired. He closed his eyes, and Will slapped his cheek again.

"Max, you can't go to sleep."

"Jesus." He didn't have the strength to argue.

Maria touched the swelling caused by Miguel's underwater punch, but the only serious damage she found was the cut to his temple. She carefully pulled away some hairs that had become caught in the blood and cleansed the wound with antiseptic before taping gauze over it.

"That'll do for now," she said. "But you'll need stitches."

She sat down at the side of the sun bed and held his hand. Max was too exhausted to notice.

He heard Will's voice. "Carlo's leaving."

Max opened his eyes as the *Infamous Five* cruised past. He thought he saw Carlo at the wheel but wasn't sure, and he dropped off to sleep—thankful that Will hadn't noticed—he didn't want another slap.

A few minutes later, shouting woke him from his doze. Stan and DG and the women were back.

Stan leapt on deck. "Is he all right?"

Max raised a weary arm in acknowledgment. "I'm OK," he managed to say. "But I feel knackered."

Stan hugged him nearly as tightly as Miguel had done when he and Max were sinking as one to the seabed, and then released him to check for wounds. Apart from the "scratch" on his temple—as Stan annoyingly called it from then on—he could see that his best friend was intact.

"He's fine," Stan said, smiling, and hugged him again.

"Jesus Christ," Max said, as DG started hugging him, too.

Lisa was entwined with Will. She'd jumped into his arms and wrapped her legs tightly around his back. Will staggered backward over the sofa arm. He hadn't the strength to stay upright, and they both toppled onto the cushions.

Max wrenched himself to his feet. He couldn't stand any more hugging. "I need a drink."

CHAPTER 24

DG rustled up two bottles of Remy Martin brandy and served it in crystal-cut glasses on a silver tray. "Drink, anybody?" He was almost knocked down in the rush. "Steady on."

Everybody drank.

After three glasses each, the shock of the past hour subsided a little, helped by the *Infamous Five*'s disappearance into the inlet, on its way back to the open sea.

"Tell us what happened," DG said.

Max finished his brandy. He knew that everybody wanted to know what had happened on the *Conchita*. Three of Carlo's men were as dead as dead could be, and yet Max and his friends were all alive. *Why was that?* Max wasn't totally sure himself. He was still partly traumatized. Now he fully understood the term "brain fog."

DG tried to help. "We saw that goon raise his gun to shoot you both. The next thing, Carlo was leaving, and you were diving into the sea. We saw Will and Maria pull a body back onboard, but we couldn't tell whether it was you or not Max. Man, to be honest, we thought you and Will were fucking dead."

"Did you say 'diving'?" Max asked. He was fumbling in his pocket. His trousers were sopping wet, making it difficult to get his hand fully inside. For a moment, his fingers couldn't locate what they were looking for, and he worried the object had fallen out during his underwater struggle with Miguel. But then he found it, secreted in the deepest corner of his pocket.

"What's that?" asked DG and Stan.

Max was holding a small, shiny object. It glinted in the sunshine. "I don't actually know," Max said. "It's a memory stick, of course, and my guess is that it holds records relating to Carlo's drug business—bank-account details, maybe the names of corrupt politicians and police officers, or something else. I don't know. But whatever, it's important to Carlo. He was willing to kill all of us just to make sure that nobody else got their hands on it."

"I scoured every inch of this boat," Stan said. "I can't believe I didn't find it. Where was it?"

"I'll show you," Max said. He walked through the main saloon doors with the others right behind. Maria hung back. "What's the best way to hide something but keep it close?" Max asked the crowd.

"I don't know," Stan said, getting irritated. He hated riddles.

DG loved them. "Easy. Disguise it."

"Jesus," Max said. "I wish I'd asked you that before."

DG basked in the admiration.

"Where's Maria's portrait?" Dannii asked.

"Oh yeah," Kylie said.

"It's gone," Tracy said.

Maria didn't speak, but like everyone else, she was looking at the blank space above the cocktail bar where the portrait had been hanging.

"Did Carlo take it?" Tracy asked, taking another large swig of the fine brandy, and thinking that would be quite a romantic thing to do.

"He didn't," Max said.

He walked behind the bar, his shoes crunching noisily on fragments of broken mirror and glass. The painting was propped up against the back wall. Max picked it up, marveling again at the beautiful image.

"The stick was fitted in here."

His index finger hovered over a narrow slit in the wooden frame. It was just big enough to take a memory stick. An advertising label bearing the name of the picture-frame manufacturer had been used to cover the opening. The label now hung loose.

Max turned to Maria. "I remembered you saying that Carlo had hung the portrait himself. I'm guessing he moved it from the master stateroom up to the bar."

"Clever," DG said. "Everybody sees the painting as soon as they walk in here, but nobody would ever guess its real purpose: it's a safe."

DG realized something else. "Hang on a minute, Max. You hadn't found the memory stick when we left for the island, had you?"

Max was silent.

"Jesus H. Christ," DG said, looking flabbergasted. "You found it after we left in the five minutes before Carlo arrived."

Max didn't know what to say. Finding the memory stick, which had most certainly saved Will's life and his, had been a complete fluke. He'd taken one last look at the portrait on his way down from the flybridge, and his subconscious had again noted the inappropriateness of putting a painting of your half-dressed girlfriend on display. Even then, Max had nearly ignored his inner voice. However, he had a minute to spare, so stood on the bar, reached up, and lifted the portrait down. The sticky advertising label was the only thing to see on the frame. He'd picked it off and just had time to tease the memory stick out as Carlo's dinghy pulled up.

Will had been thinking, too. "But Max, you must have had the memory stick in your pocket the whole time we were held at gunpoint."

Kylie understood. "What if Carlo had searched you?"

Again, Max didn't know what to say. He'd never thought of that.

"I think I'm going to be sick," DG said. "Remind me never to play poker against you."

Stan didn't know whether to be angry or full of pride. He'd always known there was something special about his best friend, and this just confirmed it for him. He chose pride.

"You told him that I'd taken the stick ashore," Stan said. "And Carlo bought it. It wasn't such a stupid assumption on his part. He'd have known we searched the boat and would have assumed we found it hours ago. What you did was either totally fucking brilliant or totally fucking stupid, and I can't quite work out which. But I know this, Maxi. You must have balls the size of melons because if Carlo had searched you—as I would have done—then he would definitely have used this." He grabbed a roll of plastic sheeting that was laid against the side rail.

"What is that?" Max asked.

"It was on the swimming platform," Stan said. "Carlo brought it over. It's a floor covering."

"Eh?" said DG.

Max was shaking inside. He knew what the tarpaulin was for. The cold reality of how close death had been was washing over him. If he had thought Carlo would search him, he would have quickly hidden the memory stick somewhere else on the *Conchita*, down the side of a sofa or above a curtain rail. That would have been much smarter than keeping it in his bloody pocket. Unbelievable. He'd been so, so lucky.

Stan explained to the others. "A Minimi machine gun fires over one thousand rounds a minute. At point-blank range, that's not healthy. The plastic sheeting was to catch Max's and Will's liquidized brains, shattered bones, and sixteen or so pints of blood. Obviously, Carlo didn't want to stain his carpet."

Dannii began throwing up.

"Don't say things like that," Tracy said, looking horrified.

Will was white as a sheet. Two days ago, he would have joined Dannii. But alone for hours in stormy seas contemplating his death—then miraculously saved—only to be taken hostage, beaten, and constantly threatened with a bullet through the head—and then tied up, bagged, and stabbed—had somewhat hardened him up.

Everyone heard a familiar noise.

"Oh fuck," Stan said.

Two seconds later, the Russian helicopter gunship lumbered over the top of the nearest hill and swooped toward them.

Will said what Max was thinking. "Carlo knows we're all back on board. It's his chance to destroy the memory stick and us along with it."

Stan charged below decks. He'd gone to retrieve another missile, but it was too late. The gunship was easing to a hover and tilting menacingly toward them, as the pilot aligned his sights. They were sitting ducks. It was point-blank range. They were about to become dead ducks.

Max felt a hand grab his. Maria was standing at his side. She was in a trance, staring straight into the gunship's machine-gun barrels. For a second, Max considered diving overboard and pulling her in, too, but the gunship would mow them down in the water. And even fully rested, he couldn't make it all the way to shore underwater. There was nothing to do.

It was all over, and Carlo had won. He realized that DG had been right all along, too: he could never leave Maria—not because she needed him but because he was head over heels in love with her.

"Look," Dannii said.

Two missiles had ripped over the same hilltops the helicopter had just appeared over. For a split second, Max thought the gunship was firing, but these missiles were from elsewhere. The long, red sticks descended steeply before levelling off over the beach, thirty feet above the sea.

One second of flight later, they simultaneously slammed into the static gunship with a sickening crunch. The now customary orange fireball was followed by a red-hot wind, which forced Max and Maria to hunker down on the deck.

And then the pressure was gone.

Max tightened his grip on Maria's hand and felt her squeezing his own in return. They were both OK. But the gunship wasn't.

Bizarrely, the stricken machine was still hovering in the very same spot, except that now instead of live pilots it contained an inferno. There was a fizzing sound, and the rotor blades, which were still gamely spinning, broke off and whirled up into the sky. Only then did the dead aircraft begin to fall. Its buckled and flaming body smacked into the sea, where it sat, burning and crackling on the surface for a few seconds before sinking out of sight.

Max checked around him. Apart from Lisa, who had apparently broken a nail, everybody was OK.

"They're not even real," DG said.

Stan appeared with an antitank missile.

"Where is it?" He looked mightily confused, and then saw the smoke pall hanging over the water, and that partially explained what had happened. He raised the tube onto his shoulder as two more black shapes cleared the hills.

"Apaches," Stan said.

"Apaches?" DG asked, peeping out of the saloon doors.

"Apache attack helicopters," Stan said, releasing a clip on the tube. Some sort of sighting mechanism flicked up. "Fucking Yanks. In my experience, the Americans are more dangerous than the Russians. They shoot more of our side than the enemy does."

Max pulled the tube off Stan's shoulder. "Jesus, they've helped us, Stan. And you've only one missile, there are two helicopters."

Stan reluctantly gave way. "Could have nailed 'em both with one shot."

The Apaches were hovering, surveying the scene. Seemingly satisfied that any potential threat had been neutralized, they descended in formation and landed side by side on the small beach. Engines were cut, rotors spun slowly to a stop, doors opened, and dark figures began jumping out, rifles at the ready.

It was difficult to see exactly what was happening from the *Conchita*, until two inflatable dinghies were pulled down to the water's edge. Men jumped in and started outboard motors. Two minutes later, the dinghies were thirty yards off the stern rail, where Max and the others were standing. A gray-haired man with a deep, New York drawl shouted over.

"Hiya, folks." He showed off a full set of shiny big teeth as he smiled warmly. "Is one of you Max West?"

"That would be me," Max shouted.

The man smiled again. "Hey, that's great. Mind if we come aboard?"

"Everybody else has," Max called back, feeling slight reassurance from being asked, rather than shot at.

The man's dinghy pulled up at the swimming platform. DG and Stan helped them tie on before leading three men up onto the flybridge. The other inflatable remained on station just off the stern.

The heavyset American appeared to be in his midfifties and had a full head of wavy, gray hair and a strong chin. He was wearing an old, checkered sports jacket; beige chinos; and a pair of brown brogues. He looked as if he were going to a lunch at his local golf club. The two men alongside him didn't. They wore padded, black jackets with the letters *DEA* emblazoned in yellow on the back.

"Doug Clark, United States Drug Enforcement Administration," the gray-haired man said, holding out a big hand.

Max took it. The handshake was warm and friendly. "Max West." He didn't bother to add "deputy manager of Spenborough Pool."

"I'm very pleased to meet you, Max," Clark said. "In fact, I'm very pleased to meet all you folks," he added cheerily, while looking around him. He was used to nervous and suspicious faces, "And very pleased, though a little surprised, to see that you're all alive."

"I guess we've got you to thank for that, Mr. Clark," DG said. "We were just about to get vaporized."

Clark smiled again. "Call me Doug. And it's not me you should be thanking. I won't take credit when it's not due. It's him you should thank." He pointed to the last man in the line behind him.

The man had been hanging back, and he cut a sorry figure. He was wearing a sweat shirt with a ragged hood, which had fallen sloppily across his face, making it difficult for him to see or be seen, and ill-fitting joggers that kept getting caught under his feet as he walked. The man was also wearing handcuffs.

One of the other agents reached over and pulled back the hood.

Max's eyes nearly popped out of his head.

"Jack!"

Max couldn't believe it. Surely Jack was in hospital being treated after the car crash—he sure looked like he needed healthcare treatment. "Is it really you?"

He was pretty sure it was Jack, but the lack of hair, eyebrows, and eyelashes, and the numerous sores and angry red spots on his face made it difficult to be certain. He also stank like dead fish.

The man nodded sheepishly. "It's me, Max."

Max was angry. "What the hell's going on here, Clark? Why is he in handcuffs? It looks like he's been tortured."

"Now, now," Clark said, a little too defensively. "He's in bracelets because he attempted to hijack my Apache."

"Hijack your Apache?" Stan asked.

Jack flinched at the sound of Stan's voice.

"He did," said Clark. "It's the only reason we're here. We'd been following the Russian gunship for over two hours but were running low on gas. I decided to return to base, but Mr. North, here, had other ideas, and stole my handgun—threatened to shoot himself if we abandoned the chase. Said he'd deserted you all once before, and he'd rather die than do it again. Kept mumbling about some place called Blackpool. I told him to fire away, but fortunately—or unfortunately, depending on your persuasion—the idiot hadn't taken the safety off. Hughes, over there, overpowered him. Just after that, we intercepted a radio message from Ortega ordering the Russian chopper to Cabrera. We resumed the mission and, as we Americans tend to do, shot first." He smiled. "We didn't land on the beach over there for a picnic. We're out of juice. I've radioed in for resupply."

Stan stepped forward and held out his hand to Jack. "You came back for us," he said.

Jack looked down at Stan's hand as if it were the greatest prize anybody could ever win—the national lottery, all the world's competitions, and a century of Nobel Peace Prizes all rolled into one. Tears ran down his face as a schoolboy smile stretched the itching spots on his cheeks. He reached out with his handcuffed hands and shook Stan's hand with utter delight.

"All right," Stan said. "That's enough. And by the way, Jack, you stink."

Jack wasn't bothered. He'd never been happier in his life. He was back with his friends, and they liked him.

DG and Will were playfully thumping Jack on his back.

"And we'll visit you every month for the next thirty years in whichever penitentiary they put you in Jack," said DG, laughing, before realizing that it might not be so funny.

Will was holding his nose.

Clark laughed at the scene. "You guys haven't been cooped up with him in an Apache. Not good, I can tell you. Uncuff him, Hughes. He deserves a break after what Masa put him through."

Then Clark became stern. "But if you ever tell anybody what you did, Mr. North, then it will be thirty years in Leavenworth."

Jack had turned away. He was rubbing his wrists and leering at the fabulous-looking girls standing by the saloon doorway. "Nice, very nice," he said, looking Lisa over from head to toe.

She screwed up her nose and went to stand with Will.

"Christ, Jack," Max said. "Some things never change, do they? Go below and get a shower, for God's sake."

"A cold one," Will said.

CHAPTER 25

T he Spanish check-in clerk beckoned Max forward. "Passport, please, sir."

Max handed over his passport and lifted his sports bag onto the scales.

"Thank you, sir."

Three days had passed since the events now known simply as "Cabrera", and it had also been three days since Max had last seen Maria. They'd sat together on the return voyage to Palma, both feeling traumatized and both unsure of what to say to the other. The conversation never got further than irrelevant small talk.

Maria had withdrawn back into her shell, her mind incapable of computing all that had happened. *Understandable*, he thought. *Her fiancé has turned out to be a drug lord rather than a coffee exporter. And, to boot, he'd just tried to murder her.*

Doctors at Son Espases Hospital in Palma had checked them all over. Max needed eight stitches to sew up his temple, and Will had needed twelve across the back of his skull, where Miguel's knife had sliced through tape and skin alike. Physically, everybody else was fine; emotionally, they were wiped out. Unfortunately, rather than rest, they were subjected to interminable hours of interviews. Not interrogation, as Doug Clark had constantly pointed out, but that's how it felt, especially as each of them were "interviewed" separately. Jack's antagonist, Alberto Masa, wasn't there; he'd been recalled to Colombia.

Finally, the endless questions had ended, and Max was cleared to leave. He'd gone straight to look for Maria, but she'd already gone.

"Left yesterday with the other women," Clark had said. "I can check if she boarded a flight."

Max wanted to accept Clark's offer, but declined. He was in love with Maria, but how could she possibly reciprocate? They'd only spent two days together, and that time hadn't exactly been an ideal get-to-know-you date. And Maria had the added confusion of her feelings for Carlo to make sense of, too. There was no point in hounding the woman—although he wanted to.

It's so strange. In just forty-eight hours, and during a series of events that most rational people would describe as a bloody nightmare, I managed to fall hopelessly in love.

His feelings for Maria weren't just infatuation—he knew that for sure—*if only they were!* Then the sensations of loss and hurt burning his insides out may not be real either, or painful—but they were.

Yes, he'd fixated on Maria's portrait like some hypnotized zombie; and yes, he'd been desperate to jump all over Maria's bones in the *Conchita's* saloon, while she was giving him the frightening lowdown on the Colombian drug cartels and the death of her father. And for those desires—at that totally inappropriate time—he felt truly guilty. But it was after that, during the storm, that everything changed. It was seeing Maria's strength in the face of overwhelming odds that had taken his breath away. He could pinpoint the exact moment: seeing her back at the *Conchita's* wheel after the great wave. Her skill and determination had saved them all from drowning. She was battered, bruised, and holding a hand across her eyes to protect them from the driving rain, yet she was unbending. Resolute. Max had never seen a person so alive, so purposeful, and so utterly, utterly beautiful. He fell in love with Maria right then and there.

But he knew it was useless.

After arriving back in Palma he hadn't really expected to see her again, but he had hoped Maria would leave a note, or at least send him a text message. *Something.* But there was nothing. The only text he got was from the EE mobile network, informing him that his data allowance had been exceeded.

Maria had disappeared from his life even quicker than she'd entered it. It was hard to take. Happenchance had brought them together—there had been no choice. But surely the turbo-charged roller coaster they'd shared merited a wave good-bye or at least a scrawl on a Post-it Note.

Carlo had gone, too—vanished into thin air. The *Infamous Five* had turned up empty in a marina on the Costa del Sol. Interpol was diligently watching the airports, railway stations, and ports, and the coast guard was searching private sailing vessels, but it all seemed to no avail.

"Our friend Carlo will be back in the Colombian jungle," Clark had said, visibly disappointed.

Carlo Ortega at liberty was something to fear, although the memory stick safely tucked in Max's pocket gave him some comfort. As agreed during a quick huddle at the hospital, the survivors of Cabrera had decided the stick wouldn't be disclosed to the police, the DEA, or anybody else. Max still didn't know what secrets it contained—he'd had no access to a laptop—but the information on it had kept them alive, and he wouldn't be giving it up any time soon—particularly as Ortega was running rings around the authorities.

The memory stick had been in his sock at the police station.

"And the police didn't search you, either?" Stan asked in disbelief.

"Nope."

"Amateurs, the lot of 'em," said Stan. "Surprised if they can find their way out of bed in the morning."

Clark had accompanied Max out of police headquarters. "A private word?"

"Sure," said Max.

For a brief moment, Max was worried that somebody had let slip about the memory stick, but it wasn't that.

"I got the impression there was something going on between you and Maria Rodriguez, or at least that you wanted there to be something going on," Clark said.

Max was surprised and too quick to deny. "Nothing went on."

Clark raised one bushy gray eyebrow. "Keep it that way, Max. And that's not the DEA talking. I don't want to see your bloated body being hauled from some goddamned river. And you should know that Maria was adamant for two days solid that the Russian chopper wasn't going to open fire. That it was there as transport."

Max couldn't believe it. *How could she possibly think that?*

He'd laughed, unconvincingly. "Thanks for the advice, Doug. But it's not needed. Nothing is going on. Maria is welcome to Carlo if she's crazy enough to want him, and I'm going home."

Clark had prodded his chest. "Bullshit, Max. Stay away. She'll get you killed. You escaped once, and I confess I have no idea how. But whatever trick you pulled, it won't work twice."

"Doug—"

"Give me some credit, boy. I've been an agent for most of your life. Whatever you did was smart, I give you that—real smart—but you've stuck a sharp stick into a tiger's asshole, and he'll be as mad as hell. Quit while you're ahead."

● ● ●

The Spanish check-in clerk handed Max his passport back.

"Have a good flight."

"Thanks," said Max.

DG was next in line.

"Any luggage to check in, sir?"

"No thanks, darling," DG replied.

The woman looked up and saw an irresistible golden smile. Instantly, she found herself smiling back.

"Oh, for God's sake," Stan said. "And do not give her your bloody toothbrush."

Tina giggled. "Go on, DG. It's really funny," she said, egging him on.

Tina had a tight grip of Stan's hand. Max thought she might never let go—ever.

"Bloody hell, buttercup," Stan said. "Don't encouragement him."

Will and Jane were standing near the back of the queue. Both had strained expressions. "We should be going British Airways," Jane said. Her tone was harsh.

Will's was harsher still. "The BA desk is over there. Off you go. And take this bloody thing with you." He shoved a Louis Vuitton chest across the floor. It banged into Jane's leg. She scowled but stayed put.

Next in line was Max's mother and Mr. Patel. He was carrying both their suitcases and was sweating profusely.

"Mrs. West," he said, "please go and sit at a table in the café while I sort the excess baggage charges. I'm afraid I may be over the limit."

Max looked at the suitcases. Mum's was twice the size of Mr. Patel's. As his mum toddled off, Mr. Patel pulled a large wad of twenty-pound notes from his wallet.

There was time for a drink before boarding. The airport bar looked out across the terminal concourse.

"One for the road," DG said.

Enrique, the barman, poured five healthy bourbons.

"A toast," DG said.

"Aye," Stan said. "And as chairman of the Bull's Head Pool Team, I'll be making it."

They raised their glasses.

"The Infamous Five," Stan said, nodding at Jack.

Jack beamed. He'd come to see his mates off.

"The Infamous Five," the five men said in unison.

"Fill 'em up, please, Enrique," DG said.

Max was feeling a little happier. "Blackpool's going to be a welcome anticlimax next year," he said.

"I was thinking we could take partners," Stan said, sheepishly.

"You would," DG said. "You won't be able to take a crap without taking Tina along from now on."

Something caught DG's eye on the concourse, and he glanced nervously at Max.

Max saw too.

It was Maria.

She was standing on her own in the center of the terminal and seemed to be the only person in the whole airport who wasn't moving. She was scanning the crowd—searching for someone. Tourists were dashing this way and that, constantly walking in front of her, and Maria's yellow cotton dress kept intermittently disappearing from view.

Max knew that she was searching for him.

"I don't know how long she's been there," DG said, but Max wasn't listening.

He was busily dodging bar tables, chairs, and drinking customers, all the time keeping one eye squarely on Maria. He wasn't going to lose her now. He burst on to the concourse as Maria looked in his direction. Max could see her emerald-green eyes flashing with recognition from halfway across the concourse. He heard her laugh and call out.

"Maxi!"

Max was truly in the moment. The noise and hubbub of the chaotic airport evaporated, and it wasn't so much blood but rather sheer joy that was pumping through his veins.

She is bothered! It meant so much.

Maria was just ahead.

He clumsily avoided an elderly couple's electric luggage trolley and bumped into a man.

"Sorr—"

Then, the real world snapped back in full color and digital sound.

Maria had screamed.

Joy and ecstasy vanished.

And Max stopped dead in his tracks.

Tourists stopped, too, but quickly moved on again as they realized the pretty lady was unharmed.

Maria was in shock; both hands over her mouth.

Max turned around as a boarding announcement resonated in the air above him.

The man he'd bumped into was Carlo. He was standing tall, imperious, and threatening, only a few yards away. He must have been watching the whole scene unfold and stepped out from behind a pillar only when Maria called Max's name.

Max glanced about him.

"Only me," Carlo said.

"Pull a gun, and the police will grab you," Max said. "They're looking for you everywhere."

Carlo was nonchalant. "Informants tell me otherwise. The search for me is over, but I'm not here to see you, Max. And you have insurance against me harming you, don't you?"

Max had just enough awareness not to touch his pocket. "The agreement stands."

Carlo nodded. "Good."

Maria was staring at both men, still covering her mouth as if another cry were trying to slip out.

Carlo moved to one side.

Max matched the movement, blocking his path to Maria.

Carlo smiled. "What you said aboard the *Conchita* was right, Max. I agree with you. It is Maria's business what she does next—her choice, and I am here to see her choose."

Carlo took a few more paces to one side. This time, Max remained where he was.

The three of them were standing in a triangle, with Maria at the apex.

Max's instinct was to go to Maria's side, but he forced himself to remain where he was. Carlo needed to know whether Maria still loved him enough to put aside the revelations of the past few days.

And I need to know too, thought Max.

He thought the question had just been answered. Surely, Maria wouldn't have come to the airport if she still had feelings for Carlo.

Or was he was deluding himself—again?

And now Carlo had reappeared like a bad dream, and more and more worries were building in his brain. The memory of Maria running out in front of Miguel's machine gun jumped into his mind.

But that was to protect me and Will, he thought. *And it took serious courage.*

He forced himself to contemplate a different scenario.

Or was Maria protecting herself? Watching her fiancé murder us both in cold blood might have been too much to forgive. Stopping the execution may have been about Maria shielding her own feelings for Carlo. Shit! How come I didn't think of that before?

The answer to that question was at least clear: he hadn't wanted to think it.

Maybe Maria does still want to marry Carlo. And maybe she really does believe that he didn't order the Russian gunship to open fire, and maybe that was true too.

Clark had admitted that he didn't actually hear Ortega give the command to sink the *Conchita*, so maybe he never had.

What is the truth?

Max didn't know but he needed to. And that's why he stood his ground.

He was primarily focusing his attention on Maria—who hadn't moved from her spot either—but he could also see Carlo to his left, in his peripheral vision. Carlo was exclusively concentrating on his fiancée. He was rubbing his fingers and thumbs together, which seemed to betray a level of anxiety. Maria's eyes were darting from Carlo to Max and then back again.

And there they were, a triangle of hope, mistrust and dilemma, as passengers wandered too and fro, all of them oblivious to the unfolding drama.

Maria understood what was required of her. She knew both men loved her and wanted her. And she knew they wanted closure. But what did she want?

A step toward either man would end it. No lengthy explanations would be required. And no second chances. If she stepped toward Carlo, then Max would immediately leave. She would never see him again. The last few tumultuous days could be consigned to history—and that would be good. But if she stepped toward Max, even if just to console him, then Carlo would also leave. He would feel humiliated—she would have humiliated him—and it would be all over between them. Making no choice was a choice in itself—if she stepped away from both men, then both would feel slighted.

Men can be so stubborn.

She'd come to the airport to bid Max farewell.

Is that true?

The Russian helicopter gunship flashed into her mind. It had swooped directly toward her, and a surprising thought had popped into her head. It still surprised her now. The deadly war machine should have frightened her; instead, she'd been filled with regret—a regret that she and Max would never make love.

She could feel the loss in her abdomen right now.

Was it the beginning of something?

Of what?

Romance?

She chided herself and a recent memory came to mind.

Neurochemicals.

Or the effect of a near-death experience—and she'd certainly had a few of those recently. The odds of a chemical reaction blossoming into lasting bonds were slim, so very unlikely. *And yet*, she thought, *all relationships must begin somewhere—perhaps even during times of trauma and distress.*

But Carlo was her rock. Bonds had truly formed. He'd cared for her and Mama, in their time of great need. And he was innocent of Papa's murder; she was certain. Mama was wrong about that. And for better or worse, Carlo was her fiancé—she'd fallen in love with him and had accepted his proposal of marriage—but that was before she'd found out about his dark side. She accepted that now. Carlo had done bad things, but everybody deserved a second chance—and she would help him become a better man, help him to use his wealth and influence to do good for others.

Or am I just frightened to leave him?

She waited to see if Papa or Mama would speak inside her head. Her parents had always been her moral compass—but there was only silence.

Her future course was hers alone to dictate.

Max could sense what was about to happen, and he needed to leave. His entire world was about to be consumed by the great chasm opening up underneath his feet. But he couldn't leave, he couldn't move; his legs were rooted to the spot. The joy he'd felt at seeing Maria on the concourse and the knowledge she'd come to search for him had succeeded only to amplify the crippling pain he was about to feel as the woman of his dreams ripped his heart out.

Carlo was visibly more confident. His hands were quiet and resting calmly by his sides. He smiled warmly and beckoned his bride-to-be.

Max recognized the expression on Maria's face. He'd seen it before. Purposeful and resolute—just as she had been after surviving the great wave.

The fingertips of her left hand were resting gently on her stomach, as if she were touching the source of her inspiration. She looked at both men in turn, one last time, still giving nothing away, and then—decision made—stepped confidently forward.

A few short seconds later Maria was standing with her choice—the other man was long gone.

"I have no idea whether I'm in love with you, Max, or whether I ever will be...but I'd really like to find out."

The End

Robert J. Cooper wrote From Blackpool to Cabrera, his debut novel, because too many of us go through life without realizing our dreams.

Robert has a beautiful girlfriend and two fantastic kids. He feels very lucky. He lives in Leeds, England.

Made in the USA
Charleston, SC
21 July 2016